W9-BEN-808

*Dear Reader,*

This Christmas, Harlequin Historicals is very proud
to be able to bring you MISTLETOE MARRIAGES,
a collection of stories written by four of our favorite
authors: Elaine Barbieri, Kathleen Eagle,
Margaret Moore and Patricia Gardner Evans.

While the settings of these stories range from the
wilds of Montana, to the ranchlands of New Mexico
and Wyoming, to a small town in Wales, each of
them captures the excitement and joy of finding love
during the most magical season of the year. We hope
you enjoy them.

All of us at Harlequin Historicals would like to take
this time to thank our terrific authors for their hard
work and talented storytelling, and our loyal readers
for their continued support. We wish you all a
wonderful holiday and a safe and happy New Year.

Sincerely,

*Tracy Farrell*

*Margaret O'Neill Marbury*

*Angela Catalano*

The Editors
Harlequin Historicals

# Mistletoe Marriages

ELAINE BARBIERI
KATHLEEN EAGLE
MARGARET MOORE
PATRICIA GARDNER EVANS

# Harlequin Books

TORONTO • NEW YORK • LONDON
AMSTERDAM • PARIS • SYDNEY • HAMBURG
STOCKHOLM • ATHENS • TOKYO • MILAN
MADRID • WARSAW • BUDAPEST • AUCKLAND

MISTLETOE MARRIAGES
Copyright © 1994 by Harlequin Enterprises B.V.

ISBN 0-373-83309-1

The publisher acknowledges the copyright holders
of the individual works as follows:

RENDEZVOUS
Copyright © 1994 by Elaine Barbieri
THE WOLF AND THE LAMB
Copyright © 1994 by Kathleen Eagle
CHRISTMAS IN THE VALLEY
Copyright © 1994 by Margaret Wilkins
KEEPING CHRISTMAS
Copyright © 1994 by Patricia Gardner Evans

This edition published by arrangement with Harlequin Enterprises B.V.

® and TM are trademarks of the publisher. Trademarks indicated with ® are registered in the United States Patent and Trademark Office, the Canadian Trade Marks Office and in other countries.

**Printed in U.S.A.**

# CONTENTS

# RENDEZVOUS

## Elaine Barbieri

To my mother and father, who taught me the true
meaning of Christmas; to my husband and children,
who brought the meaning to life; and to Holly, Siobhan
and Michael, who add a new dimension of joy to the
season and to every day.

## MOM'S APPETIZER SALAD
### from Elaine Barbieri

Mom's Appetizer Salad is a traditional part of our Christmas celebration, which I incorporated into my holiday meal when Christmas dinner shifted to my house ten years ago. The amount is easily adjustable to whatever size dinner party you are planning.

I usually use the fourteen-ounce can or jar (drained), or the closest equivalent possible, of each of the following:

> *pickled beets (save juice)*
> *marinated artichoke hearts*
> *pickled eggplant (optional—difficult to find)*
> *roasted (red) peppers*
> *sweet gherkins*
> *black olives (pitted)*
>
> *Also:*
> *one small to medium onion (adjust to preference)*
> *one stalk celery*
> *one medium carrot*

Chop all of above to a relatively uniform size—*not too small*—and combine. Moisten with pickled beet juice *if needed*. Is best if made a day in advance and is cold when served.

*Bon appétit!*

# Chapter One

*Wyoming Territory—1871*

The leaden sky continued its frozen deluge, shrouding the landscape in a curtain of white as Lydia urged her exhausted mount forward. A raging wind whipped the relentless flakes into razor-sharp pellets that abraded her numb cheeks as she bent low over the saddle, pulled her oversize hat down lower on her forehead and struggled to adjust her scarf with stiff hands incapable of the task. Abandoning the effort, she squinted into the storm, but saw only an endless sea of white through which there appeared no path or direction.

Harsh reality made slow inroads into Lydia's benumbed mind.

She was lost.

Lydia's heart lurched as her mount stumbled beneath her, struggled to regain its balance, then moved forward once more. She strained to remember. How long had she been wandering in this unwavering tempest? A few minutes...an hour...a day? Somehow she could recall only remnants of a driving urgency that had forced her to undertake the journey despite the weather's threat, and a feeling that it might already be too late. But the jagged edges of desperation had dulled as snow began falling more thickly and the moan of the wind increased to a fierce howling that easily penetrated her shabby male clothing to deaden her senses.

Lydia attempted a smile, faintly aware that her stiff lips would not cooperate. Curiously, she was no longer cold. The freezing impact of the wind on her slender frame had somehow lessened, despite the relentless battering. Instead, a comforting mellowness had begun expanding within her. Fragmented pictures of better times had flashed before her mind's eye, and warm memories had flooded back, wrapping her in a protective cocoon that denied the deepening cold. The frozen world around her had begun slipping farther away while she indulged those memories with increasing contentment and she—

Jerked back to the present when her mount stumbled again, Lydia attempted a short word of encouragement. The sound froze on her lips as she realized in a moment of abrupt clarity that her horse was going down.

The blanket of white rose up to meet her. It encompassed her as she lay helpless upon it, and held her fast. A hushed lament began within her mind. The sound grew louder, the words clearer, and her heavy eyelids slowly closed. It echoed in the rapidly expanding darkness awaiting her, becoming a resounding shout of despair....

*I came so close....*

The wild shrieking of the wind showed no sign of abating as Whit Randall pulled the ranch-house door closed behind him and faced the fury of the storm. Pulling his collar up around his neck and adjusting the brim of his hat low on his forehead, he stepped down into snow that was already knee-deep and started toward the barn. He had taken only a few steps when a persistent barking turned him with annoyance. Hunching his broad shoulders against the abusive elements, he strained to see through the whirling veil of white. The barking continued as he took a few warning steps toward the barely discernible image a few yards away.

"Quiet, Snap!"

The huge mongrel pranced toward him, pointed ears erect, wiry coat covered with snow, bright eyes trained on his face. Whit returned his stare. Damn, he was an ugly beast! It had been just his luck to stumble over the dog when the animal had been abandoned on the open range as a pup a few years earlier. He had not really regretted taking him in since that time, but there were occasions when—

The sharp barking resumed, and Whit's patience snapped.

"Quiet, I said!"

Ignoring the animal's excited lunges, Whit shook his head and turned back toward the barn. The first real storm of the year always seemed to revive the pup in Snap, but Whit was in no mood to play. He was cold, he was tired, and he was hungry. He had spent more time than his hired men out on the range prior to the storm, but here he was again, trudging to the barn through freezing drifts to check on an ailing horse.

Dismissing Snap from his mind as the animal disappeared from sight, Whit ducked his head against the snow, his gaze intent on the barn doors a short distance away.

When he had secured the barn doors behind him, Whit released a relieved breath, then pulled off his hat and shook it free of snow. After taking a moment to run a hand through roughly cut blond hair still streaked by the summer sun, he replaced his hat and walked toward the nearby stall. His tall, powerful frame was tense.

With dark brown brows drawn together over eyes as blue as a June sky, strong features intent and jaw squared, he paused to appraise the mare within. The animal had been badly clawed by a mountain lion a week earlier, and had been fevered for much of the time since. He had known the turning point in her condition would soon be reached, and he had approached the barn with a deepening sense of dread, knowing what he must do if things had gone bad.

The mare raised her head in a short welcoming whinny, and relief began to slowly permeate Whit's senses. He had not expected the lively tilt of the horse's well-shaped head, or the clarity of her eyes when she regarded him intently in return.

A smile touched Whit's lips, revealing the flicker of a dimple and a glimpse of natural charm further accented by his deep Southern drawl as he whispered, "So you've decided to get well. For that I thank you, ma'am."

The mare whinnied again, stretching out her neck, and Whit's smile deepened as he scratched the muzzle she offered him. His smile slowly faded. He would not have liked putting an end to this young animal's life. But he would have done his duty—as he had so many times in the past—no matter how distasteful it would have been.

Shrugging off that somber thought, Whit picked up a nearby can of salve and entered the stall.

At the doorway again a few minutes later, Whit braced himself for the onslaught of the storm still raging outside. He had spent five winters in this uncivilized territory, and the first snowfall still made him uncertain if he would ever become accustomed enough to the brutal climate to call this place home. Perhaps that was the reason he had resisted taking the final step that would tie him to the land, and perhaps—

Refusing to finish that thought, Whit pushed the door open. He was trudging back across the yard when an inherent honesty forced him to reconsider. No, it wasn't the weather...or the terrain...or material doubts...that held him back from embracing this land completely, despite his attachment to it. There was something else, something indefinable inside him that refused to accept—

That barking again.

Whit turned toward the sound as Snap bounded into sight and leaped against his chest.

Knocked a step backward as his breath escaped in an involuntary "Oof," Whit commanded harshly, "Down, Snap! What's the matter with you, boy?"

Snap's response was another wild dash back and forth that stopped abruptly a foot from him. Pausing briefly to consider the dog's strange behavior, Whit turned back toward the house. He halted once more as Snap bounded toward him again, this time carrying a long frozen cloth that he dropped at Whit's snow-covered feet. The dog's small eyes remained focused on his face until he bent down to pick it up.

A blue hand-knit scarf.

Resuming his sharp, excited barking, Snap raced back and forth, retracing his steps countless times, until Whit looked uncertainly in the direction the animal indicated. Snap barked louder, and Whit realized...

Moments later, Whit emerged from the barn, mounted. Without hesitation, he followed Snap into the encroaching darkness.

The storm continued its screaming assault as Whit steadied the motionless, blanket-wrapped body lying across the saddle in front of him with his hand. The ranch-house lights were becoming visible through the whirling snow, and he urged his laboring animal to a faster pace. It would be close, he knew. The young fellow Snap had led him to was barely breathing.

Glancing behind him, Whit saw the boy's nearly frozen mount stumbling at the end of his lead. It was a miracle that the animal had gotten up after its obvious fall. The boy had not been as fortunate.

His heart beginning a rapid pounding as he neared the ranch house, Whit jumped from his horse.

"Sam! Buck! Pete! Get out here! I need your help!"

The men appeared in the doorway, and Whit instructed tightly, "Pete, Buck, help me get this boy into the house. Sam, you take care of the horses. See what you can do for the boy's mount. He's almost done in."

With an uneven chorus of assent, the two men helped him to lift the boy from his horse. Inside within moments, Whit stripped off his outer clothes. The stiffness of his own hands was a grim reminder that it might already be too late to reverse any damage the boy had suffered . . . if he survived . . .

Whit's reaction to that thought was another command.

"Pete, get me some of that red-eye from the kitchen. Buck, get all the blankets you can find and bring them here."

The men snapped into action as Whit leaned over the bed. His mind raced while he fumbled with the boy's frozen clothing. Damn . . . the boy was so young and thin. . . . He hadn't even started to shave yet. What in hell was he doing out in a storm like this?

Whit pulled off the boy's hat, noting that it was almost frozen to the bluntly cut reddish-brown hair beneath. Ice crystals coated the young fellow's brows and lashes, as well. One side of his face was badly bruised and swollen where he had obviously struck it when he fell, while the other side was a peculiar shade of gray blotched with red. His lips were almost colorless. . . .

Whit's heart jumped to a racing beat.

Tearing at the frozen buttons on the boy's coat, Whit slipped him out of the confining garment. He then pulled off the boy's boots and started removing his shirt. His fingers growing clumsy in his haste, Whit had stripped the shirt open wide when his ministrations came to a sudden halt.

Blinking with disbelief, Whit looked up at the young stranger's motionless face, then down again at the rise of unmistakable mounds underneath the exposed long underwear.

Breasts.

It couldn't be . . . !

The sound of running footsteps preceded Buck's breathless entrance. "I got the blankets, boss. What do you want me to do with them?"

Whit motioned stiffly toward the nearby chair. "Put them down over there."

Dropping the blankets where indicated, Buck turned back, his expression anxious. "I'll help you get the kid undressed. Hell, he looks bad, don't he?"

"It's not a *he*."

"Wh-what?"

"It's a *she*."

Buck's jaw dropped in an expression that was almost ludicrous, but Whit was not in the mood to laugh. Making a snap decision, he ordered, "Get out. I'll take care of this. I'll call you when I need you."

Not waiting for the door to close behind his ranch hand, Whit unbuckled the girl's belt. He divested her of her frozen pants and threw them in the corner. Then, his jaw set, he began working at the buttons of the underwear beneath.

The strange weight that had encumbered her breathing was lifting. Lydia sighed at the release, hearing sounds she had not heard before . . . deep male voices fading in and out . . . heavy footsteps echoing against a wooden floor . . . She felt a warm liquid slip between her lips. She swallowed. The liquid stung her all the way down to the pit of her stomach, where it settled into a warm glow. She swallowed again, and the glow increased to a flame that warmed the frozen core of her.

Unable to raise her heavy eyelids, Lydia strained to hear as the voices drew clearer.

"I don't think you should give her any more whiskey, boss. Maybe some hot coffee would be better."

Another voice. "I'll get it."

Consciousness drifted away, but returned as another person spoke, this time close to her ear. "Open your mouth. Come on."

She knew that voice.

The soft drawl hardened. "Open your mouth, missy. I'm not goin' to let you give up."

Oh, God . . . that voice!

Barely managing to raise her heavy lids, Lydia stared through narrow slits at the male outline hovering over her. She struggled to focus, her breath catching in her throat when her vision suddenly cleared.

The handsome face above hers grew strained with concern. "Are you all right? Does somethin' hurt?"

Lydia spoke, but no words emerged. She tried again, managing only an incoherent whisper.

The handsome face above hers drew closer. "What did you say?" It drew closer still, bright blue eyes locking with hers as he said encouragingly, "Say it again."

"Am—am I . . ." Lydia took a rasping breath. "Am I in heaven?"

The handsome face went momentarily still. The familiar mouth quirked.

"No. You're in Wyomin'."

Lydia's eyes drifted closed. She almost smiled. No, she was in heaven . . . because she was with *him*.

## Chapter Two

**W**hit drew himself wearily to his feet as the aroma of boiling coffee and frying bacon permeated the small bedroom. He glanced toward the window and saw that morning had begun lightening a sky that was still heavily laden. Snow was still falling, but the wind had lessened, and the worst of the blizzard appeared to be over. The weather had improved enough that the men would be able to ride out to check on any stock that might have become stranded by the frozen drifts. He had worked long and hard to establish his herd. He could not afford any unnecessary losses.

Whit looked back at the young woman sleeping in the bed beside which he had sat through the long, stormy night. Fearful that each breath might be her last, he had found himself responding to every sound she made with increasing anxiety. He had jumped with a start when the first shaft of dawn stirred him from a light doze, his breath catching in his throat until he ascertained the slow rise and fall of her chest. He hoped that the worst was over for her, too, but he was not sure. Her violent trembling had finally ceased, and she had taken more liquid, but she had not awakened or spoken another lucid word.

A sound at the open doorway out of the bedroom turned Whit toward the short, stocky man standing tentatively there. The concern in Buck's gaze was obvious as he looked toward the bed. The same concern was reflected in Sam's face when the taller man stepped into view behind him. Whit drew himself wearily to his feet and walked toward them. Four years working side by side with his hired men on this ranch in the middle of nowhere had proved that they were honest and decent, well above the normal cut of drifting cowboys.

Buck's raspy voice rent the silence the moment he reached the door.

"How is she, boss?"

"She's still pretty weak, but she's breathin' normally and her color's better. She hasn't said anythin' since those first few words."

"What first few words?"

A weary smile curled Whit's lips. "She asked if she was in heaven."

"Hell…" Buck gave a short laugh. "I've called this place a lot of names, but I ain't never called it heaven."

At the sound of footsteps from the kitchen beyond, Whit turned toward the short, balding fellow, cook's apron in place, who held out a steaming bowl.

"I made some broth. It might not be the best-tasting stuff the little lady ever et, but it's hot." After a pause, Pete offered hesitantly, "I'll feed it to her, if you want."

"No, I'll take care of it while you fellas have breakfast."

Uncertain of the reason for his reluctance to surrender the care of the young woman to Pete's good intentions, Whit accepted the bowl and walked back into the room. Placing the bowl on the stand beside the bed, he appraised the worsening discoloration of the young woman's facial bruising, and inwardly winced. Sometime during the night, the earlier gray of her skin had turned a hot red. The side of her face, where she had fallen, had continued to swell until her eye was almost closed and her lips were badly distorted. The straight white teeth beneath seemed unaffected, however, and he was somehow comforted by that thought.

The woman's puffy lips parted with a soft moan, and Whit took a concerned step forward. He drew his chair closer to the bed, touching his palm to her forehead as he sat. Relieved by the normal heat there, he silently attributed his protective feelings toward this nameless young woman to the concern any man might feel for someone he had discovered almost frozen to death in the snow, most especially when that someone turned out to be female, and hardly more than a child.

Whit studied the young woman more closely, the unanswered questions in his mind growing. Why had she been traveling alone...in a blizzard...in isolated country? She looked to be passably pretty—or he expected she would, once her features returned to normal. Yet she wore her hair clipped short in an unbecoming way, and she was dressed in men's clothing. He had to admit the disguise had been more than adequate, if that was her intent. He had been fooled completely upon first glance. As bruised as she was, he supposed he might still be unaware of her true gender if he hadn't needed to remove her frozen clothing.

An unexpected heat rose to Whit's face. The slender body briefly bared to his gaze, however, had not been that of a child. Long-legged...high-breasted...flawless in line... His hands had been shaking so badly by the time he stripped away the last of her frozen undergarments and slipped her into his spare pair of long underwear that he had barely been able to fasten the buttons.

The young woman moaned softly, and Whit shook off his straying thoughts as he leaned across her to draw the blanket back up over her shoulder. Eyes as black as jet snapped open unexpectedly, startling him.

Relieved to see that those dark eyes were clear, Whit whispered, "Well, it looks like you're feelin' better."

The young woman held his gaze as her swollen lips worked in an attempt at a response. The whole of him becoming caught up in her effort to speak, Whit leaned closer.

A peculiar thrill chased down his spine when her soft voice emerged at last, stretching her words out in a drawl that was heartbreakingly sweet to his ears.

"Yes, I'm feelin' better... now that I'm here." The coal-black eyes searched his. When the young woman spoke again, her voice was more hesitant than before. "Don't—don't you know me, Whittaker?"

*Whittaker?*

Whit was momentarily unable to respond. No one had called him by his full given name since—

Whit searched the young woman's face more closely. Her eyes had filled with tears, and his heart began a slow pounding. It couldn't be...

Incredulity freezing the moment in his mind, Whit whispered, "Is it you, Cricket?" Then, abruptly certain, he gasped, "It *is* you!"

Suddenly hugging her close, elation soaring, Whit heard Cricket's acknowledging sob against his ear. He felt her tears wash his cheek. He felt her trembling and he clutched her closer still. He did not hear the shifting footsteps in the doorway behind him, or the warning cough that preceded Buck's whispered inquiry.

"Something wrong, boss?"

Turning toward the men standing there, Whit responded in a voice hoarse with emotion, "No, nothin' could be more right."

Cricket had slipped back to sleep minutes earlier. She was lying motionless against the pillow as Whit sat beside her bed, still incredulous.

Lydia Elizabeth Blackburn.

Cricket.

Whit's gaze slipped to Cricket's small, delicate hand, limp against the blanket. He picked it up and enclosed it in his. The skin was rough and chapped from her recent ordeal, and a familiar warmth, not untouched by pain, swelled within him.

A smile touched his lips. She had also been asleep and helpless the first time he saw her, so long ago. He had been a boy of ten then, an only child and heir to one of the oldest plantations in Georgia, and one of the largest fortunes in Atlanta. He had been a rascal of the first measure who could do no wrong in his father's eyes since the death of his mother years earlier. The servants' favorite, as well, he had come to accept as his due the affection showered on him. The world had centered around him at Grey Oaks and he had been confident that circumstance would never change.

Then had come the day, a week before Christmas, when his father walked unexpectedly through the front door with a heavily wrapped newborn in his arms, and introduced them all to Mistress Lydia Elizabeth Blackburn.

He had not been prepared for the announcement that the baby would be staying with them for an indefinite period, until Clayton Blackburn, owner of the neighboring plantation, was able to face his grief at having lost his beautiful wife in childbirth.

A soft, self-deriding laugh escaped Whit's lips. He had been livid with jealousy at the attention the squalling infant received that first day. Determined to see what all the fuss was about, he had awaited his first opportunity to find the babe alone and had sneaked into the nursery to make his own assessment. The babe had been sleeping as he drew back the blanket carefully.

He had been greatly disappointed at how little there was to see. Unexpectedly small, almost wizened, the babe had been overwhelmed by the delicately embroidered shift in which she was dressed. Her skin had been red and blotchy, and she had had only a faint sprinkling of dark hair atop her oddly shaped head. Curious, he had tentatively touched the babe's cheek with his fingertip. The babe's eyes had popped open then, and her searching, sightless gaze had seemed to pin him in the moment before she grasped his finger tightly.

The echo of his own startled gasp in that silent room was still vividly clear in his mind, as was his incredulity that a hand so small and dainty—half the size of his finger—could be so strong.

His life had not been the same from that moment on. Christmas had come and gone, as had the New Year. Mr. Blackburn, in deep mourning, had continued to avoid the baby who had stolen his wife from him. The days had stretched into weeks, the weeks into months, and the months into a year, until he had finally given up hope that Mr. Blackburn would ever come for his infant daughter.

He had been unwilling to admit, even to himself, that he hoped Mr. Blackburn never would.

Whit unconsciously stroked a reddish-brown strand of hair away from Cricket's cheek. The bond that had been struck between that infant girl and him that first day had continued to grow, surprising no one more than he. A word, a look, a smile, had seemed to communicate between them feelings no one else could understand, and the shy little girl had become his shadow from the moment she took her first step. Thinking back, Whit could not recall how many times Cricket had brought him her broken toys, as well as her tears, how many times he had ignored the teasing of his friends and drawn her onto his lap to soothe those tears away, or how many times he had awakened in the middle of the night to find Cricket's small, warm body curled up against his back.

But the consolation had not been all one-sided. Locked forever in memory were the long hours the sober three-year-old had sat by his bedside during his serious bout with pneumonia, softly "reading" to him from her picture books. The sound of her childish drawl had been strangely comforting in a world of burning fever and unrelenting weakness. It had lulled him to sleep when he was too helpless and too disconsolate to do else. Her devotion to him constant, she had been his own little cricket on the hearth.

Whit's smile dimmed. His own father had remained a widower until the day he died, but Mr. Blackburn had not. With a new wife in tow, he had come to Grey Oaks a year later to take his four-year-old daughter to live with him. The stricken look in Cricket's eyes just before the door of Grey Oaks had closed behind her, separating them, was still vividly clear in his mind.

Whit sighed. He had been fourteen years old then, tall and well built, on the verge of manhood...and so full of himself that he was mortified by his sense of loss. It had taken him three weeks to manage enough honesty to admit, even to himself, that he missed Cricket. Unable to avoid the truth any longer, he had finally saddled his new gelding and ridden to Windmere to see her, only to be stunned and hurt by Cricket's silent reception. His eyes had been as full as hers when she finally raised her small chin to whisper with a solemn dignity far beyond her years that she would not allow herself to be happy to see him unless he promised never to forget her again. He had made her that promise, and he had kept it...

Until the War.

Painful memories returned and Whit unconsciously frowned. Talk of secession had been everywhere, inflaming passions to a fever pitch. Proud and idealistic at nineteen, he had been deeply stirred by the voices claiming a need for separation. He had been determined to defend the principles of the newborn Confederacy at any cost.

Clothed in military gray and bright visions of glory, he had ridden off to war a short time later. It had not taken him long to come of age in the climate of gunsmoke and bloodshed that had followed.

Strangely, it had only been in his letters to Cricket that he was able to confess his stupidity in believing that such a war could ever be truly "won" by either side. Cricket's letters in return, written in a child's hand, had held a maturity and understanding that brought tears to his eyes.

The war had finally ended. Neither his father nor Grey Oaks had survived Sherman's march through Georgia. Windmere had been badly damaged, but had remained standing. Clayton Blackburn, his wife having succumbed early in the war, had greeted him as a son when he returned. Cricket had welcomed him with all the love in her thirteen-year-old heart.

But the ghosts of the past had been too much to bear. With only the burned ruins of Grey Oaks remaining and carpetbaggers in residence on his land, Whit had turned his back on the South forever.

A familiar, gut-wrenching pain returned, and Whit forced the memories away with sudden anger. He would not allow himself to suffer old sorrows against which he had no defenses! The past was over and done. It could not be relived or restored. He had put it behind him.

Suddenly realizing that his hand had closed in a tight fist around a bluntly cut strand of Cricket's hair, Whit released it.

He stood up abruptly, his gaze lingering on Cricket's still form.

Stirring at a sound at her bedside, Cricket fought to raise her heavy lids. Her eyes were narrow, indiscernible slits beneath heavy lashes as Whittaker stood over her, his expression solemn. Her heart began a slow singing. She had hoped for and dreamed of this moment for so long. The picture of Whittaker as she had seen him that last day, six years earlier, had never left her mind. But he had changed. He was taller, broader in the shoulder and chest. His hair was more blond, his eyes more blue, his smile more beautiful. Lines of maturity had tempered the former youthful smoothness of his face, adding new character and depth. He was still the handsomest man she had ever seen...yet he was now so much more.

Whittaker remained standing over her, his blue eyes intent, stirring the memories that were never truly distant. She could not recall the first time she had seen those brilliant eyes watching her, but she knew what they had meant to her in the uncertainty of her early years. In them she had seen understanding of a need she was unable to express, and instinctive concern far above the many kindnesses shown to her at Grey Oaks. Whittaker had always been there when she needed him. A kind word, a teasing remark, a tug on the hair or a warm lap had revealed to her a side of him few others ever saw. She had been a child, but she had not been too young to feel what she was not able to put into words. And when her father took her back to Windmere and she thought Whittaker had forgotten her, he had then come to promise that he never would.

She had believed him, because she had known he meant every word.

But then the war had come...

A soft sobbing began inside Cricket. Whittaker had been so handsome in his uniform, and so anxious to fight for his beliefs. Everyone had been so proud of him and all the other young men who rode away with him that day, and Papa had scolded her severely when she said she didn't want him to go. He had told her that the Union soldiers could not hold out long against the brave, stouthearted men of the South and that the war would be over quickly. She had lived for that day, treasuring every letter Whittaker wrote, offering him consolation from the bottom of her heart.

She had welcomed him home from the War with all the love in her heart...but it hadn't been enough. With Grey Oaks and everyone on it gone, as well as the life he had always known, the pain had been more than Whittaker had been able to bear. She remembered the tremor of emotion in his voice when he had came to say goodbye. He had

whispered over her sobs that her letters had helped bring
him through the War, that she held a place in his heart that
was hers alone, and that he would never forget her. Her
arms wrapped around his neck, she had remained silent,
vowing in her heart to love him forever.

Letters from Whittaker had become less frequent as the
years passed. Two years before Papa died, a broken man,
the letters had ceased. Waiting only until her papa had been
put to his final rest, she had packed up what was left of her
meager possessions, knowing what she must do—for she
had loved Whittaker since she grew old enough to know the
meaning of the word. He was a part of her that had been
wrenched away. She had not been whole in the time since.

Now a grown woman, she had set out to find him again.
She *had* found him...

Whittaker suddenly turned away from the bed and walked
toward the door. In a few seconds he disappeared from
sight, but his image remained before Cricket's mind as a final thought trailed across her mind.

...if it was not too late.

# Chapter Three

Outside the ranch house, the sun shone brightly, glinting on lazy flurries floating on the clear morning air. Within, Whit sat beside Cricket's bed, holding her hand.

Cricket breathed deeply, enjoying her dream come true. It mattered little that the picture was slightly off kilter—that she was dressed in the same shabby male clothing she had worn during her months of traveling, that her hair was bluntly cut, that her face was still marked by the bruises of her fall...and that, instead of the love she had envisioned seeing in Whittaker's eyes, she saw only concern. She had survived her close brush with death, and she was with Whittaker. That was all that mattered.

*Almost* all.

Cricket's mind returned to their present soft exchange of conversation as Whittaker pressed her gently, asking, "You had no one to help you with your affairs when your papa died?"

Cricket shook her head. "There wasn't much left to worry about. Papa had already sold off most of the land to pay back taxes. We hadn't been able to repair the house, and only a part of it was livable—the part closest to the kitchen." She smiled. "It was the only part of the house where the roof didn't leak."

But Whit did not smile in response. Instead, his brown brows knotted over the incredible blue of his eyes. "What about Judge Parker? Couldn't he help you?"

"Judge Parker isn't a judge anymore."

Whit's lips tightened. "Thornton Phillips was always a good friend of your father's. Surely he—"

"Mr. Phillips lost his land a year after you left. Then he packed up the family and moved away." Noting the deepening of Whit's frown, Cricket offered gently, "It was all right, Whittaker, really it was. I was prepared when Papa died, you know. Winton Moseby had been tryin' to buy what was left of Windmere for years, and he—"

"Winton Moseby." Whit's cheek ticked with restrained anger. "Of course. That damned carpetbagger already had Grey Oaks...."

A familiar sadness tightened in Cricket's stomach at the haunted look that had come into Whit's eyes. She whispered, "He treated the land well, Whittaker. He raised a new house where the old one stood before, and he kept the land together, instead of cuttin' it up as some of the others did with the land they bought. Grey Oaks was beautiful again."

"Moseby stole that land from my father before he died."

"It was all legal and—"

"He stole it!"

"He took advantage of those terrible years, but he was kinder than the rest."

"He was 'kind' because he wanted your land, too."

"I know."

"And you sold it to him anyway?"

"I had no choice."

The fierce intensity of Whit's gaze flickered, and Cricket held her breath. She hadn't traveled all this way to revive the pain of the past for Whittaker. She had only wanted—

"I'm sorry, darlin'." Whit squeezed her hand. "Sometimes I forget how many years ago all this happened ... and that nothin' can change it." He forced a smile. "Tell me what you did then."

Cricket paused in response before answering, "I sold what was left of Windmere, saddled Lucy, and started out to find you."

"To find me." Whit's gaze locked with hers. "How did you know where to look?"

"Your last letter was from Wyomin' Territory."

Whit's eyes widened with incredulity. "That was all you had to go on...a letter that was over four years old? Didn't you stop to think that I could've been anywhere by now— that you could've come all this way for nothin'? Didn't you realize how dangerous it was for you to travel alone in this country?"

Cricket shrugged. "I suppose..."

"How long did it take you to find me?"

"Almost a year."

"A year—" Whittaker swallowed thickly. When he spoke again, his voice was strained with emotion. "Cricket...darlin'...why did you take such a chance? Why didn't you stay where you were and try to locate me by mail first?"

Cricket's throat filled when she saw Whit's pained expression. Why? How could she tell this man that she had loved him since she was a child? How could she explain that she had dreamed of him, awake and sleeping, all the years they were apart? How could she make him comprehend that as she matured, she had begun to hear in those dreams the echoes of his heart calling out to hers? And how could she make him understand the urgency that sound had raised within her...or her solemn vow to answer that call, even if it took her dying breath?

She knew, at that particular moment, that she could not.

Instead, Cricket responded simply, "Because you were all I had left."

* * *

The knot in Whit's throat tightened to pain as he swept
Cricket's sober face with his gaze. Cricket...dear, loving
Cricket. She was no longer the small, sober-eyed child who
had persistently dogged his heels, or the misty-eyed nine-
year-old who had sent him off to war. Neither was she the
thin, pale young ally whose radiant tears had welcomed him
home...or the disconsolate young girl who had trembled in
his arms when he bade her that last farewell. She was now a
young woman, despite her present incongruous appearance. Yet she was still Cricket...the person who had been
able to see into his heart better than anyone he had ever
known.

The gnawing ache inside Whit expanded. Cricket had
risked her life to find him, and he would take care of her.
She was his Cricket on the hearth, a consolation like no
other, and a link to a part of him he had thought forgotten.
It was a part of himself that was filled with pain. He
wished—

Whit smiled. "Are you sure you feel strong enough to get
up today?" He swept her face assessingly, unconsciously
touching the bruised skin of her cheek with his fingertips.
"You're sure you don't want to rest for another day?"

"I'm fine, Whittaker, really I am."

Whit searched Cricket's face more closely. He saw that
the shadows underneath her eyes had not yet completely
faded. He saw that her skin was pale where it was not
bruised or chapped by long exposure to the freezing wind,
but he also saw a familiar glint in the dark eyes returning his
gaze. He recognized that light of determination, and he
knew arguments were useless against it.

"All right, let's go."

Taking Cricket's arm as she stood up, Whit walked with
her toward the bedroom door. Her arm was surprisingly
fragile underneath the rough cotton shirt she wore, and her
step was more unsteady than she cared to let on—but her

chin was high and firm. Emotion swelled within Whit as he stepped through the doorway and into sight of the three men waiting there.

Whit paused, surprised at the unexpected expressions of discomfort each man wore in varying degrees as they glanced between Cricket and him. Sliding an arm around Cricket's narrow shoulders, he drew her against his side in a spontaneous protective gesture. Cricket leaned against him, familiar and comfortable in the circle of his arm, and a slow warmth expanded within him. It touched a part of him that had been cold for longer than he could remember. It put him in mind of a time when he—

"So, there you are, Whit!"

The clear feminine voice that rang in the silence of the room turned Whit toward the kitchen doorway with a snap. He felt Cricket stiffen slowly when a tall, golden-haired woman stepped clearly into view. Cricket took a subtle step that freed her from the curve of his arm as the woman approached them with a confident sway that spoke more clearly than words. In a moment her lush warmth was tight against him, and her lips were meeting his. Her arm slid familiarly around his waist as her lingering kiss ended and she stepped back to look down at Cricket with a cool smile. "I had thought the weather was the cause of Whit's neglect this past week, but from what I've been told, an unexpected guest occupied most of his time. You must be she." Looking up at Whit again, she said, "You must introduce me to your *friend*, Whit."

Whit gritted his teeth at the beauteous woman's caustic tone. Cricket's dark eyes turned up to his as he said, "Cricket, darlin'..." He paused, somehow reluctant, before continuing. "I'd like you to meet Miss Jayne Tillis, my bride-to-be."

His cheek twitching with annoyance, Whit watched the two horsemen as they turned out of sight on the horizon.

Jamming his hands into his pockets, he ignored the bright sunshine glimmering on the frozen landscape, hunched the broad expanse of his shoulders against the cold and started back toward the house. The heat of Jayne's parting kiss had obviously been calculated to overcome his unexpressed anger by stirring another basic emotion, but it had left him cold. Unable to speak freely in the presence of the ranch hand waiting to accompany her home, he had kept his silence, but he knew his anger had not gone unnoted.

Damn! It had been a hell of a morning! At that particular moment, he was uncertain how he had ever come to accept and even admire Jayne's particular brand of aggressiveness. But the truth was, she had used it well in the past. He had been flattered by her open display of interest when they first met, two years earlier. He had been startled when she instituted their first intimate contact, and he had been as overwhelmed by her sexual abandon as he had been by her beauty. She had been a fantasy come true for a man with only bitter memories to keep him company on a lonely ranch in the middle of nowhere. He had been pleased to have such a handsome, passionate woman both on his arm and in his bed. When she led him to the point of commitment, talking of the promise of the future they could share in the eventual joining of her father's land and his, and sealed her words with a heated joining of another kind, he had dismissed the lingering doubt in the back of his mind and set the date of their marriage for early spring. He had been pleased to finally have taken a positive step toward restoring hope to a future that had once seemed hopelessly bleak.

At times like that just past, however, when Jayne's aggressiveness took another course, his doubts returned.

Stepping in from the cold, Whit was hanging his coat in the alcove by the door when he heard Buck's solicitous voice in the room beyond.

"Here, Miss Cricket, let me do that for you."

"No, please don't bother. I'm fine, Buck, really, I am."
Cricket's familiar drawl, and her inherent Southern courtesy, tightened his throat. Its tone brought back, in bittersweet reminiscence, all that the South had once been to him. Stepping into sight, he saw that the short, stocky ranch hand stood looking down at Cricket with the same respect and instinctive warmth that were reflected on Pete's and Sam's faces, as well. He had seen a look of another kind in Buck's knowing gaze whenever he looked at Jayne. It was not difficult to comprehend that, despite her rough appearance, Cricket had won his men over completely with a few softly spoken words and her inborn air of gentility as Jayne never could in a lifetime.

Whit allowed that thought only a few moments in his mind before Cricket drew herself slowly to her feet. She turned toward him as he approached, but her smile was forced. "I'd like to go out to the barn to see Lucy now, if you don't mind."

Their breath frosty puffs on the frigid air as they trudged toward the barn moments later, Whit watched Cricket for signs of weakness. She had shuddered when hit by the first icy blast, and he had had a moment's doubt as to whether she was yet up to facing the bitter cold. Gripping her arm when she stumbled on a slippery patch at the barn door, he was about to voice that concern when Cricket raised her eyes to his and whispered, "Whittaker, I'm so sorry...."

Whit's concern was obvious as he drew her into the warmth of the barn, then responded, "Sorry? Sorry for what, sugar?"

Cricket did not immediately reply. She was sorry for so many things she could not tell him. She was sorry that it had taken her so long to grow up. She was sorry that when she finally had, it had taken her so long to find him. She was sorry she had believed when she awakened and saw Whit's face hovering over her that all her dreams had come true.

But most of all, she was sorry that all the while she had been indulging those dreams, it had already been too late.

"Cricket?"

Cricket swallowed tightly. "I'm sorry...that I caused you some difficult moments with Jayne this mornin'."

Whit's expression stiffened. "Jayne can be very difficult when she wants to be."

"She's a beautiful woman."

"She is."

"You're a lucky man."

Whit raised his hand to Cricket's cheek. He touched it lightly, then smiled. His smile melted her heart as he whispered, "Yes, I suppose I am."

A soft whinny from the rear of the barn interrupted their exchange, and Cricket turned her head toward the sound. Her heart leaped as the whinny sounded once more. Beside the rear stall a minute later, Cricket stroked the soft muzzle thrust eagerly toward her, her voice husky as she spoke to the happy mare. She looked up at Whit, her eyes filling despite herself. "It was so cold, and we were both so tired. I thought we were both done for when Lucy went down, but I guess I should've known better than to sell her brave Southern heart short."

Turning at a sound in the doorway, Cricket gasped at the sight of the huge dog lunging toward her. In the space of a moment, he had covered the distance between them and had leaped up against her, his wet tongue swiping at her face. Laughing aloud, she fended him off with her arms outstretched as Whit grasped the dog's collar and pulled him back with a stern command.

"Down, Snap!"

"So, this is Snap!" Bending down, Cricket patted the animal's huge, wiry head while Whit held him in place. She spoke into the small, bright eyes trained on her face.

"You're the fella who saved my life, aren't you, boy? I don't suppose I can ever thank you enough for that."

Snap responded with quick swipes of his tongue at her hand, and Cricket laughed again. Looking up, she saw that Whit was smiling, as well, when the released animal disappeared back through the doorway, as quickly as he had come.

A faded memory returned to Cricket's mind.

"Do you remember old Wilbur Parson's dog... the big red one that liked to swim?" Immediate recollection registered in Whit's gaze as she continued, "Do you remember the time he followed us to the swimmin' hole and jumped in on top of me?"

"I remember, all right." Whit laughed. "You almost drowned. You were all of six years old and mad as a hornet when I pulled you up, sputterin' and chokin'. You gave that poor old dog some scoldin'."

"Yes, I did... and he made me feel so guilty when he hung his head like he did that I fed him all my sandwiches."

"Then you ate half of mine."

"Yours were better than mine! Hallie always packed chicken sandwiches for you."

"That's because I was always Hallie's favorite."

"You were her favorite because you brought her peppermint drops every time you came to visit! I never had any candy to give her. Papa wouldn't let me have any. He said it was bad for my teeth."

"Poor Cricket... who got only bread-and-butter sandwiches."

"No, that isn't true." Cricket winked. "I always got half of yours."

Laughing again, Whit sat abruptly on a nearby stool. He pulled Cricket down onto his lap, as he had done so many times in the past. After tossing off her hat and his to avoid a clash of brims, he curved his arm casually around her waist and leaned toward her. The bright gold of his hair glinted in a shaft of light, and she could smell the clean, male scent of him as he whispered into her ear, "I never did tell you that I told Hallie you didn't like chicken sandwiches, did I?"

"You did that?" Aghast, Cricket stared at Whit's sly expression. "Why?"

"Because I figured there was only enough chicken for me . . . that's why."

"You didn't!"

"I did."

"And I always thought you were so honorable!"

"I wasn't honorable. I was smart."

"Oh, Whittaker . . ."

Cricket looked into the brilliant blue of Whit's eyes, so close to hers. Her heart filled to bursting at the warmth there, she rested her forehead briefly against Whit's, the words she spoke coming from the heart.

"I missed you so much when you were gone, Whittaker. When you went off to war, I followed your route on the map in my room, markin' off the spots where your letters came from. I remember the day Grey Oaks burned. The fire lasted long into the night, and my heart ached, knowin' what you would suffer. I begged Papa not to write to you that it was gone, but then, when your papa died . . . well, we couldn't hide the truth any longer."

The torment of that day returning, Cricket whispered, "I wished with all my heart that I could spare you the sight of Grey Oaks in ruins. When you came home, I knew deep inside you wouldn't be stayin' long. I couldn't forget the pain in your eyes when you left that last day. It stayed with me . . . in my dreams. I knew I'd never be able to be truly happy unless I knew *you* were happy again."

Cricket paused, her heart completing the words she could not say, that *she* had wanted to be the one to make him smile

again. Instead, she continued, "I'm glad you're happy...
that you've found someone...and some place to call home."
She took a strengthening breath. "Now, when I leave, I'll be
able to remember the good things, too...not only the bad."

Whit stiffened. "What are you talkin' about? What do
you mean, 'when you leave'?"

Cricket paused. She had known the moment Jayne appeared what she must do. She loved Whit too much to stay
and watch his married life unfold, knowing that he was
holding another woman in his arms, knowing that another
woman would bear his beautiful children, knowing that this
other woman would be living out her lifelong dream of be-
longing to Whit.

Cricket forced a smile. "My papa always told me that a
lady never overstays her welcome. I'll be leavin' when the
weather changes enough so Lucy and I can make it safely.
We—"

"You're not goin' anywhere. You're here, and here's
where you're goin' to stay."

Cricket's smile tightened. She averted her gaze. "No, I
can't."

"Yes, you can."

"Whittaker, I—"

"Cricket, look at me." Turning her to face him again,
Whit whispered, "You don't really expect me to let you
leave, do you, to let you wander off alone, not knowin'
where you'll be?"

"It won't be like that. I'll keep in touch. I'll write."

"No."

"But Jayne—"

"Jayne will understand."

"No, she—"

Whit's expression grew tense. "You always were stubborn when you got somethin' into your head, and you never

did know what was good for you. I do. You're goin' to stay here . . . now . . . indefinitely. . . . Do you understand?''

Whit's light eyes blazed with anger, and Cricket sighed. She hadn't wanted to disturb him so, especially not after the warm moments they had just shared. Her regret for the uneasiness between them strong, Cricket ran a tentative finger along the tight line of Whit's jaw. It softened under her touch, and she whispered, "I'll stay until Christmas, at least. It's only a few weeks away."

"Cricket . . ."

"All right. I suppose it's too early to talk about leavin', anyway."

The straight line of Whit's lips ticked. "Stubborn . . . you were always so stubborn. Nobody could ever make me more angry than you."

Cricket responded in immediate challenge. "That's not true, Whittaker. What about the time Abner Potts shot your cat by mistake? You were fit to kill!"

"Poor old Whiskers . . . Potts, the old fool, thought he was a raccoon."

"And what about the time Beau Sellers stole your clothes when you were swimmin'?"

"That was different, he—"

"And the time your papa made you clean all those fish you caught in a net that day, because he said you had taken unfair advantage of the poor creatures? And later, when he told you you had to *eat* all of them, too? You were so angry! I thought—"

"All right."

"And the time when—"

"All right, you win!"

Lifting her to her feet, Whit stood beside her. Suddenly grinning, he slipped his arms around her and hugged her tight before releasing her to whisper huskily, "Did I tell I'm happy you're here, Cricket, darlin'?" He brushed her cheek with his lips. "Damned happy."

And Cricket's heart sang, because, somehow, she knew he meant every word.

# Chapter Four

"You didn't have to do that, Miss Cricket, but we sure do appreciate your thinking of us."

A frigid gust whipped the snowcovered landscape as Cricket turned toward Sam Little. Wrapped to the ears in her scarf, her hat pulled low on her head and two layers of clothing underneath protecting her from the winter chill, she handed him a cup of steaming coffee from the rear of the Bar WR wagon. She liked the tall, graying cowboy. He was quiet and sincere and appreciative of small considerations. He had been the most difficult of Whit's hired hands to come to know in the two weeks since she arrived at the ranch, but she had sensed from the start that she had an ally in him.

She responded, "It's a cold day, and Pete made a big fresh pot of coffee. I was in the mood for a ride and some good company, so I brought it out to y'all." She poured another cup and held it out to Buck as the short, stocky cowboy rode up behind Sam. Waiting until Buck had accepted the coffee with a grateful nod, she poured a cup for herself and sat back on the wagon. She raised the cup to her mouth and looked out over the icy landscape. The brilliant afternoon sun had turned the land to glittering hills of silver as far as the eye could see. The brilliance overwhelmed all color, contrasting vividly with the blue of the sky in a scene of stupendous beauty. She breathed deeply of the crisp air and took another sip of the hot liquid, her gaze unconsciously searching. She turned toward Sam when he spoke again.

"If it's the boss you're looking for, he went down into the draw up ahead to see if there were any early calves that might be needing help. That draw seems to be a favorite spot for calving heifers, but it isn't as safe as they seem to think it is. We lost a few down there in deep drifts last year. The boss isn't about to let that happen again." Sam paused. "I'll go get him and tell him you're here, if you like."

"It's kind of you to offer, but that isn't necessary." Cricket smiled. "Pete bundled the pot up like a newborn babe. The coffee'll stay hot for a while, and I'm in no hurry."

"Yes, ma'am." Sam bobbed his head. "That's fine with me. Buck and me appreciate the company, especially company that improves the scenery like you do."

Cricket gave a surprised laugh. "Well, I do thank you for that compliment, Mr. Little." She indicated the worn male jacket she wore and stretched out legs clad in the same baggy trousers she had been wearing when found unconscious in the snow. "It's truly appreciated, especially since I haven't been at my best in recent weeks."

"Well, ma'am, it's my thinking that your worst is probably as good or better than some others' best—without a word of a lie."

"You are too kind, Sam." Cricket's smile broadened. "And I always thought Georgia men were the smoothest talkers around."

"Well—" Sam's light brown eyes remained sincere "—I'm not a Georgia man, but I do know that if clothes don't make the man, they don't make the woman, either, and I've traveled far and wide enough to recognize a real lady when I see one."

Cricket nodded her thanks. She was blinking back the sudden heat under her eyelids when a sound turned her toward the draw in the distance just as Whit's broad figure popped into sight over the rise. He spotted her immediately and started toward them, steadying the calf lying across his saddle in front of him.

Drawing up alongside, Whit frowned. "What're you doin' out here, sugar? You're a long way from the ranch. It's not safe for you out here alone."

"I'm not alone." Cricket smiled and patted the rifle lying in the wagon beside her. "There's no chance of my gettin' lost, either. It's easy to follow a trail in the snow, you know."

"I suppose." Whit's frown remained for long moments before he looked into the wagon behind her. "What've you got there?"

"Coffee . . . nice and hot. Pete thought you might appreciate it right about now."

"He did?" Whit's light eyes caught and held Cricket's. The music in her heart started again as his smile flashed for the first time. "It's funny that Pete never gave much thought to whether or not we might be appreciatin' somethin' nice and hot out here before you came."

"Now don't you tell me that." Cricket felt the heat of a flush warm her cheeks. "I just won't believe it."

Dismounting, Whit accepted the steaming cup Cricket offered him and held her gaze. The singing in Cricket's heart grew louder. Whit was such a beautiful man, superior in every way. He was taller than most, over six feet and three inches, she was sure. He was more powerfully built than most, with shoulders broad and erect. He was more handsome than most, with hair that glinted pure gold in the sun, eyes so bright and clear that she felt they could see right through her, and a smile that was quick and true. The sweet scent of home rose in her mind, and Cricket knew the reason was simple. Home was wherever Whit was. She had always known that . . . as well as she had known that love walked in Whit's steps…for her, anyway. That would never change.

But Whittaker had found someone else to love....

"What are you thinkin' about, darlin'?"

"Thinkin'?" Cricket shrugged. "I was thinkin' that it's beautiful out here and that you made a good choice when you chose this place to put down new roots. I was thinkin' that if somebody looked really hard at the blue of that sky, he might be able to see right into the eye of God."

Whit was momentarily silent. "You think so, huh?" Surprising her, he slid his arm around her and hugged her against his side, his voice dropping to a conspiratorial whisper as he looked down at her. "Do you know what *I'm* thinkin'? I'm thinkin' my Cricket has the heart of a poet underneath all those layers of clothes."

*My* Cricket.

Cricket held Whit's gaze for long moments. "Whit, I—"

"Oh, no…here *she* comes." Buck's low groan turned Cricket toward him as he assessed the approaching rider in the distance. He shot Cricket an apologetic glance. "Sorry, ma'am."

No apology was necessary. Recognizing the rider with a sinking sensation in the pit of her stomach, Cricket steeled herself against Jayne's approach.

Jayne's marvelous gelding snorted as she drew up alongside and dismounted. She walked directly to Whit and kissed him on the mouth, then turned caustically to the others standing there.

"Well, if I had known there was a party going on out here, I would've come sooner."

Embarrassed, Cricket forced a smile. "Not really a party…just some hot coffee on a cold day."

"So, you're Pete's messenger, then. How *nice*."

"Yes, it was nice." Whit's expression was stiff. Appearing unaffected by the heat of his intended's kiss, he continued, "But Cricket's goin' to have to be startin' back to the ranch now." He turned toward Cricket. "I'd appreciate your takin' this calf back for me, if you would. His mama abandoned him. He won't last another night out here in this weather."

"Oh, Whit, really." Jayne raised her brows impatiently. "All that trouble for a calf."

"Yes, that's right, all that trouble for a calf." The granite stiffness of Whit's jaw was a warning Jayne did not ignore. She maintained her silence, with visible effort, as he turned to Cricket once more.

"I'd appreciate it if you'd do that for me, sugar. Pete can put him in the barn for you. It'll save me some time."

"Yes, you do that, 'sugar.'" Jayne's smile was stiff. "Whit and I can use that time to talk."

Waiting only until the calf had been loaded onto the wagon, Cricket started back in the direction she had come, relieved to have left the beautiful but furious Jayne behind her. A tear trickled down her cheek as she recalled the familiar manner in which Whit had wound his arm around Jayne's waist, despite his obvious irritation.

Foolish Jayne...didn't she see? "Cricket"... "darlin'"..."sugar"... They were all pet names for a woman who would never be more than a little girl in Whit's eyes. Foolish Jayne...lucky Jayne, who had claimed Whit for her own.

The motherless calf bawled loudly in the wagon behind her, and Cricket glanced back at the animal's sad face. She sighed, a voice in her mind whispering, *Cry for me, too, little fella. I won't waste my tears, because it's already too late.*

Waiting only until Buck and Sam had ridden off at his harshly barked orders, Whit turned toward Jayne with barely controlled irritation. He saw the challenge in the bright green of her eyes, noting that they were more beautiful still with the fire ignited there. Creamy skin, perfect features, a warm, inviting mouth, the body of Venus...

And the tongue of a viper.

The softness of his tone belying the anger boiling inside him, Whit said from between gritted teeth, "You've been actin' like a jealous shrew since Cricket arrived on the Bar WR. I'd like you to remember that Cricket is my guest."

"Your guest? And I'm your intended, but you seem to have forgotten that little technicality in the past two weeks. I've seen you exactly twice during that time."

"The weather's been bad."

"Not that bad!"

"And you've been actin' worse."

"Have I?" Jayne paused, her gaze warming unexpectedly as it dropped to linger on his mouth. Her lips parted to expose the pink tip of her tongue. He remembered what that tongue could do, and his heart began a slow pounding.

"That's right, you're remembering, aren't you, Whit?" Jayne pressed closer, her voice turning to a husky purr. "I love you, Whit, and I admit I'm jealous of your little Cricket. You've been paying more attention to her than you have to me, and I don't like it. I've been dreaming about you every night... about the way it was when we were in Cheyenne the last time... and the way it was when you sent your men off for two days last month and I came to stay. I'll bet your bed was never warmer than it was then. I can make it like that again for us... every night... until we're both too exhausted to do anything else but sleep."

Whit felt the slow rise of a familiar emotion as Jayne slipped her hand underneath his jacket and stroked him brazenly. Curving her hand around the bulge below his belt, she looked up into his eyes. "It's cold out here and there's not a damned bit of shelter, or I'd remind you right now how it is between us. Tonight, Whit, darling. Come to my house tonight. You can sleep over until morning. Papa will be glad to let you use the guest room." She stroked him more boldly. "But you won't be alone there for long...."

Whit's breathing was ragged. Jayne was right. He was remembering. He was remembering the softness of her flesh beneath him, the heat of their joinings, the way Jayne had of using every bit of herself to taunt and tantalize him, just as she was doing now as she rubbed against him slowly, rhythmically...

Whit steadied himself and shook his head. "I can't come tonight."

"You can."

"No."

"Yes."

The persuasion continued.

A full silver moon hung brightly in the cloudless night sky, casting an iridescent path across the snow, as Cricket stood looking out the bedroom window. The house was quiet. The only sounds had been the deep snores echoing through the darkness from the bedroom the three hired men shared on the other side of the house, and the rustle of her own twisting and turning in bed as she struggled to sleep. Whit had commented on his plans to erect a bunkhouse for the men as soon as the weather turned warm enough. It was Buck, however, who had told her that Jayne had openly declared she had no intention of sharing the house with hired men after Whit and she were married.

Cricket had smiled and commented that newlyweds liked privacy. Buck had responded with a twitch of his full mustache that as far as he and the other men were concerned, Jayne could have all the privacy she wanted.

The ache inside her tightening, Cricket recalled Whit's return from the range that afternoon. Contrary to his mood earlier in the day, he had been irritable and tense. He had declared that he would be riding over to Jayne's for supper, and that he probably would stay the night. He had left shortly afterward.

Sam's comment as she watched Whit ride out of sight had been succinct. "It's always sad to be reminded that even an intelligent man don't always do his thinking with his brain."

With those words resounding in her mind, Cricket glimpsed her image in the washstand mirror. She supposed Sam was right. The slight young woman reflected there, her thick brown hair short and awkwardly cut, her heavily lashed dark eyes her only distinctive feature, suffered greatly in comparison with Jayne's fair, patrician beauty and exceptional womanly charms.

The dinner table had been silent after Whit left. She had been aware of the glances of the men, and their unspoken disapproval of Whit's departure. She had appreciated their concern, but she had retired to her room early, her heart in her boots.

The low bawling of a calf echoed through the stillness of the night as Cricket's gaze flicked toward the barn. She had delivered the poor creature to the ranch that afternoon as Whit had requested. Pete and she had settled him as comfortably as possible in the barn, but the little fellow wasn't happy. He didn't like being alone.

The calf bawled again, and Cricket reached instinctively for her clothes. She was dressing before she consciously realized her intent.

The icy night air buffeted Cricket's face when she stepped out into the darkness of the yard. Raising the lantern, she walked across the yard, head tucked down into her shoulders, leaning into the wind. Relieved when the barn door creaked closed behind her, she started toward the bawling that continued from the rear stall. The sound stopped as she came into view, and Cricket could not help but smile at the lost expression of the animal staring back at her.

"What's the matter, little fella? Lonesome and hungry?" She shrugged. "I suppose I can understand that."

The calf bawled once more, and Cricket's smile became bittersweet. "Well, there's not much I can do about findin' your mama for you, but I know that bottle's around here somewhere.''

Reaching into a bucket nearby, Cricket found the bottle Pete had used earlier. She pulled off the oversize nipple, walked to the rear wall and filled the bottle from the bucket of milk there. The calf, a fast learner, was ready and waiting for her when she returned.

Leaning against the side of the stall, Cricket watched the calf as it suckled eagerly. The soft, steady sound of the animal's gulping, the scampering of tiny feet in the corners and the battering of windy gusts against the outside walls lulled her into a lethargy that left her unprepared for the sudden jerk of the calf's head that pulled the bottle from her hand. The bottle thudded onto the floor and disappeared from sight in the shadows as the impatient calf renewed its noisy complaint. Desperate to silence the animal, Cricket dropped to her knees. She was searching the shadows on all fours when a hand closed on her shoulder and jerked her to her feet. Turning with a gasp, Cricket met Whit's angry gaze.

"Don't you have any sense at all?" At her confused silence, he continued heatedly, "That calf's hungry and scared. Crawlin' around like that on the ground, you'd be done for with one kick!"

"I was watchin' him!"

"No, you weren't!"

"Yes, I was!"

"No, you weren't, damn it!"

Reaching down into the shadows, Whit retrieved the bottle.

Cricket gasped with surprise. "How did you know where that bottle was?"

Whit answered her question with one of his own. "What are you doin' out here this time of night?"

Cricket paused, then shrugged. "I couldn't sleep, and neither could the calf, so I came out to see what I could do." The calf bawled again, and Whit shoved the bottle into

Cricket's hand. The calf was suckling noisily when Cricket turned back to Whit. "What are you doin' home? I thought you were goin' to spend the night at Jayne's house."

"I decided not to."

"Why?"

"That's none of your business."

"Oh." Cricket's lip twitched. "You had an argument . . . about me."

"We didn't argue about you."

"Yes, you did."

"No, we didn't!"

"Yes, you did. Jayne doesn't like me, and I don't suppose I blame her."

"You don't blame her. . . ."

"How could I blame her? You work hard, and you had little enough time to spend with her as it was. Then I came along, and you had even less."

"No, I didn't."

"Yes, you did, with havin' to take care of me after you found me."

"You've been well for two weeks now."

"And feelin' you had to entertain me."

"I haven't been entertainin' you."

"You have."

"No, I haven't."

"You—"

"You've been entertainin' me."

"I've been entertainin' you?"

"That's right." Whit paused, frowning. "You brought me a touch of home that I realized I've been missin' for a long time. A man has a right to enjoy the company of friends, and the woman he loves should understand that."

*The woman he loves.*

Cricket felt a new depth of pain. She concealed it determinedly as Whit turned her toward him, speaking more gently than before. "I don't want you worryin' about the way things are between Jayne and me. It has nothin' to do with you. Jayne's used to gettin' her way. Her daddy spoiled her from the day she was born, and she just naturally expects that I will, too.''

Cricket held Whit's gaze soberly. "I suppose a woman has the right to expect to be spoiled by the man who loves her.''

"I suppose. But a man has a right to expect some things, too…like havin' his woman respect him and his wishes, even if she doesn't always agree. Jayne's havin' trouble with that one.''

"Oh.''

Whit tilted Cricket's face up to his. His expression softened. "Don't worry, sugar. Jayne and I had a long talk, just like she said she wanted.'' A smiled twitched at Whit's lips. "Well, maybe not *exactly* like she wanted…'' Sober again, he continued, "But we straightened some things out. She's goin' to try to be…nicer.''

"Oh, Whit, you didn't tell her to—''

"I didn't *tell* her anythin', darlin'. I just explained some things…very clearly.''

"And everythin's all right?''

"Everythin' fine. Jayne's comin' over for dinner tomorrow night.''

"For dinner…with all of us?''

"That's right.''

Cricket swallowed hard. "That's good.''

"When she gets to know you, she'll love you. I know she will.''

Cricket's smile was weak. "Of course.''

"And you'll like her.''

"Of course.''

"And we'll be one big, happy family, the way it should be.''

*Never…*

"Cricket?''

"Of course.''

Pausing to search her face one more, Whit slipped his arms around her and hugged her close. His embrace lingered as he whispered against her hair, "Don't worry, darlin'. Everythin's goin' to be fine. It'll be Christmas in a few weeks, and it'll be the best one we've ever had. I promise you that."

Whit's warmth enveloped Cricket like a dream that had not quite come true. Cricket indulged it with growing emotion and replied in a shaky voice, "Bein' here with you is enough, Whittaker. You don't have to promise me anythin'."

Drawing back, Whit stared silently into her eyes before whispering, "No, I suppose I don't." He stroked a wisp of hair back from her cheek. "But that doesn't change anythin' at all." Whit leaned down and brushed her lips lightly with his. She felt the brief contact down to her toes, a yearning for still more surging inside her in the moment before he drew back and looked into the stall, where the calf stood silent at last. He turned back to Cricket. "I think that little fella will be all right until mornin'. Come on, let's go back to the house and get some sleep."

Cricket was walking toward the barn door in the curve of Whit's arm when he repeated, "Don't worry, sugar, when Jayne gets to know you the way I do, she'll love you."

Silent, Cricket stepped out into the cold.

The bedroom door closed behind her, and Cricket closed her eyes.

Never . . . never, never, never. Jayne would never accept her, much less come to love her. Whit was entertaining a fantasy that would never materialize. She knew the eventual pain of indulging such self-deception.

Peeling off her clothes, Cricket dropped them onto the nearby chair, then slipped into the worn shirt she had been using as a sleeping garment since she arrived at the ranch. It was Whit's shirt, and the most precious article of clothing she owned. It closed around her, and she sighed, climbing into Whit's bed and pulling his blanket up over her. She laid her head on Whit's pillow, knowing Whit would never lie beside her there. She would never feel his arms around her, his flesh warming hers. She would never know what it was to be loved completely by Whit, to be made a part of him as she had dreamed, because his love belonged to another woman. He had told her so, in clear words that neither her heart nor her mind could refute.

Yes, she knew what she must do. Whit had promised her Christmas. She owed it to him to let him give her that, so that they might part with warmth. By that time she would have found a plausible excuse to leave. Whit would accept her leaving then. He would have no choice.

Not conscious of the tear that trailed from the corner of her eye, Cricket took a steadying breath. In the meantime, she would make the best . . . the *very best* . . . of the time she had left with Whit. She would store memories for the long, empty years without him ahead of her, and she would love him silently, with all her heart.

Closing her eyes, Cricket smiled at the handsome, blond-haired image that remained clear in her mind. It was the last thing she saw as, exhausted, she finally slipped off to sleep.

The low sawing sound of Pete's snores echoed in the room as Whit closed the door behind him and slipped into the bunk bed awaiting him. It had been a long, trying day . . . more difficult than he had imagined it could possibly be. The most trying of those hours had been those he spent with Jayne a short time earlier.

Whit unconsciously shook his head in recollection. Jayne had been at her best . . . and her worst . . . both of which were formidable. Beautiful as always, she had seduced him with her gaze, with her walk, with her tone. Her lips had promised more . . . much more. . . .

Whit paused in his thoughts, uncertain. Strangely, he had walked through Jayne's passionate machinations as if from a distance. Untouched by it all, he had waited until she had exhausted her attempts to win him with her wiles and until she had vented her furious frustration at her failure. He had then told her, in a flat, emotionless tone, that Cricket was a part of his past that he would not put aside for anyone. Silent and fuming, Jayne had accepted his declaration, as well as his invitation to dinner the following night. She had been trembling with rage when he bade her good-night and walked out the door.

Curiously, even now he was uncertain why he had been so determined to leave.

It had been a damned cold ride home, and he had cursed under his breath when he saw a light in the barn. He had entered expecting to find a problem. He had found Cricket instead.

A familiar flood of warmth returned as the image of Cricket's small, sober face flickered across Whit's mind. His smile slowly faded. Jayne was a grown woman, and Cricket was little more than a child, yet he had read more understanding in Cricket's dark eyes in those few moments when they talked than he had seen in Jayne's furious gaze in all the time he spent with her that evening. And damned if he hadn't felt more true warmth in Cricket's brief, spontaneous return of his embrace than he had felt in Jayne's deliberately provocative manipulations!

Whit recalled the moment he had brushed Cricket's lips with his. It had been the briefest of contacts, but it had been incredibly sweet. She had rested her head against his shoulder as they walked toward the barn door, and it had felt good... so good.

Cricket... darlin' Cricket... An extraordinary warmth stole over him. He'd make everything up to her, the years of deprivation and loss, the sadness, the long years of separation. He'd give her a Christmas she wouldn't forget.

His weary eyes closing, Whit indulged the return of Cricket's dark-eyed image. His generosity was not selfless, he knew. As had always been true, in giving to Cricket, in hearing her voice, in knowing she was near, he somehow gained so much more than he gave.

It was strange ... inexplicable ... and so very, very precious.

# Chapter Five

A strong morning sun warmed Cricket's shoulders as she rode along the snow-covered trail. Heavily wrapped in the male garb she had worn for longer than she cared to remember, she maintained a leisurely pace. She turned and glanced at the horseman riding beside her.

The nip in the air faded from Cricket's mind as she allowed her gaze to linger. Broad-shouldered and erect astride his black gelding, his handsome face sober, Whit had been silent for the major portion of their ride since they had left the ranch house. She wondered what he was thinking.

It had been almost a month since she arrived at the Bar WR. In the time since, the havoc the blizzard had wreaked on Whit's struggling herd had been nullified by Whit's and his ranch hands' unrelenting work. Marooned cattle had been rescued with few losses, calving heifers had been driven to pastures close by so that they might be watched more carefully, sick cows had been doctored, and the upper pastures had been carefully patrolled to make sure the livestock there was wintering well. Each man had done his job instinctively and efficiently, and Cricket had shared in Whit's obvious satisfaction at the state of affairs.

At the state of *ranch* affairs.

As for other matters . . .

Unconsciously wincing, Cricket recalled the evening just past. Jayne had arrived in the late afternoon with the ranch hand who was to accompany her back home. A middle-aged, gruff-voiced fellow, he had said little as he took a place at the supper table, obviously as uncomfortable as the others with the ritual that had been foisted upon them by Whit's good intentions.

Jayne, beautiful in a green dress that lay against the curving line of her body in a way that was almost breathtaking, had carried the bulk of the conversation, just as she had during her series of visits since Whit's talk with her weeks earlier.

*One big happy family* they were not.

Cricket suppressed a groan. It wasn't as if she hadn't tried. She had begun by attempting to participate in the conversation Jayne instituted at the table by adding small, significant comments, but she had learned early on that Jayne did not appreciate interruption. She had tried waiting to be invited into the conversation, only to discover that Jayne had commented to Whit on her lack of friendliness. She had attempted to solve her dilemma by involving others in conversation so that Whit and Jayne might have an opportunity to speak to each other, only to reap another of Jayne's disapproving stares.

They were formidable stares, indeed.

Cricket was not alone in her discomfiture, however. Under other circumstances, she might actually have been amused by the manner in which Buck's jaw seemed to lock the moment Jayne entered the house, or by the way Sam's head seemed to sink down into his shoulders when she approached him. As for Pete . . . she had strong doubts about whether the dinnerware could withstand another of Jayne's visits, if he continued his clattering comments on Jayne's presence at the table. The way the men had taken to scattering as soon as supper was over during Jayne's visits had become almost embarrassing. The result was a series of tense, awkward evenings seemingly enjoyed by no one.

That same routine had been followed each time Jayne visited, the only difference being the lengthening periods of time Whit and Jayne had taken to spending alone together before Jayne left. Those periods of privacy, sought by both of them, had spoken more loudly than words could have, affirming the painful truth that Whit loved Jayne, and nothing would change that.

A familiar knot tightened in Cricket's stomach as she allowed her gaze to linger a moment longer on Whit's profile, etched against the glittering silver of the snow-covered landscape. Christmas was fast approaching, and with it her undeclared time of departure. The time was growing short—painfully short. It would be difficult to say goodbye.

Whit turned toward her, and Cricket forced that last thought from her mind. He smiled suddenly, and Cricket's heart took wing. This outing had been unexpected, as unexpected as the day off Whit had given the men from their work. Not bothering to remain behind to see how they would entertain themselves, Whit had surprised her by saddling up her horse, as well as his own, and taking her off for a morning ride. If he had been uncommunicative in the time since, the brilliance of his smile now more than compensated for it as he prompted her, saying, "You're awfully quiet this mornin', sugar."

"*I'm* quiet?" Cricket gave a short laugh. "You were the one who looked like his mind was a million miles away."

"Did I?" Whit shrugged. "Maybe not a million. I was just thinkin' about that clump of trees up the trail—there at the head of the draw."

Cricket was momentarily puzzled. "About a clump of trees?"

"They aren't ordinary trees, you know."

Cricket strained to see into the distance as Whit's horse broke into a trot. Reacting instinctively, Lucy twisted her neck and shook her head, sidestepping as she strained to follow suit. A smile breaking across her lips, Cricket gave the frisky animal full rein, her breath catching in her throat when Lucy broke into a gallop, leaving Whit and his gelding in their wake.

Quick to take up the challenge, Whit spurred his horse forward, and the race began!

Snow swirled up from Lucy's hooves in a stinging spray as the excited animal flew across the frozen ground. The cold wind whipping her face, Cricket shouted with excitement when Whit closed in rapidly behind her. Breathless as they rode neck and neck, she leaned forward to urge her eager animal on.

Her heart racing as the wooded patch drew closer, Cricket glanced beside her. She suddenly realized that instead of urging his mount on, Whit was struggling to hold the powerful animal back to her smaller horse's strides. Taking pity on horse and rider alike, Cricket reined Lucy back to gradually resume a more modest pace. Whit did the same, and she grimaced when she caught his eye.

"There was a time when you would've died before you'd let me think I could keep up with you in a race, Whittaker Randall!"

"Is that so?" Whit's grin widened. "I must've been a damned arrogant piece in those days."

"You were."

Whit gave a short laugh. "And you were an annoyin' little pest who never gave up."

"I was."

"I can see you have a good memory." Whit's gaze suddenly pinned her. "Let's see just *how* good it is. Next week is Christmas...."

"I remembered *that*."

"Think back.... What do you remember most about the Christmas season at home?"

Cricket sat back in her saddle, smiling as a parade of
memories marched across her mind. "There's so much to
recall.... I remember the excitement and the singin', and the
sweet smells of bakin' that never seemed to cease as Christmas approached. I remember that everybody seemed to enjoy all the things that led up to Christmas almost as much
as the day itself...like when you and Papa took me with y'all
when you went out to cut pine and cedar branches in the
woods to decorate the house."

"You remember that, do you?"

"Oh, yes. It was such great fun. I always got cold, but I
never really cared, because you let me help you pick out the
branches to be cut, and then you let me help you collect
them and put them in the wagon before we went back to the
house. I can almost smell those branches now...."

"Breathe deep, darlin'."

Cricket breathed deeply, her breath catching in her throat
at the strong fragrance of cedar and pine. Whit's smile
broadened as her gaze darted to the grove up ahead. Motionless for a moment, Cricket kicked Lucy into a gallop,
this time reining back only when she reached the grove and
the fragrance swelled around her.

Her eyes filled to brimming as Whit drew up beside her,
Cricket gave a choked laugh. "These trees don't look the
same as the cedars back home, but they smell the same. Are
you goin' to let me pick out the branches, Whittaker?" She
laughed again. "You know I always choose the most difficult ones."

Whit dismounted, reached up and swung her down from
the saddle. Standing over her for a few silent moments, he
whispered, "Darlin', I'll get you any branch you want. You
just pick it out."

"Oh, Whittaker... Why are you so good to me?"

His handsome face growing slowly sober, Whit stroked
her wind-reddened cheek. "Damned if I know."

Whit lowered his head and brushed her lips lightly with his. He drew back slowly, his gaze meeting hers as he paused briefly before turning abruptly toward his horse. He was back beside her in a moment, saw in hand, his smile firmly fixed.

"Pick out those branches, darlin'. But remember, we don't have a wagon to carry them back."

"Oh, Whittaker! You're spoilin' all my fun!"

Her lips still warm from his kiss, as she wished they always would be, Cricket slid her arm under Whit's. Together they walked deeper into the grove.

A herd of antelope walked tall and proud, resplendent in white-and-tan winter coats as they trailed across the hillside above them. Whit silently grasped Cricket's arm. Pointing, he waited for her spontaneous gasp of appreciation, and his heart warmed at the open wonder in her expression. Stepping back, he took a moment to enjoy the peace of sunlight glinting on untrodden snow and the rise of majestic mountains in the distance. A tranquillity swelled inside him that he hadn't felt for many years.

The past few hours Cricket and he had spent in the draw had been balm for the soul. They had watched the flight of cedar waxwings spooked from their perches by their arrival. They had seen deer in shaggy winter coats eye them speculatively, big ears stiffly erect, before walking away in disdain. They had cut branches loaded with blue juniper berries and tied them on the backs of their horses, and he supposed he had never seen anything more beautiful than Cricket's expression as she buried her face briefly in the fragrant branches.

Sitting on a nearby log, Whit breathed deeply, inhaling the crisp, spice-scented air. Cricket sat beside him, and he slipped his arm around her. He drew her closer, ignoring the little prickles of awareness shooting up his thigh as her leg pressed warmly against his. Contentment warm and full inside him, he looked down into her sparkling eyes.

"Happy, darlin'?"

Cricket's dark eyes met his, and something tugged deep inside him. When she spoke, her voice was a husky whisper. "Yes, I suppose I am."

"You suppose?"

Cricket averted her gaze. "I suppose it's hard for me to realize that I'm really here, after thinkin' and dreamin' about bein' with you again for so long."

The strange tugging inside Whit grew stronger as he cupped Cricket's chin with his hand and turned her face to his. "Was it hard for you...after I left?"

Cricket shrugged. "Papa did the best he could. We didn't go hungry or anythin' like that...but things weren't the same."

"I know."

"I wished you were there with us."

Silent, Whit looked into the sober darkness of Cricket's eyes. "I wasn't the fella you had been expectin' when I returned from the War, darlin'. I was tired...deep inside. All I had been wantin' after all the bloodshed of the previous years was to go home, but when I got there, my home was gone. Everythin' was gone."

"*I* was there."

Whit's small smile came from the heart. "I know. If you hadn't been there, I don't know what I would've done. But I couldn't stay, not rememberin' things as they had been and seein' them as they were. I had to leave."

"I know."

"The only trouble was that I took it all along with me when I left...the pain and the bitterness. I had traveled hundreds of miles and turned my back on dozens of places when I finally realized that I had to put the past behind me. I pushed it all out of my mind then, even you...everythin'

I associated with what had once been. I settled here and was determined to make a new life for myself."

"I suppose that was the best thing to do."

"I thought so at the time."

"And now?"

"Now? When you came, darlin', I realized I had put the past out of my mind, but not out of my heart. The truth is that I missed you, too, Cricket, more than I realized. Now you're with me again, and that's the way it's goin' to stay."

The misting of Cricket's eyes brought a mist to his own. Whit saw her swallow thickly, once, then again. The huskiness in her voice raised an indefinable yearning within him as she replied, "For a while..."

Cricket's sweet breath was warm against his cheek, and her parted lips were so close. He touched them lightly with his and a jolt went through him when he tasted the moistness of her mouth. He drew back, confused by the growing urgency inside him. He whispered, "I want you to be happy, darlin'."

"I know."

"I want—"

A nervous whinny broke the silence around them, snapping Whit's gaze toward his gelding. The animal was tugging at his tether, his eyes bulging. Immediately alert, Whit searched the area.

"Oh, no..."

"What's the matter?"

Cricket attempted to stand, but Whit held her firmly in place. "Don't move."

Seeing for the first time the small black-and-white animal making careful tracks around the anxious gelding, Cricket froze. Her eyes widened as she whispered, "Skunk. If he gets nervous..."

"That'll be the end of our sweet-smellin' branches...and everythin' else that's sweet-smellin' around here."

Remaining perfectly still until the animal continued its slow progress across the clearing and disappeared from sight, Whit stood up abruptly.

"Come on, let's get out of here ... before it's too late."

Standing beside him in a moment, Cricket accepted a foot up onto her saddle. A moment later, they left the draw behind them.

They were riding briskly, the fragrant boughs tied to their saddles, when Whit realized that they were at least an hour ahead of schedule in returning home. They would be too early....

Annoyed by the absurdity of his sudden panic at the sight of a harmless skunk, Whit frowned. His last statement returned to his mind, taking on new meaning, despite his efforts to avoid it.

*Let's get out of here ... before it's too late.*

And he wondered ...

Her heart singing, Cricket rode contentedly as the ranch house came into view. Darting a glance toward Whit where he rode beside her, she smiled. Whit had lapsed back into silence after they left the grove, but she knew that meant little. This morning they had spent together had been one of the loveliest she could remember. The reasons were myriad, with one overwhelming all the rest—that the morning had been Whit's and hers alone.

Cricket swallowed against the lump that had formed in her throat. Her hand tightened on the branches tied to the saddle in front of her. Without realizing it, Whit had given her a memory she would cherish, one that no other could replace. She would use it to fill the empty days and nights without him.

Cricket glanced at the midday sun overhead. Whit and she had been out all morning. She was cold and hungry, but reluctant to see the end of their special interlude. Out of the corner of her eye, she saw that Whit's expression was sober. She had no reason to believe he regretted the end of their short idyll as much as she, but somehow . . .

Whit glanced toward Cricket unexpectedly. His smile flashed. "Glad to be home, darlin'?"

Unable to speak words so contrary to her thoughts, Cricket nodded. She felt Whit's perusal and averted her gaze. Her smile was firmly fixed as they drew up in front of the house. It grew more genuine as she began untying the fragrant boughs from her saddle. It widened as she walked toward the house, arms loaded. She was grinning by the time Whit kicked open the door and they walked in.

"What the—?" The sweet fragrance of baking filled the air, mingling with other delicious aromas that set her stomach to rumbling. The furniture had been moved to clear the center of the living room floor. Sam and Buck, halting temporarily in the act of extending the dining room table with rough planks, turned toward her. Entering the room from the kitchen at that moment, his apron stained, Pete stopped short at the sight of her. He growled at Whit, who was standing behind her.

"What are you doing home so soon?"

After looking from one man to the other and seeing no explanations there, Cricket turned back to Whit in confusion.

"What's goin' on here?"

Dropping his boughs on the floor near the door, Whit took Cricket's from her arms and placed them nearby. He took off his hat and threw it on a nearby chair, then did the same with hers. He then grasped her shoulders, the clear blue of his eyes holding hers fast.

"You thought I had forgotten, didn't you, sugar?"

Incredulous, Cricket was unable to speak. Her eyes filling, she bit her lips against the great swell of emotion rising within her as Whit continued, more softly than before.

"How could I ever forget the day my father walked through our front door with a scrawny little infant in his arms?'' Whit wrapped his arms around her and drew her tight against him. He whispered huskily, ''Happy birthday, darlin'.''

''Are you ready in there? The guests will be arrivin' soon. Cricket, darlin', you're goin' to miss your own party!''

Cricket glanced up as Whit's inquiry rang through the bedroom door for the third time. Her courage failing, she responded, ''I'm almost done.''

Ignoring the grumbling that ensued, Cricket glanced out the window to see the afternoon sun shining on the snow. The early hour of the party was in deference to the weather and the need for guests to start the long ride home before the frigid cold of late evening, she knew, but that thought offered little consolation for the realization that she could not put off the moment much longer. Turning back to the washstand mirror, Cricket studied the reflection there. She saw a slender young woman in new white undergarments, a young woman who was above average in height, but average in every other way.

Cricket touched the short, shiny reddish-brown hair she had washed, teased into a semblance of curl and pinned behind her ears in an effort to modify its awkward cut. She studied the line of her slender white neck—too long to suit her. She eyed the swell of her bosom above the pristine garments she wore—meager compared to Jayne's womanly proportions. She traced the curving line of her body, briefly closing her eyes. Thin…unimpressive compared to Jayne's eye-catching curves.

She had not thought Whittaker would remember that during better days, a lavish birthday party for her had signaled the beginning of the Christmas season at Windmere. But he had remembered everything, even going so far as to have found the time to slip into town to outfit her from the skin out for the occasion.

Cricket turned toward the bed to gaze once more at the blue gown lying there. It was beautiful . . . too beautiful for a woman who was too average in appearance to do it justice. She had been avoiding the moment when she must finally don the splendid garment and have that fact confirmed in Whit's disappointed gaze.

She could escape the moment no longer. Cricket's hands trembled as she picked up the gown and slipped it over her head. Her heart pounded as it settled onto her shoulders, and she twisted and turned, managing at last to fasten the buttons down her back. Summoning the courage she had lacked before, she raised her eyes slowly to the mirror to again assess the image reflected back at her.

Cricket's breath escaped her in a gasp. She could not believe her eyes! The average young woman was gone! The delicate fabric of the gown had imparted a fragile, almost iridescent glow to skin that had before appeared pale and colorless. The off-the-shoulder neckline framing the gentle slope of her shoulders and the curve of her neck lent a subtle grace and beauty to their line. The bodice hugging the gentle swells beneath accented their fullness as it nipped the minute expanse of her waist. The fullness of the skirt, expertly draped, added an element of elegance to a total picture that she had not, in her wildest dreams, expected would ever be hers.

Picking up the small cluster of blue juniper berries she had snipped from the boughs Whit and she had cut that morning, Cricket pinned it behind her ear and stepped back. The glitter of tears rose to her eyes when she viewed the finished image there. She was Mistress Lydia Elizabeth Blackburn as her father had one day hoped she would appear— the realization of a dream she had believed gone with the luster of the past, never to be regained. Whittaker had realized this dream for her. It was one of his many gifts . . . one of his many precious gifts.

Cricket turned toward the bedroom doorway. Her heart filled to bursting with love for the man who waited on the other side, she drew the door open.

The music of an energetic fiddle and the scrape of dancing feet filled the cedar-scented room. Animated conversation punctuated by soft bursts of laughter, the clatter of dishes and cups and the clinking of the dipper against the bottomless punch bowl completed the merry din. It was a marvelous party!

Unable to draw his eyes from Cricket's slender figure as Charlie Barker danced her carefully past the buffet table Pete had set up with his feast of common but delicious fare, Whit felt a sense of wonder expand within him. Could the lovely young woman dancing in Charlie's arms, the gracious, delicate beauty who had so enchanted his guests, truly be his little Cricket?

Cricket turned momentarily toward him, the glow in her dark eyes stealing his breath, and Whit's sense of bemusement grew. It had seemed to him that he waited a lifetime outside the bedroom door, dressed in his best, before Cricket finally emerged hours earlier. A sense of urgency had been building in him from early morning, and he had held his breath as the door slowly opened and Cricket stepped out into the room.

Whit's throat tightened again as it had at that moment of sweet revelation. Beautiful...Cricket was beautiful... Momentarily dumbstruck, he had seen the uncertainty in Cricket's eyes the second before he stepped forward and took her hand. He could not remember what he had said to her then, but he knew no words could adequately have conveyed the scope of the emotions that assailed him. Wonder, pride, joy, and a strange, indescribable hunger—he had felt them all, only to turn and see his ranch hands, as spit-and-polished as he had ever seen them, staring at her agog.

His guests had begun arriving shortly afterward. His pride had swelled as he had introduced Cricket to them, as she had responded to each new face with an instinctive Southern charm that stirred him deeply. She had won them all over, even his austere neighbor and future father-in-law, Bart Tillis, who had obviously escorted his daughter to the party only with reservations. Despite Jayne's clinging presence at his side in the time since, Whit had not seemed to be able to get enough of looking at Cricket. Her small, delicate features had held his gaze captive. The clear velvet of her skin had called for his touch. The warm, natural rose of her lips had brought back with disturbing clarity the sweet taste of her mouth that he had sampled so briefly, and he had been hard put to strike the thought from his mind.

Cricket turned unexpectedly toward him in that moment, her eyes shining. An overwhelming swell of emotion compelled him to step forward, his heart pounding, only to be stopped by the pressure of Jayne's slender fingers as they dug into his arm.

"For heaven's sake, Whit, you look like a besotted fool, the way you've been staring at that child!"

The coldness of Jayne's tone effectively restored a sanity that had momentarily left Whit. He gave a short laugh. "I suppose I am a little besotted. Cricket looks beautiful, doesn't she?"

"Beautiful?" Jayne stiffened. "I suppose there is a pathetic kind of beauty in a drab little wren outfitted like a peacock."

"Jayne, damn it!"

"Well, you asked, didn't you?"

Anger rose hot and quick, coloring the tight lines of Whit's face. "If you say anythin' like that to Cricket . . . if you spoil this night for her in any way . . ."

The lush fullness of Jayne's breasts swelled above the green velvet of her bodice as she drew herself up angrily. Regaining control a moment later, she raised her perfectly shaped brows and smiled tightly. "Whit, darling, would I do that? I know 'Cricket' is just another stray you've taken under your wing. You've made a pet out of her, just as you did that obnoxious beast Snap, and the girl obviously idolizes you."

"Jayne... I'm the only family Cricket has left."

"Yes, dear, I know. You're her father, her brother and her guardian all combined, the person she's looking toward for guidance now that she's all alone in the world. You feel a great sense of responsibility toward her. You feel it's your duty to take care of her." The fine line of Jayne's lips twitched. "I suppose I should admire you for that, but the truth is, I'm annoyed." Jayne suddenly smiled. "But I suppose I can force myself to endure her presence here for a while longer. With the scarcity of women in this country, it shouldn't be too difficult to find a man for her." Jayne turned back toward the cleared section of floor as Willie Filmore's fiddle slowed to a halt. "Charlie seems quite smitten, don't you think?"

Whit looked up to follow the line of Jayne's gaze. His stomach tensed as Charlie leaned forward to whisper into Cricket's ear. Cricket laughed, her eyes sparkling, and the tenseness tightened to a knot.

"Your little 'Cricket' seems to be doing quite well with your guests... most especially the *male* guests."

Whit's jaw grew rigid. "If you're implyin'—"

"Implying?" Jayne moved closer, her expression suddenly sobering as she looked up into his eyes. "I'm not implying anything that you wouldn't see yourself if you weren't too caught up in the past to see her clearly. But I don't want to talk about Cricket anymore, Whit." Jayne took a step closer, the crush along the cleared area of the floor providing her the excuse she sought to press herself intimately against him. Her gaze moved to his lips, where it lingered. "I want to find a spot where we can be alone for a few moments, if that's possible. Then I'll give you something to think about that will clear that lost little wren out of your mind."

Startled to realize that Jayne's suggestion left him cold, Whit managed a smile. "I have guests, Jayne."

"Guests..." Jayne gave a harsh laugh. "You know very well that if this wasn't such a culturally deficient part of the country, you would probably never have struck up a conversation, much less a friendship, with any of the people here." Jayne's classical features drew into a sneer as she looked around the room. "They're so common—all of them. Look at them. Bill and May Seymour over there in the corner... Everybody knows May has Indian blood in her, for heaven's sake! Then there's Joe and Emma Black standing by the table.... I don't think I've ever heard that woman utter a word that didn't first come out of her husband's mouth. And, of course, Steven and Sally Rutledge... who don't have a year's schooling between them."

Whit's smile was stiff. "I had forgotten.... You were educated back east, weren't you? So you're a class above all us common folk."

Jayne's lips tightened. "Don't put yourself in the same category with those people, Whit. You're leagues above them, and you know it." Jayne rested her palm warmly against his chest. "You're educated, and you're a gentleman. If it hadn't been for that damned war, right now you'd be—" She halted, suddenly smiling. "But I suppose I should be thankful for that war, or you wouldn't be here with me now, would you?"

"I see you've exempted the Walshes and the Barkers from criticism. That wouldn't be because they have unmarried sons?"

Jayne's short laugh was almost shrill. "You read me so well, darling. There would be no point in running any of them down in your eyes, would there, especially since one of those fellows may soon come courting?" Jayne glanced over her shoulder. "Do look at your little 'innocent,' dear. She's doing quite well with Charlie Barker, isn't she?"

Whit looked back at Cricket once more. Willie Filmore had abandoned his fiddle for the punch bowl, but Charlie hadn't seemed to notice. His gaze was intent on Cricket and his hand rested at her waist. Whit felt a slow heat rise within him as that damned hand lingered.

"Whit, you're staring!"

Whit's gaze snapped back to Jayne. He spoke softly, his temper strained.

"Be careful, Jayne. You're tryin' my patience."

Jayne's eyes brimmed. True distress was in her voice as she whispered, "I can't seem to do anything that pleases you anymore, can I? And I do want to please you, Whit. I want that more than anything in the world."

Restraining a sigh of regret for Jayne's distress, Whit curved his arm around her waist. He felt her trembling as he whispered, "I'm sorry, Jayne. I haven't been fair to you lately. I apologize for that."

"I don't want your apology, Whit." A single tear trailed down Jayne's flushed cheek. "I want your love."

Another tear followed the path of the first, and another. Tightening his arm around Jayne, Whit searched the crowded room, seeking a place of privacy where her tears would go unnoticed. Finding none, he drew her along with him toward the nearest doorway. He had been preoccupied and inattentive to Jayne, and he had been unfair, but it had not been his intention to cause her anxiety. Despite her shortcomings, she was the woman he loved, and his intended.

Damn...

Pushing the bedroom door open, Whit ushered Jayne inside and took her into his arms.

Her heart an aching lump in her breast as the door closed behind Whit and the beauteous Jayne, Cricket forced a smile.

"Is something wrong, Miss Lydia?"

Turning, Cricket met Charlie Barker's concerned gaze. She forced her smile to brighten as she looked up into his pleasant, boyish features. "I'm fine, Charlie. Just a little tired, I suppose. I haven't done this much dancin' since the last birthday party my papa gave me when I was a child."

"Well, I'm sorry to hear that." The lines at the corners of Charlie's small brown eyes deepened as he smiled and leaned closer. "This is hard country, but I'm thinking that when the weather clears up a bit, we might be able to offer you a bit more entertainment. As a matter of fact, I'll make it my aim to do just that in the months to come, if you'll allow me the privilege."

"You needn't trouble yourself on my account, Charlie."

"It would be my pleasure, ma'am."

"Oh, Charlie..." Cricket's smile faltered. Charlie was such a nice fellow. How could she tell this young man that one thought alone had been the impetus of everything she had done in her life up to this point in time—the hope that one day Whit would look at her in the way he now looked at Jayne? How could she tell him that this beautiful evening Whit had arranged for her, with its bevy of welcoming friends, good food and music, was all the more painful for the realization that she would soon be leaving it all behind? And how could she tell this fine young fellow that there was no future to the interest she saw shining in his eyes, because the only man she would ever love had disappeared through that nearby doorway a few minutes earlier with the woman *he* loved?

Feeling the rising of a familiar despair, Cricket touched Charlie's hand lightly. "Will you excuse me for a few minutes? There's somethin' I must do."

Grateful for the silence of the kitchen when she entered moments later, Cricket avoided Pete's concerned frown as she walked toward the bucket in the corner. Scooping a handful of water into a nearby basin, she began washing her hands. She was scrubbing fastidiously when she heard Pete's raspy voice in her ear.

"I'd take some care there if I was you, Miss Cricket. You scrub any harder on them little hands and you'll be taking off the skin."

Her throat tight, Cricket picked up a nearby cloth to dry her hands and turned toward the bewhiskered cook. "It's a lovely party, Pete. You've worked so hard...everyone's worked so hard to do this for me. I don't know what I've done to deserve it."

"I'd say just being you is enough." Flushing under her surprised gaze, Pete spoke with an unexpected perception that eliminated all pretense. "You just keep your chin up, you hear? That woman's got the boss wrapped around her little finger, what with batting her eyes at him and tossing herself around like she does. Hell, he— Oh, excuse me, ma'am." Pete's flush deepened as he continued determinedly, "That woman ain't got no shame. She saw what she wanted and she went after it, using everything she's got. The boss wouldn't be a man at all if he didn't respond to the way she's been throwing herself at him for the past year."

"I suppose we should admire Jayne for lovin' Whittaker so much that she—"

"Miss Cricket—" Pete's expression was pure exasperation "—Miss Jayne don't love nobody but herself!"

"Whittaker loves her."

"That woman's got her claws into him, all right, but she ain't the woman for him."

"Whittaker loves her."

"Miss Cricket—"

"Thank you, Pete." Unable to bear any more of the well-meaning words that were slowly breaking down the last remnants of her control, Cricket looked directly into his compassionate gaze. "But the truth is that I didn't come here to set Whittaker's life on end. Whittaker loves Jayne. He wants *her*, not me." When Pete again attempted to interrupt, Cricket's small smile flashed. "I don't know very much about the ways of men and women, but I remember somethin' my papa once said to me. He said that when you love somebody—really love him—you should be able to put that person's happiness before your own. He said when a person didn't, he usually ended up regrettin' it for the rest of his life. I believe that to be true."

"Miss Cricket—"

"But you're right. Knowin' what I have to do doesn't make it all any easier." Her voice dropping, Cricket rested her hand lightly on Pete's arm. "What does make it easier is knowin' that there are some who understand and care more than I realized. Thank you, Pete."

"You don't never have to thank me, Miss Cricket."

"I know."

On impulse, Cricket leaned forward and kissed Pete's cheek. She did not wait to see the sincere regret in his eyes as she turned away.

Jayne's tears had ceased. The heady fragrance of her perfume filled Whit's nostrils; her voluptuous warmth filled his arms. With his back to the bedroom door through which they had entered minutes earlier, and with Jayne's lips separating eagerly under his, Whit heard the music in the next room begin again, and his mind drifted. Was everything going smoothly with his guests? Was the punch bowl still full? *Was Charlie Barker's damned hand still lingering at Cricket's waist?*

"What's the matter with you, Whit?"

Jayne jerked herself back from Whit's embrace. "You're as stiff and unresponsive as a dead fish!"

A smile flicked across Whit's lips at Jayne's heated analogy, and her anger deepened to fury. "It isn't funny!"

"I wasn't laughin', Jayne."

"Yes, you were! You were laughing at me!"

Instantly sober, Whit shook his head. "No, I wasn't. Truly I wasn't."

"You're so damned caught up in making things nice for that sweet-talking *child* outside that you can't think straight!"

"Cricket's had a hard time, Jayne. She may still be hardly more than a child, but she went through more than most women would to find me."

"She's running you around in circles, Whittaker Randall!"

"Jayne—"

"You're a damned fool, Whit! This whole evening is a joke! It's homage to the past! You're trying to resurrect a way of life that's dead and buried! Your 'Cricket' is a relic of the past, too, and if you're not careful, you're going to sacrifice your future for something that's irretrievable. Then, when you wake up one day and realize what you let slip out of your hands, it'll be too late!"

Whit felt his jaw harden. "Are you threatenin' me, Jayne?"

"You're damned right I'm threatening you! I could've had any man I wanted around here—"

"I never said you couldn't."

"But I chose you."

Whit paused. "That's surprisin'. I thought I had chosen you."

"This isn't a time to split hairs, Whit, and you know it!" Jayne's brilliant eyes shone with fury as she continued, her control rapidly waning. "I'm telling you now that I won't stand for much more of this. You had better pry yourself out of the past before you lose your future. If you're smart,

you'll give that thought more than a moment's consideration before you close your eyes tonight.''

Whit stiffened. ''All I've asked is for you to be a little
understandin'.''

''I've been as understanding as I intend to be!'' Her eyes
shooting emerald fire, Jayne raised her chin. ''If you don't
want me, there are plenty of other men who will!''

''You're behavin' like a child, Jayne.''

''Am I? Considering your recent shift in taste, perhaps
you might like me better that way! But whether you do or
not, I suggest you think over everything I've said. You may
not get another chance!''

Turning, her head high, Jayne pulled the door open and
strode back out into the crowded room. Within a moment
she was at her father's side. Bart Tillis's gaze rose stiffly toward him as Jayne whispered into his ear, and Whit inwardly groaned.

Out in the brisk cold minutes later, Whit helped Jayne up
into the carriage, while the elder Tillis maintained a stony
silence.

Whit's response to Jayne's rigid fury was succinct. ''I
apologize for upsettin' you, Jayne.''

The carriage snapped into motion with a crack of the
reins, leaving Whit in the darkening twilight. After watching until the carriage moved out of sight on the trail, Whit
turned back to the house. Once inside, he walked directly to
the punch bowl, filled his cup and swallowed the contents in
a gulp. Choking as the fiery liquid burned all the way down
to his stomach, he snapped his gaze toward the kitchen
doorway, where Pete was looking at him with an innocent
expression that did not deceive.

Whit refilled his cup and raised it slowly to his lips, silently grateful for the steadying effect of Pete's homemade
brew. He had emptied the cup for the second time when he
felt a light touch on his arm.

"Is somethin' wrong, Whittaker?" Cricket's eyes were dark with concern. "Jayne looked upset."

"No, she . . . she was tired and decided to go home a little early, that's all." Whit touched a bright strand of hair that curled around Cricket's ear. "Are you havin' a good time, darlin'?"

Cricket's gaze searched his for a silent moment before she gave him a smile that lit his heart. "It's a beautiful party."

"Not as beautiful as you are, sugar." Noting an approaching figure out of the corner of his eye, Whit stifled a groan. "If I'm not mistakin', Charlie is on his way to—"

"Excuse me, Whit." Suddenly beside them, Charlie grinned boyishly as he took Cricket's hand. "I think this is my dance."

The fiddle squeaked louder as smiling couples danced past, Cricket and Charlie among them, and Whit's spirits sank gradually to his toes. Had he imagined it, or had Cricket actually seemed sorry to leave him?

Uncertain . . . of so many things . . . Whit refilled his glass.


Standing beside Cricket in the doorway as the evening sky lit the snow with the brilliance of day, Whit waved a brief goodbye to the Barkers. The Christmas carols had faded for the evening, along with the strains of a final happy-birthday song. The party was over. The relentless Charlie and his parents were the last of his departing guests, and, relieved, Whit closed the door behind them. He turned toward Cricket as she spoke.

"It was a lovely party, Whittaker. One of the best I've ever had."

Whit did not immediately respond. The unidentifiable ache that had begun inside him earlier in the evening tightened painfully. Cricket's smooth cheeks were flushed, and her dark eyes were glowing, and Whit realized he would never see any woman lovelier than she was at that moment.

His little Cricket had turned into a woman before his eyes. The simple truth of it was that he was overwhelmed.

"Whittaker—?"

"You've become a beautiful woman. Did you know that, sugar?"

Not waiting for Cricket's response, Whit slipped his arms around her and drew her close. She was so slender in his arms, a fragile, graceful willow. Her hair was a fragrant silk against his lips as he whispered, "This has been a special day for me, darlin'. I'll never forget it."

Drawing back, Whit saw that Cricket's eyes had filled. Her lips parted in a failed attempt at response, and the desire to still the trembling of her lips with his own was suddenly painfully strong. Startled by his reaction, Whit released her. His voice was unnaturally hoarse as he whispered, "It's late. You've had a big day. Go to bed. The boys and I'll clean up here."

"No, I—I want to help."

Cricket's dark eyes held his, and the gnawing ache inside Whit expanded. Sweet, darling Cricket, so warm, so close…so damned innocent. She didn't know what she was doing to him when she looked at him that way. He wanted . . . he needed . . .

Shocked at the direction of his erratic thoughts, Whit fought to regain control.

"Whittaker . . ."

"Go to bed, Cricket."

Cricket's gaze searched his only a moment longer, before she turned away with a soft good-night.

The house was dark and silent as Cricket lay awake in her bed. Sleep eluded her. The events of the day ran over and over again across her mind. It had been a wonderful day and a marvelous party. Whit and the men had worked hard to make the event of her nineteenth birthday memorable, and they had succeeded. Whit's friends had welcomed her warmly and made her feel she was one of them. Everyone had seemed reluctant to have the party come to an end.

But one thought was inescapable. Somewhere, somehow, something had gone wrong....

It had all started so well. Recalling the moment she had first stepped through the bedroom doorway into sight in her new finery, Cricket briefly closed her eyes. Joy swept over her once more. It had been as she had always imagined it would be. Whit, tall and incredibly handsome in a dark jacket that emphasized the breadth of his shoulders and the sunstreaked gold of his hair, had stepped toward her, his blue eyes bluer than any she had ever seen, seeing only her. She had read approval in his eyes, and so much more, as he took her hand and raised it to his lips. It had been a dream come true....

Almost.

Jayne had arrived a few minutes later, magnificent in green velvet that accented the extraordinary color of her eyes, and her dream had come to an end. Dear, attentive Charlie had monopolized her time for the majority of the evening, relieving Whit of the need for a careful balance between the past and the present in his life. In a sad way, she had been grateful. She had enjoyed the party, she truly had, but a basic truth could not be avoided. She had spent the evening dancing in one man's arms, while longing to be in another's.

It had been obvious from the start that Jayne did not share Whit's enthusiasm for the party. Cricket had been startled, however, to see Jayne make an early exit shortly after Whit and she slipped off for a few moments alone together.

Had it been then that the tension began building in Whit's gaze? As many times as she had reviewed it all in her mind, she was still unsure. Tears again hot under her eyelids, Cricket knew that her only certainty was that a strange kind of sadness . . . or need . . . had replaced the joy she had previously sensed within Whit. That same emotion had been too strong at the end of the evening for her to say more than a simple good-night. In the hours since, however, she had regretted that lack of communication between them with all her heart.

Something . . . somewhere, somehow . . . had gone wrong.

A sound of movement from the living room broke into Cricket's thoughts. She heard the front door click closed with a soft snap.

Throwing back the covers, Cricket hastened to the window in time to see Whit's unmistakable figure slip out of sight as it headed toward the barn.

Her heart beginning a heavy pounding, Cricket turned toward the worn clothing piled on the chair nearby. Fully dressed moments later, she jammed her hat onto her head and drew the door of her room open before a conscious decision was made.

Closing the barn door behind him as he entered, Whit hung his lantern on a nearby nail. He breathed deeply of the odors assaulting him, taking comfort in their familiarity. A cold nose nudged his palm, alerting him to the presence of the animal suddenly at his side.

"All right, Snap. Did I wake you, boy?"

The dog's response was a soft whimper before he returned to his warm corner. Whit unconsciously smiled. He had not thought he would ever envy a poor, dumb animal, but there were times . . .

Whit removed his hat and slapped it down on a bale of hay beside him, then ran a frustrated hand through his hair. Damn . . . damn, damn, damn. It had been a hell of a night.

Walking slowly toward the rear stall, Whit appraised the small mare within. He eyed her flank and saw that the wound that had nearly ended her life was well healed. He scratched the muzzle she stretched out to him. His consternation deepened.

He hadn't been able to sleep a wink during the hours he had lain abed, and he was damned confused. The party had gone well. His neighbors had been delighted, claiming the celebration had added to the festivities of Christmas, just a week away. They had welcomed Cricket with open arms, and he knew she had been warmed by their reception. His guests had enjoyed the party so much that they had been reluctant to leave, despite the long ride home most of them would have to endure before they sank into bed that night. Jayne's and her father's early exit had been the only exception, but he knew he would have no true problem there. A visit the next morning, a few whispered promises and warm reassurances, and Jayne's smile would be restored. Jayne loved him, and he loved her....

Didn't he?

Cricket's small, sober face appeared before his mind's eye, and Whit felt the peculiar knot in his chest tighten. Somehow, Cricket's image had replaced Jayne's each time he sought to summon it through the long hours past. The memory of the taste of her lips—so incredibly sweet—had taunted him mercilessly. Causing him the most anxiety of all, however, was the soul-wrenching hunger which returned with the memory of Cricket's reed-slim body against his.

Cricket... no longer a child...

He—

The barn door creaked behind him, and Whit turned abruptly to see Cricket's slender figure step into the light. She walked hesitantly toward him, and he was torn between a spontaneous joy at the sight of her and an emotion so close to pain that he was momentarily paralyzed by its depth. The blue gown she had worn earlier had been abandoned for her previous male attire, but she was still beautiful. The light of the lantern was reflected a hundred times over in the warm glow of her hair as she came closer. Her sober gaze stirred a silent cry of longing within him. His

heart was all but rent in two by the bittersweet joy of all that
was Cricket when she stopped a few feet from him to whisper, "Are you angry with me, Whittaker?"

"Angry?" Whit steeled himself against the slow trembling that had begun inside him. "No, I'm not angry. I
could never be angry with you, darlin'."

"Tell me what's wrong, then." Cricket took a step closer.
Her eyes trailed his furrowed brow, the tight contours of his
cheek, the straight line of his lips, and Whit's heart began a
new pounding. Sensing his torment, Cricket raised her hand
to stroke his cheek.

"Don't touch me, Cricket."

Cricket's hand dropped immediately to her side. Her eyes
filled. "You *are* angry." Her voice quivered as she continued softly, "Tell me what's wrong, Whittaker. I want to
know."

"Nothin's wrong." Whit attempted a smile. "Go to bed.
Everythin' will all right in the mornin'."

"I don't want to wait until mornin'." Cricket's chin grew
stubborn. "Neither of us is able to sleep, and I'm not so
much a fool that I can't see that whatever's botherin' you
has somethin' to do with me." She took a short breath.
"Are you upset because Jayne left the party early?"

"No."

"It's my fault, I know, and I'm sorry. But there's nothin'
I can do to make her like me." Cricket sighed. "I suppose I
can talk to her the next time she comes and explain—"

"I said it's not Jayne."

Cricket paused. "It's me, then, isn't it? What did I do to
make you so sad, Whittaker?"

"Sad? Is that what you think, that I'm *sad?*" Frustration, incredulity and a nameless, mounting emotion turned
to sudden anger within Whit. "You're such a damned innocent, Cricket! You traveled across this country all alone
to get to this wilderness territory, risking your life a hun-

dred times over, and you almost died in the attempt . . . but you didn't learn a thing, did you?''

Cricket stiffened. "I—I learned a lot!''

"Did you? What did you learn? Tell me.''

"I learned . . .''

Whit took an angry step closer as Cricket's voice faltered. "Tell me what you learned, Cricket.''

Cricket's lips tightened. "I learned that the world is a cold, hard place. I learned that there are more people in it who will take advantage of your ignorance than there are who will help you. I learned that there's only one way to accomplish what you want to do, and that's to push on, every day, without lettin' anythin' get in your way. And I learned . . .''

Cricket's voice trailed to a halt as a single tear made a shiny path down her pale cheek. She was shaking visibly, but something inside Whit would not let him relent.

"Yes? What else did you learn, Cricket?''

"I learned that after all the torment and pain, things don't always turn out the way you wanted them to.''

"Meanin'?''

Cricket shook her head.

*"Meanin'?"*

Cricket did not reply.

"Tell me!''

"Meanin' that a dream can fall flat—that it can all turn out to be for nothin'!''

"What do you mean, for nothin'?''

Cricket took a hard step forward, her body trembling violently. "You know what I mean! You know!''

"No, I don't. Tell me!''

"I mean that when you reach the end of the trail . . . the place you always wanted to be, you . . . you sometimes find out that there's no real place for you there at all!''

"No place for you . . .''

"And nobody really wants you! *Nobody!*''

Suddenly trembling as violently as she, Whit rasped, "Is that what you think?"

Her eyes wide saucers of anguish, Cricket turned abruptly. She had taken two quick steps toward the door when Whit grasped her arms and turned her back to him. His throat hoarse from the emotions he was suppressing, Whit rasped again, "Is that what you think, that nobody...that *I* don't want you?"

The soft sob that escaped Cricket's lips all but destroying him, Whit crushed her tight against him as he murmured, "Oh, God, darlin', I only wish that was true."

Lost to her grief, Cricket sobbed in his arms, and Whit drew her closer still. Whispering soft, almost unintelligible words of comfort, he stroked her back, her hair, the nape of her neck. Stirring in his embrace, Cricket raised a tear-streaked face to his.

"Tell me what's wrong, Whittaker, please. I have to know."

"Oh, darlin'..." Whit's voice was a rough whisper. "Don't you know?"

Trailing the shiny path of her tears with his lips, Whit found Cricket's mouth at last. Exhilaration rose within him as he tasted its sweetness, as his kiss pressed more deeply than before. He heard Cricket's soft murmur as her lips parted under his, and his exhilaration rose to a pounding joy that thrust all rational thought from his mind.

This was Cricket...*his* Cricket. She felt so right in his arms...so good. Her fragrance was born to be breathed by him, her skin made for his touch, her slenderness shaped to fit his strength.

Whit took Cricket up into his arms. She was light as a feather as he carried her to a shadowed corner nearby. She was pure beauty as he laid her gently against the straw and covered her mouth with his once more. She was youth and glory, a wonder beyond measure, as her arms slid around his

neck and his kiss surged deeper. And she was love...
returning kiss for kiss, caress for caress, yielding, giving, as
hungry as he for the riotous sensations enveloping them, as
his shaking hands stripped away the layers of clothes between them, baring her smooth white skin.

Cricket's gasp echoed in the silence when Whit ran his lips
against the white column of her throat, against the curve of
her shoulder. His mouth closed over the pink crest of her
breast at last, and a hot elation swept his senses. The sensation grew stronger, wilder, as he suckled the warm
mounds, caressed them with his mouth, and Cricket responded with soft sounds of mounting passion that raised
him to a new level of loving assault. Cricket cried out in
protest when he abandoned the soft flesh, but he stifled the
sound with his kiss, caressing her tongue with his, searching the hollows of her mouth, wanting as he had never
wanted before, needing as he had never thought he could.

His hands freed the baggy trousers from her hips and he
stripped them away. Pausing briefly, he looked at the total
perfection of her in the semi-light. He met her gaze, speaking a wordless, endless litany of love with his eyes as he
stripped away his clothes, as well. Poised above her, his
chest heaving with emotions held barely in check, he whispered softly, "Tell me you want me, darlin'. I need to hear
the words."

Emotion flushed Cricket's face. She attempted a reply
that would not come. When words failed, she extended her
arms slowly toward him, a single word escaping her trembling lips.

"Please..."

Whit swallowed the word with his kiss as he filled her
waiting arms. He took her gasp deep inside him as their
warm flesh met. He reveled in her soft whimpers of passion
as his manhood pressed against the warm, moist delta
awaiting him, and he gasped aloud as he thrust home within
her at last.

At rest within her, Whit raised himself above Cricket and looked down into her passion-filled countenance. He heard her rasp his name, and he heard the wonder in the sound. It resounded in his heart, raising his joy to new heights as he thrust within her again and again, as the rhythm of love mounted, rapidly overwhelming his mind, raising him to ecstasy so supreme, so blinding...

Release came quickly, passionately, rapturously. Clutching Cricket close, Whit savored the precious moments as he breathed in the warm scent of her.

Still joined with her, although their passion had stilled, Whit raised himself to look down into Cricket's face. Her heavy lids fluttered weakly, and he caressed them with his lips. The damp paths of happy tears stained her cheeks and he wiped them away with his kiss. Her love-bruised lips moved with a whispered word of love, and he consumed them.

And the loving began anew...

A cold chill trailed across Cricket's bared shoulder, disturbing her sleep. A heavy warmth oppressed her, and she moved beneath it. She moved again, a slow joy coming to life within her as her eyes slowly opened to the sight of Whit's head beside hers on the warm bed of straw.

Looking down, she saw Whit's body and hers lovingly entwined, his arm draped possessively across her as he lay on his side and his leg stretched across her ankles. She savored the sweet intimacy as the aura of love swelled over her.

Whit loved her. He really loved her. He had proved it in so many wordless ways as he had worshiped her body with his. They would never be apart again.

Inching closer, Cricket brushed Whit's lips with hers. A hot flush rising to her cheeks, she trailed her tongue along his lips, her heart beginning a new pounding when Whit's eyelids flickered, then slowly rose. The blue-eyed gaze that met hers was momentarily disoriented.

"Whittaker, darlin'..."

Whit's gaze slowly cleared. An unreadable emotion gradually registering in his eyes, he looked at her for long, silent moments before turning abruptly toward the gray light of dawn slowly penetrating the darkness.

"Damn..."

Drawing back abruptly, Whit ordered, "Get up, Cricket."

"But—"

"I said, get up."

Helping her to her feet, Whit swept her nakedness with his gaze for a tense moment before retrieving her clothes.

"Get dressed."

"What's wrong, Whittaker?"

"Get dressed!"

Pulling on her clothes with shaking hands, Cricket turned to find Whit fully clothed beside her, his eyes cold.

"Hurry up. I want you back in the house before the men wake up."

"If you're worryin' about what they'll say, I don't care. I—"

"Maybe you don't care what they'll think, but I do. Get movin', damn it, and be quiet about it!"

Whit rushed her across the frozen yard in hurried steps, then stayed her outside the front door of the house. Her bewilderment deepened when Whit pushed it open and glanced cautiously inside.

"All right, it's clear."

Pulling her in behind him, Whit drew her to the bedroom door. An indefinable emotion flickered across his sober face before he whispered, "I'm sorry, Cricket. Damn... I'm so sorry."

Whit pushed the bedroom door open behind her, forestalling the need for response. With no other recourse, Cricket turned and slipped inside.

Standing stock-still as Whit's footsteps faded away from the door, she closed her eyes.

It was over.... Oh, God, it was over...and she didn't know why.

## Chapter Six

Whit urged his mount forward through a pasture muddy with melting snow, his gaze intent on the two men checking a limping heifer a few yards away. Pausing a few feet from them, he took off his hat and wiped his arm across his forehead, more in reaction to his silent anxiety than to the warm wind that rocked him with surprising strength.

Sam and Buck had already loosened their coats and unwrapped their mufflers, and Whit gave a harsh laugh. As if his world hadn't gone crazy enough, a chinook wind had blown up, hot and dry with southern air that had raised the temperature more than ten degrees in the past five minutes. He knew that twenty minutes from now the weather would probably be almost balmy, in contrast to the former frigid cold, and that it would remain that way until the wind blew itself out overnight. But he also knew that a chinook often brought a blizzard in its wake, and that in all probability they would pay dearly for winter's brief, teasing lapse. That phenomenon had amazed him during his early years in this particular part of the country, as had the displays of northern lights that usually accompanied it at night.

Whit swallowed against a further tightening in his throat. Had things been different, he would eagerly have anticipated sharing with Cricket the incredible ribbons of light— red, green, white—shooting high into the sky and then falling back, only to shoot moonward once more, shimmering and waving in an unmatched aerial ballet. But that possibility was now nil. He had been avoiding Cricket, his guilt overwhelming, since the night of her birthday, the night she had spent in his arms.

But guilt... shame... disgust with himself... that wasn't the worst of it. Because the truth was that the scent of Cricket was still in his nostrils, the taste of her was still on his lips. His body trembled still at the memory of the moment when the moist inner core of her had welcomed him in with innocence and joy, when she had become a part of him so completely that—

A silent groan echoed in Whit's mind.

Another truth was that he had been avoiding her because he truly feared that once she was within arm's reach again, looking up into his eyes with that gaze that touched his soul, he would not be able to keep his hands off her.

Oh, God, what had he done?

Memory returned to taunt him.... Cricket, her eyes filled with love, her arms outstretched toward him. He had teased her untutored body with his loving, with his need. He had given her a glimpse of what could be, had made her taste the glory... and he had then told himself she wanted him as much as he wanted her.

Dear, guileless Cricket... so young, little more than a child... She had trusted him. She had risked her life to find him again, and he had paid her back by taking advantage of her when she was most vulnerable. Cricket had been deserving of better from him. He had stolen her innocence. No matter the depth of his regret, he could never give it back.

Christmas was two days away, but nothing was the way it had been supposed to be when he promised Cricket a beautiful Christmas. He had ridden to see Jayne the day after the party. He had told her simply, without embellishment, that he no longer believed there was a future for them together.

Jayne's fierce pride had called that exchange to a halt shortly afterward, and he had been grateful.

He wished he had had the words to say to Cricket, as well, but they had not come. *I'm sorry.* He had repeated that phrase over and over again to her, knowing each time how pathetically inadequate it was.

Other words, straight from the heart, had gone unsaid.

*I wanted you, Cricket. I needed you more than I had ever needed anyone before, and, somehow, when you were in my arms, I couldn't look beyond that need.*

He had looked beyond it since. He had seen himself as he truly was, and had despised himself for failing to protect Cricket, most especially from himself.

The sound of low cursing and the frantic thrashing of hooves interrupted Whit's thoughts when the heifer Buck and Sam had subdued broke free and squirmed to its feet. Buck turned toward him, cursing again as the animal beat a hasty retreat.

"That damned animal ain't got nothin' wrong with her at all! Look at her run! I got half a mind to—"

Making a sudden decision, Whit interrupted Buck's growling complaint. "Forget it, Buck. Let's go home."

"Home!" Buck shot Sam a sideward glance. "But we didn't even do—"

"I said home."

Not waiting for Buck and Sam to mount, Whit turned in the direction from which they had come earlier in the day. It was time to set things straight with Cricket. To tell her that he . . .

The crash of breaking crockery echoed in the silent kitchen, simultaneous with Cricket's sharp gasp. Kneeling to pick up the broken pieces of the bowl she had knocked to the floor, Cricket whispered embarrassed words of apology that were met by Pete's reassuring smile as the balding cook knelt beside her.

"Don't you go worrying none about that bowl, Miss Cricket. Accidents happen, and that old bowl's seen better days, any which way you look at it."

Sitting back on her heels while Pete took the broken pieces from her hands, Cricket swallowed the tears that had always been close to the surface in recent days. "You're too kind to me, Pete."

"I ain't no such thing." Pete stood as Cricket rose to her feet. He tossed the broken pottery into a box by the door and smiled more widely. "Don't you go worrying about it, you hear? It won't even be missed."

*Like me, when I leave...*

Pete's small, bleary eyes studied her intently before he offered boldly, "And don't you go worrying about anything else, either. I don't know what's been bothering the boss the past few days. He's been real quiet like, but he ain't been talking much to nobody, so I wouldn't take it personal."

A hot color flushed Cricket's cheeks. So the men had noticed Whit's stiffness with her. If they knew—

"Come now, Miss Cricket..." Pete patted her hand gently. "I happen to know that the boss went to see Miss Jayne the day after the party. You know she left early, with her nose out of joint, and I'm thinking they had a little argument, that's all. It's just taking him longer than it takes most to realize that she ain't the woman for him, but when he does..."

Pete's intended words of comfort cutting her deeply, Cricket turned toward the stove and the pot boiling there, tears welling. "The stew's boilin'. Would you like me to make the biscuits? My papa said I had a light hand with them."

"You do whatever you like, Miss Cricket."

Incapable of response, Cricket nodded and reached for the flour. She was unaware of Pete's sympathetic gaze as her trembling hands worked at the familiar task. Pete's comment echoed in her mind.

*You do whatever you like, Miss Cricket.*

If she could, she would talk to Whittaker and say what was in her heart, but she could not. The few words they had exchanged had been too painful.

*I'm sorry, Cricket.*

Oh, God . . . he was sorry.

*I hope you can forgive me.*

He wanted her to forgive him.

How could she respond? How could she explain that, however briefly Whittaker had loved her, those moments had been beautiful beyond measure, and she would treasure them forever? How could she tell him that to lie in his arms had been the fulfillment of a dream that she had hoped would continue the rest of their lives? And finally, how could she declare the love that filled her heart and mind, when Whit's heart and mind were filled only with regret?

She could not.

But, despite it all, hope remained. She smelled it in the scent of cedar and pine that filled the house with fragrance. She sensed it in the plans for the Christmas holiday that Whittaker refused to abandon. She felt it touch her each time Whittaker's gaze wandered toward her, however briefly. It tormented her each time Whittaker came near, each time he said her name. It lingered, despite her better judgment, teasing her with the thought that perhaps that very afternoon Whittaker would ride back to the house and say to her—

The sound of hoofbeats interrupted her thoughts, and Cricket turned toward the window. Her heart leaped at the sight of Whit returning, riding slightly ahead of his men, so tall and handsome in the saddle that her heart ached at the sight of him. He drew closer, and her heart plummeted. There was something about his expression . . .

"Well, what do you know!" Pete's exclamation of surprise broke the silence of the kitchen. "What do you suppose those fellas are doing home so early?"

Not taking the time to respond, Cricket wiped her hands on a nearby cloth and walked toward the front door. Her jaw was tight with tension as the door opened abruptly and Whit stood outlined against the white landscape beyond. Cricket's heart jumped to a racing beat when he finally spoke.

"Will you take a walk with me, Cricket? There're some things I think we should talk about."

A silent sobbing began inside Cricket as Whit moved aside to allow her past him. Snatching her coat from a hook by the doorway, she slipped through, glancing up briefly when Whit fell into step beside her.

It occurred to her as they started up the melting trail beside the house that walking thus, side by side, was another dream that had been realized, only to be as off kilter as the rest since she had found Whittaker again. Her heart twisting in her chest, she feared, however, that this time, this walk, would mean...

The wind whistled through the trees as Whit shortened his pace to match Cricket's on the muddy trail. Warm and dry, it buffeted them, flaying Cricket's small, sober face with shiny strands of hair while she continued steadfastly forward. He knew that expression. She was waiting for him to speak. He could put the moment off no longer.

Whit halted abruptly, silently grateful for the unexpectedly mild weather that had enabled them to get away where they could speak privately, while still in clear view of the house. Coward that he was, he knew he could not trust the inexplicable weakness that even now tempted him to wrap his arms around Cricket, to cover the line of her lips with his kiss, to know again the sweet wonder of Cricket's loving response and to feel her—

Damn!

Cricket looked up. Her dark eyes met his with unexpected sadness, and Whit felt a new depth of pain. *He* had done this to Cricket. He had put sadness where there had formerly been joy. He had destroyed her faith in him, and, in doing so, had broken her heart, as well. He wanted . . . he *needed* to restore the joy there—somehow, some way.

"Cricket . . . darlin' . . ." The endearment raised the shine of tears in Cricket's eyes as Whit continued softly, "I know I haven't been fair to you the past few days. I have no excuse for the way I've been avoidin' talkin' to you, except to say that I've been goin' around in circles, tryin' to think things out. The truth is, after all this time I still don't really know what happened that night...how I could've..." Whit paused, then whispered, "I can only tell you that I regret what happened, with all my heart."

Cricket's dark eyes flickered, and Whit felt her pain. He ached to take her into his arms and assuage her despair, but he knew he could not. Instead, he continued, "I wanted to talk to you so I could tell you that you don't have to worry that it'll happen again. I did you a terrible wrong, darlin'. You trusted me, and I took advantage of that trust. You were vulnerable, and I took advantage of that vulnerability. The fact that I had no conscious intention to do it doesn't change the result. I'm older than you . . . more experienced . . . I should've . . . I could've . . ." Whit paused again. "But I didn't."

Cricket was no longer looking at him. Her gaze was fixed on a point in the distance, her face available to his scrutiny only in profile. It was a beautiful profile that raised a longing in him so deep . . .

"Cricket . . . look at me, darlin', please."

Cricket turned obediently toward him. The devastation he read in her face sliced at his heart. At the point of despair, he rasped, "You know how much you've always meant to me, in so many ways. I want to make this up to you. I *need*

to make this up to you. I want to take care of you the way I
should have. I want to keep you safe the way I should have.
I want to strike what happened from your mind. I want you
to feel safe and secure with me, the way you did before. I
want to give you the kind of Christmas I promised."

Cricket did not respond, and Whit gave a short laugh. "I
know what you're thinkin'. This talk about Christmas
doesn't mean much to you anymore . . . not now. But I *want*
it to mean somethin' again, because I know if it does, it'll
mean that you've forgiven me. I need that forgiveness,
darlin', because the truth is—" Momentarily unable to go
on, Whit took a steadying breath "—because the truth is
that I doubt that I'll ever be able to forgive myself."

When silence was her only response, Whit pleaded, "Say
somethin', sugar . . . please."

Cricket's lips moved in an attempt at a smile. "What's
there to say that hasn't already been said?"

"You can say you'll forgive me."

Cricket's smile became a pained grimace. "I'll try."

*I'll try.*

The words were a double-edged sword that cut deeply,
drawing blood. Whit took Cricket's hand in his. It was incredibly fragile in his callused palm, and cold despite the
growing heat of the afternoon. He held it gently, then raised
it to his lips.

A tremor shot through Whit's veins as his lips touched
Cricket's skin, shaking him badly. Straining for control, he
released her hand.

As if by mutual consent, they started back toward the
house, but Whit knew the damage had been done . . . for the
yearning had begun anew.


The bedroom door closed behind Cricket, shutting out the
pain of her conversation with Whit a few moments previous. She walked to the window to stare out at the land beyond. A pine tree in the distance danced in the warm wind,

brushing the endless blue of the sky. In the lower pasture the snow had shrunk visibly, dotting the landscape with brown patches of earth. The snow was weeping, as was her heart.

Cricket raised her chin higher, fighting an almost debilitating sadness. She had spent a lifetime dreaming about one man... only to awaken to a dream that had suddenly become a nightmare.

*Forgive me, Cricket...*

Cricket's heart responded with the words she had not dared utter in return.

*Forgive you, Whittaker...my darling, my love? If I must try to forgive you, it mustn't be for having loved me so briefly. It must be because you don't love me enough...with your whole heart and soul, as I love you.*

Oh, Whittaker...

Raising her hand to her mouth, Cricket pressed her lips against the spot still warm from Whit's kiss. Whit's torment had deepened visibly after that kiss, and she had been able to avoid the truth no longer. To remain would be to prolong an endless agony of regrets for the man she loved.

Two days until Christmas... a day bright with the birth of hope and joy.

Two days that must last a lifetime.

# Chapter Seven

A frigid wind swept the frozen path that had a day earlier been deep with mud. Walking cautiously toward the barn, Whit looked up at the sky and frowned when the cloud bank over the mountains appeared to thicken before his eyes. He gave a low, disgusted snort. He had seen similar cloud banks clustering there many times before. He knew what they meant.

Glancing back at the house, Whit unconsciously sighed. He had hoped this special day, Christmas Eve, would dawn bright and clear so as to facilitate his plans. Everything else had seemed to be going so well since Cricket and he had had their talk . . . at least on the surface.

His spirits sinking, Whit looked up at the trail behind the house that he and Cricket had climbed two days earlier, remembering. Cricket had spoken little, but her words, *I'll try,* had seemed to exemplify everything she had done in the time since.

After retiring briefly to her room following their talk, Cricket had emerged with a smile that had seldom left her lips in the time since. He had strained to convince himself that her smile was real, but in his heart he had known that Cricket was trying as desperately as he to restore some of the joy of the past to a Christmas where the present had become too painful to endure.

But, despite it all, joy, however bittersweet, had begun to seep through.

It had begun simply, with the scent of gingerbread baking. The fragrance had been so reminiscent of Christmas in the busy plantation kitchens that Whit's heart had ached. He had entered the kitchen shortly afterward to find the table piled high with a white mound of recently popped corn, and the incongruous sight of Pete working with great concentration beside Cricket to string the corn into an endless winding strand. He hadn't needed anyone to tell him what came next.

Dragging in the tree he had cut and mounted earlier in the week, he had set it up in the living room and worked side by side with Cricket as she wound the garland around it with meticulous care. Gingerbread men, properly decorated, had taken their places on the branches soon afterward. With each decoration she placed on the tree, Cricket's enthusiasm had seemed to grow.

Cricket's enthusiasm, somehow contagious, had appeared to infect Buck and Sam, as well. He could think of no other reason for the contribution those two gruff men had presented Cricket with that morning, a roughly cut miniature stable and hand-carved nativity figures that had left Cricket at a loss for words.

It had been then when Whit determined that Christmas services at the small church in town would be graced with a beautiful newcomer dressed in blue on Christmas morning. Despite the traveling time involved, he knew nothing would bring back the true warmth of Christmas more clearly than the sound of Christmas carols echoing from the rafters of a church, no matter how humble the building was in comparison with the graceful Southern structure Cricket and he both remembered.

He had also decided that he would give Cricket her Christmas gift there, where memories would enfold them as he fastened his mother's small gold locket around her neck.

Whit frowned. Strangely, he had never considered giving his mother's locket to Jayne. It was only since Cricket's return that he had realized against whose skin that locket had next been meant to lie. Neither had he divulged to anyone the cancellation of Jayne's and his marriage plans, knowing that neither he nor Cricket was up to facing the obvious questions that would follow.

The heavily laden clouds in the distance had expanded rapidly during his brief moments of introspection, and Whit groaned aloud. The picture he had formed of Cricket and him seated side by side on one of the hard wooden pews of the frontier church was rapidly fading. The wind was already rising, and if he did not miss his guess, the approaching storm would arrive before afternoon and would dwarf the blizzard that had delivered Cricket to them more than a month earlier.

The sound of heavy footsteps behind him announced Sam's and Buck's approach. Jerking the barn door open, Whit commented wryly, "It looks like the weather doesn't have any respect for the season. We're goin' to have to get the rest of those heifers out of the upper pasture and put them where we can keep an eye on them durin' the storm."

"We're way ahead of you, boss." Buck's expression was dour. "Real poor timing, too. Miss Cricket was just showing Pete how to make some kind of sugar candy with them nuts Pete's been hoarding. I kinda had my mouth set to taste the first piece."

Whit could not suppress a smile. "Looks like that'll have to wait for a few hours."

Mounted minutes later, Whit glanced back at the house. The thought trailed across his mind that a few hours was too long a time to spend away from Cricket today.

Whit hesitated a moment longer at that strangely sobering concern, then kicked his mount into motion.

Large, heavy flakes of snow had begun falling, and the wind was already rising. Looking out the kitchen window, as she had countless times since Whit and the men rode out an hour earlier, Cricket frowned. The open circles of brown earth that had popped through the snow during the brief thaw were already covered with a new blanket of white... a pure new beginning, somehow symbolic of the day they would begin celebrating at the stroke of twelve that evening.

Cricket's smile slowly faded as reality returned. She had grown quite adept at pretending in the past few days, so much so that she had almost been able to convince herself that the warmth she had read in Whit's eyes had not been stirred solely by the common memories of the season Whit and she shared. She had almost succeeded in convincing herself that the joy would remain when the holiday was gone, but she had not. Jayne and her father would arrive for Christmas dinner early this afternoon, as previously planned. With them would come the arrival of harsh reality, and the reminder that she had no place in the home the man she loved would soon be sharing with another.

Her thoughts halting abruptly with the appearance of an approaching wagon in the distance, Cricket slowly stiffened. The blond hair of the woman seated beside the driver was unmistakable.

No, it couldn't be Jayne. It was too soon! She wasn't up to facing Jayne's biting scrutiny without the buffer of Whittaker's presence. Her wounds were still too raw. She—

Suddenly furious with her childish panic, Cricket raised her chin with determination. She was a woman now, and the future of the man she loved hung in the balance. Despite Whittaker's assessment of the situation, *she* knew the real truth. Without conscious intent, *she* was the one who had taken advantage. She had leaned heavily on memories dear to Whittaker's heart, and in doing so had stirred powerful emotions within him. But those emotions had not been based in reality. Reality was that Whittaker loved Jayne in a way he could never love her...and that he had asked Jayne to be his wife. The final reality was that within forty-eight hours she would be gone, never to return, and Jayne would remain.

If she was the woman she hoped she was, if she loved Whittaker as much as she believed she did...

Affixing a smile on her face, not conscious of Pete's assessing stare, Cricket walked toward the door.

The snow whirling behind her with increasing fury, Jayne stood imperiously in the doorway. Her welcoming smile stiff, Cricket was momentarily disconcerted by Jayne's obvious rage as she advanced into the room, shook the snow off her woolen wrap, tossed it on a nearby chair and stated flatly, "I want to talk to you."

"Whittaker's not here. He—"

"I know he's not here! My men saw him riding out into the upper pasture. I said I want to talk to you."

"Why?"

"You know damned well why!" Her gaze suddenly jerking toward the kitchen doorway behind Cricket, Jayne snapped, "Get out of here, Pete. I want to talk to 'Miss Cricket' alone."

Jayne turned abruptly toward her driver, who stood behind her. "You, too! Out! You can wait for me in the barn! What I have to say won't take me long. We'll be leaving in a few minutes."

Embarrassed by Jayne's condescending manner, Cricket responded, "Whit won't be home for a few hours. He—"

"That's exactly why I came, and I'll be damned if I'll leave before I say what I've come to say." With another enraged glare at her hired man and Pete, Jayne shouted, "Get out of here, both of you!"

Pete walked to Cricket's side, his lined face emotionless. "Do *you* want me to go, Miss Cricket?"

"You bastard!" Jayne's gaze pinned the older man with open hatred. "You never liked me, did you? For all I know, you were part of this whole thing...you and those other two. You may have gotten your way, but there's one thing I know. Whit would never stand for your defiance of my wishes...under any circumstances...so when I tell you to get out, you had better move fast!"

"Miss Cricket—"

"I told you to get out!"

Unwilling to subject Pete to further abuse, Cricket attempted a smile. "Please do as she says, Pete. Everythin's all right. Jayne just wants to talk to me in private for some reason." The heavy pounding of her heart belying her calm exterior, Cricket saw the momentary indecision in Pete's expression and urged, "Please..."

Waiting only until the door closed behind the two men, Jayne rounded on Cricket sharply.

"I suppose you think you've won! Well, you haven't!"

Cricket's response was a bewildered shake of her head. "I don't know what you're talkin' about."

"Don't lie to me, you conniving witch! I don't know what you said to Whit the night of the party that made him break our engagement, but I—"

"Break your engagement?"

"Don't pretend you don't know!" A sob escaped Jayne's lips in a temporary lapse. "He visited me the next morning. I never saw him so upset...so terribly beaten... He told me that he couldn't marry me...that circumstances had changed, and it wouldn't work out between us."

"I didn't know—"

"Liar! You, with your innocent face and mewing ways... I knew what you were up to the first minute I saw you! You wanted Whit then, and you want him now. You think you've got him, too, but you'll never be able to make him happy!"

"Jayne, I didn't know—"

"You've ruined him, did you know that?" Jayne's piercing stare intensified. "With Whit's land and mine joined together, we would've had an empire that far surpassed what Whit lost because of that stupid war! He would've been wealthy...powerful... He would have regained the position in life he was always meant to hold. There were no bounds to what he and I could've accomplished together. Instead, you've consigned him to mediocrity...to the bare essentials of survival in this wilderness." Jayne paused briefly in an attempt to maintain her waning control, then continued in a hiss, "But worst of all, you've robbed him of the woman he loves."

"I didn't!"

"You did! He told me—" Jayne breathed deeply. "He told me that he loved me...that he'd never love anyone the way he loved me. He said giving me up was the hardest thing he ever had to do...but he had no choice. He said he couldn't marry me because you had come between us."

"No—"

"He said you were dependent on him and he felt a responsibility to you."

"No!"

"He...he *cried* when he asked me to forgive him."

Cricket closed her eyes.

"You're pretending again, aren't you?" Cricket's eyes snapped open as Jayne continued with increasing venom. "You don't fool me. All you care about is yourself. You don't really care about Whit. If you did, you'd let him go on with his life as before. You'd let him look forward, instead of making him look back. You'd let him be happy."

"I want Whittaker to be happy. I want that more than anythin' in the world."

"Then leave! Go away and never come back! When he's free again, he'll come back to me, because he loves me...and I love him. I'll make him happier than you could ever make him. I'll keep him satisfied and content. I'll fill his bed and his heart, just as I did before you came."

Cricket's face drained of color.

"Yes, that's right." Jayne's expression became exultant. "Whit and I were lovers, and he told me it was better between us than he had ever known it could be. He—" Jayne swallowed tightly, then raised her chin. "He told me before he left that he'd *never* stop wanting me."

Cricket was silent, unable to form a word of reply.

Staring at her for a few moments longer, Jayne reached for her woolen wrap. She shook it off again, then covered her head.

When she spoke, her voice was devoid of its former heated emotion. "I'm going. You may tell Whit what I said, or you may not . . . whatever you choose to do. I don't care. You've already ruined Whit's life. Nothing could make things worse."

Through the doorway with a few quick steps, Jayne climbed onto the wagon and within minutes was on her way back in the direction from which she had come. The heavily falling snow had all but blotted her from sight when the sound of Pete's voice awoke Cricket from her distraction.

"Miss Cricket . . . are you all right?"

Her head snapping to Pete's concerned gaze, Cricket attempted a smile. "I . . . I'm fine. Jayne was angry. You were right. She and Whittaker had an argument and she blamed me, but now that I know what was the cause of it, I can take care of it."

The lines of concern on Pete's grizzled countenance deepened. "Don't you believe anything that woman says, Miss Cricket. She's a viper. She—"

"She's the woman Whittaker wants to marry."

"Yeah, but—"

"He loves her."

"Miss Cricket—"

"That's all that's important."

Pete attempted to speak once more, but Cricket stepped back, her smile forced. "I...I think I'll lie down for a while, Pete...if you don't mind."

"Of course I don't mind!" Pete smiled his gap-toothed smile. "You rest just as long as you like. The boss'll be back in a few hours, and he'll straighten everything out. He wants you to be happy, you know."

"I want him to be happy, too."

"I'll be busy in the kitchen finishing up. If you need anything, you just call, you hear?"

"Thank you, Pete."

Moments later, behind the bedroom door, Cricket closed her eyes.

The pretense was over.

Her time was up.

Oh, God, it was done.

# Chapter Eight

Whit stared at Pete's flushed face, his heart hammering in his chest. "What do you mean you didn't even know she was gone?"

Whit's frustration mounted. A strange uneasiness had driven him to ride back to the house ahead of the men as they herded the last of the heifers through a winter storm rapidly reaching blizzard proportions. He had arrived a few minutes earlier and knocked repeatedly on Cricket's bedroom door, only to go inside and find she wasn't there. The blue gown he had bought her had been spread out carefully on the bed, but her few personal belongings had been missing. After a few words with Pete, he had gone immediately to the barn and found Lucy gone, as well, and his apprehension had turned to fear. Disbelief had brought him back to Pete for an explanation the older man was not able to give.

"I'm telling you, I didn't know!" Pete's agitation was apparent. "Miss Cricket just said she wanted to lie down for a while after Miss Jayne left."

Whit stiffened. "Jayne was here?"

"She was, and she was madder than a hornet, too."

"What did she say to Cricket? Did she make her angry?"

"I don't know what she said."

"Damn it! What *do* you know, Pete!"

Pete's worried frown darkened. "I should've knowed something was really wrong. Poor Miss Cricket, she was as white as a ghost when Miss Jayne left."

"Damn you, Pete, I thought you said—"

"I don't know nothin', I told you! Miss Jayne drove up with that hired man, Chuck, and she stamped into the house like a storm cloud ready to pop. She told me to get out because she wanted to talk to Miss Cricket alone."

"And you did it!"

Pete's jaw stiffened. "Miss Cricket asked me to."

"You should've—"

"I *told* you, Miss Cricket asked me to."

"All right. What happened then?"

"I didn't hear what they talked about." Pete's expression grew defensive. "I couldn't listen at the door, you know, especially with Chuck standing right there . . . even if I had a mind to! Anyway, Miss Jayne came out a little while later, climbed back onto the wagon and drove off, and when I went back inside . . . well, Miss Cricket and me talked for a little bit, that's all."

"What did she say?"

"Nothing meant for your ears."

"What's that supposed to mean?"

"It means she didn't say nothing you was supposed to hear."

"Damn you, Pete!" Whit gestured toward the heavy snow falling outside the window. "Look out there! If Cricket's out there somewhere, she—" Whit took a steadying breath and began again. "You know Cricket's not really familiar with this country. Hell, there're miles of open land out there, with the snow fallin' so thick that you can't see your hand in front of your face."

"I know that! I ain't stupid, you know! What I'm telling you is that Miss Cricket didn't say nothing that made me think she'd leave." Pete paused, his expression briefly hopeful. "You sure she ain't just out for a ride? I mean, she was upset—"

"She was upset." Whit briefly closed his eyes. God, what had he done? His throat tight, he glanced toward the Christmas tree Cricket and he had decorated the previous day. He remembered the warmth between them as they had worked on it side by side. He recalled thinking that she had forgiven him and had put that night behind her...even if he had found himself increasingly haunted by the beauty of the emotion they had shared. He—

An envelope propped at the base of the tree caught Whit's eye and his thoughts came to an abrupt halt. He snatched it up and tore it open, recognizing Cricket's careful script as he read:

My dear Whittaker,
It is hard to say goodbye. The timing is difficult, but I hope you will believe that I haven't chosen this moment to leave in order to cause you additional distress. I know you were sincere when you said you loved me as you have since I was a child and that you wanted to take care of me. The only problem is that I'm not a child any longer, and I can't let you sacrifice your happiness for me.

I know Pete will tell you that Jayne was here. Please don't be angry with her. Everything she said and did was done out of love for you. I suppose that I, better than anyone else, understand.

Merry Christmas, my dear Whittaker. I hope you will respect my decision to leave and that you will remember me with the same joy that fills my heart when I think of you.

With love,<br>Your Cricket.

Whit's trembling hands tightened on the neatly scripted missive.

So polite . . . so civilized . . .

So *damned foolish!*

Panic flushed Whit's senses. Didn't she know the danger she faced in this storm? Hadn't she learned anything the first time she barely escaped with her life? Didn't she realize that if anything happened to her, his life would end, as well? Didn't she know that he—

A sudden shudder shaking him, Whit glanced up at the silent, thickening curtain of white beyond the window. Unconsciously crushing the letter in a furious grip, he shoved it in his pocket and turned toward the door. In a moment, he had mounted and turned his horse into the storm.

The frozen deluge continued as Cricket urged her struggling horse forward through the shifting, knee-high drifts. The unrelenting wind whipped her with icy pellets of snow, rocking her as she bent low over the saddle in an effort to maintain her seat. Stretching out her hand, she patted her mount's neck, mumbling words of comfort through stiff lips almost incapable of the task.

The screech of the wind increased in volume, and Cricket pulled her hat down lower on her forehead. She adjusted her scarf across her mouth, her body and mind numb from the chilling onslaught as she peered into the deepening storm.

Unable to see more than a few feet in front of her, Cricket felt a slow panic assail her. No, this couldn't be happening again. . . . The snowfall had been modest when she had left the house. She had not anticipated any difficulty in finding her way back to town along a trail that had been clearly outlined against the melting landscape a few days previous. How . . . when had that delineation disappeared, leaving her surrounded by the same endless sea of white that she had floundered in once before?

The curtain of snow thickened, and Cricket was struck by a sudden, heart-stopping realization. She was traveling as blind and ignorant of direction as the laboring animal beneath her!

As if in response to her thoughts, Lucy stumbled briefly, emphasizing the irony of a situation Cricket realized would be laughable were it not so sad. After the incredible hardships and desolation of her journey to this raw frontier, after the exalting highs and devastating lows of finding Whittaker again, after the emotional upheaval of being held in Whittaker's arms, of becoming a part of him, of having her dream come so close to realization, only to have it snatched away once more…she was now back exactly where she had started.

She was lost.

Cricket's heart assumed a ragged beat. She was becoming irrational and confused. She had already lost her concept of time, and she was dwelling too long on what might have been, when she should be concerned with what *was*…a blizzard that sought to lay a final claim to her.

Her mount's sudden jerk on the reins drew Cricket sharply from her muddled thoughts. She clutched the reins tighter, her frozen hands almost incapable of sustaining their grip as she assessed the hesitant animal silently. Was Lucy floundering, as well? Would her stout heart finally succumb?

Halting abruptly as Cricket urged her forward, Lucy jerked harder at the reins, shaking her head with a whinny of protest.

Cricket leaned forward to speak into Lucy's ear, her voice hardly discernible over the howl of the wind. "What's the matter, girl?"

Twisting her neck to look back at her, Lucy shook her head again and took a few halting steps, just as a lull in the shrieking wind allowed the vague outline of a shack to waver briefly into view some distance to the left. The outline was gone a moment later, leaving Cricket as uncertain as before. Robbed of breath by another freezing blast, realizing time was growing short, Cricket took the only option left to her. She allowed the reins to fall slack.

Her mind growing number by the minute as Lucy moved forward once more, Cricket was struck by a familiar, bittersweet thought that summed up her heartache in a few succinct words. . . .

*I came so close.*

The shriek of the wind grew louder, its force more intense. Enclosed in a yowling, freezing rage of white—the sky, the landscape, the earth, swallowed up by the driving storm—Whit forged relentlessly forward. There was no doubt in his mind that Cricket had started back toward town, a journey that would take a few hours under the best of conditions. Under the worst of conditions, however, such as those that she now endured . . .

Whittaker felt a sharp stab of panic. Cricket could be anywhere! The trail had disappeared beneath the snow during the first half hour of the storm, with the force of the wind raising drifts that distorted the landscape until now even he was occasionally uncertain of his direction. Making matters worse, Cricket's abrupt departure could not have allowed her to adequately prepare for the violence of the storm.

Whit's heart began a frantic pounding. Somewhere in this white, ever-changing void, Cricket was wandering . . . lost, cold, needing him . . .

As he needed her.

Whit felt his throat tighten. Reality had struck him with staggering force the moment he entered Cricket's room and saw the blue gown carefully arranged on the bed. The message it conveyed had shaken him to the soul. Cricket had returned his gift to her, and with it, all that it symbolized . . . the new maturity he had acknowledged the night he first saw her in the gown, the incredible hours of loving passion they had shared, and the silent promise of a tomorrow that had dawned filled with regret.

A rush of rage momentarily dulled the effects of the frigid wind that buffeted Whit. Why hadn't Cricket, always wise beyond her years, realized that his world had come full circle in the short weeks since she had reappeared in his life... and that he had been momentarily paralyzed by the emotions evoked? Why hadn't she recognized his difficulty in learning to face memories that had formerly brought him only pain, and in accepting the realization that hope for the future did not necessarily exclude all that had gone before? And why... why hadn't Cricket sensed that the love consigned to a hidden chamber of his heart had been held secret even from him... awaiting the necessary passage of years for her to reach maturity... and that that love would be as difficult for him to acknowledge as it had been for him to comprehend?

Stunned by the impact of that last thought as it emerged clearly in his mind for the first time, Whit caught his breath.

Could it be that he had loved Cricket all his life, without realizing it?

*Yes, it could.*

Could it be that the lovemaking they had shared had merely been a natural progression of that love, and not the betrayal of trust that had shamed him?

*Yes, it could.*

Could it be that he wanted the matured Cricket with the same depth of commitment and love he had had for her as a child?

*Yes, he did.*

His bay's sudden whinny interrupted Whit's thoughts. The screech of the wind increased in volume, frustrating his efforts to see... to hear... when another whinny from his bay elicited an echo of a whinny in return.

Elation flashed across Whit's mind. Taking a steadying breath, he rasped, "All right, boy. Find her."

Hunching his shoulders against a violent gust that threatened to thrust him from the saddle, Whit resisted the urge to spur his mount to a faster pace as the animal moved slowly forward. His agitation increased when the animal stopped abruptly. He was close to despair when the outline of a shack became momentarily visible a few yards away.

His heartbeat increasing to a thundering in his ears that rivaled the rage of the wind in volume, Whit recognized the abandoned shack that stood on the far western corner of his property. He was startled to realize the distance he had wandered from the trail, and was certain Cricket could never have made it this far. Then another whinny sounded from the rear of the dilapidated structure.

His bay responded in kind, and hope surged bright and keen once more. At the door of the shack within minutes, Whit paused, realizing the shuddering of his powerful frame was due more to raging emotions than the raging elements and recognizing that his hopes and dreams lay in what he would discover on the other side. His hand trembling, he pushed the door open with a sudden thrust.

Darkness...without a sign of life...met Whit's gaze. Stepping inside, he scanned an interior covered with the dust of years and the litter of abandonment. His heart sank at the sight of broken furniture scattered across the floor, a dented kettle nearby, a potbellied stove standing blackened and cold in the center of the room.

But in the corner—

The shadowed mound on the floor there moved. It unfolded, stretched out to human length, and turned stiffly toward him. His heart leaping, he heard a hoarse voice rasp, "Whittaker...is that you?"

Shuddering violently, her mind numb from the cold that had settled deep inside her, Cricket stared uncertainly. Was she dreaming, or was the broad, snow-covered figure standing outlined against a blustering wall of white in the doorway really—

A few quick steps, and Cricket's question was answered by the strength of Whittaker's arms as they clasped her close. His warmth surrounded her, his gruff words met her ears. She heard the anguish in his tone, and her arms slipped around him in return, comforting him as he comforted her, until anxious words turned to kisses, the comfort to loving, and the shuddering to passions held barely under restraint.

Drawing back from Whit's embrace with sheer strength of will, the heat between them negating the cold of the storm still raging without, Cricket rasped, "No, Whittaker... please. We've been through this before, and it's brought us only regret."

"Regret?" Whit's eyes held her, their incredible blue color mesmerizing her with its brilliance as he whispered, "I have regrets...yes. But my regrets aren't what you think. I've been a damned fool, Cricket. I didn't want to trust anythin' associated with the past, because I was afraid the heartache would start again. But I didn't know... I didn't realize..."

His voice failing, Whit lowered his mouth to hers. He drew deeply from it, appearing to gain the strength he sought as he pulled back at last to stroke her face with a trembling hand.

"I just didn't know how much I loved you, darlin'. I didn't know that the love would come alive inside me the minute I touched you, or that it would overwhelm me before I had time to realize that you were a part of me that had been hidden even from myself."

"No, Whittaker." Cricket shook her head, certain she read guilt in his words. "It was unfair of me to come here. You had made yourself a new life. You had a brilliant future ahead of you, and I spoiled it."

"No, you—"

"Please, Whittaker, don't say any more." A tear slipped from the corner of Cricket's eye. "I know the truth. Jayne told me."

"What did she tell you?" Whit stiffened, his expression hardening. "What did she say?"

"She told me the truth."

A familiar knot inside her tightening into pain, Cricket sought to avoid his eye, only to have Whit grasp her chin to turn her back to meet his gaze.

"Tell me what she told you, Cricket."

"She...she told me about the plans for the future you had made together. I ruined them all, and I robbed you of the woman you love."

"*You're* the woman I love, Cricket."

Cricket shook her head. "She said you told her you couldn't marry her because *I* had come between the two of you."

"Cricket—"

"She said you felt a responsibility toward me because I was dependent on you."

"Cricket, please believe me—"

"Oh, Whittaker...she said you *cried* when you asked her to forgive you."

"No...no..."

"She said you told her you'd never love anyone the way you loved her...that you'd never stop wanting her."

"Lies, Cricket...all lies!" Whit's gaze grew desperate. "Listen to me, darlin'. Let me explain." Whit paused briefly, refusing to surrender her gaze. He began softly, "I wandered for a long time after I left the South behind me. Then I came to this country and settled here...but I still wasn't at rest. Somethin' had gone cold inside me. I had no sense of belongin', of bein' a part of it all, despite every-thin' I had begun to build. When I met Jayne I thought puttin' down deeper roots would be the answer, but I knew in my heart that somethin' wasn't right, somehow. Then you came back into my life, and that spot that had been dead inside me started comin' alive again. I began rememberin' the good in the past instead of only the bad. And I started rememberin' that I had loved you as a babe who was always under my feet, that I had loved you as a child who seemed to know me better than I knew myself, and that I had loved you as a young girl who had welcomed me home and who had loved me without reservation.''

His voice growing deep with the passion of his words, Whit whispered, "But it took me longer... almost too long... to realize that I also loved you as the woman you had become. Cricket, darlin'..." His voice failing once more, Whit paused, then continued in a husky rasp, "You're everythin' to me. I know that now. You're my link to the past and my path to the future... a lovin' path, darlin', that I want to travel only with you." His brilliant eyes growing moist, Whit whispered, "I love you, my darlin' Cricket. I want you to be with me always... as my friend, my helpmate, my lover, my wife... for the rest of our lives."

"But Jayne—"

"There is no Jayne, Cricket, only you and me. Let me prove it to you, darlin'."

Drawing her close into the circle of his arms, Whit began his argument slowly, convincingly... lovingly. Sliding her arms around his neck as his lips met hers, Cricket welcomed his passionate logic with all the love in her heart.

Daylight dawned, a bright, clear day. Lying in Whit's arms, the chill of the abandoned shack dulled as much by the love that burned in her heart as by the fire that burned in the rusted, potbellied stove a short distance away, Cricket opened her eyes to the sound of a gentle whisper.

"Merry Christmas, darlin'."

Her flesh warm against Whit's, Cricket touched the locket that lay against her breast. Her eyes misted as she whispered in return, "I have nothin' to give you that's as beautiful as this, except…'' Sliding herself closer, a tear slipping down her cheek as happiness swelled sure and deep within her, Cricket whispered, more softly than before, ''Except the gift I've saved for you all my life. Merry Christmas, Whittaker…with all my love.''

Silent as their lips met once more, Whit accepted Cricket's tender tribute, knowing in his heart that the greatest gift of all was the one they would share together…for the rest of their lives.

*     *     *     *     *

## *A Note from Elaine Barbieri*

*Dear Reader,*

Christmas is wonderfully hectic in the Barbieri household. It starts with a traditional Christmas Eve dinner at my mother's home, then Midnight Mass. It continues on Christmas morning with a gathering of the huge Barbieri clan at my husband's family homestead, then a return to my own house for a day-long celebration with happily squealing grandchildren, non-stop taped Christmas carols, mountains of presents and food, food, food.

The joy of the season seems to have multiplied with the addition of each new child to our household over the years. I consider myself a very fortunate woman to have been so blessed.

I'm especially happy this year to be able to share the joy of the Christmas season with my readers by writing a Christmas story that, hopefully, will add to the enjoyment of the holidays.

"Rendezvous" is my Christmas gift to you. With it comes my genuine wish that each of you will experience the true joy and love of the season, this year and always.

*Elaine Barbieri*

# THE WOLF AND THE LAMB

## Kathleen Eagle

For my niece, Abby, who's five years old this
Christmas. Don't grow up too fast!

## MEGA BROWNIES
### from Kathleen Eagle

The fare from my kitchen is rarely fancy. The food I put on the table is generally simple, quick and hearty. I'm always on the lookout for good recipes along those lines. When I find one, I like to experiment. Often I'll try a substitution when I'm missing an ingredient, and I'll come up with a whole new dish. Okay, so sometimes it's a flop, but that's the way of experimentation.

Here's a recipe that meets my requirements. Use it for emergency baking over the holidays. Everybody has at least one of those occasions, don't they?

> 1 brownie mix (I like to use one with nuts)
> 1 cup semisweet chocolate chips
> 1 cup coconut
> 1 cup raisins or currants or $1/2$ cup each drained, chopped maraschino cherries and raisins
> (Or try something else. Use your imagination. I do!)
> 2 tsp rum flavoring

Mix according to package directions. Fold in the rest of the ingredients and bake according to package directions. Pan will be heavy; brownies will be moist; husband and children will snarf them up.

Wasn't that easy? Happy holidays!

# Prologue

On the thirteenth of June in 1879, the day she reached the matronly age of thirty, Miss Emily Lambert received a wondrous birthday gift. The widower Charles Tanninger, who owned house, land and livestock in the far West and with whom she had corresponded briefly after answering his advertisement in the *Boston Herald,* had proposed marriage.

"I suggest that we be wed forthwith by proxy, my dear Miss Emily," his letter said, "and that you hasten to join me and my two motherless daughters on my estate in this beautiful Montana Territory, for I fear that some other beau might snatch you away from me if we wait to tie the Blessed Knot after you arrive."

"The Blessed Knot" struck her as a charming phrase, almost as charming as the face in the photograph accompanying the proposal. Charles Tanninger was clearly a distinguished gentleman, "neither callow youth, nor dotard," with a well-groomed mustache, gentle eyes, hair graying at the temples.

And he was a Westerner! Emily had never been farther west than the Berkshires, but she had read a great deal about the people who lived in the Territories and the adventurous lives they led. Mountains whose peaks disappeared into the clouds, and meadows so vast that their carpets of wildflowers rolled beyond the horizon...such vistas challenged the limits of her considerable imagination. Before another birthday rolled around, she vowed she would see them.

Granted, she was taking a gamble in this venture, possibly the first real risk she had willingly undertaken in the entire predictable course of her thirty rather sheltered years. While her sister, Susan, had accepted the first proposal of marriage that had come her way, Emily had chosen to study classical literature, Romance languages and the viola at Wellesley. When her father could no longer afford her tuition, Emily had accepted employment, much to her father's dismay, as a governess. She liked children. She had held comfortable positions within the households of two well-respected Boston families, and she had enjoyed a certain sense of independence. Her third position had been less satisfying for her. The time had come for a change.

She wanted a home, a husband and children of her own and, despite the fact that she was still a ''handsome'' woman, as her present employer had recently noted—much to her discomfort—she realized that she was past prime ''marriageable'' age. No matter. Out West the opportunities were plentiful. There, surely, a clever woman might be appreciated for her resourcefulness. And there, her fundamentally timid heart buoyed by the spirit of adventure, Emily would make her mark.

Vowing to reach her new home in time to make this Christmas a very special time for two young girls in need of a mother rather than simply a governess, Emily took deliciously secret satisfaction in giving her notice.

# Chapter One

"Pardon me, sir, but I think you ought to wake up now."

Had the voice been an octave lower or a decibel louder, Wolf Morsette might have pulled his pistol and shot someone. But since it was barely strong enough to tickle his ear, he only growled. That should have been warning enough.

"Pardon me, but, you see, we've stopped at a roadhouse, and I believe we might have something to eat if we go inside. The driver said . . ."

Wolf opened one eye as he shifted his shoulders into the corner of the stage's unpadded and wholly austere interior. The fine-featured woman bunched her fingertips together and brought her hand toward her mouth, eyeing him eagerly. "Food," she said. "Inside."

Condescending as the gesture was, it was almost pretty. He'd seen only one other hand as smooth and as pale as this woman's was, and it had belonged to a high-priced whore in St. Paul. The whore had also shown some concern for his hunger—the kind that earned her a living. This woman didn't stand to earn a penny for her trouble. Had he been in a better mood, he might have spared a smile.

She raised her voice enough to compensate for any hearing impairment he might have had. "Do you speak any English?"

Wolf grimaced and shut his eye again. Noise and food were equally unwelcome at the moment. "Some," he grunted.

"Very well, sir, in light of your self-inflicted infirmity, which one can easily detect in such close quarters as these, I should think it would behoove you to eat some—"

"Not *that* kind of English." He folded his arms over his chest and settled deeper into the corner, muttering, "In plain, simple, *quiet* English, I ain't hungry."

"I see."

He felt a tugging beneath his boot heels.

"Then release my skirt, please."

Wolf opened his eyes and glanced down the considerable length of his legs, which stretched to the opposite corner of the coach.

"You are stepping on my skirt, sir."

"*Pardon.*" Unconsciously he allowed the accent of his upbringing to soften the word, for he remembered his parlor manners only in the Canadian French his parents had spoken.

"*Certainement,*" the woman quipped, her tone brightening considerably. "You speak French, sir?"

"Only in bed." Wolf raised his heels a couple of inches off the floor of the coach and offered a menacing smile. "Better hightail it into the roadhouse before, in my self-inflicted state of weakness, I take a notion that's where we are right now."

"I beg your pardon, sir." With a deft flick of her wrist she jerked the bottom of her black skirt out from under his heels. "I am a married woman."

"Minor detail. I can overlook it if you can." He nodded toward the open window and the soddy that stood beyond it. "You'd better get in there and grab a plate before your man eats your share."

"That man is certainly *not* my husband." Her indignation was directed toward the soddy first and the passenger who had already gone inside, then at Wolf. "Despite your rudeness, sir, and since this might well be the only opportunity I shall have, I feel it my Christian duty to inform you that—" Again she glanced toward the windowless hut that sprouted buffalo grass and thistles from its roof. "I believe our traveling companion may have picked your pocket."

Wolf arched an eyebrow her way. The information interested him less than the fact that she had seen fit to share it with him. Another surprising show of courtesy from a woman whose people rarely saw fit to show his kind much of any consideration.

She lifted her slight shoulders as her slender fingers fluttered about the pink and white cameo pinned to her tucked white blouse, just at the base of her throat. Her blue eyes failed to meet his as she spoke, barely above a whisper. "I have seen pickpockets at work before, on the streets of Boston. When this abominable conveyance lurched to a stop, our companion—Mr. Johnston, I believe—jostled you, and I am quite certain he slipped his hand inside your coat."

The shared confidence earned her half a smile. "It's a rare woman whose eyes are as sharp as her tongue."

Briskly she adjusted her gray wool jacket as she lifted her small, pointed chin. "And a foolish man who succumbs to stuporous sleep in the presence of strangers."

Wolf laughed and shook his head as he straightened. "You're no stranger, Miss Emily Lambert." He flashed a knowing look. "*Married* woman."

"How did you know my name? My *maiden* name."

"Heard you tell the stationmaster back in Deadwood."

"Old habit." She dismissed it with a wave of her left hand, flashing the thin gold band on her third finger. "Less than two months married, and I'm still unaccustomed to my new name. Mrs. Charles Tanninger."

"Miss Emily Lambert sounds nicer." Wolf eyed her appreciatively. He figured her for a proxy bride, in which case

*Mr.* Charles Tanninger was in for a pleasant surprise. She had a little age on her, and she was pretty high-headed, but she was easy on the eyes.

He jerked his chin toward the coach window. "Go on in and get yourself something to eat, Miss Emily. You need to be puttin' some meat on those bones before winter."

"I'm from New England, sir. I'm well acquainted with cold winters."

"You might know snow, but you've got no acquaintance with wind, Miss Emily. Out here, the wind'll cut right through a wispy frame like yours. You need to tie on the feed bag." He reached out and pushed the door open for her, enjoying the look of indignation on her prim face. "Johnston came up empty-handed, but thanks for the tip, Miss Emily."

He watched her through the window, admiring the smooth way she walked, shoulders back, head held high. He liked the way her skirt swished in the grass and the way the ends of the bonnet ribbon tied in a bow to the left of her chin fluttered over her shoulder.

Boston. Long ways away, probably a whole different world. Gave a man pause to wonder whether a woman from Boston would even recognize him as a mixed blood.

Emily had not anticipated such a long and bumpy ride on the stagecoach. She had traveled as far as she could by train, then connected with the Deadwood Stage Line in Dakota Territory. As she had anticipated from her sundry readings, the farther west she had traveled, the rowdier the communities she had encountered. It was rather exciting.

Deadwood, a rickety gold miners' settlement tucked into a crevasse in the pine-covered Black Hills, had been the rowdiest so far. The residents consumed more whiskey than water, discharged their firearms simply to make noise, bet anything they owned on any challenge anyone cared to offer and took it for granted that every woman had her price.

Emily's short stay had proven to be quite interesting. She had never received so many improper advances from such a plentiful variety of scoundrels. And now she could have added her fellow traveler to the list, except that he had not mentioned his name.

It surprised her that he'd bothered to take note of hers. She'd thought he might be related to the Red Indians somehow, but if that were the case, his remark about speaking French in bed was a bit confusing. She had never met anyone quite like him—not that she had actually *met* him. Dressed in buckskin pants and a wool coat with fringe at the shoulders that looked at though it had been fashioned from a blanket, he had purchased his ticket in silence and boarded the stage the same way. It was Emily's sensitive nose rather than the man's behavior that told her he was either drunk or suffering from the aftermath.

But it was the third passenger in the coach who truly made Emily feel uncomfortable. He was a fast talker with little to say, and his attention shifted constantly, as though he'd lost something and thought it might reappear anywhere at any moment. As the afternoon light dimmed and the evening shadows lengthened across the low-lying hills, Mr. Johnston's evasive eyes became more and more disconcerting. The passengers spoke less, bounced around more, and the interior of the coach gradually darkened as the dark, enigmatic man dressed in buckskins slept on.

Suddenly the coach hit a deep rut, first the front wheel, then the rear. Emily bumped her head on the ceiling, then fell back to her seat with a teeth-gnashing thud. The driver whistled and popped his whip, and the coach lurched, then surged forth, dumping Johnston onto Emily's lap. He shouted. She yelped. During the chaos his hands were all over her, everywhere at once. His sheer weight knocked the breath from her lungs, and she couldn't get it back, not even a little. She hadn't the voice to order him off, hadn't the strength to push him away.

But the weight was finally lifted. A glint of metal flashed in the shadows, and a cold, steely click arrested all motion.

"You know what, Johnston? You've overstayed your welcome."

Johnston stiffened as he slid away from Emily. "What're you talking about? I can't help it if this road's got more holes than—"

Gasping for air, Emily shrank back as she groped for the edge of the seat.

"You were gettin' off anyway, weren't you? Assuming you found something on one of us worth makin' off with." The man Emily had thought to be sound asleep jerked Mr. Johnston close beside him on the seat opposite hers and menaced his ear with the barrel of a pistol. "You want to make your apologies to the lady before you take your leave?"

Emily gasped. "You can't—"

"You're damn right, Miss Emily, a man sure can't get much sleep when there's a snake in his bedroll. Now you can either jump out, or I can hold this gun right where it is until the next stop." He paused, looked Johnston in the eye and slowly grinned. "'Course, we hit another good rut, it just might go off." The grin vanished. "If it doesn't, we'll see what the Deadwood Line does with weasels who—" he reached into Johnston's coat pocket and pulled out a gold watch and chain "—steal from its passengers."

"That was pinned inside my jacket," Emily exclaimed as her hands flew from the pocket in the lining of her wool jacket to the one in her skirt. "My purse is still..." She pulled against the drawstrings and shoved her fingers inside the small satin pouch. "You managed to take the money out and leave the purse? How remarkable, Mr. Johnston."

"You can't prove nothin'."

"Whatever you've got on you must be hers." The gun barrel touched Johnston's temple. "You got nothin' off me."

"But I *had*—"

"Empty your pockets."

With unsteady hands, the man complied. Emily claimed her small roll of paper money and the six twenty-dollar gold pieces she'd had when she left Boston. "The rest is not mine," she said quietly.

"You sure you're not missin' anything else?"

"No, I—" Peace of mind, perhaps. Dignity. In a matter of moments Johnston had managed to assail her person, her private self, with his quick, invasive hands. Her fingers trembled as she touched the brooch at the base of her throat. "Yes, I'm sure."

"What'll it be, Johnston? Take your chances with the coyotes, or deal with the wolf?"

"Wolf?" Johnston turned his head toward his captor. "Wolf Morsette?"

"Forget the formalities," Morsette said. "I've got my hands full, and yours are shakin' pretty good already."

"So... you just gonna let me go?"

"You're going to make him jump out—" Emily looked out the window, into the desolate, deepening dusk "—here?"

"*Here* keeps changin'," Morsette blithely pointed out. "It's gettin' pretty dark out, Johnston. Pick your spot before I change my mind."

They were slowing down for a hill. "Looks good here." Johnston opened the door and paused long enough to tip his bowler hat. "Sorry for any inconvenience, ma'am, but a man's gotta use whatever talent he's got. Morsette's got his, I've got mine."

"Mr. Morsette, you must let the law handle this," Emily pleaded.

"This is the law out here, right here in my hand." And the barrel was pointed at the man who was already on his way out the small door. "It says, 'Thou shalt not steal a lady's dowry.' It's gettin' drafty in here, Johnston."

"Damn your soul to hell, Morsette."

"Reckon I'll see you there."

"Remember to roll when you hit bottom," Johnston muttered to himself as he balanced the balls of his feet on the threshold and prepared to spring. "Pleasant jour—"

One bootheel kicked the flapping door.

"Oh, my—"

"Nice jump." Uncocking his pistol, Morsette grabbed the door and pulled it shut, thwarting Emily's attempt to see what kind of a landing the man had achieved. "That fella's had himself some practice."

"I know he's a thief and—" She sat back, staring at her remaining traveling companion in disbelief. "And a scoundrel, but what about the Indians?"

"Indians?" Morsette tucked his pistol under his coat. "The thieves and the scoundrels have cleaned them out already. They've got nothing left for a pickpocket to steal. Don't have to worry about them."

"Are there no wild Indians close by for *him* to worry about?"

"A few, yes."

"How close?"

"Quite close." He leaned forward. "Close enough to make out the color of your eyes, Miss Emily."

"Then—" she gestured toward the window, sputtering dramatically "—putting that man out on the road was an unconscionable thing to do. They might—"

"They won't bother. They don't give the slightest damn about the color of *his* eyes. But yours..."

"It's too dark to see my eyes."

"Wild Indians see very well at night." He sat back with a self-satisfied smile. "You have pretty eyes, Miss Emily."

There was a pleasant lilt in his voice, a cadence unlike the drawl she'd heard in Deadwood. But she thought surely his English was too good to be that of a Red Indian. "I am *Mrs.* Charles Tanninger, sir. It would behoove you to bear that in mind."

"My name is not 'sir.' It's Wolf." He cocked an admonishing finger her way. "And you'll want to bear in mind that my name fits me well."

Billings, Montana, was a ramshackle town surrounded by rimrock and scrub pine. The November wind had driven everyone indoors. No one came to meet the stage. There was no husband with a fresh shave and polished boots, no little girls dressed in their Sunday best waiting on the landing at the depot.

Emily's inquiries at the mercantile and the land office were met with cold stares. "The Tanninger place is out in the hills west of town," the telegraph operator told her. "Ol' Tanninger keeps to himself. He ain't picked up his mail in a month or more."

She decided to rent some manner of transportation at the livery, even though she was uneasy with the thought of trying to find her own way in the wilderness. From what she had seen, what passed for a road in this country was little more than a cow path over rugged terrain.

"A buggy will do nicely," she told the white-haired man with the tobacco-stained beard.

"Ain't got a buggy for rent." The man folded his arms over his chest, turned his head to the side and spat into the dirt, barely missing the spotted dog that was curled up just outside the doorway.

"A buckboard, then."

The man shook his head.

Emily glanced pointedly at the wagon that was clearly visible through the back door of the big, dilapidated barn.

"This is a matter of some urgency. I would be willing to pay—"

"Is the bride running out on the honeymoon?"

Familiar though it was, the deep voice startled Emily. When she turned, dark, smiling eyes unnerved her. The spotted dog scurried out of the way of the black horse at the end of Wolf Morsette's lead. "I'll give you twenty-five, Harding."

The bearded man stuck out his hand for Morsette's money. "Don't matter what you'll pay, missy. If you're on the run, anything you take outta here, you got to *buy* outright. I'll sell you a good horse at a fair price, like I just done for this here feller." A gap-toothed grin separated the mustache from the mottled beard. "Think you can fork a horse, missy?"

"Fork . . . a horse?"

"He means *ride,*" Morsette said.

"Even more worrisome," Harding added, "will somebody be chasing after you?"

"Of course not." Emily bristled, staring down each man in turn as though he'd taken leave of his senses. "There has been some confusion, some simple misunderstanding, or else—" Harding's attention had strayed to the row of stalls, presumably in search of another horse to sell. Emily turned the last of her explanation on Morsette, but she was losing conviction as her tone softened. "Or else perhaps Mr. Tanninger has been unavoidably detained."

"Then *perhaps* you ought to take a room at the hotel and wait for him," Morsette suggested.

Emily shot a quick glance at Harding as she stepped closer to the man who had shared the stage ride with her. His methods might have been questionable, but it was thanks to him that she had any money at all for the purchase she was about to be forced to make. "The people I've met here thus far have seemed less than friendly," she confided. "I have asked about Mr. Tanninger, about the location of the farm.

Is it too much to expect a simple how-do-you-do and welcome from these people?''

"In my case it generally is."

"But your reputation precedes you."

"What reputation?"

"Your reputation as a fast gun," Emily said solemnly, hushing her tone. "The man on the stage whispered your name in fear. I don't think I've come across it in the stories I've read, but then . . ." She stepped closer. "Did you know Wild Bill Hickok, by chance?"

"Nope. Never crossed his path."

"But you *are* a gunman," she concluded. "Are you, by chance, between jobs?" He arched an eyebrow, offering her the chance to justify her question. "Are you available for hire, that is?"

His eyes brightened, presumably with interest. "What do you need, Miss Emily?"

"I seem to need a guide." She glanced at the toes of her shoes. "And I'm in a rather poor bargaining position since you know exactly how much money I'm carrying."

"I didn't count it." The black horse shifted restlessly. Morsette patted its neck. "I'm just passin' through here. I don't know Tanninger, don't know where his place is, don't really—"

"But I'm sure you could find it." She stepped to the side, turning her back to Harding to shut him out of earshot. "It's not that I'm incapable of managing on my own, and I have read a great deal about the territory, but I think it unwise to venture out without really knowing—" a nervous glance toward the dusty, deserted street betrayed her waning confidence "—where I'm going."

"I think you've already done that, Miss Emily."

"Mrs. Tanninger," Emily corrected.

Wolf smiled.

"This mare's easy-ridin'," Harding called out from the second to the last stall. "Let her go for thirty bucks, plus another thirty for a saddle."

"Forty-five for the lot," Wolf said. "The lady's new in town, Harding. Show some hospitality."

"Take it you learned horse tradin' at your daddy's knee," Harding grumbled. "And horse *thievin'* from the other side."

"Careful, old man. The mention of my name strikes terror in most men's hearts." His friendly wink surprised Emily. More astonishingly, it pleased her. "Guess my reputation hasn't preceded me this far."

"Don't ask no names, don't know no names," Harding recited as he led the mare from her stall. "That's how come I've lived this long. I'll take your price if you pay in gold."

"Half in gold," Wolf said. "That's as good a deal as you've seen since spring, Harding. And if that mare's hardmouthed, you're gettin' her back. Which way to the Tanninger place?"

"West of town about fifteen miles. Follow the trail into the hills out there, you'll run right into it." Harding accepted Emily's money in exchange for the dun horse. "Tanninger generally fires off a couple of shots at anyone who comes too close, but he don't shoot to kill."

Morsette handed Emily the black horse's lead in a wordless invitation for her to hold his horse. She accepted without question. "You sure he knows you're coming?" he asked as he took the mare from Harding.

"Of course. He..." Emily hoped. She *trusted.* "He knows."

Morsette slid one hand along the mare's foreleg and lifted the hoof for a quick inspection. "We'll have to do some hard ridin' if we're gonna cover fifteen miles before nightfall. You sure you're up to it?"

"We haven't agreed on your—"

"Sounds like the place is on my way." Continuing his inspection of the mare, he felt through the thickening winter coat for saddle sores. "Maybe your husband will put me up for the night if I bring his bride to him, safe and sound."

"I should hope so." Emily gave a tentative nod. "I should certainly hope so, Mr. Morsette." He turned to her with an admonishing look. "Wolf," she corrected.

"Shh," he warned as he drew on a rawhide glove. "Somebody'll be wantin' to draw down on me, just to build up a reputation like mine."

"Indeed? Perhaps you need an alias."

"Why don't you think one up for me?" He smiled. "One for the books."

The autumn season had been one for the books this year. Wolf had spent the summer in Dakota Territory, picking up jobs where he could find them. He was Métis—a mixed-blood Cree who also had French and Scots relations in the Red River Valley on both sides of the Canadian border. He'd been a buffalo hunter, trapper, guide, interpreter and, yes, a hired gun on occasion. But ever since the Sioux had whipped Custer at Little Big Horn, the whites had got real touchy about Indians, and the Indians—all the different bands who had lived on the Plains as far back as anyone could remember—were being herded from one little square on the map to another.

It was hard for a man like Wolf Morsette to figure out which way to turn from one job to the next. He was a wanderer by nature as well as by trade. Or *trades*. He was adaptable. If a handsome woman needed a little shepherding, hell, he didn't mind helping her over the hard spots. She was, he thought—eyeing the open front of her jacket and admiring the way her breasts bounced to the rhythm of the mare's mincing trot—an entertaining diversion. A plucky little wayfarer whose dilemma had given him an amusing way to turn, at least for a day or two.

"Couldn't we either speed up or slow down?" The question bounced exactly the way her breasts did, and Wolf's laughter brought a scowl to her face. "I'm neither properly dressed nor properly equipped for this, and it's quite uncomfortable."

"Don't wanna play the horses out," he said with a smile. "Don't wanna drag our tails, either."

"How much—" she grabbed the saddle horn and adjusted her seat "—farther?"

He nodded toward the clear blue horizon. "I'd say just over that hill."

"The *next* hill? From here it's hard to tell where it begins and ends."

"Maybe it doesn't. It's a big hill." Feeling a little devilish, he nudged the black's flanks with a moccasined heel, extending the trot. "But you can handle it, Miss Emily."

"Certainly, I can." She lifted her chin. *"Certainement."*

*"Bien."* Again, he flashed her a smile.

Her first glimpse of the log house gave her an eerie feeling. The queer chill in the back of her neck had nothing to do with the numbness in her fingers and toes. Neither was it due in any way to the fact that the house was considerably smaller than she'd pictured it, nor to the unharvested squash and pumpkins that were visible amid the frost-blackened vines in the garden at the side of the house. But the large bird circling over a distant grove of pines lent a sense of heaviness to the silence in the brown and yellow valley.

"Turkey vulture," Wolf said, his eyes following it, too. "Sick livestock, maybe."

"That must be why he couldn't come to town."

"Must be." Wolf raised his voice as they approached. "Hello, the house!"

The front door opened just a crack. Twin shotgun barrels appeared.

"Don't look like your new husband's got much height on him," Wolf muttered as he reined in his horse and signaled for Emily to let him ease in front of her. "Take it easy, now," he called out. "You sent for a bride, and here she is."

The shotgun protruded farther through the crack.

"If this ain't the Tanninger place, we'll be on our way." Wolf raised the palm of his gun hand to show that it was empty while he eased his weight toward the left, visualizing the move he'd have to make if the situation turned any uglier. Dismount, scare the mare to the trees and cover the woman's back as she fled for safety.

"Mr. Tanninger, it's—"

"Just sit real tight, Miss Emily," Wolf warned softly. "We'll go or stay, whatever you say," he called out. "But put up your gun. It's makin' me a little nervous."

"Who are you?" a small voice shouted from the house.

Wolf glanced at Emily, who seemed, impossibly, to recognize the voice, to warm to it instantly and take it to heart, though its owner's face was yet unseen.

"I'm Emily Lambert," she said eagerly. "Emily Lambert *Tanninger.* Are you little Lisette? No, you must be Marie-Claire."

"Lisette's hidin' under the bed," the voice reported.

"This is Mr. Morsette," Emily explained. "He was kind enough to help me find my way here. Please put the gun down, Marie-Claire. We're not strangers. I have letters from—"

The double-barreled gun was slowly lowered and laid across the threshold, then the door squeaked on its iron hinges. A young girl emerged. She had a woman's eyes set in a childlike face. Her eyes were the same dark color, the same hooded almond shape as Wolf's, and her skin was nearly as brown. He dismounted as she descended the single wooden step.

"Mr. Morsette, I believe I need some assistance," Emily said quietly. "My legs feel a bit unsteady."

Without a word he reached up to help her down. The slight weight of the woman in his arms and the fear he saw in the child's eyes combined to stir some protective part of him. The woman had come a long way to be a stepmother to mixed-blood children. He glanced from her face to the girl's and back again. If it had come as any surprise to her, it didn't register on her face.

"Now that I have purchased a horse, I shall practice daily." She turned to the girl, who stood waiting, tears slipping silently down her cheeks. "Marie-Claire and I shall practice together. Do you enjoy riding, Marie-Claire?"

"I think she's glad you're here, Miss Emily."

"And I am most certainly…" She pulled off her glove and gently touched the girl's jaw with the backs of her fingers, then cupped her hand over the side of her head, smoothing a straggly braid. "Lisette is hiding under the bed, you say? We must allay her fears at once. Would you mind if we—"

Wolf held both horses' reins. "Where's your papa, Marie-Claire?"

The girl took a swipe at her tears with one hand and pointed past the house toward the stand of pine trees with the other.

The black-and-gray turkey vulture wheeled overhead, stretched its wings in a shallow V, then flapped once, twice, easing its dismal descent toward the treetops.

# Chapter Two

"Take Miss Emily inside, and tell your sister it's gonna be all right," Wolf said quietly.

Marie-Claire couldn't seem to pull her focus away from the pine trees. She drew a long, shuddering breath, and her lower lip trembled. "I put him by Mama, but I didn't make it deep enough."

"I'll see to it." Wolf untied one of his saddle packs and gave it to Emily, along with a shuttered look. "There's food in here." He glanced at the stone chimney. "Is there no wood for a fire?"

"I can find some," Marie-Claire offered. Clad in a long-waisted calico dress, she wrapped her arms around herself as though the reminder had given her a chill. "We ran out, and I was kinda scared to go lookin'."

"I'll bring wood. Is your sister sick?"

"No."

Wolf nodded once, and his eyes finally betrayed something—relief, maybe—as he mounted the black horse and instructed Emily "Water the mare and tie her up somewhere. I'll hobble them both where they can graze, soon as I see to—" He pulled his hat lower, hiding his eyes as he finished softly, "Mr. Tanninger."

Wolf returned to a roaring fire, a kettle of hot water and a cake of lye soap, which he sorely needed. Two little girls with wet hair and clean faces were chewing on his hardtack and jerky, and Miss Emily was buttoning her own cuffs. Without a word, she filled the basin for him while he hung his capote and hat on a peg near the door and began stripping himself down to the waist—down to his parti-colored *l'assomption* sash, which was the badge of his heritage.

The need to wash himself was so strong it nearly made his hands shake. Imagining what Marie-Claire must have gone through in trying to lay her father to rest had nearly undone him. The child's best efforts to do the impossible had fallen short, leaving Wolf's namesakes to do their worst. There had been little left of Mr. Tanninger, and the smell of death had been hard to stomach, even on a cold night. He hadn't been a young man—that much Wolf had discerned—nor did it appear that he'd been shot.

Wolf leaned over the basin and scooped handfuls of warm water over his thick hair, then rolled the soap in his palms and scrubbed hard. He closed his eyes and worked the soap over his shoulders, his arms and his chest, straightening after a time and letting the water trickle down his weary back even as he kept washing.

"I'll help you rinse when you're ready."

His eyes flew open. Three pairs of female eyes stared at him. Miss Emily was ready with a bucket of water. She glanced away, but not before she'd given his bare chest a quick appraisal. The spark of admiration in her eyes made his chest swell. He wanted to smile.

But instead he bent over again. "Douse me good," he told her.

The water sluiced over the top of his head, splashed into the basin, over the tabletop and across the rough plank floor. A rivulet ran down his back and got trapped in the wide sash, but it felt good. He couldn't remember the last time he'd had warm water for bathing. A quick shake of his head showered the room with drops and made little Lisette giggle.

It was that sound that made Wolf smile.

"It feels like it's raining inside," the little girl said.

"That might be for the best." Emily took after the puddle with a broom. "The house needs a good scrubbing, top to bottom. I found wood for a fire, but there's not much food here."

Wolf gave Lisette a passing wink as he moved closer to the fire. "No jerky left for a hungry man?"

"Oh, yes, there's that, but not much else."

"We don't need much else. I see squash outside. We could make soup."

"We have some beans and some salt pork," Marie-Claire reported. "But a wolf got the chickens after Papa took to his bed."

Wolf ruffled his thick hair with both hands as he sat on his heels and hunkered close to the fire. "When did he get sick?"

"He's had a pain in his belly for a long time."

"You mean, more than a few weeks?" Emily asked.

"More than a year."

"Did he go to a doctor for it?"

Marie-Claire shook her head. Her voice barely rose above the crackle of the fire. "Papa said no doctor could fix it. Either it would go away after a while, or it would kill him. It never went away. Just got worse, and finally he took to his bed. He said our new mama was comin' soon, and that I should be there to meet the stage when it came. But the horses ran off, too. Or else somebody stole them." She looked at Emily, apologizing with her eyes, as though she had failed to keep a promise. "And then I forgot what day it was that I was supposed to..."

Emily laid a comforting hand on the girl's slight shoulder. "It's all right, dear. Mr. Morsette found the place with no trouble."

"While I was tryin' to look after Papa and Lisette, the place just went to pot. I couldn't keep up."

"How old are you?" Wolf asked.

"I'm eleven now," Marie-Claire boasted. "My sister's almost six."

"I'd say you've done just fine." Wolf reached for the hardtack and jerked meat Emily offered. Her fingers brushed his, and their warmth distracted him for a moment. Their eyes met, and he read her wish that she could make more food—or better food, or hot food—the kind of nourishment that gave a woman a sense of satisfaction, he supposed. He felt an unsettling sense of pleasure simply in taking it from her hand. Softly he thanked her. Flame shadows danced across her face, and her smile was even softer.

Turning his face to the fire, he reminded himself that he'd just buried this woman's husband—husband at least in name—and that she was suddenly a widow. And then he reminded himself that he was Métis.

"What did Mr. Tanninger tell you of his first wife? Anything at all?"

"Only that she died when Lisette was a baby."

He turned to Marie-Claire. "Your mama, was she Métis?" When the girl didn't respond, he lifted one end of his *l'assomption* sash. "Was she a half-breed, like me?"

The girl shrugged as she glanced away. "We ain't supposed to talk about that."

"Look at me, Marie-Claire." If the sash meant nothing to the child, surely his deeply tanned face would make his point. "Was she dark-skinned, like me?"

"She was part Cree." Marie-Claire glanced from Wolf's face to Emily's and back again, as though this bit of information must go no further. "We never went to town much because people there say things about us."

"You're a very pretty girl," Wolf told her. He smiled when Lisette stopped gnawing on her jerky long enough to analyze her sister's prettiness. "Both of you."

"That's what Papa said. He said the new mama would teach us woman things. I already know how to read." Marie-Claire shrugged and reconsidered. "Well, pretty good. Papa was teaching us because they wouldn't let us go to school. They said we had to go to an Indian school."

"Where's the Indian school?" Emily asked.

"I don't know. Wherever the Indians live, I guess."

"And you don't know where that is," Wolf concluded.

Marie-Claire looked at Emily. "Are you disappointed?" she asked. Quickly she elaborated, "Papa said when you got here, things might not be the way you thought, and you might be disappointed."

"I regret Mr. Tanninger's passing. I regret that very, very much." She knelt beside the two girls, touching Marie-Claire's knee, smoothing back Lisette's damp hair. "Tomorrow, we must make plans, and for that we shall all need a good night's sleep."

The girls were asleep in the tiny loft. Wolf spread his bedroll near the hearth while Emily hovered nearby, almost as though she expected to share his bed. Of course, he knew better. But the only place left for her to sleep was on the rope bed with the straw mattress in the far corner. It was to have been Emily's bridal bed, but presumably—Wolf pivoted in a squat, his hand braced on one knee, and scrutinized the cheerless piece of furniture—it had been Charles Tanninger's deathbed.

"Would you rather sleep here, close to the fire?" he asked her.

"You're welcome to use the bed if you wish." She dragged one of the cabin's two ladder-back chairs across the floor and set it at the foot of his bedroll. "I thought I'd sit up for a while and just...ponder all this."

She sat in the chair. He sat cross-legged on the bedroll and began filling his small clay pipe.

She tried to watch the fire, but her gaze drifted to the bed, and she stared, entranced. "He sent me his picture. He wrote wonderful letters about Montana. He made everything sound so . . ." She pressed her lips together, then gave her head a quick, dismissing shake. "He should have *told* me."

"He needed a mother for his children. You wonder why he didn't send *their* picture?"

"No, of course not. That never occurred to me." *That* was left unclarified. "But he should have told me that he was ill."

"Would you have come sooner?" Perversely he preyed on the guilt he saw in her eyes. "Or not at all?"

"Do you think he knew he was dying?"

"I'd say he must have had it figured weeks back." He poked the glowing end of a piece of kindling into the bowl of his pipe and puffed several times before adding, "Maybe months."

"Was there no help for him close by? Why wouldn't anyone help?" When he offered no answers, she sighed and concluded, "He probably didn't tell anyone."

"I'll take you back to town in the morning."

"I don't suppose we could—" she surveyed the cabin's sturdy rafters and its plank floor "—stay here."

"We?"

"I am Mrs. Charles Tanninger. Legally." Tentatively she added, "This . . . this *is* my home."

"Does it feel like home to you?"

She shook her head. "But I could—"

"No, you couldn't." Abruptly he tossed the kindling into the fire. "There's nothing here to eat. It's November." He eyed her sternly. "No, you couldn't."

"We'll find a place in town, then."

"Wonder if Tanninger left any money behind." Either the prospect or the notion that he'd come up with it seemed to surprise her, but out of habit he interpreted the look in her eyes as an accusation. "For his *family*. I'll do what I have to do to get by, Miss Emily, but I won't steal from a woman or from children."

"I didn't think you would, Mr. Morsette." She looked at her small hands, primly folded in her lap. "I shall seek employment."

"What can you do?"

"I have been a governess." At a glance she could tell that not only was he unimpressed, he wasn't even sure what that was. "Or I can be a schoolteacher."

He raised one eyebrow, acknowledging the latter as a legitimate vocation.

"I shall take care of them." She squared her shoulders and looked to him for approval. He only puffed on his pipe. "We shall find a place in town, and in the spring perhaps we shall return here, replant the garden, buy some livestock..."

Her voice drifted for lack of any practical mooring, but he had no reassurance to offer her. "I admire your spunk, Miss Emily. But you know damn well you haven't got a prayer of makin' it work." He leaned back on one elbow, stretched out his legs and eyed her pointedly. "Not without a man."

She bristled. "Mr. Tanninger discovered himself unable to make it work without a woman."

"With two little girls to raise, it didn't take a genius to figure that one out. The wonder is that he didn't go lookin' in the real obvious places." He plucked the pipe from his mouth. "Wonder how he met up with his first wife and why he didn't go back to the same place for a second one."

"He was originally from New York."

"That explains it," he said, discovering the need for another light. He reached for more kindling. "Likely he learned a lesson about stickin' with your own kind."

"I don't know about that. Sometimes a person who seems to suit one perfectly..." Intent upon watching him relight his pipe, she seemed to briefly lose her train of thought. "Sometimes that person isn't suitable at all."

"It helps to start out with certain things in common."

"What would those things be? Proximity, family background, an interest in education and children and dreams of..."

A wistful smile crept into her eyes, and he was drawn into it, trying to imagine a very young Miss Emily strolling on the arm of a dapper gentleman. He'd met a few such men in St. Paul, and he'd taken no pleasure in their company. "A list like that oughta get you started," he allowed, soothing unexpected bitterness with a puff of smoke.

"Not if a prettier face with better breeding comes along."

Wolf gave a caustic chuckle. "You mean there's better breeding than full-blooded white?"

"There are all kinds of breeding and all kinds of blood."

"There's red..."

"And there's blue. Yes, indeed, sir, I once had a beau." The forced lightness in her voice was counterpoint to his dark scowl. She smiled too brightly. "'Had while he was mine,' to paraphrase Mr. Shakespeare."

The thought appealed to him less with each passing moment. "Then along came a demoiselle whose papa made your beau a better offer?"

"Just so." She gave a small, self-deprecating shrug. "Accepting the proposal of a man I had never met seemed, from my experience, no more hazardous than trusting a man I *thought* I knew." A fluttering gesture dismissed her remembered folly. "For, you see, in the end, all that we had in common was not worth a fig."

"There is one very important thing you and Mr. Tanninger lack in common." She allowed him to make the obvious point. "You're alive, and he's dead."

"I must look quite the fool." She laughed and gave her head a quick shake. "You wouldn't buy a horse without assuring yourself first that it was sound. I, on the other hand, have traveled two thousand miles, only to find—'' She waved her hand toward the empty bed. ''Perhaps all it takes is desperation to turn an intelligent human being into a fool.''

''And Mr. Tanninger was desperate.''

''Perhaps I thought I was, too.'' She lifted her chin, then her gaze, toward the loft and spoke solemnly. ''But now I cannot afford foolishness. I must remember that I am, first and foremost, an intelligent human being, and I must decide how best to provide for these children.''

''You won't do it by staying out here.'' He sat up and leaned closer. ''Did you see the look on that child's face when we first came, Emily? That was desperation. You try to make a go of it out here, she'll have that look on her face again, real soon. And so will the little one.'' He paused, assessing the concern in her eyes. It was, he truly believed, all for them. ''And so will you.''

She nodded like a chastised young girl brought to her senses by the reminder that she was, after all, a woman. For all her courage, physically she was still quite vulnerable. ''If you would take us back to Billings tomorrow that would be very helpful, Mr.—'' She looked into his eyes and nodded almost imperceptibly. ''Wolf.''

Marie-Claire rode behind Wolf, and Lisette sat in the saddle in front of Emily. The cold, crisp air turned their breath to steam, and the pale gray sky seemed to droop overhead as the day wore on. By the time they reached Billings, Emily's bottom was so sore she made a private vow to spend an entire night in a hip bath once she secured lodging at the hotel in which, lacking adequate transport, she had previously stored her baggage with the intention of returning to collect it with her new husband's wagon and able assistance. The remembrance of her naïveté almost made her weep. It was as though years had passed since she'd last laid eyes on the hotel sign.

"I'll be makin' arrangements at the livery," Wolf told her. "The girls will help me get the horses bedded down while you get your room."

"Won't you be renting a room, too?"

"Like I said, I'll be makin' my arrangements at the livery."

"If it's a matter of adequate funds, I certainly owe you—"

"It's nothing to do with money." He glanced contemptuously at the hotel's pretentious false front. "I'm used to sleeping out under the stars most nights. There's a wood stove over at the livery stable, and I've got a friend there. This ain't my kind of town, I can tell you right now."

"After we get our bearings, the girls and I will seek out long-term lodging, but for now—" the thought made her smile "—food, a tub of hot water and a bed will do nicely."

"I'll be taking my supper at the saloon."

"Oh."

"And I'll be leaving tomorrow. Headin' north."

"Oh." She couldn't ask him to do otherwise, but the announcement gave her a strange, hollow feeling. "You won't leave without saying goodbye, will you?"

"I'll be hung over and feelin' mean, Miss Emily. Sure way to ruin your day, so, uh..." He dismounted quickly, and wordlessly offered to help her down, leaving Lisette in charge of the mare.

Emily's rubbery legs were in no hurry to carry her away, and Wolf's hands were in no hurry to let her go. They stood between the horses—she looking up, wondering, he looking down, resolving. "I'll be claimin' my goodbyes right now."

"You'll be—"

He lowered his head slowly, so that she might have backed away if such a thing had occurred to her. But there was no threat in the dark depths of his eyes, and the idea of the impending touch of his generous lips to hers was suddenly more enticing than the thought of food. She heard his heels slide against the hardpan street, and through her skirt she felt the pressure of his thighs. She closed her eyes and drummed up the notion that there was no wantonness on her part if she couldn't see it coming.

His lips lit softly, like a butterfly, and his kiss invited her to take flight. The soft groan could not have been hers, for she had no breath for sound. The hungry response could not have been his, for his tongue had found its way past her lips, taking its fill of the taste of her.

Then it was over, and she imagined fleetingly that she had dreamed it all. But his laughing eyes laid claim to every nuance of her dream.

She stiffened with counterfeit indignation. "Mr. Morsette!"

"Wolf," he reminded her with a lopsided smile. "Miss Emily Lambert."

He chuckled to himself as he transferred Marie-Claire to the other horse. "You girls can ride double on Miss Emily's mare while she gets you set up with a place to stay." He mounted the black while Emily stepped back, still staring, still trying to recover. "You might want to take your meals in your room," he advised as he neck-reined his mount. "There might be some objection to, uh, children in the dining room."

Emily sat in the hip bath soaking the soreness out of her lower half until the water turned cold. It took some time to dry and coif her long hair, dress and prepare to enjoy a hot meal. All the while she mulled over her problem—or *problems,* each one sure to create two or three more—and cast an occasional glance at the street below, wondering what had become of Marie-Claire and Lisette. It was nearly dusk, and still they had not returned from the livery stable. After supper it would be their turn for a bath, and then . . .

And then what? Without ever having been a wife, Emily was suddenly a stepmother and a widow. It was simply too much to handle all at once. She would have to take it apart and deal with each piece separately—the death of her husband, the woeful condition and legal circumstances of his property, the arrangements for herself and the children—all matters that would not easily be resolved. She had limited funds and few resources. But she had one advantage. She was accustomed to earning her way.

# Chapter Three

"Mr. Morsette?"

The big barn was quiet but for the sound of horse jaws working over a mouthful of grain in one of the far stalls. Dim lamplight glowed behind the single door that stood ajar. Emily pulled it open cautiously.

"Wolf? Are you…" Three pairs of dark eyes beamed up at her. "What's this?" she asked, but she could see that this was where Mr. Harding kept his tack and his potbellied stove, his worktable and apparently his guests. "What are you doing? I thought—"

"I'm feeding the girls some supper," Wolf said, explaining the obvious as he soaked up the last of his stew with a hunk of bread.

"But I thought they were coming over to the hotel after they helped you take care of the horses."

"They said we couldn't stay with you at the hotel," Marie-Claire muttered as she, too, turned her attention to the contents of her tin plate.

"Who said that? I told the clerk that I had two children with me who would be along any time, and that they should be directed to—" Emily gestured toward the hayloft, then folded her arms around herself tightly "—my room."

Marie-Claire spoke with her mouth full. "The man said no Indians could stay there."

"Are we Indians?" Lisette asked.

"Mama was mostly an Indian, so that means we're mostly Indians."

"Well, we shall see about this. I paid for a room, and it is certainly my prerogative to—"

Wolf finished off his bread, then set his empty plate on the workbench. "What name did you register under?"

"Why, Emily—" She remembered her signature, and her voice dropped considerably. "Lambert."

"Old habits die harder'n old husbands," Wolf said as he fished around under his capote for his pipe bag.

"Mr. Morsette!" She cast a pointed look at the girls, then stared him down vehemently. "Why should it make any difference whether I registered under my maiden name or—"

"Because if you'd used your *married* name, you probably would have been told there was no room at the inn." His curt nod served as punctuation. "Miss Emily."

"There *is* room."

"Don't push it. The girls can stay here."

"The girls most certainly may *not* stay here, Mr. Morsette. Why, that would be *most*—" tucking the pipe bag under his sash, he took her by the arm and scooted her out the door before she could finally utter "—improper."

There in the shadows it was his turn to stare her down, nose to nose. "Miss Emily, you have a room at the hotel, and if you wanted to take a man up to that room, strip down and bang the bedstead against the wall all night long, nobody'd try to stop you. They wouldn't think there was anything improper about that at all."

Her mouth dropped open.

"But they won't let you have those two little Indian girls sleep up there with you. No way in hell."

"That's absurd."

"Maybe so. But that's the way it is."

"What about you?"

"I can go into a saloon in one town, order up a drink, have myself a game of cards, no questions asked. Go to another town, they might point to the No Indians Allowed sign and send for the sheriff. All depends on what they want to see when they look at my face." He squared his shoulders, swept his long coat back and hooked his thumbs in his beautifully woven sash. "Or whether they think I might be in a mood for trouble."

When she caught herself admiring his hands, she quickly looked up and found the challenge in his eyes equally disturbing. "And if you are in such a mood?"

"I once held a barkeep at gunpoint while I drank a whole bottle of Taos Lightning, then walked out the front door without missing a step." He gave a jaunty smile. "At least, that's what they tell me."

"You don't remember?"

"I remember the halfway mark on that bottle and the way that barkeep's Adam's apple kept bobbin' up and down every time I tickled his temple with my gun barrel." She stepped against the wall, and her eyes widened. He braced his shoulder next to hers and gave her an off-center grin. "Tell you what, though. I can get myself a room in any jail house in the territory without even askin'."

"Mr. Morsette, *you* are a rogue."

"And *you*, Miss Emily Lambert—" she closed her eyes against his admonishment "—have a lot to learn."

He laid a warm fingertip against her temple, and she wondered what a cold steel barrel would feel like there.

Not good, she decided, and her eyes flew open. "If you knew all along that we might have had this problem at the hotel, why didn't you—"

"I didn't think they'd—" He drew his finger away, then rolled his shoulders against the wall and rested his head. "Those two pretty little girls. I thought maybe they'd get past the desk on your good name and their innocence, after you were checked in."

"I've already paid for the room."

"Then use it." He straightened, gesturing toward the outside door. "I'll pass up my visit to the saloon. They'll be fine here. Harding gave us some blankets. We've got a stove and plenty of wood." He encouraged her with a smile. "All the comforts."

Emily shook her head. "It wouldn't be proper."

"*For you* it wouldn't be proper." With one hand on her shoulder he guided her toward the door. "Go on back and get some sleep. We'll figure something out tomorrow."

"Figure something out," she grumbled as she marched away from the livery and across the dark street. Piano music tinkled several doors away, and rowdy laughter poured into the street. Wolf would rather be there, she told herself. That's the way he would prefer to spend his evening, and who could be certain that he would not, once the girls were asleep? Who could predict anything in this cold, austere, unfriendly, *unruly* locale? *She*, Emily Lambert, certainly could not.

Nor could she predict the weather. When next she marched across the street, lugging two carpetbags, it was snowing.

The girls were asleep, and Wolf was having a smoke when Emily appeared once again in the doorway. She plunked both bags on the threshold at once, then adjusted her bonnet as though the gesture itself were some kind of an announcement.

Wolf pulled his pipe from the grip of his teeth as he levered himself off his straw-cushioned blanket. "Don't tell me the hotel gave Miss Emily Lambert the boot."

"They did not. I informed them that the accommodations were unsuitable. I demanded that they refund my money—all but the twenty-five cents for the bath."

"Did they?"

"No."

"They will." He indicated the straw pallets. "Are these accommodations more to your liking?"

"Under the circumstances, I believe certain practical considerations must take precedence over comfort. Marie-Claire and Lisette need an adult female chaperon." Primly she straightened her wool jacket. "So you may consider yourself relieved of duty, Mr. Morsette, if you feel an urge for... sport."

He wasn't sure where it came from—maybe the blue-gray evidence of fatigue beneath her eyes—but he felt an urge to bed her down next to the girls and simply watch over them all while they slept.

"We were listening to the music a little while ago, while we watched the first snowflakes fall," he told her as he snatched his blanket up, stepped over her bags and led her away from the warmth of the small room toward the heavy door that faced the rutted street. He draped the blanket over her shoulders. She thanked him with a look.

They stood together in the doorway, a block and tackle hoist dangling overhead from a roof beam that jutted from the loft.

"It's been an open winter so far, but we're gettin' it now."

"It's pretty." She looked straight up and watched until the dancing flakes made her dizzy.

"You like snow?"

"Tomorrow is the first of December. It's time for snow." She pulled the blanket close, shawl fashion. "Soon it'll be Christmas. I had hoped and really planned to hang pine boughs and decorate a spruce tree in my own home this season." She tipped her head to the side, as if the angle gave her a better view of her dream. "I thought I'd light the yule log in my own hearth and sing carols. We wouldn't have missed having a piano or a violin after I'd served Thomas Lambert's secret grog recipe."

"Grog?"

"It's a hot drink, made with a bit of rum," she admitted as she watched Wolf light his small pipe. "My father was an old sailor, then a shipwright. He used to recall how the sailors would grumble whenever the captain would cut the rum with water. They called *that* grog. But during the holiday season, a bit of rum mixed with hot lemon and sugar water was a part of his merrymaking." She smiled, remembering. "My mother never disapproved as long as he permitted her to do the mixing."

"Maybe he added an extra kick to his own on the sly."

"Perhaps," she allowed as she untied her bonnet. Her smile was for him this time. *"Peut-être."*

*"Peut-être,"* he echoed as he puffed on the clay pipe. "My great-grandfather was a *voyageur,* a man who plied his trade on the waterways up north. But his boat was a canoe, and his language was mostly French. My grandfather was a Métis trip man, who manned the oars of a york boat on the big Canadian lakes."

"And your father?"

"Ah, that's where my boating heritage came to an end. My father worked for the Hudson's Bay Company for a time, but as the forts and the jobs became fewer, many of the Métis lost their jobs, and he was one of them." He leaned against the big, rough-hewn doorframe. "And so what French I know comes from the schooling I had off and on from the priests who followed our camps when I was young. My people call their language *Michif.* It's a little like French and a lot like Cree."

He stole a glance at her between puffs on his pipe. "My mother was Cree. My father brought her from Canada to Dakota."

"Are you American or Canadian?" She looked up, as though seeing him for the first time. "Or Cree, or... or is that the same as Red Indian, or..."

"I am Métis. Mixed blood." He suffered her bold perusal of his face, wondering how she saw him now, what she thought. He saw no judgment in her eyes.

He gave a nod over his shoulder. "And so are those little girls. What do you intend to do with them?"

"I intend to provide for them somehow." She looked at the bonnet she'd taken off and fingered the satin ribbon on the brim. "Perhaps we might return to Boston."

"Not before spring." His pipe had gone cold. He jerked it out of his mouth and gestured into the snowy night. "I'm headin' north. I've got an urge to dance to some fiddle music and drive a *cariole* through the snow and feel welcome at any fireside."

"You're going home, too, then? North to Canada?"

"From what I hear, I've got some relations living this side of the border on the Milk River. That's where I'm headed." He shifted his weight from one foot to the other, feeling pressed to say something he was far from sure was the right solution.

Trouble was, he'd thought long and hard, and it was all he could come up with. "I can take the girls with me and find a family for them."

"Among your mixed-blood relatives?" He had managed to astonish her. "How do you know they would be welcome there?"

"They are Métis." He slapped his pipe against his palm, and the ashes scattered. "We know one thing for sure, Miss Emily. They're not welcome here."

"You've only *heard* about these relatives of yours? You don't know them?"

"There were some families that left the Red River Valley a few years back and headed west, following the buffalo. Families I'm related to."

"Following the buffalo? They sound like nomads." He questioned the word with a look, and she assumed he needed a definition. "Wanderers. They have no home."

"Home is wherever your people are. Your relations. The people who open their doors and tell you to come on inside, no questions, no charge." It was the kind of reception he'd yearned for since the autumn chill had set him on the move.

"Do these Métis people of yours *have* doors?"

He smiled patiently. "With a good supply of logs they can raise a cabin in a day, working together."

"How do they get their living?"

"We hunt, trap, trade, sometimes farm a little plot of land. The game used to be much more plentiful, but now that it's harder to find, we make do." There was no need to elaborate. He knew the art of wandering better than she did, and she knew that the tools of the hunter had many uses. "We find ways."

"I should think I would be able to find ways, too."

"Tanninger's land must belong to you now," he suggested cautiously. "I don't know how much he had, but it must be worth something. You could sell it."

"Whatever it brought would rightfully belong to Marie-Claire and Lisette."

"That's pretty generous thinking." He touched her hand. She glanced up, and he smiled. "You ought to be thinking about what you'll need to see you through the winter here and get you back to Boston in the spring."

"Winter...here?"

"Here in town," he said, directing her attention to the hotel at the other end of the street. "Come wintertime, nobody usually goes anywhere. Indians have their winter camps. Métis have *hiverant* camps." He shrugged. "You've got this town."

Where she didn't know a soul.

"How far is the Milk River?" she wondered, listening absently to the merry tinkling of the piano.

"It's a good distance. Probably take us ten days to a fortnight, if the weather holds."

She assumed the full measure of her height, tipped her chin up and looked him in the eye. "I cannot let you take those two little girls, Mr. Morsette. It would not be proper for them to travel in your company without a chaperon."

"You got a better idea, Miss Emily?"

She nodded once. "I shall have to accompany them."

"What for? Come spring, you'll be free to light out on the first stage and never look back."

"Knowing that I had shirked my duty, I would never be able to stop looking back." She paused to take a brief, silent inventory of her feelings about her decision, then gave a nod. "You're right, Mr. Morsette. The girls need a good home, and clearly there is no acceptance for them here. Nor, I think, for me." Which, she realized, didn't bother her in the least. "I'm going with them."

"And after we reach our destination, what will you do then, Miss Emily?"

"I'm not certain. I only know that Mr. Tanninger was counting on me. And he did write fine letters. He may have omitted a few details, but he gave me such lovely things to dream about." She glanced down the street and confided quietly, "I do not relish the notion of spending Christmas alone in that hotel, Mr. Morsette."

The dismal prospect was one that had haunted him, too.

"You keep forgetting my name," he said.

"Wolf." She smiled, feeling braver now that she was set on a course of action. "I confess, the name Wolf does give one pause. Since you say that it suits you, I am given to wonder how."

He returned her smile. "If you travel with the Wolf, you will see for yourself."

# Chapter Four

It took several days to prepare for the journey. Wolf and Emily pooled their resources to buy a packhorse, a gentle mare for the girls and supplies. Following a two-day hunt, Wolf traded fresh kill for cured pelts, sinew and pemmican, which was counter to his customary trading practice. Pound for pound, bargaining with raw goods went against his grain, for a Métis hunter knew the value of cured pelts and dried meat.

But he had no time for the intermediary steps. He needed to fashion fur-lined mitts and moccasins for his three female charges. In time he planned to make a few more items from the materials he had left, but the hands and feet needed immediate protection. Embracing the challenge ahead, he assured Emily that in her situation she could do worse than hook up with a "born nomad." Every drifter had his methods, but the Métis had honed their wandering skills to perfection.

They set off early one brisk, rosy morning, while much of the town still slept. Harding Livery's resident rooster perched on a corral post and crowed farewell to his fellow boarders. Emily had no idea where she was going, but she was not saddened to leave this frontier town behind. She told herself that in putting her life in the hands of this handsome nomad—she used the word with a deferential smile—she was risking no more than she did whenever she consigned her safety to the driver of a coach or the engineer of a train. At least Wolf was not a total stranger.

An enigma he surely was, but perhaps that was simply a function of his being male.

They were headed almost due north. The wind in their faces sometimes made their eyes tear. There was snow in the draws, but the hilltops, swept clean by the wind and bathed in winter sun, were nearly bare. As long as the weather stayed mild, Wolf resolved to ease Emily and the girls into the routine of strenuous travel, progressively increasing the amount of time they spent in the saddle. At first, even though they stopped several times a day for a brief rest, the three were exhausted by the time they made camp at dusk. They were all healthy, Wolf assured himself as he continued to push hard. They would adjust to the demands of the trek sooner or later.

Each night he asked that they gather the firewood and prepare the food while he built a shelter that was as cozy as any cocoon. The four of them slept in a tight bundle, children snug in the middle, their feet warmed by the embers of the camp fire. When it burned too low, Wolf would build it up, then return to his place. He would lay his arm over the children, and in her sleep, Emily would reach across them, too. Their arms met, forming a warm, protective arch, and Wolf smiled as he permitted himself to drift on the outer shell of sleep.

"Tonight we will make bannock bread and tea," Wolf announced triumphantly several days into the ride. He brandished his string of grouse, unabashedly seeking female approval. He had been rationing the flour, but roast fowl was a particular favorite of his, and his girls were in store for a feast.

"I know how to make bread," Marie-Claire offered.

"And I know how to make tea." Taking a turn around the birds, Emily silently speculated that the tea would be the easy part. "But here's the important question." Wolf's eyes danced as he handed Emily his catch, pretending not to notice the way she grimaced and held them at arm's length. "Which one of you is the best poker player?"

"Poker?" Marie-Claire shook her head, then brightened when she thought of an alternative. "Papa taught me to play whist with a blind man as a partner."

"You notice they're gutted," Wolf told Emily in an aside. "All we have to do is roast 'em, then skin 'em."

Emily uttered a small sound of relief.

Wolf turned to Marie-Claire and merrily challenged her with arms akimbo. "Now, just where would you find a blind man to play cards with?"

"You couldn't see him, and he couldn't see his cards. That's why he played so dumb. But Papa had Lisette for *his* partner, and that was the same as having a blind man."

Lisette wound up to smack Marie-Claire's hip. "I ain't the same as no blind man!"

"Well, you were practically a baby then," the older sister chided, forestalling Lisette's hand.

"I ain't no baby!"

"I knew a blind man once who played poker with marked cards," Wolf said. "Marked them himself with little pin pricks you could hardly notice. He never got to deal, so he never touched anyone else's cards until they laid down their hand. Then he got to check and see what they had."

"Couldn't you feel the marks when you dealt the cards?" Emily asked as she carefully laid the string of birds on what had been designated the table rock when they'd made camp.

"Nobody knew what they meant. You could hardly even find them. He had fingers like an eagle's eyes." Wolf chuckled, remembering. "Skinned the pants off me every time, that ol' blind man." He cast Emily a repentant glance. "So to speak."

"I'm not sure that poker would be a proper pastime for two young ladies," Emily averred, accepting his contrition with the properly prim nod.

"It will where we're goin'." Wolf rubbed his hands together, warming them by the fire. "Everybody plays cards. Everybody plays the fiddle, and everybody dances. You know how to do a Red River jig, Lisette?"

"I know how to skip-to-my-Lou." She demonstrated, skipping around in a circle until she drew a round of applause. Then she bobbed a fitting curtsy.

"Very nice," Emily said. "That last part will be quite useful in many dances."

Clearly torn between taking up skipping in the hope of earning a similar response or practicing mature restraint, Marie-Claire asked, "When we get to where we're going, will there be dancing?"

"Plenty of dancing," Wolf said.

"Whoopsie!" Dizzy from her performance, Lisette planted a fur-mitted hand on the table rock to steady herself. "I want to see Wolf dance with Miss Emily."

"Oh, yes, will you?" Marie-Claire asked him.

"Tonight!" Lisette demanded.

"I'll surely ask her." Thoroughly charming Emily with his smile, he asked the girls in an aside, "What do you think she'll say?"

"Yes!" they squealed in unison.

"I'm sure I shall need instruction," Emily allowed. "I believe I was fairly adept at Lisette's dance when I was a girl, but I've not learned much dancing since."

"Let me teach you a step or two after supper."

"Teach me, too!" Lisette pleaded.

"We can watch," Marie-Claire suggested, recovering her sensible-older-sister tone. "Let Wolf first teach Miss Emily."

Wolf gave a lesson in coal-roasting game birds, sparing them the finger-freezing job of plucking the feathers. Then the girls helped Wolf make the bannock bread, while Emily played the novice onlooker. The recipe was simple enough, but Emily was not accustomed to the heavy texture and bland flavor of skillet bread.

"Fills the hollows," Wolf said as he watched her taste it. "I've had raised bread before, mostly when I've been in places like St. Paul and St. Louis. I'll bet you like raised bread better."

"I do, but this is a clever way to make it on an open fire." She scooted closer to the warm flames, immersing herself in the simple joys she'd once taken for granted. "The roasted bird is wonderful. I don't believe I've ever had it cooked this way."

He laughed. "You're finally tasting the best there is, then." His expression turned boyishly hopeful. "You know how to make raised bread?"

"Yes, I do. Several ways." She eyed the skillet and the remains of the flat bread. "But I've only used an oven to bake it."

"How about a Dutch oven?"

"I could try that. Do you have one?"

"Not on me. But I'll get us one if you'll make us some raised bread." He flashed her a quick smile, laced with rare shyness. "Sometime."

She imagined a kitchen.

He envisioned a tripod standing in a big stone fireplace.

She wondered whether they'd both heard the word *us* in the same intimate way.

"It might take some practice," she said, "but I'm beginning to think I can master almost anything."

He grinned as he set his empty plate aside. "How about a two-step?"

She studied the bits of brown leaf floating in her tea and shook her head. "I've always tended the children while other people danced."

"Tended them where? Don't the children come to the dances, too?"

"Not in Boston."

"Not in St. Paul or Deadwood, either," he recalled. "At least, not that I saw. Not that I was invited to many dances. But at the Milk River camp, I will be. We all will be. Big people, little people, young and old." He braced his palms on his buckskin-clad thighs as he stood. "So we'd best get ourselves in practice. Stand up, you two, and learn from the nimble-footed Wolf."

The girls leapt to their feet.

Emily clutched her tin cup in both hands, searching one face after the other for a sign of good sense.

Wolf swept one side of his open capote behind his hip and made a courtly bow. "Miss Emily, may I have the honor?"

"Without music?"

The tune he hummed was not one she recognized, but his deep, sonorous voice rendered the melody irresistible. Emily abandoned her search for good sense. With a smile she rose gracefully and allowed him to take her in his arms. He provided the music and the pattern of movement, but she was half a step behind at every turn, for it was a lively dance.

"One-two, one-two, that's it," he instructed, and then resumed the tune.

Her next misstep elicited a giggle from the sidelines.

"You two smarties follow along," Wolf ordered. "This arm so, this arm so, and one-two, one-two." There were more giggles as the girls copied the pose. "Come on, I can't count and provide the music both." He entreated Emily with a charming smile. "One-two, one-two."

"One-two, one-two," she recited, even as her feet faltered in the snowy grass.

"Or here's a waltz. A little slower, now. One-two-three, one-two-three, yes." And he hummed a gliding tune.

Emily might have caught on faster had his lithe step not been so distracting. Only their arms and hands actually touched, but she could feel the power in his thighs simply in the way he moved, and the arms that carefully guided her felt impossibly strong. He was doing all the work, and she could not help but follow, if stumblingly.

"Is this right, Wolf?" Marie-Claire led Lisette in a close approximation of the dance step. "One-two-three, one-two-three."

He continued to hum as he nodded.

"Sing the words," Lisette pleaded.

Wolf made a funny face and shrugged, still humming.

"There is only the melody," Emily interpreted. Wolf nodded. "Our Wolf is a complete orchestra."

*Our Wolf.* His eyes brightened. His hum became a bellowing "da-da, da-dee" as he whirled Emily round and round on the energy infused in him by the heady claim she'd made on him.

Marie-Claire laughed. "I think he's turning into a tornado!"

"Ouch!" Lisette hopped on one foot. "You stomped on my toe."

"Just as I have done to my poor partner," Emily confessed. Wolf spun her in a circle. Her head flopped like the lid of a tobacco tin, dislodging her hat. Still tied beneath her chin, the bonnet dangled down her back, doing a wild dance of its own. "Oh, but our Wolf is so busy being an orchestra, he can't howl in protest."

"Ayooooo!"

The dance party dissolved into fits of laughter.

"The Wolf can always howl," he assured them as his spinning slowed to a halt. "And the only instrument I can be is a fiddle. Don't I sound like a fiddle?"

"You have a wonderful voice." Emily pressed her hand to her chest in a reflexive attempt to check any unseemly rise and fall. "That's why Lisette wanted to hear the words." On a deep breath she wagged a finger at Wolf. "But now, before you come up with more ways for me to make a fool of myself, I think we must stoke up the fire and put these children to bed.''

Emily used warm water from the leather boiling bag to clean the girls up while Wolf arranged their bed, stripping pine boughs of their needles to make an insulating mat inside the lean-to. Once the girls were tucked in, he and Emily lingered near the waning fire, sharing the last of the tea, enjoying the quiet beauty of a starry winter night from their comfortable seat on the fire-warm flat rock that served as their only piece of furniture.

"Did you feel foolish, dancing with me?" Wolf asked, the vast darkness nearly overwhelming his hushed voice.

"Only because you're so good at it, and I seem to have wooden feet."

"If we practiced together, we would learn to move one with the other. You wouldn't have to count. You wouldn't even need to think. Your body would learn the rhythm from mine."

His words made her feel a delicious flash of warmth. She closed her eyes briefly and let the feeling flow through her.

When she opened them again, she encountered his knowing smile.

She cast about for subject matter. "Do you play the violin?"

"I fiddle a little." His rhyme made her smile in return. "Or used to. Haven't touched a fiddle in a long time. Not since I left home."

"Which was a long time ago in a land quite far from here," she recalled.

"Sometimes my childhood home was far from here. Sometimes not. We traveled across northern Dakota, into Canada." As he gestured expansively, he noted the interest in her eyes, the earnest attempt to understand *home* as he described it. "You and the girls and me, we take this camp with us as we go. We set up in a new spot, and we make it ours for the night." He considered the serenity he saw in her face—the sleepy eyes, the fire-flushed skin, the dewy mouth. "You feel good here tonight. I can tell."

"How can you tell?"

"By the way you smile. It comes more easily than it did when I first met you." He edged closer. "Do you remember when I kissed you?"

"You were saying goodbye."

"This time I'm saying thanks." He took her shoulders in his hands and drew her to him. "*Merci*, Miss Emily."

His kiss was slow and smooth, never faltering, at once bestowing blessings and gratitude. Then abruptly it was withdrawn.

"For what?" she managed to ask, self-consciously turning her face aside.

"For the dance." His lips skimmed her cheek, his breath warming her skin. "Now this is my thanks for the kiss."

His second kiss claimed her breath, her brain and all her senses. He engulfed her in an embrace that made her feel marvelously warm and safe. It surprised her that she could take comfort from someone whose size and strength so completely overwhelmed her. But she could. She *did*. And she thrilled to the pressure, the stimulating motion, the delightful taste and the unexpected softness of his lips.

"This could go on and on," she said breathlessly when he permitted her to speak.

"That's the idea. One kiss leads to another."

Stubbornly she kept her eyes shut tight. Perversely she croaked, "It can't."

"Of course it can," he said silkily. "Exactly the way you know you want it to."

She groaned. Her shoulders sagged in the parenthetical grip of his hands. She shook her head quickly.

"You do understand, it simply cannot lead from one to another because…" She searched for some innocent way to express what she imagined his far-from-pure thoughts to be. "Because I think you would want more."

But when he released his hold, it only left her in doubt.

Too quickly, she sought reassurance. "Wouldn't you?"

"I would." *He did.* "But wanting and having ain't hardly the same." He levered himself off the rock and stood up, making a production of stretching his long legs as though he'd just had a pleasant nap. "And right now I have other matters to attend to."

"Oh?"

He gave her a sly smile.

She hopped down from her perch and straightened her skirt. "I mean, *good.* We should...we *must* attend to other matters, so that we do not think about..." Flustered, she snatched up a stick and poked it into the fire, stirring flame from the coals. "About matters that we should not think about."

"Thinking and *doing* ain't the same, either." He chuckled behind her back. "And you can't stop a man from thinking about one matter while he's attending to another."

They both had matters to attend to that neither wanted the other to see. They were private matters that would spawn surprises when the time came. Christmastime. It meant something a little different to each of them, but it also meant something miraculously, wondrously the same. Not wanting or having, but giving. And in order to create something special to give, they both had work to do.

It wasn't easy. They had been on the trail for eight days. If their luck held out, they would soon reach the big bend in the Milk River, and it would be none too soon, for in this country, fair weather could not hold through December.

Wolf was making himself a pair of snowshoes, so by all apparent accounts his creative efforts were being poured into that undertaking. Each night after supper he set about shaping the frame and stringing the web of sinew while he sang snatches of French voyageur songs that had been passed down through generations of Métis who no longer plied the north country waterways.

Meanwhile, Emily ducked into the back of the lean-to he put up each night. The shadowed firelight barely illuminated her work, and her stiff fingers were barely useful in manipulating a needle, but there she applied careful stitches to the muslin and flannel she'd bought in Billings. When the girls announced that they were going to take a peek and see what she was doing, Wolf bade them join him in song. It was an invitation they could not resist, and patiently he taught them strange new words and lively old tunes.

After Emily called the girls to bed, it was Wolf's turn to craft in secret. He expected his fur hats to be a welcome change from flimsy felt bonnets and woolen shawls. He had some ideas for toys, too. It had been a long time since he'd done any whittling, but he successfully revived the knack he'd once had, and all done in cheerless silence so that he would not wake the children. Or the woman.

Ah, the woman. She was a rare breed, no doubt about that. She had as much courage as any man he'd ever met, and she was far more honest than most. More honorable than just about anybody he might care to name, including himself. But they had as much in common as fish and fowl. He knew it was a mistake to let a woman like her get under his skin, even slightly, even briefly.

But be damned if he could think of anything better to do. Except maybe find a way to get under hers.

Wolf recognized the signs of a Métis community. The twenty-five cabins were built in a circle around a larger building. The circular arrangement of the camp was inspired by their Indian heritage. The clay-plastered walls and stone fireplaces he knew he would find within most of the cabins were proof of their European ancestry. The dance hall in the center was pure Métis.

But the lack of smoke issuing from the chimneys was not a sign of any heritage. It was, he feared, a sign of nobody home.

Emily and the girls could feel the emptiness, too. From a distance, the abandoned village looked peaceful, as though everyone might be asleep. But as they drew near, the winter landscape silently attested to complete desertion. That they had come all this way only to be greeted by utter quiet was unspeakably heartbreaking.

And so, for long moments, no one spoke.

The horses' dogged plodding announced their arrival. Not one face appeared in a doorway. Finally, Wolf called out, *"Métis ici? Mou nou si Morsette."*

"Don't they speak English?" Marie-Claire asked.

"If they were here, many of them would. They would jabber your ears off." With the broad sweep of an arm he voiced the bitter irony of their journey's reward. "You wanted a house of your own, Miss Emily? Take your pick."

"They've all moved away?"

He dropped his arm to his side. "Sure looks like it."

"But why?"

"Wish they'd left someone behind to tell us. Doesn't look like they did." His hand signal forestalled her dismount. "Let me check things out first."

He moved from house to house, flinging doors open, kicking the last three out of frustration. *"Rien,"* he called out, shaking his head dejectedly. "Nothing. Not a soul."

He headed back to one of the first cabins he'd checked, signaling with a jerk of his head that they were to follow him. "This one's clean as a church, and they left the bedsteads behind."

They unpacked, gathered firewood and found that there was plenty of grass for the horses—a sign, Wolf said, that the camp had been abandoned all summer.

After sharing a somber evening meal and arranging bedrolls over the rope webbing on the beds, Marie-Claire withdrew quietly to bed. Lisette had fallen asleep on the floor, with her head in Emily's lap. Wolf lifted the little girl into his arms and tucked her into bed with her sister. It would be a tight squeeze if Emily chose to sleep with the children. She would. As he stepped away from the bed, Wolf took visual measure of the sliver of space left and made a silent bet with himself on it.

"One thing bothers me," he mused, joining Emily on the floor by the fire. "We haven't cut much sign in the last couple of days."

"Sign of what?" She handed him a tin cup of hot tea.

"Anything moving, either on hoof or wing. Anything living or breathing."

She sighed. "You're saying, nothing to eat."

"I'll go out and find meat tomorrow. If it's out there, I'll find it."

"I know you will. With you as our guide, the girls and I haven't had to worry about food or shelter. Things I once took for granted, but now..." She dipped herself a cup of tea from the boiling bag, then sat back and savored the scent of the steam and the warmth of the cup in her hands. "I see that it's a mistake to take life's essentials for granted. If suddenly they're not there, the pampered individual has no notion of how to provide."

"If they're *not* there, only God can provide."

"Indeed." She looked at him curiously. "I would not have taken you for a religious man, Mr. Morsette."

"You would not have *taken* me at all, Miss Emily. I was your last resort. Just like the livery stable, and just like..." His observation made them both uncomfortable. He glanced away, finishing on a doleful note. "This hapless journey. Your guide has brought you to a ghost town."

"There is ample precedent for finding hope in a stable, Wolf. And for persevering even though the prospects seem limited. Tomorrow there will undoubtedly be manna from heaven. Or deer." Her optimism drew his gaze to her, and her smile instantly buoyed his spirits. "Or a heavenly hare, how would that be?"

She touched the back of his hand. He was totally unprepared for the way his heart suddenly skittered against his ribs.

He cleared his throat and effected a diffident shrug. "The Métis are given to moving on. They might have left just because they were tired of the place."

"I thought Mr. Tanninger was my last resort." Her fingertips stirred over his hand. "You, Mr. Morsette, are something else entirely."

"And what is that, Miss Emily?"

"I don't quite know. An unexpected—" she smiled wistfully "—messenger, perhaps. Pathfinder. Conveyer. Catalyst. A bit of sand working his way into my shell."

He leaned closer. "If I break through, there'll be hell to pay when I whisper my message in your ear, Miss Emily."

"Is that so?" She stayed her ground, her nose only inches from his. "You've yet to answer the question about whether you are a religious man."

"You didn't ask a question. You made a statement." And it was he who retreated, staring into the fire as he spoke. "Anyway, I don't have an answer. See, I'm a mixed blood. There are two sides to me. The Métis always have a Black Robe around telling everybody to get married and get their children baptized. If you were to ask the Black Robe, he'd tell you I'm a sinful man. On the other side—the Red Indian side, as you call it—hell, I'm just a man like any other. I do believe in God."

He turned to her and spoke so quietly, she had to strain to catch every precious nuance. "I guess if you're wondering whether a man's got any religion, you've got to watch how he behaves, see if there's love in him somewhere."

"What if he's hiding it?"

"If it's there, you can find it. You just have to know how to look. You have to keep in mind who he is and where he comes from."

She took a deep breath and released it slowly. "What if he holds a gun to someone's head right before your very eyes?"

"What if he doesn't pull the trigger?" They exchanged a look of frank acknowledgment devoid of common ground. Then Wolf turned his attention to the fire. "Sometimes a man's hard-pressed when it comes to standing up for what needs defending."

"Sometimes he goes too far."

"Sometimes he doesn't go far enough." Again he shrugged. "Either way, I guess that's why he needs some religion. Because sometimes he's just too damned weak and too damned hard-pressed."

"This is harsh country. That much I can surely see."

It was his turn to touch, experimentally, the curve of her skirt-draped knee. "Too harsh for a gentlewoman like you?"

"I have two sides, too," she said quietly. "I'm finding more strength than I knew I had."

He stretched out close to her, bracing one elbow on the floor, his face only a hand's breadth from the lap where he longed to lay his head the way Lisette had earlier.

"What sort of a house do you want?" he wondered. "What kind do you dream about?"

She tipped her head slightly, considering. "One that's mine to put the trimmings on."

"Woman frills." With a forefinger he touched the bit of lace that encircled her wrist at the end of her otherwise plain white sleeve. "My mother always beaded everything. Anything she could sew a bead to ended up covered with flowers."

He pictured a leather wall pocket beaded with blue and red blossoms sprouting from curly green vines.

She imagined yellow wallpaper flocked with tiny pink rosebuds.

"I would have curtains in the windows and rugs on the floors," she said.

"How many floors would you need?"

"One." She caught his eye with a teasing smile. "In each room."

"How many rooms would you need?"

"I would only *need*—" she gestured with an easy flourish "—the essentials, now that I'm no longer a pampered individual. But I would make it comfortable."

"So comfortable you'd never want to leave?"

She nodded.

"Not even if someone said . . ." He lifted his hand to her cheek and cradled it in his palm, entreating softly, "'We have to go, Emily. You can take your curtains and your rugs along, and I'll build you another house, but we have to leave this one behind.'"

"It would depend on who that someone was." She stroked the back of his hand. "And whether I could depend upon him to keep his promise."

After Wolf stoked the fire, he turned to find that Emily had, indeed, wedged herself in with the girls. So he went to bed alone and watched the fire shadows flit from rafter to rafter until the darkness finally swallowed up all but the glow of embers. He closed his eyes and wished for sleep, but he was cold. In all the nights he'd spent sleeping under all kinds of circumstances, he'd known plenty of cold. But not like this.

"Emily?"

"Hmm?"

He was deep-down glad she hadn't managed to fall asleep, either.

"I was gettin' sorta used to us sleeping close," he confessed, knowing damn well how forlorn he sounded.

"I'm not far away."

"Feels like you are."

Silence.

"I like being able to touch you, just to know you're there." He sounded like a lovesick kid, and he knew it. But it was worth a try.

She was so quiet, he wasn't sure she was breathing.

Finally, she whispered the word he longed to hear.

"Wolf?"

"Hmm?"

"The truth is, I like that, too."

He smiled. The rope bed groaned as he turned toward the sound of her voice.

"But I'm staying over here."

## Chapter Five

Wolf was busy setting a rabbit snare when his sixth sense told him he wasn't hunting the river bottom alone. He hadn't heard anything. He hadn't cut any sign. He just knew. And he knew his company had to be one of his kind—either Indian or mixed blood. Otherwise the proof of the presence would have been more substantial. He cocked his pistol and turned slowly.

"You *bonjour* man?" The watcher appeared to be Chippewa or Cree, but he could very well have been a mixed blood himself. The man had some nerve, Wolf thought, calling *him* the disdainful term some Indians used for the Métis.

But since, for all Wolf knew, this man might well have friends close by to back him—and since Wolf had not a one, save a gentlewoman and two little girls—he gave a grunt that might be taken as assent, and he lowered his gun.

The newcomer opened his buffalo wearing robe to show that he meant no harm. His knife was sheathed. His rifle was still in the scabbard, strapped to the Appaloosa standing behind him. "Berger coming back already?" the man asked.

"Berger... Back from where?" Wolf had an uncle from Pembina named Pierre Berger. He wondered if the Indian could be referring to the same man.

"Back from a better place."

Wolf scowled. "What, heaven?"

The Indian laughed. "When I find a place *that* good, I keep it for myself." He gave a chin jerk, indicating the river bottom. "There is no game here. Last spring, those *bonjours* down there, they were looking—" he nodded toward a pine sapling "—pretty skinny. Even their dogs. So I told them, better hurry up and get to gettin', before the whites get every good place there is."

"Do you know where they went?"

"Sure, sure, I showed them." He pointed westward. "Not too far. Maybe five days' ride without those *bonjour* wagons." He clapped his hands over his ears and mimicked the infernal squeal of the Red River carts' greaseless axles. Wolf's hearty laughter didn't fit with the pistol, so he put it away.

"Hurt your ears, do they?" Wolf gasped, the last ripples of laughter still tickling his belly.

"Only a man who has no enemies makes such noise."

"Must be why it's been so long since I drove a Red River cart." Absently toeing the rawhide loop he'd been triggering as a trap, Wolf scanned the frozen river's lazy curve. "There's still no game here?"

"Hard to find any."

"So why are you here?"

"Saw your smoke. Thought Berger came back, maybe. Or maybe somebody wants to trade."

"I've got nothing to trade." He jerked at the loop with his heel, spending his snare in disgust. "I was looking for relations, come over from Dakota. Or so I heard."

"I can take you there."

"We've already come a long way. I have—" Wolf nodded in the direction of the village and gave what seemed the simplest, safest account "—my family with me."

"They go hungry this winter, you stay here. I can take you to Berger, leave tomorrow." By way of explanation, the man grunted in disgust. "The missionaries come to our camp and make Christmas."

"Oh, ho, I see." Wolf planted hands on hips and gave an appreciative chuckle. "You'd rather hear some fiddle music."

"I like to kick the heels with the *bonjours*."

"And New Year's is the best time for that." With a wave of his hand, Wolf invited the man to mount up and follow him. "We'll see what Emily says."

Emily's response was unequivocal. "I will not be moved."

"Thank God I left Bear Catcher standing outside. I told him..." He gestured in exasperation. "I told him you were my woman. Told him we had two daughters. Where are they, anyway?"

"They're fetching water in which to boil the meat you promised you would bring back with you."

"I tried creating antelope out of clay, but I thought it might fall apart in the pot."

She would not be intimidated by sarcasm. "Who is Bear Catcher, and why on earth would you tell him that you have a wife and children?"

"Because I thought it sounded good!" He raised his palms in abject surrender. "All right? I wanted to see what it felt like to say it, so I said it." A gesture indicated the man beyond the door. "He offered to lead the way. I didn't want to explain it all, so I just told him..." He glanced away with his confession. "The first thing that popped into my head."

"How interesting that a lie should be the first thing."

"Yeah. Interesting." He realized that the *nature* of the lie was more than interesting. "It would save me some embarrassment if you would act—" He looked her in the eye and tried not to demean himself further with an unbecoming plea. "If you would go along with me, the way any good wife—"

"Good wife! I beg your pardon, Mr. Morsette, but you have persisted in addressing me as *Miss* Emily. Fairly rubbing my nose in my status, despite the fact that *legally* I *have* been a married woman, however briefly. And now, you make a mockery of that fact, blithely claiming me as *your woman*, when we have not even . . ."

"We have shared a bed," he reminded her quietly, taking mean-spirited satisfaction in shattering her usual decorum.

Her eyes widened in horror. "Are you going to compromise the integrity of that experience, as well?"

"I said you were my woman. Any details would be just between you and me."

She stared, tight-lipped, clearly doubting his word. His heart hardened again. "It's not like the details would be something you'd never take part in. You *did* come out here looking for a husband."

"I *had* one."

"You had a dead one." He turned away, muttering, "Now you've got me."

"From a dead husband to a fake one," she clipped acidly.

He spun on his heel faster than any of her fanciful gunfighters. "I'm no fake *anything*."

Undaunted, she squared her shoulders. "And I'm expected to comply with *your* wishes to save *you* embarrassment."

She was infuriating. She was unreasonable. Damn her, she was . . . *woman.*

He glanced at the door, hoping no one would come through it and witness his mortification. He paced the length of the room and back again. The place had suddenly become too small, too tight a fit, to contain the two of them. Damn! What would the girls do if he resorted to trussing up their dignified Miss Emily and tossing her over the back of his horse?

Not a good plan, he told himself.

"Let me tell you a story," he said, and his controlled tone helped to calm them both. He took her hand in both of his and drew her to sit beside him on the bed he'd tossed around in the night before. "The Lakota tell a story about a woman who would not obey her husband when he told her it was time to break camp and move on. She sat down and refused to budge, so he had to leave her, because..." He searched for a reason she might accept, but he wasn't sure one existed. His gesture appealed to her simply to grant him the obvious. "Because it was time to go. And she's still sittin' there to this very day." He paused for effect, then looked her in the eye for the same purpose. "She turned to stone."

Emily responded with a dismissive shrug. "Like Lot's wife, who turned to salt."

"No, there was a difference. The Lakota woman had a child strapped to her back. The child shared her fate."

He knew he had made his point when he saw her lower lip tremble. He'd backed her into a corner. But somehow he felt no joy in it.

She stared at their hands, still clasped on his knee. "I don't understand this *time to go.* We just got here." Her dejected sigh nearly undid him. "And I'm so tired."

He wanted to give in and make more promises he couldn't keep, but he remembered the way his father used to answer that heart-rending complaint. "Only a little farther and we will find what we're looking for."

She looked into his eyes, hers frankly pleading. "I hardly remember what that was."

"People who will take us in."

"It's almost Christmas." She turned her attention to the fireplace on the opposite side of the room. "I could make this place feel like home, and we could at least have Christmas before we—"

"Get it through your head, Emily, this place can't be home. I can't let you think of it that way. There's no one here because there is *no food* here." He squeezed her hand.

"It's best that we go now. You have to trust me, Emily. I may not be much to you..."

He gave her a chance to object, and when she did not, he released her hand, rose from the bed and walked away. At the door, he paused, steeled himself and offered her a cocky smile. "I may not be your true husband, *Miss* Emily, but I'm all you've got. We're leaving in the morning."

"And I have no say in the matter, no choice at all."

"You can choose to remain a woman..." He nodded toward the stone hearth that seemed to hold such an attraction for her. "Or become a rock."

All right, she would go, Emily told herself as she stuffed her belongings—what he'd allowed her to take with her when they'd left Billings—and the girls' into her two carpetbags, preparing them for the packhorse. She hadn't seen him since they'd had their talk, but the girls had dashed in and out a couple of times, once for a piece of charcoal and once to deliver Wolf's instructions that she make a batch of bannock bread.

Wolf suddenly burst through the door, the look in his eyes as jubilant as that of a boy who had just made his first ringer in horseshoes. "We've got something to show you, the girls and me. Come on outside."

"I'm not finished here," she said in a small, tight voice.

Surely he could see that she'd done as he'd asked. He might have told her that he was glad to see that she'd decided to be, in his eyes, sensible. But he did not. He waited. When she finally looked up, she was sure she detected an uncharacteristic touch of humility in his eyes.

"It's kind of like a peace offering," he said quietly.

*A peace offering.*

Magic words.

He hooked one hand over the top of the door, braced the other on the doorpost and stood there awkwardly, as though he wasn't sure whether to come in or stay out. She might have mentioned the cold air coming in, but she didn't. It wasn't important now. They shared a look that would have served well between true husband and wife, apologies and forgiveness passing both ways.

"The girls helped, remember. So..." He rocked the door back and forth, making the wooden hinges squeak. "So, just so you know. They heard us arguing."

"Oh, dear."

He shrugged, almost boyishly. "It's nothing. People argue sometimes."

"But the girls will feel better when they know we've put it aside."

The look in his eyes said, *So will I.*

She read the message and nodded, then smiled. "Show me this peace offering."

It was a sleigh. A *cariole,* he explained, but he'd made it from parts that had been scattered and left behind. "I found the runners stuck up in some rafters. Somebody must have forgotten that he'd stored them away." He took a turn around the conveyance, proudly pointing out each resourceful feature. "Found some pieces of harness, a wagon tongue. And I fixed up the box off a broken cart. Filled it with some straw I found stored in a rack. Bear Catcher helped the girls make some paint, and *voilà!*"

The girls stood to one side of the sleigh with their latest instructor, Wolf to the other. All eyes were on Emily, all awaiting her approval.

Approval was surely too small a word for the emotion that flooded her heart.

"Oh, it's beautiful!" She approached the creation cautiously, as though she were afraid she might scare it away. "It's just perfect. Such wonderful, wonderful..." She examined one of the metal runners, the supporting uprights, the wooden platform, then the box itself, decorated by novice painters. "Oh, look, snowflakes," Emily marveled. "And flowers. A combination of seasons. How lovely!"

She held out her arms to the girls, and they came running, each claiming a side so that she could squeeze them both at once.

"What about me?" Wolf demanded jovially. "Peace offered deserves peace given in return."

The girls nudged Emily in his direction.

"Yes, of course . . ."

"Right here." He laid a forefinger against his lips. "The kiss of peace would sit well right here."

She stepped up to him, stood on tiptoe and gave his lips a matronly peck.

He arched an eyebrow. "Did that look as halfhearted to you girls as it felt to me?"

"Do it again, *longer* this time," Lisette advocated, clapping her hands for good measure.

"Lisette," Marie-Claire admonished. "Behave like a proper lady."

Hearing the echo of her own teaching gave Emily a warm sense of satisfaction. She thought of another bit of wisdom, and offered it gently, her eyes never leaving Wolf's mock-stern face. "When a gentleman shows such consideration, a proper lady responds wholeheartedly."

She slid her arms around his neck and pulled his handsomely chiseled face within her reach, then gave him the kind of lip-melting kiss she'd never have guessed to be part of her repertoire.

"Peace," Wolf said when he caught his breath.

Smiling, Emily responded, "Peace."

The sleigh complicated their travel at first, for the mares did not readily pull as a team, and the harness Wolf had improvised kept breaking. He was patient. He put on his snowshoes and fairly skated over snow and ice alongside the mares, coaxing them to work together. When something broke, he fixed it, grumbling only when he thought no one was listening.

At times Emily thought he was almost *too* patient, for there were some moments so frustrating that she wanted to beg him to leave the infernal contraption behind and get on with the journey. But then she would look into the faces of the two girls and remember their efforts, as he had asked her to do, and she would steadfastly hold her peace.

But after a few days the going got easier. Between Bear Catcher and Wolf there was always a hunter to provide something for the skillet or the spit. The sleigh finally proved to be an asset, especially when long stretches of frozen river offered a level path. And then, what fun! Emily taught everyone to sing "Dashing through the snow," even as they did so, and the air turned less cold, the days less tedious, the travel less arduous.

Spirits rode high until Christmas Eve came before they had reached their destination. To make matters worse, the wind at their back was picking up, and the small white clouds overhead began to bump into each other, blend together and turn gray.

"We will find them soon," Bear Catcher promised. "Before we reach the mountains. Berger does not make camp in the mountains."

"He is Métis," Wolf agreed. "A man of the prairie. He travels until he finds the best hunting, then makes his camp."

"You can see that the deer are thick here," Bear Catcher said. "The camp is not far. This is where I told him to come."

"I'll ride on ahead to look for some kind of sign. Find us a good place to camp, if nothing else." Wolf could tell that his proposal didn't sit well with Emily, but she kept her concerns to herself. He offered what encouragement he could. "Either way, I'll bag us a good Christmas dinner."

They followed Wolf's tracks until they trailed over the top of the river bluff and disappeared. Bear Catcher stayed the course along the river bottom until late afternoon, when Emily began to worry aloud. "He must have found them by now," she said. "Otherwise he'd be back, don't you think?"

"He waits for us."

Emily chucked the horses with the reins. "Do you know where?"

"A good place."

"A good place," Emily echoed. "A good place, a good place. He is testing me. He asked me to trust him, and now he thinks he must test me. And on Christmas Eve, of all times, testing my confidence, testing my...my faith."

The girls huddled close to her in their straw nest, all three swaddled in the blankets that made up the bedrolls. Including Wolf's. At least he had no plans to make camp without them, which surely meant—Emily scolded herself for thinking of it, even in the negative—he had no plans to desert them.

She looked up, seeking more substantial assurance from the new friend who had taken over Wolf's shepherding duties. "You believe he's somewhere up ahead, waiting for us, just...*waiting* for us?"

Bear Catcher's expression was both intent and inscrutable. "*Bonjour* man always finds a good place."

"I hope it's the place we're looking for," she muttered as she flicked the reins again. "I hope he's finally found those people."

"He finds *something*." Bear Catcher nodded downriver, toward a place where the high bluffs seemed to support the sagging clouds. "Look there."

At first only the smoke was visible. Then the cave in the rocky river bluff came into view, its tall, narrow portal festooned with pine boughs. Close by, Wolf could be seen tending something on the fire. When he saw them, he waved and motioned them over, grinning like a man who had found treasure. And to be sure, he had, for in the face of a gathering storm, the cave was as welcome a sight as the house of Emily's dreams ever would be.

It might have been a castle. A yuletide fortress, really. Wolf had trimmed it, inside and out, so that the scent of pine filled the interior, and the fire held the chill at bay. If Emily wanted an extra room, she had it now, for there was a second opening, where he'd built the fire, and enough space to accommodate the horses.

"You're awfully big to be a Christmas elf," Emily teased happily.

Wolf laughed as he welcomed them into his glorious find. "Do you mind spending Christmas Eve in a cave?"

"I believe there's some traditional precedent for a cave that shelters both man and beast." Her cheerful tone obscured the anxious look meant only for him. "No sign of the Berger encampment?"

"This is as far as I've gone. It was far enough for you to travel today." He slipped his arm around her shoulders and drew her close. He was still shaken by the overwhelming sense of relief that had flooded him the moment he'd caught the first glimpse of them, moving slowly down the river. He'd hated leaving them, but his choices had been limited, and he hadn't been comfortable with the one he'd made until he had them in his care again.

"The Métis are close by," he assured her. "I know it. Only a little farther."

"This is wonderful, Wolf." Emily surveyed his work, breathing deeply of the scents of pine and fire. "It's so festive. It feels like Christmas."

He squeezed her shoulders, and he laughed when Lisette suddenly grabbed his leg and hugged for all she was worth. "I don't want you girls getting attached to a cave, now, so tell me if you start thinking it feels like home."

"I think it does, a little, now that we are all together." Emily looked up, then reached out to touch his smooth chin. "With the ominous clouds gathering overhead, I did wonder ... did fear for your safety, Mr. Morsette." He scowled, and she smiled softly. "Wolf."

"I'm not about to stray." Reluctantly he backed away, for there was still work to do, but he lifted an admonishing finger her way. "And I'm not about to forget that I made you a promise."

"What promise?"

"Have *you* forgotten, then?" He shook his head, offering Bear Catcher a man-to-man look. "When a promise slips his woman's mind, a man should keep his mouth shut and count himself lucky. It doesn't happen often."

"A woman's head is made to store these things," Bear Catcher agreed.

"You see, Emily? What is between a man and a woman is the same no matter where they live or what clothes they put on." Such talk drew him back to her for another quiet word, fingers laid briefly against her cool cheek. "Or the color of their eyes or face or hair. We never get to see your pretty hair, Miss Emily. It's always covered or knotted up somehow."

"I like to keep it neat, and, um ..." He was pushing her bonnet back, touching her hair as though he had a sudden need to make sure it was still there. "Wolf," she whispered, desperately torn between propriety and the soft glow in his eyes. "My goodness."

"Your goodness." He gave a quick nod. "That's something I don't doubt."

It was her turn to back away, for this time the sense that all eyes were on her made her feel flustered. Awkward. She wasn't sure what response would be appropriate. Surely not the ardent kiss she was half-inclined to bestow upon his dear, welcome face.

"Look at this Christmas feast," she exclaimed dramatically, taking into account the sizable chunks of spitted meat dripping over the fire. "With all this—" her gesture included the spruce tree he'd stood in one corner and the pile of boughs he'd stripped to be made into beds "—you have certainly outdone yourself, Mr. Morsette."

He tucked his thumbs into his sash and grinned. "Your goodness must be rubbing off on me."

"And yours," she said, touching his arm, "on me. I have another song for tonight, and I have surprises." She smiled at the girls. "Gifts."

"So early?" Wolf asked.

"What is your custom? Do you save them for Epiphany?"

"It's been so long…" Wolf shook his head and laughed. "The priest would hold Mass and tell us, 'No fiddles, no dancing, you Métis! This is a night for quiet prayer.' And so it was. But then came the visiting from house to house, and gifts and music and racing the *carioles*. We know how to make a celebration last."

"It sounds wonderful, doesn't it, girls?"

"We have some fun in store," Wolf promised. "We'll unload the straw and bed the horses down. Is everyone hungry enough to eat my cooking?"

After supper Emily taught the lyrics to "Silent Night." Wolf's strong voice lent rich, haunting depth to the hymn. In the distance, a whole choir of wolves joined in, and the horses' patient presence reminded the group of the part the animals played in their lives, this night and every night. Wolf and Bear Catcher were hunters, as their fathers and their fathers' fathers had been, but they never took the meat or the hides for granted, and their horses were like brothers to them.

And so when Emily told the story of Christmas, she made special mention of the donkey, the ox and the lamb. In all the years that she had heard the story, she had been most thrilled by the vision of golden angels and most charmed by the serenity of mother and child. The "lowly manger" had been a familiar but meaningless phrase before this night.

Now she understood what it meant to huddle together—man, woman, child and beast—simply for the need to stay warm. She looked at her companions, and for the first time in her life she understood what it meant to be a stranger in one's own land, now ruled by a conqueror who lived in a faraway place. Never before had she traveled so far, made do with so few comforts and sought nothing more than ა safe haven and unqualified acceptance.

And, after the long day's journey, never before had she been so content to be where she was with what she had.

When Wolf came to bed, he discovered that Emily had claimed the cold berth, the one close to the wall, leaving him the spot nearer the fire, with the girls to be snuggled, as usual, between them. Not tonight, he decided. He tucked the blankets around Marie-Claire's feet, then stepped over the three. The pine needles rustled beneath the cozy nest as he insinuated himself between Emily and the cave's rock wall.

She stirred and made a soft sound of protest, lifting her head just enough so that he was able to give her his arm for a pillow.

"Shh." He positioned his lips close to her ear, put his other arm around her and pulled her against him. "Tonight the Wolf shall lie down with the lamb."

"Oh," she said, and he could tell that she wasn't sure whether he was man or dream.

He brushed her hair aside and kissed the edge of her ear. "You'll sleep warmer this way, and I'll sleep happier."

"But, Wolf—"

"Hold my hand," he suggested as he trailed it down her arm, seeking her hand. "Hold it tight, now, don't let it stray, the way it will in my dreams."

"Wolf, you are such a . . . wolf!"

"Shh, love, you could tame me," he crooned in her ear. "I could be your lapdog." He traced the curve of her ear with the tip of his tongue and felt a shiver shimmy through

her. "Your watchdog. I would let no man come near you."
Delicately he nipped her downy nape, and she gasped.
"Your hunting dog," he whispered. "I could provide for
you."

"What must I do in return?" she whispered.

"Don't make me sleep outside."

"Oh, Wolf..." She squeezed his hand and tucked it
against her belly. "You once told me that you were accustomed to sleeping under the open sky. You said—"

"Did you know that it was a woman who first tamed the
wolf for a pet?"

"It was?"

"The wolf found her sleeping in the woods one night, and
he thought she was beautiful. He lay down with her to keep
her warm." Wolf snuggled as close against her back as he
could get with their clothes in the way. "Like this. Just before the sun rose, he slipped away. Each night he would seek
her out. Some nights he would find her in the woods, and he
would curl up next to her. On cold nights when she slept inside, he would stay outside her door. During the day he went
into the hills, but at night he wanted to be near her. Soon he
began to long for her company, day and night.

"He hid in the trees one day and watched her gather
cherries until she filled her baskets. Then she tried to lift
them, but the weight of the full baskets was too much for
her. She stumbled and spilled the cherries. When she picked
herself up and started collecting them off the ground, the
wolf noticed that she was crying, and he knew he had a
choice to make. He could either go back to his own kind, to
the wolf people, or he could stay with the woman and ease
her burden.

"In his heart the choice had already been made, but when
he came out of the woods, he frightened her. She'd never
seen him in the daylight, and he looked quite fierce. He
thought she was repulsed by him, and he wanted to die. But
she did not hiss at him or throw rocks to make him go away,

the way a man might do. Instead she stood very still. Then, finally, she held out her hand, palm up. He came to her and licked the salt of her labor from her hand, licked her until her calluses melted away. And he offered to carry her baskets on his back."

Emily gave a soft sigh. Then she moved his hand slowly, slowly, letting it trail lightly along the center line of her body until his fingertips touched her chin. She lowered her head and pressed her lips to the back of his hand.

Wolf closed his eyes and finished his story in a husky whisper.

"To this day, the dog is a friend to the women of the Cree, the Lakota and the Chippewa. He bears their burdens, and he asks little in return."

"What a wonderful story," Emily said softly. "Tomorrow you must tell it to the girls."

First one giggled, and then the other joined in.

"We heard."

"I didn't hear the first part," Lisette insisted.

"You didn't have to make up a big story, Wolf," Marie-Claire admonished. "Miss Emily would never make you sleep outside."

Wolf chuckled. "I didn't make it up. The grandmothers tell that story."

"My grandmother told it another way," Bear Catcher informed them from his corner of the cave.

Emily had to bite her lip to keep from laughing aloud. Wolf could feel her shaking with it. He playfully nipped the back of her neck, but still she managed to contain herself, which was more than he could say for himself when she reached back and tickled him in the ribs.

The night wind whistled and stirred the snowfall, while inside the warm cave the voices in the dark took turns telling stories. First Bear Catcher launched into his grandmother's wolf tale. Then Emily whispered a fairy princess tale, followed by Wolf's dream-catcher story.

It was Christmas Eve. No matter whose customs they would follow, it was gift-giving time.

And the best gifts of all were the stories.

## Chapter Six

Christmas Day had a dreary dawning. The world outside the cave was ruled by wind and snow. But inside there were two young girls who took no notice of the weather. They were too busy exclaiming over the miraculous appearance of gifts made especially for them. There were fur hats and wooden string puppets whose legs jackknifed when their strings were pulled. There were two soft-bodied dolls with calico dresses and pretty muslin aprons, one for each of them.

Emily helped them try on their Cossack-style hats and showed them how to tie their aprons. She admired the little puppets' remarkable mechanism and praised the cleverness of the carver who had fashioned them.

The two men quietly smoked their pipes, enjoying the proceedings with male reserve until Wolf announced that it was Emily's turn to be surprised.

The girls sat her down on their bed.

"Close your eyes, Miss Emily."

Emily could hear Wolf whispering to each girl. Intrigued, she shut her eyes even tighter and listened closely, trying to imagine what he was handing them and which girl approached her from the left and which from the right. A fur hat was the first gift. Emily could easily guess by the careful way she handled the fitting and hair arrangement that Marie-Claire was the designated giver. Emily lifted her hands to touch, parted her lips to praise, but Wolf's voice delayed her response.

"Don't open your eyes yet. We're not finished."

She sensed that it was little Lisette who came up behind her and draped something soft and fuzzy around her neck, topping it off with an exuberant hug and a whispered "Merry Christmas."

"Say it the way Wolf told you," Marie-Claire instructed.

*"Joyeux Noël!"* Lisette shouted, jumping with considerable joy of her own. "Open your eyes! Open your eyes, Mama!"

Lisette didn't notice the startled expressions in the faces around her, but her innocent excitement bridged the awkward moment, and Emily quickly fell to petting the fur pieces and fawning over the girls, who hovered close by.

"Lisette's just a baby," Marie-Claire whispered apologetically. "She never knew our—"

"It's all right," Emily said, warming Marie-Claire's hand in hers. "It's perfectly all right."

"You look like the beautiful fairy princess," Marie-Claire said. "Doesn't she, Wolf? From the story last night."

"I don't know much about fairy princesses. She reminds me of the woman in *my* story." A smile danced in his dark eyes. "The one who tamed the Wolf."

"But I wouldn't tame him and then take his fur."

"These are made of fox fur, not wolf. The skins were small. I only had enough for—" Laying a hand on her shoulder, he smoothed the triangular fur scarf the girls had arranged about her neck. "What would this be called?"

"I think they used to call this a fichu." Emily tucked her chin into the fur, looking down her nose to admire as she patted and primped. "They used to wear them when the dresses had very low necklines."

"I don't know much about ladies' fashions."

"I shall be happy to revive this fashion. It's wonderfully warm and soft." She looked up at him and smiled. "Very practical. Thank you."

"When my cousins see you, the women will all want one of these. When we find them..." He knelt beside her, bracing his arm over his knee like a suitor, eager to offer credible reassurance, which he knew to be the gift she needed most. "*When* we find them and we get settled in, I'll make you a cape. Or a coat. Which would you like?"

"I'm very pleased with what I have."

"What you need is a wearing robe, like Bear Catcher's."

Emily's gaze followed Wolf's, and together they included the man who still lounged on his sleeping pallet, smoking his pipe. "Why, yes, I have admired—"

"Careful," Wolf warned quietly. "He's liable to give it to you if you tell him how much you like it."

Bear Catcher laughed. "I like very much your saddle and two of your blankets, *bonjour* man."

"Just trying to make you look good," Wolf teased.

"I'm looking plenty damn good already." Bear Catcher tapped a forefinger to his temple. "Plenty damn smart, too."

"Well, I have a gift for *you*, Bear Catcher," Emily announced. She opened one of her carpetbags and produced two flannel shirts. "And one for Wolf."

The shirts looked exactly alike—both red and black, both collarless, buttonless boxy styles, but they fitted. And the men seemed genuinely pleased.

"Oh, my, you do look handsome, both of you. You could pass for brothers."

"Half-brothers, maybe." Wolf tapped Bear Catcher's shoulder. "You think the Indian agents would believe I'm your brother, Bear Catcher? This side of the Canadian border, there's no Métis. There's either white or Indian." He held out his hand, displaying the back of it for proof. "And I sure ain't white."

"*Half*-brother, maybe," Bear Catcher allowed.

"See, so that makes me Métis. Not *bonjour* man." Playfully he jabbed an elbow into Bear Catcher's ribs, and Bear Catcher returned the gesture, adding a sparring maneuver. In their look-alike shirts they might well have been two rowdy boys. Their audience rewarded them feminine giggles.

"'Course the government's making reservations for you Indians. Your half-brothers don't qualify." Wolf slapped Bear Catcher's shoulder. "Where's your agency, Bear Catcher? Is there room for me on the rolls?"

Bear Catcher shrugged. "If I go back to Dakota and put my name in their book to be counted, they say I will have an agency and annuities."

Emily considered the curious requirement. "You mean, you're supposed to return to the country where you were born so that a census can be taken?"

"Just like in the Christmas story?" Marie-Claire asked. "Just like Mary and Joseph?"

"Governments have their business to do. Since time immemorial they have made it a project to count people and determine their..." Emily searched for the proper word. "Origin, I suppose."

"When they come to count us, we'll be with the Métis." Wolf chucked Marie-Claire under the chin, drawing out her soft, sweet smile. "Right, girls? If they don't have Métis on their list of choices, they can count us as Indians who play the fiddle and dance a Red River jig."

"And wear beaded moccasins and hunt buffalo," Emily supplied, admiring Wolf's moccasins, then Bear Catcher's.

"Buffalo are gettin' harder to find these days, but not beads." Wolf stuck out his foot for a better view. "We've still got the beads. So they can call us Chippewa or Canadians or *bonjour* men if they want, but we'll still be Métis."

"And where shall I be?" Emily wondered.

"For the rest of the winter, you'll be with us. After that..." He shrugged, his glance skittering away from her face and purposely avoiding the two girls'. "I guess you can be wherever you want to be."

"If we find your people—"

"*When* we find them."

"When we find them," Emily obliged, "are you planning to finally settle down?"

"I'm used to makin' my way as I go. I've never done much planning." He planted one hand on his hip and gestured in her direction with the other. "Well, look at you, Miss Emily. You made your plans, and they didn't work out. Looks to me like a plan ain't something you can always depend on."

The crackling fire was the only sound filling the abrupt, awkward silence.

"I guess you're right about that." Taking her own time, Emily rose to face him.

But not in anger. She mirrored his stance, arms akimbo, and challenged him with a fierce smile. "Guess that's why a man needs some religion," she drawled in a passable imitation of Wolf Morsette. In her natural voice, she added pointedly, "And I guess that's why a woman does, too."

Wolf was momentarily dumbfounded.

Emily stood her ground, still smiling.

He laughed. Then he looked at her, shook his head and laughed some more. "Hell, that sounds like something a wise man once said!"

"He has his flashes of wisdom, along with his moments of weakness." Emily lifted Lisette into her arms and gave her puppet string a quick tug. "And from the looks of it, he's been planning for Christmas for some time."

"Damn right. I might not know just where I'll lay my head from one night to the next—" he ruffled Lisette's hair and treated Emily to a wolfish wink "— but I know what I'm givin' my girls for Christmas."

When the storm abated, Bear Catcher rode out with a promise to locate the Berger camp. When he didn't return, Wolf roundly cursed the man's entire ancestry.

But Emily was worried about their friend. "Perhaps he's lost."

"Lost? Indians don't get *lost*. He doesn't wanna miss any part of the New Year's celebration, so he's just takin' his time, just fillin' up his belly." Wolf kicked at the last of the firewood. "He's probably keeping his mouth so full he hasn't gotten around to telling anybody that we're out here waitin' on him."

It was easier to grumble than to think of bundling the women up and taking them out on what could well prove to be another fruitless journey.

"I don't think Bear Catcher would let us down." Emily laid a consoling hand on his arm. "You don't, either."

"We'll see." From the cave door he scanned the frozen stretch of river below. "The weather's on our side now."

And so was the granter of Christmas wishes. They'd traveled no more than half a day when they came upon a party of Métis hunters. Riding in the lead was their friend, Bear Catcher.

"You don't trust my word, *bonjour* man?"

Unable to suppress a broad grin, Wolf rode up beside his Indian friend and clasped his arm. "Hell, I thought somebody might have mistaken you for a renegade Sioux and shot your damn tail feathers off."

Bear Catcher laughed. "Not even a one-eyed white man could mistake a Chippewa for a sneaky Sioux."

"Then again, I thought you might have gotten caught up in the fiddle music. But Miss Emily knew better."

"They got a Black Robe, these *bonjours*." Bear Catcher smiled at Emily as he gave Wolf fair warning. "If she's not your woman, she will soon be mine."

"You *wish*," Wolf said, his sense of humor suddenly in short supply. His horse pranced restlessly as he wheeled to greet the party of horsemen strung out along the river-bank.

"Are you Wolf Morsette? Joseph Morsette's son?" A man with a salt-and-pepper beard offered Wolf a hand-shake. "You sure favor your mother, boy."

"So I've been told."

The older man motioned for the rest of the party to gather in close, then leaned back in his saddle, taking in Wolf's appearance from head to toe. "Heard you made yourself a reputation with a pistol. What kind of a thing is that for a Métis? A little six-shooter. A man needs a good buffalo gun. A good rifle."

Squinting into the bright winter sun, Wolf agreed, indi-cating his rifle scabbard with a nod. Next to his pipe and his knife, the rifle was a Métis man's most prized possession.

"You got the law on your tail, son?"

"Not that I know of."

"I'm Pierre Berger. Don't know if you remember, I'm a half-brother to your father, from over by—"

"I remember my uncle Pierre," Wolf said, smiling.

"Where you been keepin' yourself?"

"Been knockin' around the Territories since I can't re-member when. Thought I'd head up this way, look up some of my relations."

"See you brought your family."

"I, uh—" Wolf backed his horse up a couple of steps, reining his head toward the sleigh. "This is Emily. The lit-tle ones are Marie-Claire and Lisette. What we need is—"

"What we need is some fiddle music, Mr. Morsette." Emily took off one of her gloves and extended her hand to the elder man. "Please say we haven't missed the celebra-tion, Mr. Berger."

"Missed it?" Berger dismounted in order to greet Emily properly, taking her hand in both of his. "No, no, we've got plenty to celebrate. This place Bear Catcher told us about, this whole basin, the game is plentiful. Good land here. We got twenty-five families, and the trader, Janeaux, he says he'll put us up a trading post." He looked at Wolf. "We're calling it Spring Creek."

"Spring Creek," Emily repeated, as though the words were almost sacred. "Oh, Wolf, it has a *name*. Girls, your new home is called Spring Creek."

Just as Wolf had promised, they had found people who would take them in. And, as Pierre Berger had promised, the holiday celebration was still in progress when they reached the camp, which looked quite similar to the one on the Milk River. But here the hearths were warm, the laughter merry, and the big hall was jumping with music.

The dancing was even livelier than anything Wolf had demonstrated. The men, especially, were the most tireless dancers Emily had ever seen. The new dance hall's as yet only partially mud-plastered log walls fairly trembled with the rousing hoots and yelps that punctuated the music of fiddle, washtub and clacking spoons. The plank floors shook from the stomping heels. The parti-colored *l'assomption* sashes tied about most of the men's waists whipped around the room like trailing banners. Emily would have judged Wolf the most agile, most graceful, surely the most remarkable dancer in the crowd, but he termed himself "rusty." She could see why when the contest winner was able to perform thirty different jigging steps.

Bear Catcher had his own version of each dance, but the Indian influence on the blended heritage of the Métis was readily apparent in his steps. One young woman seemed particularly interested in teaching him to waltz. And even the smallest children were fine dancers. There was no shortage of dance teachers for Marie-Claire and Lisette, who had known a dearth of playmates in their young lives. But that was about to change.

For Emily there was only one dance partner. She thought perhaps Bear Catcher's comment had given Wolf pause. He had come home at last. Not to a place, but to his people, with whom he had a lot of catching up to do. Still, he was as attentive to her as the most ardent suitor. She loved the feel of his hand on her back as he guided her effortlessly about the floor. She would have been pleased to spend the rest of her life dancing with him thus.

"Nothing would please me more," he whispered in her ear, "than to dance with you until the sun comes up, Miss Emily."

The declaration surprised her, so close had it come to her own thoughts. He looked into her eyes and smiled knowingly. Unless he was a mind reader, she'd unconsciously made her wish aloud.

"Or until you agree to be my wife," he said. "Whichever comes first."

"Marriage means settling down, doesn't it? Making plans?" She gripped his shoulder tighter than she meant to as she recalled his every infuriatingly evasive word. "You said that in the spring..."

"There will be no spring. Not unless you marry me." The hand at her back slid to her waist, taking a possessive hold. "At least, not for me. I've had winter in my heart for such a long time, I didn't know any better." He glanced over her head, then quickly back, his eyes pleading with hers. "Marie-Claire and Lisette belong with us, Emily. Don't speak of leaving me—"

"I was thinking more that... *you* might not stay."

"Woman, don't you know how much I love you?"

They stood together in the middle of the floor, dancers whirling in the periphery of her stunned awareness. *He loved her?*

"And... I promised to build you a house."

She found only a small piece of her voice. "For all of us?"

"And then some. As many rooms as it takes to make you happy." He pulled her against him and whispered, for her ear only, "And as many babies."

"Oh, Wolf, I love you. I didn't imagine…I dreamed, yes, but I could not think or hope—" she tipped her head, needing to see his face through the tears gathered in her eyes "—that there might be a husband for me, and love, too."

He touched her cheek solicitously. "How else would you have it?"

"No way else," she declared, hugging his neck, seeking his lips. "No one else. Oh, Wolf…"

"They've gotten started kissing in the New Year," someone shouted.

"*Sacre coeur*, wait, wait…"

A hand on each of their shoulders drew them out of a blissful kiss. Like two dreamy-eyed children they blinked at each other, then at Uncle Pierre's laughing face.

"What is this, you want to start your own tradition?"

"What tradition?" Emily's question ended in a funny little croak.

Wolf laughed and squeezed her affectionately.

Pierre waved his hand in the air. The music had stopped, and the room was filled with chatter, both *Michif* and English, flavored with hearty guffaws and happy giggles. "Father, we should have the blessing," Pierre announced.

"I think these two must have the blessing." A priest robed in a black cassock appeared at Pierre's side. He addressed Wolf solemnly. "If all you have is a country marriage, my son, I can give you the Church's blessing tonight."

Wolf took no offense at the priest's assumption. He simply grinned at his bride-to-be. "None too soon for me, Father."

"Wolf." She rose on tiptoe and whispered in his ear. "We ought to have a proper wedding."

"She's right." Tucking her hand under his arm, he turned to the assemblage to make his announcement. "Miss Emily has tamed the Wolf. She is a very proper lady, and she deserves a proper wedding. And a proper house.'' He gestured with his free hand. ''And all this family.''

Cheers filled the dance hall. The fiddler added his chords of approval, and the washtub player rattled a resounding tattoo.

''People who will take us in,'' Emily said with a smile. ''No questions asked.''

''Considering our special circumstances, Father, would you mind dispensing with the banns and such?'' Wolf entreated Emily, making no attempt to mask the eagerness in his eyes. ''Let's have our proper wedding after we kiss in the New Year. New Year's Day is a good time to make vows.'' Then he whispered, ''The sooner we marry, the sooner you will have your house.''

''Then let's turn this party into a wedding feast,'' Emily agreed.

As the head of the group, Pierre received the priest's New Year's blessing, which he passed on to his wife and each of his own children in the form of a kiss. Once the New Year's kissing started, it continued throughout the group, a blessing joyfully shared. The mood was right for a wedding, then, and Pierre's wife brought out a treasured length of cream-colored embroidered cutwork linen, which served as Emily's veil. Pierre magnanimously offered the use of his cabin for a honeymoon.

The house-to-house visiting, the *cariole* races, the dancing, the music—all the festivities continued without the newlyweds. For three days they listened to the sounds of the celebration going on outside the walls of their borrowed lovers' bower. Food appeared regularly on the doorstep, and periodically someone outside would shout in *Michif* a close approximation of *Toujour l'amour!*

"You're missing the Métis festivities," Emily teased as she fed her husband a bite of the raised bread she had baked for him and dipped in stewed plums. He licked the plum juice off her fingers, then shared the sweet taste from his lips to hers.

"I'm *making* Métis festivities," he told her. He smiled lustfully as he dispatched the buttons on the yoke of her white flannel nightgown. "Would you rather make them here by the fire this time, or under the bed covers?"

"If you touch me there..."

"Where?" His thumb flicked across her nipple. "There?"

The sweet ache he'd been tutoring her to love took her breath away, made her eyes drift closed, made her smile.

"Yes, I think so," he whispered against her neck. "I think you want me to touch you there."

"I think so, too," she said. "And I think it's too late to move to the bed."

There were races going on outside. Wolf had half a mind to race a little, too. On a bet he knew he could shuck his sash, pants and moccasins before she could get her nightgown over her head. But his Emily liked it better when he took her slowly. When he teased her and touched her and kissed her until all her thoughts were quite improper—that was the way his Emily loved to be loved.

He smiled when he heard another victory shout. "Noisy fellow," he grumbled. "Maybe I should just go out there and give him a run for his money, hmm?" He bit her nipple gently and sucked air between his teeth until she shivered with the tingle he took pleasure in creating for her. Chuckling, he pushed her nightgown over her shoulders and down, down until he'd stripped her bare.

And bare she lay on the soft fur rug. He knelt beside her, grinning at the lovely picture she made, her skin already flushed from the fire and from his ardent attentions.

"Would you mind if I ducked out now, just for a little race?"

She tugged on his sash, drawing him back to her. "Not if you wouldn't mind sleeping outside."

He gave a wolfish whimper as he nuzzled her, rooting around her breasts. Moments later he growled as she took her time freeing him from his pants.

And finally, as the moon rose over the New Year's festivities in the Métis winter camp, Miss Emily's Wolf gave a thrilling, thoroughly heated-up howl.

Within a month, Miss Emily had a house of her own.

And within nine more, Marie-Claire and Lisette had a baby brother.

*     *     *     *     *

## A Note from Kathleen Eagle

*Dear Reader,*

Some of my most treasured gifts are the ones my
children made for me when they were little. On my
desk sits the pencil cup made from an orange juice
can decorated with yarn, the decoupage paperweight,
the lopsided ceramic bowl that holds my business
cards and the one-of-a-kind gargoyle candy holder.
I have three plaster casts of five-year-old-size hand-
prints, and on the back of each is the poem most
mothers have seen a time or two—the one about the
small fingerprints on the wall. Those hands, all three
pairs, are bigger than mine now, still leaving their
fingerprints on the wall, but now it's makeup and
motor oil rather than mud pies. It's hard to believe
how quickly those hands have grown.

At Christmastime we take out the decorations the
kids have made over the years, along with those
we've collected for each of them, and we replay the
memories. They outgrow their clothes and their toys
in the blink of an eye, and before you know it,
they're not bringing handmade gifts home from
school anymore. But they don't outgrow Christmas.
Nowadays they give their parents music—the payoff
for all those piano, guitar and violin lessons. They
give us help with dinner, a shoveled driveway, a ride
to the mall, a call when they're going to be late
getting home.

Our gifts to them? Over the years the wish lists
have run the usual gamut from dolls and bicycles to
stereos and snowboards. Santa has done his share of
fretting over those lists at our house. Some years
have been fat, others lean. But the value of so much
of that holiday booty fades quickly, and what remains
a treasure is the child's handmade gift, the keepsakes

and memories of holidays past and the simple gifts of kindness, thoughtfulness and respect.

If the holiday season is a special time to cherish the children, let's remember *all* our children. Let's remember that it takes a whole community to raise a child. And let's realize that the best gift we have to give our children is peace, starting in our own homes in our own neighborhoods. From there it must spread throughout the nation and the world. But it can only come through kindness, thoughtfulness and respect, for doesn't that add up to love?

Thank you, dear readers, for your wonderful letters, for the bears some of you have sent for the Eagle "Bear Tree," for the recipes, the poetry, the books, newspaper clippings, anecdotes and more, but especially for your continued friendship and support. I wish you a blessed holiday season.

My gift is my story, and this one's for you!

*Kathleen Eagle*

# CHRISTMAS IN
# THE VALLEY

## Margaret Moore

To my family

## SPICED APPLE JUICE
### from Margaret Moore

36-48 oz apple juice
1-2 cups orange juice
$^1/4$-$^1/2$ cup brown sugar (to taste)
approx. $^1/4$ tsp nutmeg (to taste)
1-2 cinnamon sticks
1 sliced lemon

Heat to boiling. Simmer and serve.


## PEPPERMINT BARK
### from Margaret Moore

1 pkg. (8 oz) semisweet chocolate squares
$^1/3$ cup crushed candy canes (about 3 medium)

Melt chocolate in heatproof bowl over hot—*not boiling*—water. Remove from heat and stir in crushed candy canes. Spread in thin layer on waxed paper.

When cool, lift paper and candy into airtight container. Break into chunks to serve.

# Chapter One

*Wales—1870*

Gareth Williams lifted his cap and once again tried to smooth down his unruly curls.

"Stop preening, man," his friend Iolo Rhys-Evans chided as they walked along the narrow street of the Welsh village. "Like a peacock you are, and no need."

"Not wanting any coal dust about me," Gareth replied, his expression suitably serious.

Iolo halted and turned toward Gareth, his eyes even with Gareth's broad, muscular shoulders. "I've got no coal dust on my face."

Gareth grinned.

"This will be the last time I go to the tailor for you, if this sort of talk is to be my reward," Iolo muttered when they started on their way again. "That suit is something a deacon would wear. Ashamed I would be to be seen in it."

Gareth didn't bother to comment on Iolo's sartorial criticism. "Time would have been short to get ready if you had not. I was wanting to finish a letter. Never thought it would take so much writing to make a union."

"We must have as many join as we can."

"Right you are there, Iolo. I heard the owner's son is to be the Superintendent of the colliery."

"His *son* the Superintendent?"

"To learn the business, they say."

"Huh! Then we cannot be too fast to get things organized. But you should have asked my sister to run your errands."

"Rhiannon might have taken the favor to mean another favor," Gareth answered, his voice gentle but firm.

Iolo shrugged good-naturedly. They stopped at the butcher's shop to make way for some women coming out the door. Inside, they could see Mervyn Davies and his father bustling about trying to fill orders before the shop closed for Christmas Eve.

"Our Mervyn may not be up to his usual standard for the rugby game tomorrow," Gareth observed. "Exhausted he'll be."

"He said he would be at the open house," Iolo replied, surveying his reflection critically in the window. He straightened his new hat with his good right hand.

"And he will be having too much ale, in all likelihood. Having to have a small chat with him, me."

"It's Christmas Eve, Gareth," Iolo protested. "I know you're the captain but—"

"But we want to win, don't we?"

Two girls passed by, carrying baskets full of holly with which to decorate their homes for the holiday. They eyed the two young men, and Gareth gallantly tipped his cap. The gentlemanly gesture caused the girls to burst into giggles before they hurried onward.

"Famous you are, Gareth," Iolo said, his face somber although his dark eyes were full of laughter. "Think now, if you would only enter for a solo in the *eisteddfod*."

"Pride goeth before a fall," Gareth quoted sagely.

In truth, Gareth would rather cut off a limb than stand alone and sing in front of an adjudicator at the annual festival of songs and poetry. A choir of neighbors and friends was one thing. But alone? Never.

"A pity it is you won't join us singing on the street to-night, either," Iolo said when they left the main road through the village.

"Not wanting to catch a chill running about the streets in the middle of the night."

"Your voice will be missed, Gareth."

"I will do my singing at the open house."

Iolo nodded, content, until Gareth reached up to try to smooth down his curls again. "Are you trying to drive me mad?" Iolo demanded.

"Did I not hear you telling Mervyn there would be plenty of pretty girls at your house tonight?"

"There will be, and now I'm wondering what I was thinking, inviting you. The women flock around you like bees to honey." Iolo sighed as if the troubles of the world sat on his shoulders. "There would have been hell to pay from Rhiannon had I not."

"Wanting me to stay home, and let you go to hell?"

Iolo shook his head. "No. We must have the best tenor in the valley to sing."

Gareth smiled contentedly. If Iolo only wanted him to sing and drink and eat, and he did not have to talk, he would enjoy himself. He would let Iolo, who had a rumbling bass voice, shine in his glory for the young women. And let him talk to them, too.

There had been only one girl who had ever touched his heart and she had left the valley years ago.

The stones of the street were cold against his shoes as they hurried on. Gareth pulled up his tweed collar against the wind. The cloth scratched his freshly shaven cheeks, and he felt like a little boy going to chapel. His mother had always scrubbed his face as if his entrance to glory depended upon it.

The windows of the houses they passed cast bright light through their frosty panes. From inside came the sounds of merriment and the smells of celebration—wassail and cake and strong, homemade ale.

They reached the cottage of Iolo's family, a small building perched on the mountain far above the village, the colliery, the blackened water of the river and the slums of the Irish.

Here, the air was clear and fresh. Music and rich laughter spilled across the night, and voices called greetings to the young men when they entered the cottage and stamped the snow from their boots.

"Needing a drink, first, before the singing," Iolo said. "To the kitchen, Gareth, for some ale." He frowned gravely. "Oh, I am forgetting the rugby team is to have dry throats tonight."

Gareth punched Iolo playfully on the arm. "One or two glasses won't matter," he said.

Then he heard a laugh. Rich and full and lovely as the call of the nightingales in the mountains it was, the kind to make you want to laugh, too. A woman's laugh, of joy and friendliness and a deep sensuality that was to the ears what velvet is to the touch.

Gareth's breath caught in his throat and he slowly wheeled to look into the crowded front room. Holly and mistletoe decorated it. A Yule log burned in the hearth. The sounds of a harp and piano mingled with the talk.

He noticed nothing except the young woman standing near the window, silhouetted in the lamplight. No queen in all her finery looked more regal and more lovely than Kitty Maude Jones did at that moment.

A red ribbon which matched the ruby of her lips bound her dark hair. Her shining gray eyes glowed with frivolity above a shapely nose and a delicately pointed chin. The pink of her plain silk blouse was like the bloom on her cheeks. One slender hand rested on the back of the chair where Iolo's old uncle Sion sat, and the other hand lifted a glass of wassail to her lips.

A shaft of joy and desire and pain shot through Gareth while he watched her, filled with envy for even the glass that touched her beautiful lips.

So, Kitty Maude Jones had come back, and come back a woman, no longer a girl with a quick laugh and quick temper who had sat near him at the little village school, and him too shy to say a word.

Several times he had been caned for not minding the teacher because he had been staring at Kitty Maude's bowed head of dark hair, the white, slender nape of her neck, even the graceful way she wiped her slate.

But it had not only been her beauty that touched him. She took care of the younger children, and on the days some of the poorer ones came to school with no lunches, she had given away her own.

He recalled a time when some of the older boys had teased young Morgan for the patches on his clothes. How Kitty Maude had flown at them, her eyes blazing and her cheeks burning with indignant passion! He had been ready to strike the boys himself, but there had been no need. Kitty Maude's words had proven just as effective—and perhaps more so— than any blows.

How much he had wanted to speak to her then! To tell her how good she was, how noble, how brave.

He had said nothing.

Suddenly Kitty Maude looked toward the door, her eyes widening as if something or someone had startled her. For an instant he feared he had made some sound, but nobody else seemed to notice if he had.

She saw him. Gareth practically bolted toward the kitchen.

Iolo's sister, Rhiannon, stood beside a large oak table and handed him an ale. With an eager, flirtatious smile, she let her fingers brush against his.

Although Rhiannon was a plump, merry girl with twinkling dark eyes and a ready laugh, she would never be anything to him except the sister of his best friend and workmate, because Rhiannon thought only of herself.

Unfortunately, Rhiannon's hopes were as plain as a Welsh Not, a board tied round the neck used in the schools to punish children who forgot and spoke their native tongue.

"Winning the game tomorrow, do you think?" she asked. "It may be a long, cold day."

The annual Christmas Day rugby game would go from after breakfast until dark. Rhiannon's prediction about the weather was likely to prove correct, but Gareth smiled anyway. "We will win. Mervyn is a good forward."

"Is he?" she replied with little warmth. "There is good. You will surely be beating the other team then."

"We will all be doing our best."

"And the choir in the *eisteddfod,* too. Grand, you'll be getting. A pity it is, though, Gareth, you won't enter the competition for a solo. Winning for sure, I am thinking."

"Uncle Sion wants some ale," a young woman said.

Gareth stood still as a pillar of coal when he heard Kitty Maude's achingly familiar voice.

"Of course," Rhiannon replied with a surfeit of sweetness. She took hold of Gareth's arm in an iron grip and turned him to face Kitty Maude. "Remember Gareth?"

He found himself looking into Kitty Maude's limpid gray eyes. Like clouds they were, which promised welcome rain from the summer's heat, or the mists of the mountain.

Then—oh, with a look that kindled flames long banked—she said, "Yes, I do. How are you, Gareth?"

"Good. I am good," he managed to say.

"Kitty Maude's going to Canada. She's staying with her uncle Hywel until she leaves. Week after next, isn't it?" Rhiannon asked, sly as the serpent in Eden.

There came a flash of indignant fire to Kitty Maude's eyes that Gareth remembered well. "Yes."

"Is that so?" Gareth said, his voice calm although a coldness like the inside of a tomb numbed his heart. He took a gulp of ale that went down his throat the wrong way, and he began to cough.

Rhiannon grabbed his sloshing glass while Kitty Maude pounded on his muscular back.

To be asked if she remembered Gareth! Kitty Maude mused angrily. Why, she had been aware of him before she saw him, as she had when they had been at school together, even though he never said a word to her.

She had often observed him surreptitiously in the school-yard. He was the younger boy's champion, the first picked for the games and the unquestioned judge of disputes. It wasn't his size or his muscles that made him a leader there, but his unwavering, absolute sense of justice. Everyone recognized it and knew Gareth could be counted on to decide what was right and fair.

The teachers had also discovered a core of inner strength in Gareth Williams that could not be made to yield to injustice. One day an English teacher had berated a child named Tafline who arrived at school with holes in her stockings. She had fallen, Tafline tried to explain. Afraid, she spoke in Welsh. The teacher had commanded that she stand in the corner of the yard the whole rainy day with a Welsh Not around her thin neck. Gareth Williams had approached the teacher and told him Tafline would catch her death if she stayed outside. He would take her place.

Very calm and quiet Gareth had been. The teacher ordered Gareth to his class and told Tafline to do her own penance. Instead, Gareth had escorted Tafline to the door of the school as if she were a princess and he her knight, and then had returned to the yard to stand in the corner.

The teacher said no more, and miraculously Gareth did not fall ill. The next morning, though, Tafline's father and six brothers called at the school. People said the teacher would be on crutches for the rest of his life, but everyone knew that if Gareth had not taken Tafline's place, the man would have been dead.

How could she forget such a boy, now a man whose fearless eyes made her heart race in response?

"Enough!" Gareth cried, straightening. "You are going to have me black and blue!"

Kitty Maude promptly moved away while Rhiannon clutched his arm firmly.

"Mrs. Rhys-Evans' ale is strong," Gareth remarked.

"She says strong men need strong ale," Rhiannon replied coyly. She handed Gareth another glass and straightened the lapels of his jacket, incidentally shoving Kitty Maude out of the way with her broad hips. "Iolo says you're the strongest man in the colliery."

"You are a coal miner?" Kitty Maude asked. She struggled to keep disappointment from her voice. Gareth Williams had been one of the cleverest scholars in the village school. There had even been talk of his parents sending him to be a solicitor or a doctor. She had often wondered what had become of him, but she had never expected Gareth to waste his mind in the colliery.

"Yes, he is a cutter," Rhiannon said. "Oh, I was forgetting you don't approve of miners."

"It is the work I hate. The men I pity."

"Why pity?" Gareth demanded.

"The danger."

"Every job has a danger."

"Not like that one."

He shrugged. "It is a place to work, like a factory, only darker."

"My da and my brothers were killed in the colliery," she reminded him. It had been one of the worst accidents in the history of the valley. "Brought up in a box that sat light on the men's shoulders."

Gareth looked about to reply, but before he could respond, Rhiannon spoke. "Miners make a good wage," she offered, her hand still on Gareth's arm. "And there's accidents in factories."

"So that makes the dangers no account?"

"We are forming a union to improve things," Gareth said quietly.

"Tell that to the widows and orphans," Kitty Maude retorted. She marched from the kitchen.

When she reached the parlor, she paused awkwardly. Old Uncle Sion was looking at her with disappointment. She had completely forgotten his ale.

Gareth came into the room, a glass of ale in his hand. She refused to acknowledge him, even though he walked straight toward her. Disregarding her, he handed Uncle Sion the ale, then moved silently across the room. To her relief, of course.

Someone started to play a familiar tune on the piano. Soon the whole room was singing a Christmas carol in rich harmony.

In the blending of splendid voices, Kitty Maude detected a melodious tenor whose tone seemed to reach out and caress her. She glanced at the corner from whence it came—and encountered Gareth's steady gaze.

She looked away quickly, remembering her resolution to have nothing to do with miners. To give your heart to one was to live in fear or poverty all your days.

But even as she fought to ignore Gareth, Kitty Maude's resolve weakened.

If only Gareth was not...Gareth. If only his eyes had not said so plainly that he admired her, until she had found out he was a miner. If only she did not feel as if she had been half-dead these past years and only come back to life when she saw him standing in the door. And if only she didn't suddenly sense that to go from here would be to leave a part of her soul behind.

She wanted to marry a man who would live a safe, clean life above the ground, not a fellow who might die suddenly in an explosion or accident. Or die slowly because coal dust clogged his lungs.

Not even if he was bold, strong and handsome, with eyes full of fire and passion.

Mervyn Davies entered the room and made his way to her rapidly. Everyone expected Mervyn, a good-looking fellow, to take over his father's shop. Uncle Hywel and Aunt Olwen had been hinting in no very subtle way that Kitty Maude could do worse than marry such a fine young man.

But there was no promise of anything except pleasant, predicable geniality in Mervyn's face. Nonetheless, Kitty Maude smiled sweetly and let him stand beside her while they sang.

Then she realized Gareth had gone.

Gareth was trying not to get drunk in the kitchen.

He was very tempted to drink himself into a congenial frame of mind, but he had the rugby match tomorrow. The team from the ironworks in the next valley had several members who weighed at least two hundred pounds, so it was no game to be played in a fog. One slip and you would be trampled in the mud—where Kitty Maude Jones, with her gray eyes like stars of morning and her ruby lips, wanted to consign honest men making an honest wage.

Rhiannon pressed against him, her breasts hot and heavy on his arm. "Warm in here, it is," she whispered in his ear. "Needing some air, me."

He took another drink. "Go and get it."

"There is cruel you are, Gareth Williams," she said, pouting. "Wanting some company is all."

Gareth was sure Rhiannon would stick to his side like a burr all night and try to get him alone sooner or later, so he pushed away from the wall and headed for the door, Rhiannon close behind.

Outside, he looked at the stars, little dots of light in the coal-black sky. Voices singing in the house and from the other cottages nearby sounded like choirs of unseen angels.

Rhiannon pulled him toward the shed at the back of the garden where her father and brothers washed after work.

Gareth planted his feet firmly on the path and lifted her fingers from his arm. "Wanting to have me killed?" he asked, his tone as icy as the ground beneath their feet. "Your father would take a shot at me if he found us alone in there." *Or make us marry,* he reflected sourly.

"We can say we were only fetching more ale," Rhiannon tempted.

"No. You wanted air. I am going inside."

"To make a fool of yourself staring at Kitty Maude Jones?" she asked savagely.

Gareth didn't bother to respond.

"If you speak to her, I will tell Iolo you tried to get me alone in the shed!" Rhiannon warned.

Gareth turned around slowly. "You would lie?"

Rhiannon sauntered close to him again, her eyes greedy and her smile bold. "Gareth, don't you like me?"

"Not so much now as I did before," he answered.

"Because of *her?*" Rhiannon asked contemptuously.

"Because of what you have said and done and threatened to do."

"Have you got another cask?" Iolo called from the doorway. "Parched we are in here from the singing."

Ignoring her brother, Rhiannon marched toward the house. Gareth went to the shed and fetched the ale, all the while telling himself he certainly could and would forget Kitty Maude Jones.

After all, she was once more leaving the valley. He would never see her again.

# Chapter Two

Kitty Maude rose cautiously, trying not to disturb her younger cousin Elizabeth, whose bed she shared. Her cotton nightdress provided little warmth in the chilly room, so she drew her thick woolen shawl around her shoulders. After tiptoeing across the cold, bare wooden floor toward the frost-covered window, she raised the sash.

She watched the bobbing light of the torches the men and boys carried as they dashed about the streets. Their boisterous laughter and joyful singing made her smile.

She might have known better than to try to sleep on Christmas Eve, she thought wryly. The custom of caroling long into the night before the early-morning Christmas service was not so strong in Cardiff. She had forgotten how long the young men and boys of the villages would carry their torches and how loud they would sing, especially on a bright, moonlit night.

Occasionally doors would open and groups of singers would be invited into a house for oatcakes soaked in broth or hot milk, cakes, cold meat and, of course, ale.

Her uncle entertained such a group now. They had come to the door after Kitty Maude had already gone to bed. Nevertheless, she knew some from their voices. Iolo, thick from drink. Mervyn, high with excitement. A few others she recognized. And one that made her heart race and her body warm despite the frigidity of the room.

In the street, a group of young men who had been conferring on a nearby corner started to sing. Kitty Maude drew warmth from their fellowship. It would probably be difficult for *them* to leave the valley. Like Gareth, they surely had many friends here. Perhaps their families had lived on the surrounding mountains for generations, too.

Their families had not been destroyed, leaving a mother and her only surviving child to make a living somehow. Their mothers were probably at home in cozy cottages preparing for Christmas Day, not lying beneath the frozen ground, dead too soon from worry and overwork.

Suddenly Kitty Maude had the distinct sensation that she was being watched. She glanced over her shoulder at the bed, but Elizabeth had not stirred.

Then she realized someone was in the doorway. "Uncle Hywel?"

"No."

Gareth Williams stepped inside the room. He closed the door.

"What do you think you are doing?" she demanded quietly. "My uncle would kill you twice to find you here."

"Will you go again from the valley?" he asked urgently.

"Are you mad, Gareth? They will have me judged by the deacons!"

"I would not let anyone try to shame you, Kitty Maude. But I must know. Is it true?"

"Of course it is. I have had enough of death and coal, Gareth. I am going far away."

"There is a pity."

"What I do should matter nothing to you."

"It does."

He stepped into the light that came from the open window. A wintry blast blew into the room, reminding Kitty

Maude that she had on nothing more than her shawl and her nightgown. "I . . . I shall call my uncle."

"No, I will go."

Neither one moved toward the door.

"I have loved you since the day you defended little Morgan at school," Gareth said after a long moment, his voice full of anguish. "Do not go from the valley again."

When she did not answer, he reached out and with arms made strong from his work, embraced her fiercely. His lips found hers, and kissed.

Such a kiss! His mouth took hers firmly, possessively, as if she had always been his and always would be.

For the first time she realized that there had only been one man she wanted for her husband and he was kissing her. With no thought of shame, or the deacons, or her uncle and the others below, Kitty Maude returned the kiss. And the passion. And the possession.

Their tongues entwined and their hands touched and caressed. She felt the strength of his body beneath the rough tweed of his jacket and delighted in the motion of his hands on her back. He slipped her shawl from her shoulders.

Then Elizabeth stirred in her sleep.

"There is ashamed you should be, Gareth Williams," Kitty Maude whispered anxiously, slipping from his grasp.

"I am not." He touched her cheek. "Nor are you. Promise me you will not go."

She was tempted to give him her word. But . . . "Would you give me your promise to quit the colliery?"

He looked at her for a long moment, then turned and left the room. The cold air—and his silence—pierced her like a knife as she stared at the back of the door.

She should be horrified that a man had dared to come to her room, and she only in her nightclothes. She should be shocked that he had the effrontery to close the door. She should be angry that he had kissed her. She should be ashamed that she had enjoyed his kiss and his caress so much.

Instead, almost unbearable disappointment overwhelmed Kitty Maude. Slowly she went to the window to close it, the carolers a nuisance now.

Her gaze went to the pithead and the slag heap, the mound of loose refuse from the mine that grew steadily higher every day, blighting the beauty of the valley.

Above the music, she could hear the machinery that kept the colliery pumps going. Like a whisper of a heartbeat they were, but a heartbeat of death, not life.

She looked at the snow-capped mountains and fought the memories of the long, desperate wait at the top of the colliery pit, the broken bodies of her family and the grief-stricken wails of her mother.

The group of singers left the house, Gareth among them, and Kitty climbed back into bed.

Yes, she must go from here. Away from the mines. And the power of the mountains that could snuff out a life so quickly and so mercilessly. The mountain and the coal didn't care if a man was handsome or young or strong or admired.

It would kill him anyway.

As soon as the sky lightened, Kitty Maude stopped staring at the ceiling and got out of bed. She dressed and helped little Elizabeth put on her good clothes before going downstairs to the kitchen.

Aunt Olwen and Uncle Hywel were there, and the kettle already boiling.

"Come you, I mustn't be late for chapel this morning of all days," Uncle Hywel chided gently.

Kitty Maude drank her tea, the only thing she would have until after chapel.

Scrutinizing her teacup, Kitty Maude asked, "How do you think the valley men will do at the rugby?"

"With Gareth Williams for captain, we cannot lose." Although Uncle Hywel would never permit himself the sinful luxury of attending the Christmas Day rugby game, he still cared greatly about the outcome.

"Gareth Williams, is it?" she asked innocently.

"An excellent young man. A model he would be, if he would only come to chapel."

"He doesn't? Why?" Kitty Maude braced herself to hear that Gareth had taken to drink or prizefighting or some other loathsome pursuit that would tell her he had truly fallen from grace.

Uncle Hywel sighed. "Mr. Powyss-Jones."

Kitty Maude put down her cup. "The minister?"

"An orator he may be, but having no sense sometimes. When Gareth's parents died of influenza, he told Gareth it was the fulfilling of God's holy will. Dear me! Gareth shouted such blasphemy, the people heard him in the streets. After that, Gareth wouldn't come to chapel anymore."

"Oh."

"I fear he will be getting himself in trouble soon."

"Why?"

"The union could mean strikes and hardships and bad feelings." Uncle Hywel sighed softly. "Perhaps it is well you are leaving Wales, Kitty Maude. Change is coming to the valley and no man can see which way it will lead. But enough talk of trouble. It is Christmas Day."

The chapel windows glowed with the light of the candles women had made to adorn it. Many had been intricately decorated with twisted bits of colored paper. Kitty Maude had made a candle, but she did not look around to compare hers to the others.

She was too afraid that if she did, she would encounter the steadfast gaze of Gareth Williams.

He was here because it was Christmas Day, surely. It could be nothing else, so there was no need for her heart to pound like a piston or her hands to shake.

Uncle Hywel sat at the front beaming at the young man. He would have had a much different expression if he had come upon them kissing in his house.

Here, now, Kitty Maude could easily imagine how terrible it would be to be called to the front of the chapel to face the board of deacons and be denounced as a Magdalen and cast out.

Gareth had said he would not let her be shamed, but he could not give back her good name in the eyes of the townspeople once it was taken away.

Of course, she was leaving the valley, although that had not been in her mind when he kissed her. Nevertheless, she should have stopped him and not stayed in his arms, with his mouth so warm and soft and firm on her own....

When the service finally ended, Kitty Maude lingered in her pew. She wanted to commit to memory the texture of the cover of the hymnal, the sensation of the hard wooden pew at her back, the scent of the candles and the soft voices of the people. Soon, very soon, she would be gone from here and it might be a long time before she could return. Perhaps she never would.

Suddenly a great and terrible loneliness filled her.

"Kitty Maude, my little one, come here!" her uncle called, breaking into her maudlin thoughts.

She gave him a smile that slipped away when she saw Gareth Williams towering over Uncle Hywel. Gareth's expression was solemn, but there was a boldness in his eyes and a look as if they shared a secret.

He might contrive to have her shamed yet.

She was tempted to flee the chapel, but that would be a capitulation, so she straightened her shoulders and walked toward them intrepidly.

"Kitty Maude, this is Gareth Williams," Uncle Hywel said.

"How do you do?" she asked stiffly.

"Very well, thank you, Miss Jones."

"Kitty Maude is going to Canada soon. There is a pity, for the place is surely full of heathens. But no one can sway her mind."

"Perhaps you could let me try."

Kitty Maude raised her eyebrow, an arrow of anger in her glance. "I had heard you were sick, Mr. Williams," she replied, a hint of a defiance in her voice. "In the head."

"Oh? Not too sick to play today, I hope?" Uncle Hywel asked solicitously.

"I am quite well, Mr. Jones."

"It is a relief to my heart," Uncle Hywel replied cheerfully. "Well, no doubt you'll be wanting a good breakfast. Honored we would be to have you."

"Honored I will be to join you."

Kitty Maude stared at the floor and tried to think of some excuse to avoid breakfast.

Uncle Hywel started to give Gareth advice concerning the team from the next valley. Kitty Maude sensed an opportunity to flee and took it without pausing to see if Gareth followed her. Outside, she quickened her pace until she was almost running along the frozen road.

"Kitty Maude, wait! Going to exhaust me before the game," Gareth called behind her.

"Not caring one bit if I do, you bold devil!" she cried, turning on him. "Talking to my uncle as sweet as you please!"

"I wanted to be introduced to you properly."

Kitty Maude glared at him. "What?"

Gareth halted beside her and took a deep breath. "Well, thanks to God for stopping at last. I said, I wanted to be introduced to you properly, so I can court you."

"You *are* a devil! You know that I am going from this valley. I do not wish to be courted by you, introduced or no."

His smile would have been infuriating, if she had not seen true longing in his dark eyes. "That was not what was in your kiss last night."

"To hell with you, Gareth Williams." She spun on her heel and strode away.

"We are organizing a union to improve things at the colliery."

"Good for you."

"Things will get better. You will see. Safer."

"I do not care about your union. I am leaving the valley."

"Are you coming to see the game?"

"No!"

"Kitty," he pleaded softly, pulling her into a narrow alley between two shops.

"Take your hand from my arm or...or..."

"Kitty." He lowered his head.

"I will scream...." He was going to kiss her. "Gareth..." She did not, could not, fight her building desire when his lips met her own.

He drew back and caressed her cheek. "I will promise to leave the colliery if you will promise to be my wife."

The silence stretched between them, broken by the soft beating of the mine pumps and the rattle of the tram full of slag. She stepped away, confused by her own emotions and the suddenness of his proposal.

Without a word she turned and hurried toward her uncle's house.


Apparently unconcerned, Gareth watched the wagons bearing their opponents come to a halt at the edge of the field used for rugby football.

A light snow had been falling since the dawn. Puddles of sheer ice dotted the scored and pitted field. Groups of boys, many of whom were clearly dreaming of the day the honor of the valley would rest on their shoulders, scrutinized the players from the sidelines. The ironworkers were huge, with muscles on muscles.

Sweethearts of the lads on Gareth's team also waited nearby, seated on straw in carts or wagons with blankets around them and baskets of provisions. During the day, other villagers would come to encourage their team and bring fresh hot tea and the ubiquitous ale.

Gareth commanded himself to think only of his team and the game, but he was feeling like a man seeing his future slip from his fingers as water slides over a smooth stone.

Kitty Maude had said almost nothing to him all through breakfast and wouldn't even look at him.

Stupid he had been, going to her room last night, although he had been desperate to find out if she meant what she said, or if she could be persuaded to change her mind. If only she would stay, she would soon learn that things were going to change for the miners.

Even then, he had not meant to kiss her. He was not sorry he had, for that kiss had told him plainly that Kitty Maude cared about him, in spite of her harsh words.

Perhaps the most stupid thing of all had been to say he would promise to quit the mine. He and Iolo had been working long and hard to establish a union. If he left the colliery, he would lose his credibility as the leader of the miners.

The referees, one from each valley, took their places to begin the match.

Gareth stepped onto the playing field and looked toward his team's goalposts—to see Kitty Maude Jones sitting in Mervyn Davies's father's wagon.

She wore a hooded cloak that hid most of her hair. Over it she had wrapped the shawl she had worn the previous night. He could well remember the texture of it beneath his hands when he held her, and the sensation of her body against his.

So, she wasn't coming to the game? Or not until Mervyn asked her?

He tore his gaze away and fastened it on the hapless Mervyn, who, if truth be known, was every bit as shocked as Gareth to see Kitty Maude on his father's wagon. Pleased he was to have the prettiest girl in the valley there, until he saw the look in Gareth's eye—a remnant from the days of fighting the Roman invaders, of terrorizing the encroaching Normans and of rebelling with Llywelyn, the last true Welsh prince.

"There is surprised I am," Mervyn said, his voice a whine. "Not expecting to see Kitty Maude today, with her uncle a deacon."

"No matter," Gareth replied coolly, pleased by Mervyn's discomfort. And angry at himself for letting a woman distract him.

Gareth went to his position determined to think only of winning.

Unfortunately, during the game he was all too aware of the presence of Kitty Maude. He noticed when she shifted her position in the wagon, ate, drank or cheered. His attention strayed to her before every play and when his team scored a goal. He saw how her eyes glowed with excitement and how her cheeks grew more rosy in the cold afternoon air.

By now, the field was no longer frozen. The players' feet had rendered it as muddy as a river bank in the spring. They made two disastrous plays and Kitty Maude got down from the wagon.

Gareth's feet slipped. He fell heavily, dragging the other players with him. One of the men from the other team, whether by accident or design, stepped on his arm.

The referees called a halt to the play immediately. Gareth pressed his lips together to stifle a moan, the pain in his arm excruciating as his teammates carried him from the field and laid him in a wagon—until he saw Kitty Maude running across the field paying no attention to the mud splashing on her clothes or the players taking their positions.

The doctor, who had been attending the game in case his services were needed and because he was an avid rugby enthusiast, quickly and competently examined his patient. "Not bad, considering," he announced. "An arm broken. It's been snapped like a dry twig, so setting it will be easy."

Across the field, the spectators cheered loudly. "Davies has scored!" Dr. Powlett cried excitedly.

Gareth, however, was no longer interested in the game, or even his arm. Kitty Maude stood beside the wagon and she held his hand in hers. "I thought you were not coming," he said.

"Uncle Hywel wanted to know how the game went."

"So you had to stay all day?"

She blushed very prettily and her long dark lashes brushed her cheeks. He shifted a little closer to her and winced.

"Does it hurt bad?" she asked softly.

"Not so much as my heart will if you leave the valley again," he answered, his voice low but so intense that she knew he meant it as much as a man could mean anything.

She looked down at Gareth's mud-spattered face and bruised cheek. His jersey was in tatters about his muscular chest. And his eyes ... His eyes shone with such yearning that a lump came to her throat and her heart fluttered like the wings of a bird flying to freedom.

She stroked his hand. How could she go where he would not be? She would never see his face or hear his voice or witness his eyes taking fire when he saw injustice. She would never feel his lips on hers, and his hands on her body.

"I promise I will quit the mine, if you will be my wife."

Her resolution to leave the valley wavered, then disappeared. She believed he meant what he said, and Gareth Williams was a man to keep his word. Happiness blossomed inside her and she bent down to kiss him.

The doctor suddenly turned back to his patient. "What is this I am seeing with my own eyes?" he demanded.

"It is nothing wrong, Dr. Powlett," Kitty Maude answered. "We are going to be married."

Gareth's face broke into a wide smile. He pulled her toward him, unmindful of the people gathered around them, and he kissed her deeply.

Across the field, Iolo and Rhiannon and several other spectators stared. "I will tell her uncle of this shameful behavior," Rhiannon said bitterly.

"Do, and I will tell our father about that night you never came home 'til the dawn," Iolo replied firmly, burying his disappointment and ache for what he had always known was a hopeless dream. "Gareth and Kitty Maude were meant for each other."

# Chapter Three

*One year later*

Dismayed, Gareth looked around the kitchen in the dim morning light. The fire in the stove was out and Kitty Maude was nowhere to be seen.

He rubbed his tired eyes and called her name, albeit half-heartedly. Perhaps she had gone to her uncle's. No doubt she was angry because of last night.

He had held what he had hoped would be a short meeting about the union in their parlor. He had done his best to keep the discussion on the necessary subjects, but trying to stop Welshmen in the heat of oratory was not something easily done. The men had stayed and stayed, arguing until very late. Then he had drafted a letter to the man trying to organize the ironworkers. He had fallen asleep with the pen in his hand.

Now he had to hurry to be at the colliery or he would be late for his shift.

He turned when the door to the garden opened suddenly. The pale light of the early winter's morning illuminated Kitty Maude against the backdrop of the snow-capped mountains. "Where have you been?" he asked.

"Did you have a good sleep?" she retorted. She shoved the door closed.

He sighed wearily. "The meeting went long and I had a letter to finish. I must get to the colliery. Have you got no food ready for me?"

"Here," she said defiantly with a toss of her thick black hair. She banged his tin food box on the table. "You will be too tired. You could have an accident."

"Or I will not be cutting as much as I should and I will be fired. Then you would have your wish and I would have no job," he answered sarcastically. "Not getting too hopeful, I wouldn't be. The men would strike if they fired me."

She sniffed. "For one man?"

"If you would meet them, you would see how we stand together. That is the way of a union."

"Does the union love you, then?"

"What do you mean?"

"You will give your life for them in the mines, and what will they give you in return? Is there no other man in all the valleys who could lead the union except you?"

He pulled her into his embrace. "How could I represent the men who go below if I am not one of them?"

Kitty Maude stiffened in his arms. "If you will not keep your word, Gareth, I will not keep our wedding vows. I will leave you."

He barked a mirthless laugh as he drew back. "Again?"

Kitty Maude's expression was determined. "I mean it this time, Gareth. I will do what I say I will."

"I know you don't mean it. I've told you, I will keep my promise when I can."

"That day will never come."

"Yes, it will. Besides, I will be safe as long as I have Iolo beside me. Often he's given us enough warning of gas for everyone to get out until the air was clear. This is our home and these are our people, Kitty Maude. They need me."

"*I* need you. Alive. And all you can say is that I should have no fear because of Iolo."

"Things are going to be different," he insisted.

"What of cave-ins?"

"Old Mr. Ransford agreed to use more timbers for props before he went to London," Gareth replied, although her question reminded him that he must soon speak to young Ransford about the poor quality of the wood.

"No child, you, but a grown man. You did not promise to keep your word whenever *you* were ready." She raised her chin defiantly. "I have taken the chickens to Davies the Butcher just now."

Gareth stared at her, a shaft of apprehension lodging in him at the mention of this practical detail that told him she was making no idle threat. "Ah, now, Kitty-oh-Kitty," he said, wrapping his strong arms around her waist as if he would hold her there.

"If you will not keep your word now, if your union and your job are more important than me, I am leaving on the next train to Cardiff and then I will go as far away from coal as I can."

"You cannot mean it. You love me as much as I love you. You won't go. I have lost count of the number of times you have said you would and yet here you are still."

Kitty Maude faced him, her eyes burning not with rebellion, but with passionate intensity and great agony. "Gareth, every day you leave me to go down into the pit, I am so filled with worry, I can hardly think. Can't you see that we are growing further and further apart? Or must I go away to make you see the distance already between us? I will not wait to see your back bent and hear you coughing. I know that one day I will stand at the top of the pit expecting to see your corpse.

"When you are at the colliery, all I can hear is the wail of my mother's grief in my ears, all I can think of is the poor broken bodies of my father and brothers." Her voice grew soft. "They hadn't been killed quick in the explosion. They had been crushed."

Suddenly Gareth was afraid. Not of the colliery or an accident, but that today there would be no reprieve. "I cannot quit right now. Wait until after Christmas, and we can talk again. I promise."

"If you wait any longer, you will be late for your shift," she said flatly.

He reached for his jacket and cap and put his hand on the latch of the door. "I love you, Kitty," he whispered hoarsely. "I need you. Do not go."

Because he simply could not believe his loving wife would leave him, he went out, shutting the door softly behind him.

Kitty Maude went to the door and watched her tall, strong husband stride along the street.

Her gaze roved over the houses. Dirty water trickled along the gutters of the cobblestone street. Mrs. Rhodri next door uselessly cleaned the coal dust from her windows. Children played on the side of the slag heap.

Pressing her hand against the hardly noticeable rounding of her stomach, she wondered if she should have told Gareth she was having a baby. Surely he would not want his children growing up in filthy streets with a coal tip for a place to play.

She would not bring a child into the world to face what she had faced—the anxiety at the pithead, the grief of a mother widowed too young, the worry of trying to survive on what a woman could earn.

Besides, if Gareth would not keep his word for her sake alone, what kind of marriage did they have?

Taking a deep, ragged breath, Kitty Maude straightened her shoulders. No, it was better to go and let him have his colliery and his union.

Then she saw Gareth's food box, left on the table. She grabbed it and ran to the door, but he had already gone around the corner at the far end of the street.

* * *

Gareth strode toward the mine, still trying to convince himself that Kitty Maude's threat was an empty one. They loved each other too much for her to go.

Didn't they prove it nearly every night—when he wasn't busy with his union work—by making passionate love? They could not share their bodies the way they did, so freely and so completely, if there was not deep, abiding love between them.

Besides, Kitty Maude would know it would be a terrible scandal. Her uncle would have told her what had happened when Kyna Powlett-Jones, who was not married, had a baby. Her whole family had been forced out of the valley.

No one would blame Gareth for his wife's action. Kitty Maude would bear the brunt of gossip, because no decent woman ever left her husband. While she might give any excuse she wanted, all would suspect it was because Gareth would not quit the colliery. They would have little sympathy for a woman who expected her husband to give up a good job.

He struck his fists together as if he could silence gossip with a blow. His hands were empty. He had left his supper sitting on the kitchen table. He paused, wondering if he should go home and fetch it.

Then he heard someone weeping behind a nearby shed at the back of a tavern. He didn't hesitate, but went to investigate.

He found a young girl huddled on the ground. Her dirty, ragged clothes barely covered her thin, shivering body. Her arms encircled her knees and her shoulders shook with her sobs. No more than thirteen, he guessed.

"Can I help you?" he asked softly, crouching beside her.

She lifted her face. Her tears had streaked the coal dust on her cheeks. Obviously she was one of the girls who worked in the mine, and judging from her rags, one of the

Irish who lived in the hovels closest to the river where the ground was always damp and the air unhealthy.

The girl shook her head, her eyes suspicious, her nose red and dripping, her thin lips blue with cold.

"Come now, you can tell me," he said kindly. "What has happened to make you cry?"

"You are Gareth Williams," she said, slightly awed, "that's making the union."

"Trying to. Trusting me, then, is it?"

"It's...it's Mr. Ransford. He's going to take away me job, and me dad's dead and me mam's sick from the last baby."

"Why is Mr. Ransford going to take away your job?" he asked quietly.

"Because I...because I..." She started to weep again.

"Does he think you are not working hard enough?"

She gave him a sidelong glance and her eyes showed anger and dismay. "I can work as good as any of them."

"Then why?"

"He had me come to the Superintendent's office. I thought I'd done wrong...."

"And?" he prompted gently.

"Just Mr. Ransford was there."

"Oh?"

The girl's face filled with fear—very much like Kitty Maude's every day when he left for the colliery. He concentrated on the girl. "What did Mr. Ransford say?"

"Nothing."

Gareth sat back on his heels. "Nothing?"

"At the first. He...he touched me."

Gareth's hands became fists.

"I started to cry, and he said if I didn't do what he wanted, I would lose my job." Her head sank so low, it almost touched the ground. "I would not," she sobbed.

Gareth stood slowly and struggled to control the blinding fury and complete loathing within him. He believed the girl because he had often seen Ransford watching the pit women when they came from their shifts, not something a Superintendent needed to do. The women avoided him, although he was young, rich and handsome in his English way.

And Mary Dowlais's father had abruptly taken her from service in Ransford House after bragging for days about her fine new position. Mary said nothing, but there were stories of bruises and a narrow escape from a fate worse than death.

Gareth reached into his pocket and handed his handkerchief to the girl. "Dry your tears." He took out some coins, all that he had. "Take this, too, for a Christmas present, is it?"

She stared at the money in her small hand. "It's not Christmas yet."

"Almost."

The girl wiped her eyes. "Don't be telling Mr. Ransford I told, will you?" she pleaded. "He will take my job away for sure."

"Leave Mr. Ransford to me," Gareth said firmly. "Go home now."

"Thank you," she answered softly.

Gareth strode away toward Ransford House.

Gareth marched to the front door of the mansion. Large it was, and very English there in the valley. Out of place, like young Ransford himself.

A maid of about fifty answered the door. "Deliveries at the rear," she said curtly, by her accent English.

"I want to speak to Mr. Ransford."

"I don't think—"

"Please to show me in."

When she still delayed, he pushed his way past her. He gestured toward a sitting room filled with furniture upholstered in rich plush velvet, potted plants and a variety of small porcelain figurines on delicate tables. "Is this where I should wait?"

The maid looked about to faint. "No! I should say not! If you must intrude, follow me to the library."

Gareth flashed his most gallant smile and the maid thawed a little as she pointed to a book-lined room. "I shall inform Mr. Ransford. Whom shall I say is waiting?"

"Mr. Gareth Williams," he replied in the same way a man might have said the Prince of Wales.

The maid gave a displeased frown and went out, closing the door.

Gareth surveyed the room with mingled admiration and disdain. It was well proportioned, with dark paneling and shelves filled with leather-bound volumes. There was a desk and overstuffed chairs. Heavy damask curtains covered the window and hid a view of the blackened river and dead vegetation along its banks. When he was a boy, he had fished in that river.

"What do you want?" Ransford demanded ungraciously from the door.

Gareth faced the Englishman who came into the room.

From the sneer on Ransford's face, it was obvious he shared the maid's low opinion of the man in his library. Ransford had to know he was addressing a man who quite probably worked for him. A man his own age, in fact, had he cared to look a little closer, and one who was responsible, by the labor of his strong arms and back, for the clothes the Englishman wore and the fine house in which he lived.

Had Ransford paid attention to the expression in the brown eyes and the scornful curve of the lip of the man before him, he might have had the wisdom to hide some of his natural arrogance. However, he did not, so he repeated scornfully, "What do you want?"

"I am Gareth Williams. From the fifth pit."

Ransford put the desk between himself and the brawny young man with the intense gaze. Ransford actually felt quite frightened, until he remembered there was a gun in the drawer of his desk. He searched his memory and recalled that Gareth Williams was an agitator and unionist—and he was married to that astonishingly beautiful young woman he had seen in the village.

"I have come to invite you fox hunting," Williams announced.

Ransford sat rather abruptly, his hand touching the handle of the drawer.

"Fox hunting," Williams repeated. "Englishmen enjoy fox hunting, don't they? And we got plenty of foxes in the hills."

Williams crossed his arms deliberately when Ransford remained silent. "Hate foxes, do Welshmen. They prey on the helpless lambs, you see. No reason, sometimes. Except the lambs are weak and the fox is strong."

Williams's voice was cold and deliberate and inexorable as death, although perfectly reasonable. There could be no mistaking the fellow's meaning, however, and Ransford wondered which woman had talked. She would be dismissed the moment he found out.

"So we rid our valley and our hills of what would hurt and terrify the weak and helpless."

Ransford rose. "I appreciate your kind offer—"

"Nor would I try to hunt alone. Accidents can happen, see, to a man in the mountains."

"I was . . . I was planning to find you, Williams. There is a position available in the office. A clerk's position. I understand you have finished school, and it has occurred to me that you would be a fine candidate for the job."

"A clerk's position? In your office?"

Ransford smiled. "Yes. It would pay twice the salary you currently earn now."

"Twice the salary for pushing papers over a desk compared to what I earn risking my life in your mine every day?"

"Are you telling me you don't want the job?" Ransford asked incredulously. "I understand you are a recently married man, Williams. You should think of your wife and any family you hope to have."

Gareth did think of Kitty Maude and wavered. She would be happy if he were not working underground.

Yet if he took this job, he would be beholden to this swine. He would be giving his tacit approval to this man's actions. The thought was so abhorrent that Gareth didn't even answer. He simply left the room, more convinced than ever that his place was with those who worked in the colliery.

Ransford's hand still trembled as he opened the drawer and removed his gun. He replaced it. One gun would be useless against an angry mob if this fellow decided to make a fuss over some pit women.

His father never should have forced him to come here, he thought bitterly. It was a waste of his talents, his education and his abilities. He had only tried to find some kind of compensation for the indignity of the lowly position of Superintendent. Now his life was apparently at risk because of a few lower-class drabs.

Perhaps it was time to go to London and relate the truth of the matter to his father before these local agitators made trouble. Yes, that was the thing to do.

Besides, it was nearly Christmas, and surely his father would be happy to have him for the holiday.

"Gareth! You're going to be late, man," Iolo called out, studying his approaching friend and taking in everything from the missing food box to his righteously indignant countenance. Gareth told Iolo about the Irish girl and his meeting at Ransford House.

"That blackguard! To offer the job, Gareth!"

"I would sooner slit my own throat than have to be grateful to such as him. Say nothing of this to the others until we see if he takes the warning, or we will have murder on our hands as much as if we had killed him ourselves.''

"It would get you above ground, though," Iolo said thoughtfully. "Kitty Maude would be happy."

"I will keep my word to Kitty Maude soon enough."

"You had another quarrel, didn't you?"

"She said she's leaving me."

"Again?"

Gareth managed to grin, but it did not reach his eyes.

"Wishing I had a pretty wife to be angry with me. Bad luck it was, bringing you to the house last Christmas Eve," Iolo said.

"Maybe it was."

Iolo glanced at his companion. "The Joneses are all hot-tempered, Gareth. She's never meant it before."

Gareth's expression did not change.

"She will be at home later. If she's still angry at you, you can join us at the Barmaid's Arms."

"If Kitty Maude is home, I will not be wasting my time in the pub."

Gareth and Iolo arrived at the pithead and joined the line of men waiting to be taken below the surface in the cagelike elevator.

"No supper, Gareth?" Trefor the banksman observed.

"Left it sitting on the table." Gareth climbed into the cage to descend with Iolo and some of the other men on his shift. "Set us down like velvet, boy," he called.

Trefor grinned and started to work the mechanism that lowered the elevator to the main tunnel. Gareth held his breath at the beginning of the plummet, anticipating the slowing of the cage. As always, he experienced the strange sensation that they were returning up the shaft, although they were continuing their descent.

The cage came to a stop with a thump. Carrying their Davy lamps, picks, shovels and food boxes, the men scrambled out into the dank dimness of the lowest level.

Gareth and Iolo walked along the narrow space beside the tram rails to the seam they would work. Around them they could hear other miners digging and the loud beating of the pumps that brought fresh air and took away the water that would flood the mine if not removed.

Gareth removed his jacket and shirt and crawled into the tunnel. Iolo, behind him, did the same, throwing his clothes over the side of a tram cart.

A few years ago, Iolo had been a cutter, too, until his left arm had gotten crushed between two trams. After that, Gareth had asked that Iolo work with him, filling the trams with the cut coal. It was usually a task for boys, but the Superintendent had agreed because Gareth did the work of two men.

Lying on his side, Gareth dug out the coal with his pick and pushed it along to Iolo. While he worked, he thought of Kitty Maude, and the sorrow in her eyes, the fate of her family and the unyielding rigidity of her body.

He told himself he had no reason to feel the guilt that flashed through his soul. He had promised Kitty Maude he would quit the colliery as soon as he could, and he meant to do so.

She simply didn't understand. Although more miners were beginning to sense the benefits of standing united, there were still too many in other valleys who were unsure. He did not want to desert the men who were looking to him for leadership until the union was a reality.

Especially with Ransford as Superintendent. His father had gone to London, leaving his son in charge, and that was proving to be a mistake. The senior Mr. Ransford was tough, but he was just and respected for it. Young Edward Ransford was arrogant and demanding, although he clearly knew next to nothing about the day-to-day operation of a coal mine.

No, Gareth thought, he couldn't leave the colliery yet.

But was he willing to spend his life lying on his side in the confines of a seam, cutting coal for a man like Ransford, who got rich from the labor of men, women and children? Apparently their labor was not enough for him, either. He wanted to possess their very flesh.

What kind of man was *he*, that he could ignore the promise he had made to the woman he loved to make money for Ransford? To be sure, the union was important, but it wasn't more important than Kitty Maude.

He had given Kitty Maude his promise. What did she ask, after all, but that he keep his word?

With sudden resolve, he backed out of the slender shaft. "Iolo!" he called softly.

"Yes?"

"This is my last shift."

"What is that you are saying?"

"I will not come down again."

Iolo gaped at him. "You are not taking the job Ransford offered, are you?"

"I have decided I must keep my promise to Kitty Maude."

"What of the union?"

"You can lead it, and I will help you all I can."

"Kitty Maude will be home," Iolo protested. "She always is."

"No. She meant it this time, Iolo. I am going home at once." Gareth regarded his friend, sad he would not be working with Iolo again, but sure he had made the right decision. Finally.

Iolo clapped his hand on his friend's shoulder. "I suppose it is about time, after all. Have no worries about me. If Ransford takes my job, I will ask Mervyn Davies if he needs a driver for his wagon." He winked. "Mervyn will be wanting to keep on our family's good side—" Iolo cocked his head.

"What is it?"

"Something is wrong," Iolo replied quietly.

Gareth gathered his clothes and his tools. "Gas?"

"Do you hear that? Like a creaking?"

"No."

"Get the others." Iolo said urgently. He ran toward the cage. "We got to go up."

Gareth joined him and they called to the other miners on the shift to flee. They knew of Iolo's second sight when it came to danger and obeyed without hesitation.

Two cages full of men and boys returned to the surface, until only Iolo and Gareth were left waiting. The empty cage rattled swiftly down the shaft, Trefor obviously understanding the need to hurry.

"What's that?" Gareth asked breathlessly. "Is that what you heard?"

Iolo shook his head.

Gareth muttered a curse. "It's Evan Evans." He started back along the main rail and scanned the darkness for the boy of twelve.

He saw a figure crouched beside the wall, trembling.

"Evan!" he called quietly. "Come on, boy. Out with you."

Evan, unmoving, stared at the support across from him. A crack in the wood widened before their eyes.

Gareth pulled Evan to his feet and shoved him toward the cage. "Go!"

A low rumble reverberated around them. Evan needed no more urging. Clouds of coal dust swirled over them.

Gareth sprinted for the elevator. Then he tripped on a piece of wood left lying beside the rail and fell.

# Chapter Four

Kitty Maude stood on the platform of the train station, clutching her valise and ignoring Uncle Hywel, who watched her balefully from his place behind the ticket counter of the station. Others awaiting the train were at the window. They whispered and pointed at her with frank curiosity.

Uncle Hywel had been shocked when she told him she was going to Cardiff and had asked all sorts of questions that she had refused to answer. Obviously he suspected she was leaving her husband, because he had awkwardly tried to warn her about scandal and gossip. She had been tempted to explain, but she had not. If Gareth did not understand her reasons, no one else would, either.

Gareth could say what he liked after she was gone. It would not matter. She would never come back. Could never come back. Not from fear of scandal, but fear of her own weakness. Last Christmas she had given in to Gareth's pleas and his promise, and it had taken her far too long to realize that he would never keep his word.

If only she had not met Gareth again, she would have been gone on this very train a year ago. If only he had not been as she remembered him, and more. If only she had not married him, thinking she could persuade him to change.

If only he had kept his promise.

Angrily she dashed away a tear that fell on her cheek. She would not cry here. Not now. Maybe when she was alone in the train where there would be no prying onlookers.

She looked along the track. The Cardiff train was late. She might have known it would be.

She stamped her feet to warm them and pulled her large woolen shawl tighter. What would Aunt Ceridwen say when her niece came knocking on her door? No doubt her visit would not be an overly welcome surprise, yet they would not turn her out. They were family, and it was Christmas.

Kitty Maude set down her valise and rubbed her kid-gloved hands together. Inside the station it would be warmer, but inside would be Uncle Hywel and the others.

The train would not be long now, and soon she would be on it. Leaving here. Leaving the valley forever.

She turned slightly to have a last look at the village. The smoke from several chimneys drifted upward toward the mountains.

A movement caught her eye. Someone else was buying a ticket from Uncle Hywel. The young Englishman, the son of the colliery owner. She returned to surveying the tracks.

"Good day to you," a smooth, very proper English voice said behind her. "It is Mrs. Williams, is it not?"

"Yes, it is," she replied, each word a piece of ice. She was affronted that young Mr. Ransford had spoken to her at all. They had never been properly introduced and she could feel his bold, impertinent scrutiny. He wouldn't dare do that if Gareth was with her.

Undoubtedly the gossips inside the station would make much of this chance meeting. She could imagine the story that would fly through the village, straight to Gareth's ears.

"Allow me to introduce myself. Edward Ransford, at your service. Going on a holiday visit without your good husband?"

Kitty Maude tightened her lips. "Yes, Mr. Ransford."

"It is a great pity your husband is not a far-seeing man."

"Oh?" He saw years ahead to a united force of miners working in the valley; however, she had no desire to discuss her husband with this Englishman.

"I thought he would be happy to take the clerk's job I offered him."

"The what?"

"He didn't tell you? I suppose he didn't have time," Mr. Ransford replied patronizingly. "He came to my house this morning to talk of a business matter. I offered him a position in my office."

Why would this man offer a known unionist such a thing? "What was it Gareth wanted to see you about?"

Ransford's gaze slipped from her face. "Business, as I said."

The man was hiding something. It must be important if Gareth had seen fit to go to Ransford House when he had to get to the colliery for his shift—something that made this man worried enough to try to bribe Gareth when surely even Ransford could see that Gareth Williams would sooner lose his hand than take a bribe.

Whatever slight respect Kitty Maude had for the mine owner's son dwindled to nothingness. "He prefers the colliery," she said calmly.

"Does he? Well, the price of coal appears to be dropping this year. It may be that some of the men will have to be let go."

"Mr. Ransford," Kitty Maude said, giving him a look she would have given a rat had it dared to show its snout in her kitchen, "are you trying to tell me about your business, or is there something more pertinent to me in your words?"

"I was merely trying to offer you and your husband a word of advice. I cannot say what might happen to a man's job if he has refused an advancement, especially over the lies of a dolly-mop."

Venom was in the man's voice, and fear. Gareth must have gone to Ransford House because he had found out a truth in the rumors circulating through the village.

She could see Gareth now, the calmness of his controlled fury on his face but the burning anger of righteousness in his eyes. Protecting the weak was what he was destined to do, made to do, meant to do. It was why— She gasped as a realization struck like a blow to the core of her heart. It was why she had loved Gareth Williams since they had sat together in the village school.

Kitty Maude smiled at Ransford, ignoring his surprise at her expression. "In other words, since he prefers to do honest toil among his friends than go to work in the office, you will take away his job?"

"I never said so."

"You meant it just the same. I have heard you have been to Oxford, Mr. Ransford. If that school teaches you to let one of your best cutters go and to believe all those who work in the mine with him will simply say, 'So be it' and not stand by him, you are very much mistaken. The union..." She took a deep breath. "*His* union would not allow it."

She heard a rumble and felt the ground shake. She peered along the track.

A whistle shattered the winter's serenity. A long, loud, mournful blast. Not the train.

Accident! At the colliery!

Forgetting Ransford, her uncle, her valise—everything except Gareth—Kitty Maude lifted her skirts and ran from the station.

"Iolo?" Gareth called softly.

Silence.

He took a deep breath and tried to calm himself, but he choked on the coal dust clogging his throat.

He was trapped. At least he wasn't dead.

Not yet, anyway.

He had no lamp and could see nothing in the darkness. But that was good, in a way. The lamp's flame would have taken too much of his precious air.

His head ached. Gas? No, or he would be unconscious still, or dead. He tried to move, but a sharp pain shot from his foot, almost making him faint. Feeling along his leg, he encountered the unmistakable stickiness of blood. He attempted to pull his foot free slowly. A sickening, frightening sound of shifting rock told him to lie still.

Surely those who had made it to the top would come for him before the air was gone. Provided the elevator still worked and it could get to the bottom of the shaft. Hopefully the rubble was not too thick between this cavity and the main shaft. Surely the rock would hold while they rescued him.

Using his hands, Gareth learned the extent of his dark prison. A support had fallen across the shaft. For a miracle, another had collapsed in a similar manner and together the two wooden posts supported the space where he sat upright. He also felt an opening the width of his fingers at shoulder level and could only hope it reached through the fallen coal toward the main shaft so he would not suffocate.

Had Evan and Iolo made it safely to the top of the shaft? Were there others here, like him, alive? Or dead? He must find out. He struck the rocks beside him with a lump of coal in an syncopated tapping. Anyone hearing would know it had to be a man.

Nothing except the sound of his own breathing. No one could hear him, or was able to answer if they did. It was as if he were the last creature left in the world.

It should not be so quiet. He should be able to hear the pumps. If they were not working, no fresh air could come into the mine and the shafts at this level would eventually fill with water.

The men had to get through to him before he drowned. Or bled to death. Or suffocated.

He fought a wave of panic. He had been about fifty feet from the shaft when he fell. Perhaps only a small wall of fallen coal and muck separated him from freedom.

He started to dig. Once again, though, he heard more rock falling, and he realized that without anything to make supports, he might merely do harm.

He had to wait.

To stem his growing dread, he lay against the coal and forced himself to think of something other than the terrible danger he was in.

Kitty Maude and the last night they had been together. Lying in their bed with his hands behind his head, he had watched her brush her long dark hair. How it shone in the candlelight!

Despair rose again in his heart, but he pushed it away. He must believe he would be saved and he would think only of Kitty Maude.

Her rosy soft lips that he could never kiss enough. The gentle curve of her dark brows and the way the right one would arch when she was puzzled. The silkiness of her skin. The soft swell of her round breasts in the palms of his hands. The little catch in her breath when he caressed her. The dimples in the small of her back, and how she laughed when he licked them. Her delighted, seductive expression when she discovered how her own tongue could arouse him.

Her determined resolve when he left her today.

Did she know what had happened, or was she already gone from the valley on the Cardiff train? If so, she would be spared another terrible wait.

She had worried about this so long, and he, pompous, stupid fool, had always thought her worries groundless.

Who was right now, boy? What good was his broken promise doing for his men or his union or him? He had convinced himself that what he was doing was necessary for the miners and that he needed to be one of them to make a difference. He had even dared to believe himself their savior.

Alone in the dark, he admitted the truth. He had secretly delighted in the respect and admiration of the colliery workers. He had enjoyed the fear in Ransford's eyes.

Nor had he been willing to confess the true reason he did not want to leave the valley. His people had been here for centuries. The rocks of the earth were a part of him, the streams of the mountains the blood of his body. He was afraid to face the future in an anonymous place where his ancestors had never walked and no man knew his name.

But now, here, alone in the dark with the water seeping around him, he knew something more terrifying than leaving the valley, or being trapped in a cave-in.

It was never seeing Kitty Maude again.

If he got out of this alive, he would keep his promise. If Kitty Maude had already gone to Cardiff, he would follow her and beg for a second chance. For Kitty Maude, he would leave his union and his beloved valley forever.

If death did not take him first.

Along the road to the colliery, Kitty Maude joined a throng of frightened women and unnaturally silent children. A mass of unspoken, unknowing dread, they pushed through the gates and did not stop until they reached the pithead.

A man she knew from chapel, named Trefor, worked the controls of the shaft elevator, cursing and sweating with anxiety, his face ashen. Around him a group of men spoke in hushed, worried voices. Kitty Maude could tell by their blackened faces that they had just come from below. Several miners stood nearby, their wives and children clinging to them with obvious relief. Despite the whisperings of the crowd, it was strangely quiet. She heard no steady beat of the pumps. She knew that without the pumps, there would be little air in the lower levels. And the water would rise, too.

"A cave-in, it was."

"The lowest level."

"No explosion, thank God."

Kitty Maude scrutinized the crowd desperately, searching for Gareth. But she could not see him, or Iolo.

She did see Rhiannon and moved toward her. Rhiannon's chin trembled as she shook her head.

Trefor's muttered prayer of thanks caught Kitty Maude's attention. Her heart seemed to stop as the machinery creaked and groaned and started to function. The elevator came slowly into view.

Out first came young Evan. Then Iolo, coughing and choking.

Kitty pushed her way through to him. "Gareth. Where is Gareth?" she demanded anxiously, grabbing hold of Iolo's hand.

"Below," he said, coughing fitfully. "Went for Evan. He fell—then the roof give way."

"You left him?" she asked in a horrified whisper. A vision assaulted her of a body crushed and broken and without life. Not her father or her brothers this time. Gareth. Gareth, dead. "You must save him!"

The people parted to let Ransford through. "What has happened?"

Iolo stepped forward, his eyes narrow slits of rage. "The supports—the *useless* supports—gave way. We all got out but Gareth."

"Everyone should leave the area," Ransford said, so calmly it was an insult. "We shall investigate this matter immediately after Christmas Day. Trefor, you and the other mechanics will have to stay to get the pumps working again."

Ransford turned away as if there was no more to be said or done.

Kitty Maude barred his way. "What of Gareth?"

Ransford shook his sleek English head. "It is too dangerous, I'm afraid, Mrs. Williams. I would not be willing to risk the men until the pumps are working."

Kitty Maude stared at him in disbelief. "Not meaning it, are you? Gareth is there! You *must* send men to find him!"

"And since when you been caring about risk, Mr. Ransford?" Iolo asked. "I for one will go, and gladly."

Young Evans tried to pull free of his mother's restraining hand. "And me! I will go for Gareth!"

All around Kitty Maude, other men began to offer. Even the Irish, who lived apart, did not go from the colliery.

Still Ransford shook his head. "Without the pumps working, the water—"

"To hell with the water!" Kitty Maude cried defiantly. "I will not leave here until my husband is brought out."

Iolo and many of the others came to stand behind her, picks and shovels in their hands.

Ransford glanced at them uneasily. "My dear, he is probably already dead."

Kitty Maude felt a shaft of ice pierce her heart, but she straightened her shoulders rebelliously. "When my husband is found, and I know he will be, I am going to tell him I am so proud he refused your office position, I could burst. And when I tell Gareth how you looked at me at the station, you will be lucky if you get away with your life."

"We are going down, with or without your permission," Iolo said, just as determined and tough as iron.

"I will call the police."

"Do as you wish," Kitty Maude replied. "Good day, *Mr.* Ransford!"

Ransford took one look at the people gathered around her and elbowed his way out of the gate.

"My fault, it was, Mrs. Williams," Evan said, trying manfully not to cry. "He come to get me, see, before—"

"A good boy you are, Evan." Kitty Maude approached the lad. "Thank you for your offer, but you have had enough this day," she said quietly.

Evan's mother's eyes shone with gratitude.

"It might be you'll be needing someone small to get to him," the boy continued intensely.

Kitty Maude shook her head. "Not you," she said, although she knew Evan could very well be right. She straightened, suddenly sure of what she had to do. "I will go below."

Iolo took hold of her arm. "Kitty Maude! That is not necessary. Plenty of us are willing. You stay here."

She thought of the baby she carried and lowered her head, prepared to agree.

Then she raised it. She was young and healthy and strong. Dr. Powlett had told her so. She was still slim, too. She would be careful and have faith that all—all—would be well. "I am smaller than any of you. And no one here loves Gareth as I do. It is my right and my duty to go. It will be my joy to save him."

Iolo gave an assenting nod, which made her proud. "Evan," he said, "give her your trousers. There is no time to be lost if the pumps are still."

"We will be doing what we can to get them working again," Trefor called out immediately. He hunched over the machinery like a troll at his craft.

Kitty Maude took off her cloak and gave it to Evan's mother. She wrapped it around her son, who wriggled out of his trousers and handed them to Kitty Maude.

"Your fine silk blouse..." Mrs. Evans whispered.

"Does not matter in the least." Kitty Maude started toward a nearby shed to change her clothes. She paused and turned to the waiting crowd. "Go home, please. It is too cold to wait. We will give a blast of the whistle when we have Gareth safe."

She hurried inside the shed and took off her short jacket and the skirt she had worn for her journey. Everything, in fact, except her drawers, chemise and blouse. She drew on the boy's trousers and tied them with a piece of rope lying nearby.

When she came out, she saw that everyone still stood expectantly. She blinked back tears at their silent solidarity and went to Iolo at the cage. Two other miners were beside it.

"Is this all who are coming?" she asked Iolo.

"Too risky to take more, see? Without the pump, air will be scarce, so there's me to warn about gas, you for size and these two hulking brutes to dig. We can send for more as we go."

Rhiannon hurried to them, a tin food box and a flask in her hands. "Take these. The flask is just water. We've sent the boys to fetch beer and brandy."

Kitty Maude stared at the food box. Gareth had eaten no breakfast and he had forgotten his supper. It might be hours before they could reach him. Hours with no food or drink.

For a moment unable to speak, she nodded her thanks at Rhiannon, who smiled tremulously. "Finding him you will be, and God go with you."

Taking a deep breath, Kitty Maude grabbed the lamp Iolo offered her and crawled inside the elevator. Iolo and the others followed.

The elevator lowered them into the darkness, the shaft as black as the pits of hell.

"Good a time as any to have introductions," Iolo said quietly, his familiar face ghoulish in the dim lamplight. "This is Hu Merthyn—you saw him in the rugby game last Christmas. Scored the first goal."

Kitty Maude nodded a greeting.

"And Dafydd Evans-Ennion, sings bass in the choir."

Dafydd, holding stout pieces of wood to use for supports, touched one to his forehead in acknowledgment.

Suddenly the cage shook to a stop. Iolo peered into the darkness. "Just right," he said, and jumped.

They heard a splash. "Come, you," he called out. "No gas, and the water only to my ankles."

Kitty Maude climbed from the cage into the hot, humid tunnel. The water was not deep, but it was frigid. The air was stuffy and close, and warmer than she expected.

Iolo pointed.

They all stared at the wall of rubble ten feet in front of them.

# Chapter Five

The rescue party toiled for hours in the depths of the Rhondda valley.

Although the pumps were not functioning completely, some started to move fresh air into the upper levels. It seeped into the area below, allowing more men to join Kitty Maude, Iolo, Hu and Dafydd as they dug farther along the main rail. Even then, because of the continuing danger of cave-ins, they proceeded with excruciating slowness.

Iolo said hopefully that perhaps Gareth was in a cavity along the tramlines, where the supports were strongest. If there were openings throughout the debris, he could have enough air to wait for them.

For the present, the problem was not so much the air as the rising water and unseen gas.

Iolo, followed by a man Kitty Maude knew only as Emlyn, backed out of the narrow tunnel into the larger open space where Kitty Maude crouched uncomfortably in knee-deep water, her trousers in shreds and her blouse a tattered rag that clung wetly to her tired arms and back.

"See how far you can fit in there," Emlyn said to her softly. They spoke in whispers, always mindful that a loud noise might cause more rock to fall.

Another muddy, sweat-soaked man crawled into the opening from the direction of the elevator shaft.

"Ransford's come back. With some police."

Although her nerves were already as taut as the strings of a harp, Kitty Maude felt another sickening surge of dread.

"He said he was going to make sure the mine was shut down 'til after Christmas."

"He cannot!" she protested.

Iolo took her hand and gave it a companionable squeeze. "He dare not."

The man grinned, his teeth white in his face. "We sent them off. Him and his English police!"

Relief flowed through Kitty Maude, but it was short-lived. Perhaps she was being too selfish in her concern for Gareth. These men were risking their lives. Now she worried there might be trouble for those above. "I hope no one is going to be jailed or hurt."

"We are all in this together, for Gareth," Iolo said softly. Hu and Emlyn nodded.

Suddenly Iolo touched Kitty Maude on the shoulder. She looked at him with a smile that rapidly disappeared when she saw the anguished expression on his face. "Gas!" he said urgently. "I'm sorry, Kitty Maude. We got to get out."

Emlyn and the rest of the men began moving back immediately, casting sorrowful glances at Kitty Maude.

"Go on up," she said to Iolo. "I am staying. Gareth is here. I know it."

"Kitty Maude!" he protested quietly. "The gas."

"He is not dead! I would feel it in my heart if he were." She grabbed a pick and scrambled into the opening barely a foot tall. She did not begrudge the others their safety and was grateful for what they had already done, but she was not leaving without Gareth.

Surrounded by the rock, her heart pounded as if it would explode and her hands trembled as she crawled forward. Pushing fear from her mind, she went on until she arrived at the farthest end of the tunnel. Her fingers traced the end of the small opening the men had found.

She ignored the pain of her bleeding knees and hands and strained to listen. Iolo had told her Gareth would tap on the rocks, if he was conscious.

If he was alive. If the gas had not reached him first.

Silence. She lifted the pick and tapped.

Nothing.

"Oh, dear God, send me a sign," she prayed aloud. "Like the Star of Bethlehem. Please!"

Fighting panic and an overwhelming sense that it was already too late, she put her lips to the opening. "Gareth!" she called as loudly as she dared. "Gareth!"

The cold water, creeping constantly higher, had reached Gareth's waist.

He pressed his teeth together to still their chattering. A blanket of snow would have been warmer, and more helpful. This water didn't numb the pain in his foot, nor could he drink it to ease his thirst.

Against his will he thought of the river. It had sparkled in the sunlight like the jewels in the tiara of a queen before the colliery had poisoned it.

He forced himself to listen once more for the sounds of a rescuer. Several times he had heard noises that gave him a brief hope. It might have been merely the settling of the rubble, but he knew he dare not lose hope or he would be as good as dead. Yet no answer had come to his signal.

He did not want to die. Not now. Not buried in the coal, alone in the dark. Not without telling Kitty Maude of his decision. He couldn't bear the thought that she might never know he had been on the verge of keeping his promise.

What would become of her?

She would be left a widow. Her uncle would offer her a home, unless she chose otherwise, so she would not be left destitute.

Probably someday another man would ask her to be his wife. Some other man would live with her. Eat with her.

Watch her brush her lovely hair. Make love with her. Give her children. . . .

Rage and jealousy against this imagined suitor consumed him and he moved abruptly, as if he was trying to keep the man at bay. To his shock, his foot suddenly came free. He threw his arms over his head and waited for the roof to crash down on him.

There was some slight movement of the rubble, but not much. Renewed hope replaced his anger and he shifted a little higher, wincing with the pain his action caused.

He was so hungry and thirsty! Visions of Kitty Maude's sweet cakes, her delicious stew and the oat bread she baked every second day drifted through his mind, so real he could almost smell them.

He concentrated on keeping his breathing shallow and regular to preserve what was left of his air.

Then he heard a soft noise. A whisper. A caress. His name.

Maybe in his last moments on earth his mind was playing tricks, because it had sounded like nothing so much as Kitty Maude calling him.

It was nearly Christmas, the celebration of a miracle. He would have confidence in what he had heard. He grasped a lump of coal and tapped again on the rock.

Kitty Maude didn't dare to breathe while she listened. No, she hadn't imagined it. The taps were not rhythmic as dripping water would be. Nor were they arbitrary, like falling rubble. It had to be a signal. A blessed sign.

"Gareth!" she called again, fighting the urge to shout. She grabbed her pick and beat a similar rhythm. "We are coming! We are coming!"

She twisted around as far as she could and raised her voice as loud as she dared, wondering if there was anyone to hear her. "He is alive! We are almost to him!"

"By the saints!"

Iolo had stayed.

Iolo joined her in the tunnel and helped push back the muck and coal that Kitty Maude frantically loosened.

She choked back a sob. How could she ever have wanted to abandon a place where there lived such steadfast, loyal friends? She didn't any longer and she would tell Gareth so when he was safe in her arms.

Then Gareth's mud-streaked face appeared. Stifling a cry of relief and joy, Kitty Maude tugged at him with all that remained of her strength.

His strong arms enveloped her in a crushing embrace. "Kitty, Kitty," Gareth murmured as he held her tightly. Of all the things he had dared to hope, he had not imagined Kitty Maude down the shaft to greet him. How brave she was to come for him.

He drew back, ignoring the pain and the dampness of blood on his leg to look into her face.

"Gareth, we must hurry. Gas," she said through her tears.

"A stubborn woman you have married, man. Out with you, now," Iolo ordered from somewhere farther down the tunnel.

Gareth obeyed at once. Following Kitty Maude, he crawled along the narrow tunnel. More blood dampened his trousers and the agonizing throbbing increased, but he knew they dare not stop.

Kitty Maude paused to wait for him when they reached a larger space. "You are hurt!"

"Not bad. Go on," he ordered.

"No," she said firmly. She put his arm on her shoulder and supported him. "I will not leave you again. Not here, and not ever."

He saw the unyielding stubbornness in her eyes and heard the conviction in her voice. Today, he blessed her for them. Her perseverance had saved his life.

When they reached the main shaft, they found Iolo and the cage waiting. Gareth tried to stand up, but he couldn't put his weight on his injured leg. Iolo slipped under Gareth's other shoulder. "You are eating too well," he muttered as he helped him into the elevator.

"Not today." Gareth sat down heavily. He stretched out his injured leg and pulled Kitty Maude to sit close beside him, his arms around her slim shoulders.

Iolo got inside and signaled Trefor to bring them up.

"Never thought I'd see you again, Iolo," Gareth said softly as they rose slowly to the surface.

"And have us lose the rugby captain and the best tenor in the valley all at once? Don't talk foolishness, man."

"What is wrong with your leg?" Kitty Maude asked anxiously.

"My foot was pinned. It is nothing. Oh, Kitty, I was afraid I would never see you again! I was on my way out. I will keep my word. I will quit the mine."

She shook her head. "I was wrong, Gareth, and selfish it was of me to ask you to quit."

"Selfish it was of me to break my promise."

"I was too stubborn. I should have listened."

Iolo shifted, reminding them of his presence. Kitty Maude smiled at him. "You must like stubborn people, Gareth. You should have seen Iolo telling Mr. Ransford he would search for you in spite of the man's threats."

Iolo grinned wryly. "No, Gareth, you should have seen Kitty Maude. Some fierce she was, I can tell you. When I warned her about gas, she wouldn't quit, either."

The cage stopped and they climbed out. Just when their feet touched the ground, there was a tremendous explosion below. The cage shook like a dog worrying a rat in its teeth. Smoke billowed up the shaft as if it were a chimney. They hurried away, coughing.

The waiting crowd broke into a cheer. Kitty Maude's eyes filled with tears not just from the stinging smoke, but also with appreciation of their loyalty. Gareth smiled broadly.

"Thank you. Thank you all," Kitty Maude murmured.

Uncle Hywel made his way through the crowd. "Praise be to God! Now for a good hot breakfast at my house. And I am thinking we must have a special service of thanks at the chapel."

Dr. Powlett appeared and took one look at Gareth's leg. "This man should not be standing," he said.

Trefor produced a barrel and Kitty Maude lowered Gareth to sit upon it.

Dr. Powlett made a swift examination. "Another broken bone. Not so clean this time, but you are the fastest healer I ever saw, so we shall be hopeful." He glanced up at Kitty Maude and gasped. "Mrs. Williams, is that *you?*"

"Yes, Doctor."

"What have you been doing?"

"Rescuing me," Gareth answered for her. "An amazing woman I have married."

"A foolish one, I fear, going down there in her condition."

"I am well, Dr. Powlett."

"Condition? What condition?" Gareth demanded.

"She is pregnant."

*"What?"*

Kitty Maude took Gareth's hand in hers. "I—we—the baby and me, I mean—we will be well now you are safe, Gareth."

The people swarmed happily around them, slapping Gareth on the back and offering hearty congratulations. Then, slowly, they fell silent.

Young Ransford, a shotgun in his hands and a force of twenty policemen at his back, marched through the gate. He shoved his way through the crowd and stopped in front of

Gareth. "So, you are alive after all," he said. "Caught in your own sabotage, I suppose."

"That is a lie," Gareth replied slowly. "The damage was caused by your penny-pinching, and you should be thanking Iolo more were not hurt or killed."

"Is that so?" Ransford's impertinent gaze ran over Kitty Maude, from the top of her filthy, matted hair to the ruins of her trousers. "Your devotion to your husband does you credit, my dear."

Gareth struggled to stand up. Kitty Maude, her attention on Ransford's gun, pressed her hand on his shoulder.

"No doubt you will be a faithful visitor to his jail cell."

"Jail?" Gareth asked. "I will not be going to jail."

"We shall have to see what the judge says."

"Wanting to have a strike you are, then?" Iolo demanded. "And you having one pit already useless."

"Bad business, I am thinking," Emlyn remarked.

"The Lord has surely sent a judgment upon you, Mr. Ransford," Uncle Hywel intoned. "I would not be tempting Him any further, lest you kindle His wrath."

"If you strike, you will starve!" Ransford said angrily. A resentful murmur surged through the mob.

"This man needs immediate attention," Dr. Powlett bellowed.

That was all Kitty Maude needed to hear. Ignoring Ransford, she helped Gareth to his feet, dismayed by his pale skin beneath the coal dust. Together, they made their way toward Mervyn's wagon. Young Evan, who must have raced to fetch it, sat beside Mervyn on the seat. Quickly he jumped down to help.

"Don't go yet, Mervyn," Gareth ordered. "I am not wanting any trouble for my sake."

"Your foot..." Kitty Maude warned as Dr. Powlett climbed aboard the wagon.

"Can keep a little bit more."

"No, it cannot, young man."

"I say it will. Or tend to it here, if you must."

"Stop them!" Ransford ordered the sergeant of the police.

The sergeant was not a particularly intelligent man, but it did not take much intelligence to realize that he had only twenty men, and they were facing a sullen crowd of over a hundred brawny miners holding sharp picks and heavy shovels. He lifted his hat and scratched what was left of his hair. "Well, now then," he said slowly. "Needin' doctorin' he is, so not likely to get far. Surely you can press your charges later, eh?"

"You bloody oaf, I want that saboteur arrested immediately!"

"What evidence?"

"Evidence? What are you talking about? My word should be enough!"

"Not feudal times, Mr. Ransford," the sergeant replied coldly. "A policeman needs evidence to lay a charge. The way I see it, this man's been trapped for hours. If he was going to make mischief, I would think he'd have gotten himself away. So you can go home unless you've got something a policeman can use."

Then the sergeant ordered his men to leave, much to their obvious relief.

"*Now* may we go?" Dr. Powlett asked Gareth.

When Gareth was convinced the police were leaving, he nodded his head. The people surrounded the wagon and escorted it through the gate, leaving Ransford standing alone beside the ruin of the fifth pit.

Kitty Maude placed the cup of strong tea at Gareth's elbow on the table in their parlor. His bandaged foot rested on a low stool before him. His eyes were closed and she thought he slept. She watched him silently, drinking in the sight of him like a man nearly dead in the desert quenches his thirst at an oasis.

With a quickness that meant he had been awake for some time, he reached out and pulled her onto his lap.

"A sly boy you always were, even in school, Gareth Williams," she chided, trying to sound angry, but failing.

"You it was always causing problems in the schoolyard with your temper."

She pressed a kiss to his forehead. "And you always fighting someone else's battles."

"Not anymore. Those days are done."

"You can still help with the union."

"Yes, and I will." He held her tighter. "I want to prevent other women and children from having to wait at the pithead because of an accident. Or having a harsh life because of a man's death in the mine."

"Oh, Gareth, what a narrow escape we had! And not just down the mine. If the train had been on schedule—"

"I would have followed you to Cardiff or wherever you went. I had decided to make good my promise."

Her arms encircled him. "I was a fool to believe I could live without you."

"No getting away from me now, Kitty Maude Williams. Even with this foot, I would chase you."

Kitty Maude smiled, her gray eyes shining like the Christmas star. "I would make sure you caught me."

He gently pushed her off his lap. "Much as I am enjoying this, it makes my foot ache."

Before she started fussing over him, he said, "There will be none of this idleness when we have a baby in the house."

"Lazy you are calling me?" she asked with a flash of temper.

"Not at all." He grew thoughtful. "Perhaps I am to be called the lazy one. Not working and—"

"The doctor said your foot will be fine if you let it heal properly. And no spendthrift, me. We will have enough money for weeks yet. My uncle will help us, too, if we need it." She stooped to give him a long, lingering kiss. "You will find work when you are well. You will see."

"I am not taking any charity, Kitty Maude."

"A proud man I have married." She hesitated a moment, then continued. "There is sure to be employment at the colliery for the best cutter in the valley."

"I made a promise to you, Kitty, and was too long to keep it. I will not break it now."

"I am releasing you from it. If the colliery is what you want, I will not stop you."

"I don't want it, Kitty. I have given them my notice." A sharp rap sounded on the front door. Kitty Maude gave Gareth a surprised look before hurrying to open it. When she saw who stood on the step, her eyes widened and she stepped back with a movement that was a combination of a nod, a curtsy and a warning to Gareth. "Come in, and welcome."

Gareth had only seen the senior Mr. Ransford once. Nonetheless, he immediately recognized the gentleman by his well-cut tweed clothes, high collar and black silk top hat. Never had Mr. Ransford visited the home of one of his laborers—and since he was no longer employed at the mine, Gareth was astonished to have the man in his parlor.

Mr. Ransford removed his hat and bowed slightly. "I hope I'm not disturbing you, Mrs. Williams. Mr. Williams?"

Gareth didn't reply as he struggled to stand. This was no moment to be sitting in a chair.

"Please, remain as you were," Mr. Ransford said.

Gareth did not sit although Kitty Maude placed another chair for Mr. Ransford. "Take a seat, if you will," she said. "What is it we can do for you?"

Mr. Ransford brushed imaginary lint from his hat. "First, let me say I am grievously sorry about the accident. I have spoken with the men and I want to assure you that corrective measures have been taken." He coughed and looked away from them. "I have also dismissed my son from the position of Superintendent."

"Good, is that," Gareth replied flatly.

"I have mining interests in the Canadian north, and I think his talents will be better employed overseeing those operations." His gaze returned to Gareth. "I understand you have given notice?"

"Yes."

"I'm sorry to hear it. Perfectly understandable, of course. Regrettable, as I said, but understandable. However, I need a new Superintendent. I have decided it would be wise to hire a Welshman, so I have come to offer this position to you."

"Superintendent?" Gareth could only stare, dumbfounded. He heard Kitty Maude gasp.

"Yes."

Gareth's eyes narrowed suspiciously. "I am for the union, Mr. Ransford. Especially after what has happened, I am surprised you would think of me."

Mr. Ransford cleared his throat. "I know your opinions on labor matters, Mr. Williams. While I cannot promise I will always concur, I do think my son—that is, certain matters were dealt with in a spirit of divisiveness rather than cooperation. I'm hoping I can persuade you to take this position with a view to restoring the previously harmonious relations between labor and management."

"What the men want is reasonable, Mr. Ransford. I will not work against them."

"I will agree to some of their requests. As for the raise in wages, I will do what I can, but I am not responsible for the price of coal set by the marketplace."

"I know. You have dealt fair with us before."

"I am glad someone apparently remembers. I assure you, Mr. Williams, that I realize market conditions were not always explained." He sighed wearily. "The world is changing very rapidly, Mr. Williams. This business is not what it was."

Gareth glanced skeptically at Kitty Maude. "Many things can change in the blink of an eye," he said. "Let me see if I understand you. It is for the men's sake you are asking me to be Superintendent, so they have someone to explain things to them?" He frowned. "Please, sir, I am not a babe. If you cannot talk truth to me, I will never work for you."

"I see you are not a vain, sentimental, impractical man, Mr. Williams." The older man's voice assumed a business-like tone. "Very well, I'll be frank. I can foresee nothing except difficulties and strikes and hardship for me—and the men—if this spirit of hatred is allowed to fester. The only hope I have is to hire someone the men trust to be the Superintendent. Although this job pays considerably more than working the seams, I am not asking you to sell out your principles. I *am* asking that you consider taking this position on the understanding that I am trying to repair the mistakes of the past to ensure a profitable future. I promise to deal fairly with you, as long as you promise to deal fairly with me."

Gareth rubbed his chin pensively. He needed the work, but he had no wish to be perceived as a traitor. Yet as Superintendent, he would learn about the coal business and better comprehend the owner's circumstances. He would know if a problem was a matter beyond the owner's control or a battle worth fighting. The post was tempting—but so had been the apple in Eden.

When Gareth didn't respond, Mr. Ransford looked at Kitty Maude. "Perhaps I can enlist your aid to persuade your husband."

"No," she said at once. "Whatever decision he makes, I will stand by him."

Gareth took hold of her hand. "I will take the position with a caution to you. The first sign of bad dealings, and I will go from there. All the men will hear of my reasons, too.''

Mr. Ransford inclined his head and got to his feet. He put out his hand. Gareth shook it. ''I think we understand each other, Mr. Williams,'' he said gravely. He went to the door and paused on the threshold. ''Thank you, and a merry Christmas.''

A few days later, Gareth struggled into a sitting position in bed.

''What are you doing?'' Kitty Maude asked.

He tugged at his nightshirt. ''Getting this cursed thing off me.''

''But it's Christmas Eve and sure I am that Iolo and the others—''

''Maybe they will and maybe they'll leave us in peace. For a certainty I cannot stand to be wearing this another moment.''

''Then let me help.''

''Good God, woman!'' Gareth yelped when her hands slipped along the naked flesh of his back beneath the nightshirt. ''Call that helping?''

''Yes, I do.'' She began to caress his chest. He gave a low moan and let his head fall back. With a throaty chuckle, Kitty Maude ignored his plea to continue and stopped to pull the garment from his body.

Gareth turned with surprising swiftness and enveloped her in his arms. ''I thought you were worried about Iolo and the others coming banging upon the door for me to join them in the singing.''

''Your foot!'' she cried. ''And you'll wrinkle my best nightgown.''

''My foot is fine and pleased you should be I am not tearing your best nightgown off right now,'' he said with a devilish leer.

Just then the bedroom door burst open to admit Iolo, Emlyn and several other young men.

Gareth roared with dismay and reached for his nightshirt. Kitty Maude pulled the covers up to her chin.

The men carried in a jug that smelled of ale, apples, cake and spices. They had obviously been sampling the beverage, for they could scarcely stand upright.

"What do you want?" Gareth asked sternly, simultaneously sneaking his hand under the covers. Kitty Maude jumped at his surreptitious caress and gave him a warning glance, but she couldn't suppress the laughter bubbling out of her throat.

"If you please, we have come to drink to your health," Iolo announced, as solemn as a druid—if the druid had been drunk. "The wassail, gentlemen."

Trying to maintain a grave demeanor, Emlyn handed the huge jug to Iolo, who saluted the couple by lifting it and nodding at them before taking a gulp of the liquid. Then Iolo returned the jug to Emlyn, who also drank and passed it to the others.

Iolo sat on the bed.

"Careful of my foot!" Gareth warned. "Just got to be healing nicely and not needing you to crush it again."

"Did the doctor say how long you will be lying here like some potentate?"

"No, but I am thinking as long as I can," Gareth replied, giving Kitty Maude such a leer, she wanted to hide her face in the bedclothes.

"No more rugby?" Iolo asked mournfully.

Gareth shook his head. "Not for a long time, anyway."

"Is it true about Rhiannon and Mervyn?" Kitty Maude asked.

"Yes. They are to be married in a month."

"I am happy for them."

"Not so much as me. With a rich brother-in-law, I will not be worrying about finding work."

"Mervyn's not that rich."

"He's offered to loan me money to get my own business. Not wanting me under his feet, I'm sure."

"What business?" asked Gareth.

"I am buying the Barmaid's Arms."

"You will not have much profit if tonight is anything to go by."

Iolo's brow lowered. "It's Christmas Eve, Gareth."

"Yes, it is," his friend allowed.

"Next thing we know, you'll be finding yourself a wife," Kitty Maude remarked.

Iolo's face reddened. "Maybe."

The wassail bowl reached Gareth. "Ask him how Mary Dowlais is these days," Gareth said slyly before he took a drink.

"Shut up, you devil," Iolo muttered.

"And you telling me only the other day I sang like an angel, so I was thinking of entering for a solo in the *eisteddfod*."

"Are you meaning that, Gareth?" Kitty Maude asked joyfully. "Good if you do."

"Giving it serious thought, anyways."

"Then you must join us for a practice," Iolo insisted.

"I'm not dressed."

"No secret, that. Put on your trousers and come." Iolo stood and staggered a little. "Emlyn, lead the way!"

Emlyn nodded and preceded the men out, carrying the jug in his hands as if it were a sacred offering.

Gareth embraced Kitty Maude gently. "I will not go if you would rather I stay."

She smiled wickedly. "Of course I want you to stay—it is Christmas Eve. But Iolo is right. Needing the practice, you."

"Kitty! There is a wound to my pride to hear you say that."

She threw off the covers and got out of bed. "You have pride to spare, so a little wound will not make much of a difference."

"I will not be going anywhere if you are parading like that before me," Gareth said as he lunged for her.

"Do as you wish, but you will be here by yourself. I am going singing." She deftly eluded his grasp and removed her nightgown, ignoring his groan of dismay.

She smiled gloriously. "You have been too long away from your friends. You should go, and I am not sitting alone on Christmas Eve."

"Are you telling me what to do, Kitty Maude Williams?" he asked ominously as he slowly climbed out of the bed.

"Never again," she said, all wide-eyed innocence.

He gathered her into his arms. "You are right and we will go. But not just yet...."


A little while later, Kitty Maude and Gareth dressed quickly and warmly and went to find Iolo and their friends. They had assembled near the chapel and stood stamping their feet in the crisp, cold air. Big white flakes of snow like moist lumps of sugar fell around them.

The men greeted the arrival of an additional tenor with laughter and jokes and another round of the wassail jug.

Iolo, the unofficial leader of the choir, took Gareth by the arm and drew him aside. "Not traditional, is it, to have a woman here?" he whispered.

"No," Gareth agreed. "I will be letting you tell Kitty Maude to go back to the house, though."

Iolo shook his head warily. "Wanting to live to next Christmas, me," he slurred. "A dangerous pred... presci... example, Gareth."

"Aye. Next year Mary might want to join us."

A smile grew on Iolo's face. "Aye, you're right. Well, it is done, so let us sing."

"Did you hear about young Ransford?" Dafydd said excitedly before they could start. "Sent off to Canada. Good riddance to him—but God help the Canadians!"

"Yes, we heard something of it," Gareth replied.

"His father come from London awhile ago," Trefor said. "I was checking the pumps when he come to the mine. Right sick he looked. He said he would hire a new Superintendent."

"He has."

"Who?" Dafydd demanded. "Another relative?"

"Another tyrant?" someone asked angrily.

"Death to the English! Long live the Welsh!" Iolo bellowed.

"He hired a Welshman," Kitty Maude said loudly.

The men stared at her.

"Why would he tell you?" Iolo asked suspiciously.

"He didn't." She squeezed her husband's arm. "He has asked Gareth to take the job."

Gareth nodded, eyeing the men in their turn. "Promised to deal fair with us."

"Heard that fairy tale before," Iolo said, scowling.

Gareth grinned. "He thinks it will be more profitable to work together."

"Now *that* has the ring of truth in it," Dafydd allowed.

"Englishman or not, he is a man of his word. But if you think that would make me a traitor to you, I will tell him no. I promise you all that if I feel old Mr. Ransford is not doing what is well or right, I will speak to him. If he does not agree, I will quit."

"A Superintendent worthy of the name you will be," Iolo pronounced.

The men apparently agreed with Iolo, for the discussion immediately turned to what they would sing.

Gareth put his arm around Kitty and drew her close. The warmth of Gareth's love and the fellowship of the others surrounded her.

"So much there is that is changing about us, Gareth," she said softly. "The mine and more when the baby comes. Let us hold tight to what remains, I am thinking."

"You are right, Kitty-oh-Kitty," he answered softly.

Content, they joined with the others in a Christmas carol. Their harmonious music floated through the village. It rose above the colliery, beyond the valley and up into the mountains to welcome Christmas Day.

\* \* \* \* \*

## *A Note from Margaret Moore*

*Dear Reader,*

Every year, my family converges on my parents' house for a tradition known as "doing the tree."

We start with the lights, specifically the bubble lights, which my folks bought in 1951, a true testament to quality. About five strands of lights go on the tree altogether, however.

Then come the ornaments. My mother has saved every ornament we ever made. I'm not kidding. My poor, old—very old—kindergarten snowman's head finally fell off last year. She fixed it.

In 1976, Mom got into the "collector ornaments," which no doubt explains Hallmark and Hummel's continuing strong sales.

After a check that the tree looks "balanced," we do the tinsel. My parents grew up durning the depression. That's the only explanation I can find for the fact that they reuse tinsel.

By this point, the tree could be made of coat hangers for all anyone can see of it.

Nonetheless, with a sigh of satisfaction, we regard the finished product, a tree decorated not just with lights, ornaments and tinsel, but with traditions, memories and laughter. My father takes a picture—and then, inevitably, we find more ornaments.

*Margaret Moore*

# KEEPING CHRISTMAS

## Patricia Gardner Evans

With never-ending gratitude to my ancestors who had
the foresight to immigrate to the United States.

# CORN CHIP PIE
## from Patricia Gardner Evans

This may not sound like a Christmas recipe, but it has become one for my daughter and me the past few years because corn chip pie is fast and easy to throw together.

The recipe that is the foundation of corn chip pie has been in our family for about fifty years, ever since my great-aunt hired Chief Meyers as the wrangler at her dude ranch. No one remembers what Indian tribe Chief Meyers belonged to, but his ancestry must have included the "tribe" of Texas, because one of his nonequine contributions to the dude ranch was his Texas chili recipe.

*1 lb hamburger*
*2 medium onions, chopped*
*2 cloves of garlic, minced*
*1 qt canned tomatoes*
*1 16 oz can of kidney beans*
*1 tsp ground cumin*
*1 tsp paprika*
*up to 2 tsp ground red chili (or ground red pepper)*
*salt, if necessary*
*grated cheddar cheese*
*corn chips*

Brown hamburger, onions and garlic together. Drain fat, then add undrained tomatoes, kidney beans and spices. Simmer 30 minutes, salt to taste. Ladle chili into bowls, add cheddar cheese and corn chips and stir. Ladle the chili over a bed of chopped lettuce and tomato, add cheddar and round tortilla (corn chips) for a festive taco salad. If you *really* want to get carried away, add salsa, sour cream and guacamole. Enjoy!

# Chapter One

November 1882
Roswell, New Mexico Territory

"Thank you, Mr. Link," Karin murmured as the roly-poly man in the loud checked suit handed her down from the stage.

"My pleasure, Miss Eklund."

Karin smiled as he tipped his hat. She often shared the stagecoach with a drummer or two while traveling her own route, and Arlo Link was her favorite. He was cleaner than most—much appreciated in the close confines of a stage—and he always treated her with respect. Although he probably treated all plain-faced spinsters who were a good four inches taller than he with respect, she conceded with a silent laugh. A corset-and-bustle salesman, he had once suggested—respectfully, of course—that she might wish to try one of "Dr. Warner's new and improved dress forms, made of the finest sateen and hair, with springs, for those to whom—" as he put it delicately "—Mother Nature has been less generous." To his disappointment, she had not purchased one of Dr. Warner's padded forms—"warranted in every respect"—to give her the voluptuousness a stingy Mother Nature hadn't.

"A happy Christmas to you, Miss Eklund," the drummer called cheerily as he picked up his worn canvas valise and leather sample case and started across the street.

"And to you, Mr. Link." Karin waved goodbye, then walked to the rear of the coach, where Bert Shnayder, the driver, was unloading the boot.

"Have you bought your ticket for your next trip, Miss Eklund? The stage is crowded before Christmas, remember," he said, setting her Gladstone bag on the boardwalk beside her overstuffed carpetbag and wooden sewing-machine case.

Bert Shnayder had appointed himself her guardian when he discovered she was alone. She didn't need one, but she appreciated his concern. "Thank you for the reminder, Mr. Shnayder, but I won't be taking another trip until January. I'm spending Christmas here with a friend."

"Will I have the pleasure of your company on the ride to Seven Rivers, Miss Eklund?"

With a sigh, Karin turned around. If Arlo was her most favorite drummer, Gerald Butterbaugh was her least. Paunchy and mostly run to seed, he clung steadfastly to the conviction that bay rum was an adequate substitute for soap and water. He clung to another, too. On the frontier there were, to Gerald Butterbaugh and his ilk, two kinds of women: wives and saloon "hostesses." If a woman wasn't a wife, she had to be the other, and was treated accordingly.

"No, Mr. Butterbaugh, you won't," Karin told him cheerfully. She started walking and put a brisk block between them, then paused in front of the new hotel. She was a day early. She could stay at the hotel until Hiram Ozbun came for her tomorrow, or... Karin looked down the street, toward the livery stable. Or she could do what she really wanted to do.

A few minutes later, just inside the big open doors of the livery stable, Karin paused to whisper the name painted over the doors to herself as she saw a man approaching from the back. *Swift*. She had worked very hard to learn English. She had mastered the confusing word orders, the letter *j*, the combination *th*, and *yes* instead of *yah*, but her Swedish tongue still had difficulty with *w*'s, and the *sw* combination was especially difficult. "Mr. Swift?" she said carefully.

"Yes, ma'am, that's me. What can I do for you?"

What he did for her was rent her a horse and buggy. There was much she didn't miss about farm life, Karin thought as the big bay settled into a steady trot, but she did miss the animals, especially the horses. It was worth the extra expense to give herself the treat of a good horse. She was giving herself quite a few treats lately, the small—in this instance, very small—voice of her conscience reminded her. Karin ignored it easily. She was just giving herself an early Christmas present.

Christmas! She hugged the idea to herself happily. In the eight years since she left home, she had managed to keep Christmas each year, no matter what the circumstances. Once she'd found herself on Christmas Eve in a squalid boardinghouse in White Oaks, with a nasty catarrh that was trying to turn into pneumonia. Mrs. Sedberry, the owner, had told her to expect nothing special just because it was Christmas. In fact, she could expect nothing at all, for Mrs. Sedberry was taking herself off to celebrate at her son's, leaving her with a niggardly few lumps of coal for the tiny stove in her room, a stale half loaf of bread, and the threat of dire consequences should she do any cooking in her room. How she could have cooked—unless she broke the legs off the rickety washstand for extra fuel—Karin didn't know, but she had managed a semblance of a celebration anyway. She had read the Christmas story aloud, the Bible

verses punctuated by her racking cough. Afterward, she had
stood at the small window while she sipped the peppermint
tea she had made, in defiance of Mrs. Sedberry's prohibi-
tion, on the stove in the tin cup she carried to avoid using the
community water dipper at stage stops. With a little imagination, the silver stars in the cold night sky were the candles on a big pine Christmas tree, and, with a great deal
more imagination, the whistling wind became church bells
ringing out the news of the Christ child's birth. For Christmas dinner the next day she had, in a veritable orgy of defiance, made more tea and stewed the little packet of dried
lingonberries her mother had sent, then spread them on the
bread. No stale bread this year, Karin thought, laughing to
herself, as the road topped a small rise. This year she was
having a *real* Christmas dinner.

"Whoa, horse." Pulling back on the reins, she brought
the buggy to a stop to enjoy the view. She took a deep breath
as she looked around, the air flowing down her throat like
a drink of cool, sweet water. Open prairie stretched all
around, all the way to the low red hills on the horizon, with
not a flake of snow in sight.

Snow. Her earliest memories were of snow, an ocean of
it, right to the shore of an impenetrable green forest. The
winter sun cleared the horizon for only a few hours a day,
and summer seemed several lifetimes away. When she was
ten, her family had emigrated to Minnesota. America was a
wonderful place, her father had told her, and she just knew
that in America there couldn't possibly be snow and there
would be other colors besides green. She'd begun to worry
when she got her first glimpse of the thick forests surrounding her new home and felt them subtly closing in
around her, trying to suffocate her. By early October,
though, her father had cleared some of the green away and
built a snug cabin. The night they moved into it, it had
snowed, and by the next morning, it had been up to her

knees and still falling. She had promised herself right then that someday she would find a place where there was sun, not snow, all winter, and where there were other colors than *green* all summer.

She slapped the reins gently on the broad bay rump, and the horse took off at a willing trot. Eight years ago she had left Minnesota to fulfill that promise. Her mother had been appalled, certain that it was not proper for an unmarried twenty-year-old young woman to travel unescorted, especially on the frontier, of all places. There were dire predictions of scalpings, "fates worse than death," ruined reputations. Her father had backed her mother, but Karin had suspected that he understood that his eldest daughter had the same tickle in her feet that had led him to Minnesota. In truth, she hadn't been too certain it was proper, either, or that her hair might not end up decorating an Indian lance; what the "fate" was, she hadn't been exactly sure, so she couldn't really gauge that risk, but whatever it was, she was ready to take it.

She still had her hair, and had quickly learned exactly what that "fate" was, but she'd learned just as quickly how to handle the Gerald Butterbaughs of the world. She still didn't know if what she was doing was "proper," but she did know that she was meeting a real need, a fact that brought her no small amount of pride. She had had only one marketable skill with which to support herself—her talent with a needle and thread. Growing up, she had seen women who spent part of the year as itinerant seamstresses, staying a few days to a few weeks with area families to help with the endless task of keeping everyone clothed. A traveling seamstress should find even more work on the frontier, Karin had reasoned, and she had been right, plying her needle with success as she worked her way south, seeking the sun. The New Mexico Territory had offered a happy dearth of both snow and claustrophobic green, and plenty of demand for her skills, and she had established a regular "route" of customers whom she visited twice a year.

Not all her success was due to her sewing skill, she knew. She always made sure her carpetbag held the latest Butterick patterns, and a variety of stylish fabrics. No frontier woman wanted to be any less stylish than her city sisters, but that was impossible if all the family clothes were made out of the same drab brown or gray and followed out-of-date patterns from the local dry-goods store. Even more important, it seemed sometimes, was the less tangible asset that she brought—the company of another woman, and news and gossip from "down the road." Most of the women she visited lived on isolated ranches, and she'd found that often her customers were far less interested in the contents of her carpetbag than in finding out how the Gottesmans' new triplets were faring, was the Zemeks' two-headed calf still alive, and had the Mazlanskis heard yet from the daughter who'd run off with the drummer? Sometimes she felt like an animated version of the serial stories that ran in *Harper's Weekly* and *The Saturday Evening Post*, but she understood their avid interest. It didn't matter that they would likely never meet the people they talked about, or that the gossip might be six months old; what mattered was that it was a human connection, however nebulous, that eased the bleak isolation. Those were the same reasons that the level of literacy out here was higher than in the cities, where company was available next door, rather than in books and letters.

The buggy bumped over a rut, and Karin glanced to make sure her portable sewing machine was still secure. At fifty dollars, it had seemed like an outrageous extravagance, and she had dithered an entire year over the purchase, but it had been worth every penny a dozen times over, if only because she had met Marit Ozbun because of it. Last May, due to the increased efficiency afforded by the machine, she had finished at the Vitarellis' several days sooner than she had expected. She had been standing in the Roswell post office, debating whether to put up a notice advertising her services or go on to her next job in Dunlap and hope the Paffetts would be ready for her, when a small blond woman had approached her and asked if she was the seamstress. It was the first Swedish accent other than her own that Karin had heard south of Minnesota in eight years, and when she responded in her native language, the woman was as pleased as she was. She had stayed a week with the childless Marit and Hiram Ozbun, sewing and quilting and chattering in Swedish, to the point that all poor Hiram got was startled frowns when he dared to say something in English. At week's end, Marit had asked her to return in six months so that they could celebrate a real Swedish Christmas.

For the past six months, Marit and she had been making plans by mail, with Marit posting letters to her in care of general delivery at the stops along her route. They would make *lussekake* and *lutefisk, glogg, julekage,* and *vorttimpor* and a big *smöorgåsbord* on Christmas Eve. They were going to have a wonderful holiday.

A large cottonwood came into view, standing in lone splendor, wearing its gorgeous cloth-of-gold autumn color. The long, dry prairie grass under it rippled and flowed in the light wind like silvery watered satin. The far red hills were dotted with green chenille junipers, while nearer by the Pecos River wove in and out of feathery pink salt cedars like a blue silk ribbon. She couldn't deny the spatial silences, the isolation and threat of misfortune, and the bleak beauty of this land, but it offered colors and textures she had never imagined back in Minnesota.

The cottonwood was a signpost of sorts. The road divided around it, with the main road angling north to Santa Fe. The other half followed the river and eventually passed the Ozbuns' cattle ranch. With the river and several natural springs, the area had once been a favorite Indian camping place. Then, about twenty years ago, it had become a favorite watering stop with the cattle drovers on their way from Texas to Kansas, and it hadn't been too many years before they realized the grazing potential of the surrounding grasslands and started staking claims.

John Chisum had been the first, getting his start, some said, by driving other Texans' cattle to Kansas, then forgetting to pay the owners. Others said with admiration that he was one of the greatest rustlers in history, the locals not being morally opposed to rustling, as long as the owners were Texans. Frankly, Karin was hard-pressed to see the difference. Other men had soon followed, from Texas and Missouri, and the town of Roswell had sprung up to meet their needs.

The road wound along a marsh, and a dozen wintering cranes flew over, calling back and forth as they swooped and glided, playing on the wind. Marit had pointed out the slough as the southern boundary of Major Swathwick's ranch. Like all cattlemen, he had staked a claim to all the land from the bank of the river to the highlands in the distance. She had heard of him before Marit mentioned him; people spoke his name with respect, rather than liking, she'd noticed, Marit included. Marit was, she had confided to Karin, a little afraid of him. Apparently a number of people were, because he was the only large landholder who hadn't been forced into taking sides in the recent Lincoln County War. He'd served in the Confederate army, and a few years after the War had come to the New Mexico Territory from Missouri with some of the men who had been under his command. Hiram Ozbun had been one of his lieutenants. She'd caught a glimpse of him once in town, but had only gotten an impression of size and beard—a great deal of both.

Shadows from the cottony clouds overhead flitted over the prairie, then seemed to converge up ahead. Karin frowned at the expanse of darkness, since there was no large cloud overhead to account for it. Her puzzlement changed to horror as she realized what the blackness was. Fighting a rising panic, she urged the big bay to a run.

There were many dangers in this country, but worse even than the obvious threats of Indians, rustlers and droughts that shriveled grass and dried up water holes was fire. With little to stop them but a chance rain, prairie fires could burn for weeks, consuming everything in their way. A wagon-wide track branched off to the left, a brown scar across the ugly black one, and, despite her desperate haste, Karin pulled the galloping horse to a halt. In sickened awe, she stared at what was left of Major Swathwick's ranch. Nothing. The big barn she remembered, the corrals, the log bunkhouse, his house—all were gone. Even the massive poles that had held the sign identifying the ranch as the Running S were charred stumps. Praying that the men and stock had escaped unharmed, she whipped up the bay again.

She covered several quick miles, but the prairie was still black as far as she could see. A sudden gust of wind swirled ash into her eyes, and it was another mile before she had blinked them clear enough to see past the horse's nose. When she could, she blinked yet again to be sure the line of silvery green she saw beyond the black was truly there. Karin sagged back against the leather seat in limp relief while tears clouded her eyes again. Either there had been a providential rain, or the major had mustered enough men to put out the fire. Whatever had happened, it had stopped before it reached the Ozbuns.

# Chapter Two

Half an hour later, the Ozbuns' house came into view, the adobe an unscorched earth brown, the clapboard second story sparkling with a fresh coat of whitewash, the ginger-bread trim a bright blue and the sugar maple Marit was coaxing along a brilliant red. Karin felt another wave of relief. She'd known the fire hadn't reached here, but until she had seen Marit's house standing unscathed, she hadn't really believed it.

Driving into the yard, she was puzzled by the large number of men, so busy building a fifth corral that none of them took any notice of her. Hiram had had only two corrals in May, maybe six or seven horses and one bull, not the thirty or forty horses and three bulls she saw now. And he certainly hadn't had so many hired hands. There were at least a dozen men now, all of whom looked like the sort who spat on the floor and cursed fluently. Searching among them for Hiram's short, square shape, she was startled yet again to see two children.

She was feeling the first stirrings of unease when one of the men caught sight of her and apparently said something, because the biggest and roughest-looking suddenly turned in her direction, then started toward her. Involuntarily Karin clutched the reins tighter.

"I'm Gabriel Swathwick. Can I do something for you?"

He spoke so abruptly that it took Karin several seconds to understand what he had said. Her initial impression had been right—height and beard—and a deep voice that matched his rough appearance. "I'm...Karin Eklund. I'm—"

"The seamstress. Hiram mentioned you were coming." His mouth seemed to twist, as if he were in pain, on Hiram's name.

"Ya—yes." Her English always suffered when her emotions weren't steady. "Are Hiram and Marit here, Major?"

One thick black eyebrow went up at her knowledge of his old rank. "No. I'm sorry to tell you they're dead, Miss Eklund."

The woman's hand went to her mouth, as if to hold back the color draining from her face, and Gabe cursed himself ripely. He could have softened the blow a little. She wasn't responsible for everything that had happened.

"V—what happened?"

She got herself back under control fast, he gave her that. The hand lowered almost immediately to clench around the other. She had lovely hands, he noticed absently. "They were coming back from town when a thunderstorm blew up, and they were struck by lightning." He heard the harsh tone of his voice and tried to soften it. "They never knew what happened, Miss Eklund. They didn't suffer."

Karin stared at him, trying to absorb what he was saying. Death on the frontier, she had learned, was often swift and sudden. She hadn't known Marit long enough to develop a deep affection for the woman, but they had been instantly fond of each other, and the loss was hard.

"Would you care to step down, Miss Eklund?"

Gabe glared at Sarge for doing what he should have had the manners to do himself.

She had been vaguely aware of the other men drifting over, and now Karin saw that one of them was standing beside the buggy, offering his hand. The man was old enough to be Major Swathwick's father, but they weren't related, she was certain. The man was at least a foot shorter, post-thin and totally bald. "Thank you," she murmured as she accepted his offer. As he stepped back, she noticed that the lower half of his left sleeve was empty and pinned up.

She was one of the tallest women he had ever seen, but she still wasn't much to look at, Gabe decided. What he could see of her, anyway. A long, shapeless gray capelike affair hid her figure. Her face was just this side of plain, her eyes were some light color, and her hair, skinned back into a tight knot, looked to be blond. At least her hat was sensible and not one of those feathered monstrosities that looked like the woman had a big dead bird stuck on her head.

The older man introduced himself. "I'm Wilbur Dawes, ma'am, but most everybody calls me Sarge."

Karin managed a smile. "I'm pleased to meet you, Mr.—" He shook his head with a gentle chiding frown. "Sarge."

Gabriel Swathwick was frowning, too, but there was nothing gentle about it. A gray-shot black beard hid most of his face, but his whiskey-colored eyes were narrowed to a squint, while his eyebrows had snapped down into a solid dark line. However hospitable Sarge might be, the major couldn't wait to see the back of her. She would be glad to grant him his wish, but the bad news seemed to have paralyzed her for the moment. More to gain relief from that frown than out of real curiosity, Karin looked past him to the new corrals. The two children had left off playing, and were standing in front of the closest corral now, watching the adults. Except for the difference in their height and gender, they might have been twins. Both of them had bright auburn hair, eyes so blue she could tell the color even at this distance, and the same oddly apprehensive look on their faces. "Whose children are they?" she asked without thinking.

"The Ozbuns'," he said shortly.

Karin looked back at him uncomprehendingly. "They didn't have any children."

His frown took on a faint ruefulness. "Not that they knew of. Apparently a relative in Nebraska adopted the two of them off an orphan train for Hiram and Marit, then sent them on here. When they arrived in Roswell wearing tags with Hiram's name, the stage company agent didn't know what else to do with them, so he sent them out to me. My ranch had burned two days before the Ozbuns were caught in the storm, and the agent knew my men and I had moved over here."

His terse explanation contained more shocks. In spite of the awful reason for it, the unexpected availability of quarters for his men and his stock must have seemed heaven-sent. It might seem callous that he had taken over the Ozbun ranch so soon, but practicality took precedence on the frontier; they no longer needed a home, and he did.

Karin looked back to the little boy and girl. They had to be from New York City, because it was an orphanage there that organized the so-called "orphan trains" that carried their precious cargo to the Midwest to find adoptive homes. Several years ago she'd been in a small town in Kansas when an orphan train pulled into the station. After the children were herded to the church and put on display, the placing agent had gone down the row, announcing to the crowd each child's age and the details of her or his education, personality and character. One little girl had done a dance to increase her chances of finding a home. It had reminded her of a horse auction or—worse—a slave auction she had read about once, and she had felt sick.

In fairness to the organizers, prospective parents were carefully scrutinized, and the adoptions afforded the orphans their best hope of a real home, but she remembered the looks on the little faces of those left behind after the audience finished making their choices. She imagined she could hear their desperate cries: "Why not me?" These two poor little ones must have been happy to be chosen, yet frightened, too, to be sent off to people they had never even seen, much less knew. She couldn't imagine what they must have felt when they were told that they had again lost their parents, then were stuck in a convenient corner, like the unclaimed baggage they essentially were. "They are beautiful children," she murmured softly.

"'Yes, they—" The words came out in an impatient snap, then abruptly stopped as a crafty, almost sly look replaced the frown. "Yes, they are beautiful children," he said more slowly, then added, in a seeming non sequitur, "Hiram had mentioned that you were planning to stay until January."

Karin managed only a nod as another wave of bleakness swamped her.

"Well, I have a proposition for you, Miss Eklund." Abruptly realizing that he had an audience just dying to hear what it was, Gabe gave the men behind him a hard look. They all took the hint and beat a quick retreat back to work, all except Sarge. But then, when had Sarge ever followed an order he didn't want to? Gabe thought dryly. Finally even Sarge left, but a dirty-dog grin disabused Gabe of any illusion that he had won their staring contest.

He turned back to the woman. She didn't say anything, but there was a glimmer of curiosity in her eyes. What color were they? Gray? Maybe blue. He shook his head, impatient with himself. "I need a housekeeper, someone to look after those children, and it seems your plans have suddenly changed. How about it?"

The heartless brusqueness of his proposition brought an automatic angry refusal, but Karin bit it back. However the offer had been phrased, he was right—she had no place to go, nothing to do, for the next month. She could scare up another job, but... Feeling even more off balance, she blurted out, "I'm surprised you didn't just give them over to someone else to care for until arrangements could be made to send them back."

"I thought about it," he admitted, "but it didn't seem right, when their lives had been disrupted so much already, to make them deal with more strangers." His expression had softened; abruptly it became even harder, as if he realized he had exhibited a smidgen of human compassion and wanted to reassure her that it was only a temporary fault. "There's some question whether they are the legal heirs. When their adoption papers arrive and I see if they were signed before or after Hiram and Marit died, I'll know whether I pay the children or the Ozbuns' kin for the ranch. It's simply more practical to keep them here until then."

When she nodded her understanding but gave no response to his offer, he added, "You'll be well compensated."

He named a sum, and Karin kept her jaw from dropping only at the last second. She knew he wasn't insulting her by implying the amount would compensate her for Marit's loss; he was desperate. They would be a single man and single woman sharing a house, but the children should be adequate chaperons, and she was so far past the age of marrying that any damage to her reputation was immaterial, anyway. The money would be a nice addition to her savings account in the Roswell Territorial Bank, but the work! She'd gotten lazy the past eight years, she'd discovered. Several times she'd taken over the household when the woman she was sewing for had become incapacitated. The endless cooking, washing, ironing, housecleaning, butter-churning, gardening, and all the while keeping track of half a dozen wild puppies disguised as children—the work was back-breaking! Unconsciously she chewed her lip, while her gaze drifted to the two small figures now standing at the corner of the house. But there were only two children, seemingly tame, and no garden to deal with....

Her bottom lip was full and soft-looking; she had a sweet mouth— Gabe jerked himself back to the matter at hand. She still hadn't given him an answer.

He dragged his broad-brimmed hat off his head—he didn't shorten appreciably, and Karin still experienced the phenomenon of having to look up at a man—and slapped it against his thigh. His pants were... *tailored* enough that she could tell his legs were as straight and strong as the rest of him. "Look, Miss Eklund, I don't know what to do with them. I'm almost forty years old, and I've never been around children."

"Hmm... Almost forty." She looked at him thoughtfully. "That old."

"Not that old. I'm thirty-seven," he said stiffly. Her mouth twitched. And he'd thought that mouth was sweet? Her eyes went back to the children, and her expression grew soft. "They came over from Ireland last year. Their father was killed in a street accident not long after, and their mother found some sort of work, but it wasn't enough to support the whole family. She took Mary and Brian to a foundling home, but kept their baby brother." Watching her covertly, he added, "They must have wondered why their mother didn't love them enough to keep them, too." She swallowed convulsively. It was low, but self-respect be damned—he was desperate. Besides, there had been that "that old" remark, he reminded himself self-righteously.

Karin looked back up at him. She was well aware that he was manipulating her. "All right, Major Sv—" Oh, why couldn't he have an easy name, like Masylenki? "Major Swathwick. I'll do it."

"Good." He settled his hat on his head with a self-satisfied air. "There will only be five for dinner. My men do for themselves." With that and a brief nod to her, he strode across the yard.

He had just solved one of his chief problems, Gabe thought, congratulating himself. So why, instead of relief, did he have the suspicion that he had just increased his difficulties tenfold?

Snapping her mouth shut, Karin stared at his broad, rapidly retreating back. His name wasn't to be her only trouble, apparently. Well, she could "do" perfectly well without any additional discussion of her employment or direction from him, she decided, ignoring the sinking feeling that she'd just made a Major mistake.

# Chapter Three

Propping her elbows on the tabletop, Karin rested her forehead on her clasped hands and stared down at the paper she had been scribbling on. It wasn't enthusiasm for her new job that had her getting back out of bed to look through the receipts she'd collected over the past eight years and write out a "shopping list" of ingredients she would need. Her gaze shifted to the pan on the stove. Nor was it an overwhelming urge for hot chocolate that had kept her from sleeping. It was guilt. She was much too old to be feeling sorry for herself because of the ruination of all her fine Christmas plans, and she was thoroughly ashamed.

With a long sigh, she raised her head to look around the kitchen, her gaze lingering in turn on the pump over the tin-lined box sink, the built-in cupboards, the polished pine wainscoting, the linoleum floor. To the back sat two over-stuffed chairs with a small table and brass reading lamp between them, giving the room an even cozier, more comfortable feel. Marit had been so proud of her house.

A faint sound came from overhead, and she smiled faintly. She had a real chaperone after all. As she had thought, Sarge had served under Major Swathwick during the War and continued in his "command," although she had been surprised to learn that the older man had married two years ago. His wife was off helping her daughter with a new baby, and he had come to fight the fire, then stayed on to help with the rebuilding. Insisting that she take the second bedroom, he had moved up to the tiny loft room next to the children's.

Karin took a sip from an enameled cup. Introducing herself to Mary and Brian, she had learned that their last name was O'Flynn, that Mary was six and Brian eight, and that they were not fond of sourdough or chili. Sourdough and chili were all, she'd deduced, that Sarge could prepare; majors, apparently, didn't deign to cook. The children had followed her into the kitchen and, once they'd determined that she wasn't going to make either of the offending foods, offered with shy eagerness to help fix supper.

The simple meal of fried ham with red-eye gravy, mashed potatoes, fresh slaw and biscuits had drawn far more praise than it deserved from Sarge and the children. Gabriel Swathwick had said nothing. Karin laughed wryly to herself. At least he hadn't belched.

"What are you doing up so late, sitting here all by yourself? Are you all right, Miss Eklund?"

Karin didn't quite stifle a small squeak of surprise. How in heaven's name could a man so big move so silently? "I—I'm fine, Major. I wasn't that tired, so I thought I'd make up a list of supplies I'll need." He moved, again silently, toward the stove. He peered into the pan, and belatedly she wondered if he would think her presumptuous for helping herself to something so expensive as cocoa.

"I haven't had hot chocolate in years," she heard him murmur, then was startled for the second time in as many minutes to see him reach for another of the enameled cups. "Are there any of those cookies left from supper?"

"Y-yes." She made to rise from the table.

"Don't get up. Just tell me where they are."

It was a command, but his voice was much less harsh and loud than it had been earlier, almost as soft as when he'd asked her if she was all right. "They're in the old Lipton tea tin, beside the coffee mill." It didn't surprise her that he was hungry; she had seen at supper that she would have to revise considerably upward her estimate of how much to cook. Yet, other than the clean platters, there was no evidence of his appetite. Broad-shouldered he was, but also lean-hipped and flat-bellied, a sign of how hard he worked. In fact, he could actually stand to gain some weight.

Scooping up the large tin easily in one hand, he approached the table. He'd put on his pants and shirt, buttoning the shirt most of the way, and tucking it in most of the way, too, but he was barefooted. His feet were big, just like the rest of him. He sat down, opened the tin and offered it. She shook her head, and he took out a cornmeal cookie for himself. She was surprised again when he dunked the cookie in his cocoa before popping it in his mouth. With him not fully dressed and her wearing only her nightgown and flannel wrapper, she had been feeling very self-conscious, and had, in fact, been about to go back to her room, but seeing such a big fierce man do something so... *boyish* suddenly relaxed her.

Gabe took another cookie. Despite what she'd said about not being tired, her eyes were sleepy-looking. They were blue, too, not that it mattered, of course. They were also red-rimmed, the lids swollen a little, reminding him that he'd been so wrapped up in his own losses that he'd forgotten hers. "I'm sorry about your friend," he said quietly.

Karin remembered that twist of pain when he'd spoken Hiram's name. "I'm sorry about your friend, too," she returned softly.

He shook his head with a short, harsh laugh. "He went through the entire War, and the worst injury he got was a big splinter in his bu—" Gabe cleared his throat. "Back."

With a small, sad smile, she nodded her agreement at the capriciousness of fate. Her eyes were the color of that flower his mother had liked, the one that had grown down by the slough and bloomed in the spring. What was its name?

"What made you decide to come to New Mexico Territory?" Karin asked, finding herself suddenly, inexplicably, interested in knowing more—everything—about him.

Dunking another cookie, he shrugged slightly. "My folks had passed on, and my sisters were married and settled. I'd always wanted to try the frontier, so I sold up and came here."

Karin took a long sip of her cooling cocoa. Had there been a woman who cried to see him leave? Oddly, she could imagine just how the woman would have felt.

Gabe washed another cookie down with a swallow of hot chocolate. "Why aren't you back home, Miss Eklund, married and sewing clothes for your own family, instead of for strangers?" The question was rude, based on their nearly nonexistent acquaintance, but he frankly couldn't understand why she wasn't married. The woman could certainly cook. On an intellectual level, he knew almost anything would have tasted good after a week of Sarge's chili and sourdough, but on a gut level... He smiled inwardly. His gut was ecstatic, and his mouth was already watering, thinking that if tonight was what she could do with short notice and meager supplies, what wonders would be possible when she had plenty of time and a full pantry?

And on second look she wasn't all that plain, either. She had a slim, lithe figure and a very feminine face, delicately boned, although not weak, and a lovely complexion. Her hair was out of that ugly knot and in a long, thick braid down her slender back, so that little wisps of it floated around her face. It looked as if it had been rinsed in warm sunshine, and he wondered what it would look like loose and free of restraint. He caught a whiff of warm sunshine, too, and honeysuckle.

His question was impertinent, she supposed, but the soft glow of the lamp and the genial warmth of the stove had created an . . . intimacy that would make her refusal to answer even more rude. "Nobody I loved ever asked me to marry him," she said simply. "And, like you, I wanted to see the frontier, especially—" her laugh sounded like warm sunshine, too "—the part that's not buried under snow and ice half the year."

So she would marry only for love. Had there been a man she loved who hadn't asked? No, he decided, and why that pleased him, he didn't know. Her blue eyes were clear, unshadowed by disappointment or unrequited longing. What *was* the name of that damned flower? He didn't put much stock in love himself, wasn't even convinced it existed, although he had to concede that Hiram and Marit had seemed to present some evidence of it. And, as demonstrated by Sarge and Hilda, it was apparently possible even late in life. Maybe that was why, even though he didn't believe in it himself, he was perversely annoyed with her for implying that she was far too old for the possibility of love now.

Realizing that he was staring, he shifted his eyes to her hands, clasped loosely on the table, and said what he was thinking, without thinking. "Your hands are very soft and smooth."

The smile Karin gave him was a little shy. "I keep them that way so they don't snag the silks I work with." His hand began reaching across the table, slowly. As if watching a magic-lantern show, she saw the large, rough, black-haired hand come closer and closer to the smaller, paler one. Just as it seemed they would touch, she abruptly remembered that she was watching *her* hand and *his* hand.

Gabe yanked his hand back at the same time that she snatched hers away. What the hell had he been thinking of? Shoving his chair back from the table, he stood up in a rush. "Well! It's late, and we both have to get up early."

Karin scrambled up just as quickly. "Good heavens, yes! We both should have been asleep hours ago!" Closing her door seconds later, she breathed out a ragged sigh of... something. How could one feel too warm and have goose bumps at the same time?

# Chapter Four

"Decide the beard made you look too old?"

Gabe scowled at Sarge's reflection in the shaving mirror. "Just got tired of itching," he muttered as he swiped the straight razor up his neck. Rinsing the blade in the bowl of hot water on the washstand, he fixed the older man's eyes in the mirror with a hard stare. "And don't think I don't know what you were up to yesterday, old man." Sarge had slunk back to eavesdrop just in time to catch her comment about his age.

The older man laughed as he sauntered out of the washroom between the two bedrooms. "Just don't take too long to figure out what *you* should be up to."

Sending a snort of pitying disgust after him, Gabe raised the razor and sliced his chin. Glaring at himself in the mirror, he dabbed impatiently at the nick. Flags! That was what those flowers were called. This time the sound of disgust was for himself. And weren't *flowers* a damned foolish thing to have wasted half the night thinking about?

Karin froze in front of the stove. Even after she recognized the big, dark man who'd walked into the kitchen, it was another several seconds before she could move. He wasn't repulsive—far from it. She was just shocked by the transformation. Without the graying beard, he looked a good ten years younger. His thick, straight hair was still black, with only a little silver at the temples, which actually made him look rather distinguished. She'd wondered if he wore a beard to hide a weak chin or badly shaped mouth, but that wasn't the case. His chin was strong, his face was lean and his features were clean-cut, and his mouth was fine—wide, firm, a little hard, maybe, but really quite... fine. One thing hadn't changed, though, and that was the frown.

"Good morning, Major."

He returned her greeting with a grunt. She didn't want a continuation of that disturbing intimacy of last evening, she assured herself hastily, but surely civility wasn't too much to ask for.

Apparently it was. His only words were "Saleratus?" and the pronouncement he made as he was heading out the door after breakfast. The first questioned an unfamiliar item on the list of supplies she'd given him; the second left her with her mouth open as she stared at his departing back again. "The laundry will be done today," he'd said.

*Ordered,* Karin muttered under her breath as she added another armload to the already daunting pile in the middle of the kitchen floor. Of all the drudgery that was included under the deceptively benign heading of "housekeeping," doing the laundry was the absolute worst. She would rather scrub chamber pots; at least that didn't take all day. And today wasn't even the right day for it, she thought righteously. Monday was laundry day, when the woman of the house could look forward to hauling gallons of water, heating it in a huge kettle, stirring the boiling soup of dirty clothes and lye soap, fishing out the steaming garments, hauling more water to rinse them, then wringing and hanging. To break the monotony, there was always the scrub board to take a layer or two of skin off the knuckles. She would have defied him, but he was paying her a substantial sum of money, and, even more important, Mary and Brian couldn't wait for clean clothes.

She managed a smile for the children as they made their contribution to the pile. As raggedy and meager as their outer clothes were, their underwear was worse. She should have thought to check last night so that she could have added underwear to the supply list, because she didn't think the major was going to be amenable to another trip to town tomorrow. There had been an awful lot of yelling outside before he left, and, although she hadn't been able to make out the words and it hadn't been just his voice she heard, his had been the loudest. She couldn't help wondering if some of that yelling had been because he had to take her rented buggy back to town. And even if he was willing to go to town again, he might not want to spend the money. After all, the children weren't his. Karin eyed the small foothill of dirty laundry grimly. Underwear-making had just been added to her "housekeeping" duties.

There was a certain beauty in a line of sparkling white sheets against a blue sky, just as there was in the hot, clean smell of freshly ironed clothes. Karin laughed dryly to herself. Her attitude toward laundry had undergone a change in the past few hours. About the time she hunted up the bluing, a wagon had come into the yard. The driver had announced that she had come to do the laundry, and suddenly Karin had understood that Major Swathwick hadn't been ordering, he'd been informing. Much of the fine irritation she had worked up had immediately collapsed, although she'd managed to salvage a little of it. Along with his "informing" the man might have done some explaining.

Assisted by her two oldest daughters, Mrs. Baca had made short work of the laundry, freeing Karin to give the house a good cleaning and make a doll for Mary. Mary needed clothes, but she needed the toy more, Karen had decided when she found the little girl playing with an old corncob she had named Bridget. The children did have some crudely carved animals that the ranch hands had made, and a wood-block wagon with cleverly fashioned wheels that actually turned, made, Brian said, by "Mr. Gabe." Brian was more than willing to share the toys, but a little girl needed a doll.

When she expressed her admiration for the wagon, outfitted as a traveling laundry, complete with kettles and tubs and wringer, portable clotheslines, even an ironing board, Mrs. Baca had told her that it had been the major's idea. When Mr. Baca died several years before, leaving her destitute with five children, Major Swathwick had approached her with a proposition: He would, at his own expense, provide the necessary equipment if she wanted to go into the laundry business. He had gotten convenient laundry service for himself and his men, it was true, but his offer had still been completely kind.

Mrs. Baca also solved a small mystery. The major dressed well, which made a shirt she'd found in the dirty laundry puzzling. The stripes had faded so badly that it was impossible to tell what the original color had been, and the neckband and cuffs were past turning. When she suggested that the shirt was more than ready for the rag bag, Mrs. Baca had agreed, saying that she had made the same recommendation, but the major had said no—emphatically. Karin was deciding the shirt must have been made by his mother or a lost love when Mrs. Baca dispelled her sentimental illusions by adding that he'd said it was the only shirt he had that fit right. With his size, broad shoulders and long arms, Karin could believe it.

She was taking down the last sheet when Brian and Mary, with a death grip on the new Bridget, ran up. "Do you want us to show you where the hens hide their nests now, Karin?"

Karin hid a smile. City born and bred, Brian and his sister were fascinated by all livestock.

"Just be watching out for the nasty old red one," Mary warned. Then, without waiting for a reply, she grabbed Karin's free hand and began dragging her toward the coop.

Despite the discovery that "nasty" was an optimistic description of the red hen, Karin was still in perfect charity with the world—the wonderfully laundry-free world—at suppertime. The pot-roasted beef and potatoes, the beet pickles and the spoon bread elicited the same profuse praise as last night's supper had. The round-robin of compliments to the cook stalled noticeably at the head of the table, so Mary innocently solicited the opinion of the only one who hadn't offered one so far.

"I don't like creamed turnips."

"Then there will just be more for the rest of us, right?" Karin smiled brightly at Mary, Brian and Sarge, and got three sickly smiles in return. All right, no more creamed turnips, she conceded silently, pointedly avoiding the unnecessarily smug face opposite her.

She still wasn't looking at him three hours later. He had actually once been considered smooth with women, Gabe thought sardonically. After they'd tucked Mary and Brian into their beds and Sarge had gone upstairs, she had spread out brown paper on the table and begun drawing what looked like pieces of some giant puzzle. He decided now to apologize for his loutish conduct, not just because he should, but because she was also ignoring his discreetly hopeful looks toward the leftover apple dumplings in the pie safe, as well as the hint of the big tin of cocoa he'd bought, which hadn't been on her list. He was perfectly capable of getting a dumpling or cocoa for himself, but, for some contrary reason, he wanted her to offer them to him.

"What are you doing?"

For once she'd heard him coming, probably because she was so busy ignoring him that she was acutely aware of him, Karin thought disgustedly. She breathed a silent sigh over her infantile snit. After all that had happened to him—watching his ranch go up in flames, losing an old friend, having two children dumped on him—he had a right to some curmudgeonliness. "The children need clothes, especially undergarments. I'm drafting some patterns, and I'll use fabric from the Ozbuns' clothes." Her throat closed for a moment as she indicated the folded clothing on the tabletop. "So there won't be any expense." Her voice trailed off as his face inexplicably darkened in the now-familiar frown.

He held up a pink-and-white gingham garment trimmed with white eyelet. "What is this?" he asked, his tone deceptively even.

"A petticoat."

"And you're going to make their underwear out of it?"

Karin gave him a wary look. He had himself shown her the trunk with the Ozbuns' clothes and asked her to decide how they might best be used. Her carpetbag couldn't provide all the children needed, and certainly Marit and Hiram wouldn't have objected. "Well, yes—"

"No." The gingham landed in a heap on the table. "Boys do not wear *pink*—" one long finger stabbed at the blameless petticoat "—drawers, Miss Eklund. Have a list of what they need ready in the morning. I'll buy it in town."

Karin glared at another now-familiar sight—his broad, stiff, *male* back. If he'd had the courtesy to let her finish, she would have told him that she was only using the gingham for Mary. He wasn't a curmudgeon—he was a big, boorish, churlish oaf! And what was even more appalling, a small, demented part of her actually found him *attractive*.

Gabe stepped out on the back porch, pulling the door not quite to. Breathing in the frost-nipped morning air, he listened to the murmur of voices in the kitchen behind him. The hodgepodge of accents proved America truly was a melting pot, as the newspapers were saying. He pulled cigaret makings from a vest pocket. And he was the one in the pot, stewing.

It was getting so he enjoyed fighting with her. He liked to watch her soft mouth priss up and the pink flush come into her cheeks. The little wisps of hair that escaped that godawful bun seemed to crackle around her face like lightning, and her eyes shot blue sparks. Her accent got stronger as she quit worrying about being so careful about her speech and lit into him. He enjoyed that, too. Hell, he realized with a sudden scowl, he enjoyed damn near everything about her. Except that bun.

He jerked the drawstring on the Bull Durham bag tight with his teeth and stuffed it back in his pocket. Whatever her accent, her vocabulary was impressive, especially for someone who wasn't a native English speaker. She frankly put him to shame, reminding him how his own speech had deteriorated. After just a few days' exposure to hers, though, it was improving. He licked the edge of the cigaret paper. Whatever her vocabulary, her accent was adorable.

The tobacco spilled over his boots. Adorable? *Adorable?* Since when did he use the word *adorable?* Hell, next he would be saying *delightful, charming* or—God forbid—*precious!* If that was vocabulary improvement, he wanted none of it!

"Major! We're fixin' to head on over to the Runnin' S! You ridin' with us?"

Now that was good plain *men's* speech. "Go on without me!" Gabe shouted back in answer to Masak.

The door opened behind him, then closed.

Sarge paused to settle his hat on his head. "You got someplace else to go?"

"Town." Gabe gave him a look. "And I suppose you have an opinion on that?" Never without one, Sarge had even more opinions lately, all of them involving the new housekeeper.

Sarge looked at him innocently as he started toward the barn. "Me? An opinion? No, not me."

His snort of disbelief was just fading when the door opened again. He didn't need a footstep or voice to warn him; the drift of sweet scent was more than enough.

"Here is the list you requested, Major."

He took it with a grunt.

Instead of going back inside, she folded her arms across her chest. "Tell me, Major, were you promoted because you could yell louder than anyone else?"

Her tone was so sweet, the lilt of her accent so delight—*different* that the words almost didn't register. "Why, no, Miss Eklund. I was promoted because I was the meanest," he said silkily.

With an exaggerated tip of his hat, he strolled off the porch, then turned around on an afterthought. "You don't have to address me as 'Major,' Miss Eklund."

Her chin went a notch higher. "Your men do."

He gave her a kind look. "You didn't serve under me."

*Under me.* She might be unmarried and a virgin, but the women she sewed for, glad of another woman to talk to, even one inexperienced in "marital" matters, talked. She had the second-hand knowledge, if not the firsthand experience, to put another meaning to those two innocent words…a scandalous, titillating—oh, why had she thought of *that* particular word? Karin moaned silently, as her dress suddenly seemed several sizes too small over her chest.

*Under me.* Gabe felt his face flush at a sudden mental image. Thankfully, she was too proper and upright—oh, Lord, he didn't need *that* image, either—and innocent to guess what he was thinking. He sneaked a peek at her. Her cheeks were bright pink. Proper and moral, he was sure, but maybe not so innocent.

She cleared her throat at the time he did. "I, ah—I've got to get back inside."

"I've got to get to town."

When the back door slammed, he was already halfway across the yard. Stewing. Oh, hell—he was at full boil.

# Chapter Five

"Karin, Santa Claus will find us here, won't he?"

Karin rearranged the milk pans on the springhouse shelf to give herself time to think of an answer to Brian's question. "Did he find you last year?" Coward that she was, she hoped Brian would say no, because that would give her an easy way to say no, too.

"No, but we didn't know about him last year," Brian said, with the perfect logic of children.

"The kids at the home told us about him," Mary added.

Wishing those children a chronic case of laryngitis, Karin latched the door of the springhouse. She had been going to ask Gabriel Swathwick what kind of Christmas celebration he had planned, when she'd overheard a hand mention something about the Christmas dance in Roswell to him. Those living on the frontier used any excuse—housewarming, wedding, store opening—to gather for food, dancing and simple human companionship, and Christmas was the premiere excuse of the year. People thought nothing of traveling hours, even days, in bad weather and over worse roads, but his answer had indicated that he wouldn't waste a single minute going to the dance. His answer had also answered her question: There would be no Christmas in his house that year, there was never any Christmas in his house, and she had resigned herself to a repeat of her "celebra-

tion'' at Mrs. Sedberry's boardinghouse. The sole consolation had been that Brian and Mary probably wouldn't know
Christmas was coming and so wouldn't miss it.

A naive assumption, Karin realized now; they not only
knew Christmas was coming, they were expecting Santa
Claus as well. And she was going to be the one to break their
hearts yet again. Drawing a deep, fortifying breath, she
turned to face them. "Yes, I'm sure he will."

Completely flummoxed, Karin slowly followed Brian and
Mary as they raced, whooping and cheering, toward the
chicken coop. Why, by all that was holy, had she told them
*that?* She knew why. What with the prickly-pear relationship between her and their guardian, including the fact that
she was certain he secretly laughed at her accent, she'd had
third—even occasional fourth—thoughts about staying the
past week, but then she'd looked at the two little waifs and
seen the fear and hopelessness in their eyes. Now, for the
first time, she'd seen hope, and even if it was for a fat man
in a red suit who didn't exist, she wasn't going to destroy it.
She didn't know yet quite how she was going to manage it—
and she certainly wasn't going to be practical and worry
about the very strong possibility that Santa Claus wouldn't
"find" them next year—but *this* year Mary and Brian were
going to have a Christmas to remember.

"Do you see Attila?" she asked them before opening the
gate of the pen surrounding the chicken coop.

Brian walked the perimeter of the pen. "No."

"Maybe she's sleeping," Mary whispered.

"Permanently," Karin muttered under her breath as she
unlatched the gate. She had christened the red hen Attila
because the evil bird had the same love of vicious attack as
its namesake. Brian had asked her about the name, which
had led to a history lesson and writing *Attila* on the tally
slate which was used for counting cattle during roundup and
hung just inside the barn door. When she later found Brian

scratching the name in the dirt with a stick to teach it to Mary, she realized how hungry to learn both children were. Mary had been learning to read at the home, and Brian, who'd already had some schooling in Ireland, read and figured surprisingly well. There was a nearby country school, but they would only be there long enough to make more friends they would have to leave, so she'd added teaching to her other duties. The children were so bright and eager that the lessons were fun, but with only the tally slate, brown paper, one pencil and her imagination, she wasn't sure how much they were really learning. A Blue-backed Speller or a couple of McGuffey's Readers would be worth their weight in gold.

While Brian and Mary threw corn, she scattered the oats she had sprouted for "greens" to get the hens laying well again, all the while keeping an eye out for their red-feathered nemesis. Sneak attacks were the hen's favorite.

"Did Santa Claus bring you presents in Sweden, Karin?" Mary asked.

She had told the children that she'd come to America from elsewhere, too, and told them a little about Sweden. "No, Jultomten did, a skinny little man with a bad temper. He came in a sleigh pulled by goats, and he would knock at the door and ask—" Karin switched to a gruff voice "—'Are there any good children here?'" She laughed. "I always said yes, of course, so he would give me a present."

Turning around, she saw Mary's look of puzzlement. "Why is he skinny? And why doesn't he have reindeers?"

Brian's face bore signs of serious doubt. "I thought Santa brought presents to all the children in the world."

"Well, he used to, but now there are so many children that he has to have ... helpers," Karin improvised madly. "Jultomten is his helper in Sweden, and of course Santa Claus needs his reindeer, so the helpers use something else."

"Sure, and even Santa Claus can't get everywhere in one night, don't you know, Mary?" Brian confirmed with the condescension unique to older brothers. "He comes to America 'cause it's the best."

The back of Karin's nose suddenly burned. After all the dreadful things that had happened to him, Brian could still say that?

Seeing she had exchanged the bucket for the wire egg basket, Brian picked up the "Attila stick" and Mary two stones as Karin eased open the door of the chicken coop. The coop was a *jacal,* constructed of posts driven into the ground and covered over with mud, with a pole roof also covered with mud and straw.

Snatches of the children's conversation drifted into the coop, and she grinned as Mary declared she was glad Santa Claus would be coming and not that "mean man." We already have one mean man to deal with, don't we, Mary? Karin added with a silent laugh. But even though it was silent, the laugh was hollow. Despite his own claim, Gabriel Swathwick wasn't mean. What she had learned and seen over the past week proved that. He'd lived in a *jacal* the first few years while he built up one of the finest cattle ranches in the area. He hadn't achieved success without some ruthlessness, it was true, but mostly he'd relied on the American values of hard work, determination, imagination and seizing opportunity. She had to appreciate that, since she believed in the same values and had, on a smaller scale, achieved success much the same way.

And he shared his success; Mrs. Baca wasn't the only one he had helped. And, completely shattering his myth of meanness, he was extremely good with Brian and Mary. Each night she told them a bedtime story after they were tucked in, which, astonishingly enough, he participated in— and unselfconsciously, too, even when Mary hugged him. And he hugged her back. After several nights of her fairy tales, the children had asked him—after carefully assuring her that they liked her stories, too—to tell them the "Patchy" story again, and she had realized—more astonishing—that before her arrival he had been telling them bedtime stories! He had looked a little discomfited then—because she was there, Karin had guessed, and gone downstairs, where she had shamelessly positioned herself in the best spot to eavesdrop.

After hearing the "Patchy" story, she understood why Mary and Brian liked it better than hers; she did, too. Not only was it wonderfully exciting, but it was true. Yet she heard something between the lines that children wouldn't. One night, shortly after he had established his ranch, Apaches had ridden off with all his horses and cattle. The loss must have been devastating, and many men would simply have given up, completely demoralized. Not him. On borrowed horses, he and his men had gone after them. After a hell-for-leather ride and a wild gun battle, they had returned with all the stock except for one cow, the only casualty. Hearing the story, she understood another facet of this complex man. Gabriel Swathwick was the kind of man who simply fought on until everyone else surrendered. She had to admire that, too.

She put the last egg in the basket. And if he didn't celebrate Christmas—well, there were worse things. Maybe his family hadn't celebrated it. Or maybe, a little imp suggested, it was because he was a curmudgeonly bachelor. She grinned to herself as she turned her back on the straw-filled coop to open the door. A big, strong, good-looking cur—Oh, no!

Gabe paused to listen to the joyful shrieks of laughter. It was the first time he'd heard Brian and Mary behaving like normal, carefree children. His mouth tightened grimly as he went back to looking for the two-man saw he already knew wasn't in the barn. Finally he gave up the pretense and leaned wearily against a stall. The letter in his pocket felt like a hundredweight of lead. They hadn't seen him ride in; he should just ride back out, but he didn't. Now Mary was chattering away about something, and the lead seemed to move to his chest. It was odd how a man could get used to the feel of little arms around his neck. The boy was more standoffish, probably because he'd already learned the lesson of orphans—not to get too close to anyone—but he knew Brian craved closeness. He was an orphan, too, though he'd become one when he should have been well past the age of needing parents, and there were times when he, too, would like the feel of warm, loving arms around him. Low, sweet laughter answered Mary's chatter. The children couldn't leave, because then she— He wiped a hand down his face. How had things come to such a pass after only a week?

More shrieks came, and he was already running even as he realized they were neither childish nor joyful.

"What happened?" He grabbed Karin to steady her as she struggled to her feet outside the chicken pen.

"Attila attacked me," she said breathlessly, then gasped as her left leg seemed to collapse under her. He snatched her up in his arms and heard another gasp.

"Attila?" He tried to ignore the firm warmth of her body, the soft breast pressing against his arm, the silky tickle against his jaw, the drugging scent.... "Who the—"

From out of nowhere a winged dervish flew at them. Lifting her out of the vicious hen's reach, he felt her arms clasp tightly around his neck while Brian went after the chicken with a stick and Mary pelted the bird with stones. It was a shame Mary was a girl, Gabe thought absently; she could have had a future as a baseball pitcher. He started toward the house with his sweet burden, the children catching up after vanquishing the hen. With Brian the main voice and Mary the chorus, he learned a number of interesting things: the identity of Attila, the solution to the mystery of the tally slate's disappearance, and that he wasn't particularly interested in putting her down anytime soon.

Setting her down carefully in a kitchen chair, he found he had to keep both hands on her when it seemed she would slide right off. "Are you going to stay in the chair if I let go of you?" he asked her gruffly. Peering up at him, she nodded with the studied solemnity of a drunk. He eased one hand away, then the other, ready to grab her again, but, good as her nod, she stayed put. What he felt was not disappointment, Gabe assured himself; it was relief.

She was not—and never had been—in any danger of falling out of the chair, Karin reassured herself, tightening her fingers over the edge of the seat under her skirt. Certainly not. That would imply a swoon, and, of course, she would never do anything so silly. It was just that...that unexpected pain in her—what was it she'd twisted again? Oh, yes! Her ankle. Right, her ankle had hurt when he swept her up in his arms, that was all.

Unbuttoning her shoe, Gabe eased it off carefully, and her foot jerked. He glanced up at her quickly. "I'm sorry, Karin. I'm trying not to hurt you."

*Hurt?* "It didn't hurt." The denial came out at least an octave higher than usual as she swallowed a hysterical giggle. Oh, no, she was feeling no pain. There were those sparks and tingles at the very slightest brush of his fingers, but they couldn't be considered hurting. They must be similar to what that electrical appliance one of the drummers peddled did, she thought vaguely. "Designed to stimulate the circulation," he said. She bit the inside of her lip on an inner whimper as his long fingers probed her ankle gently. Her circulation—among other things—was certainly stimulated.

"I need to turn your foot to make sure your ankle isn't broken, Karin, but if it hurts too much, you tell me."

Were the effects of that electrical contraption cumulative, too? She clamped her fingers tighter as the big, hard, rough hands rotated her foot and ankle with the care and gentleness of a mother handling her newborn baby. He had called her Karin twice. Strictly speaking, forgetting to call her Miss Eklund was probably just an absentminded, momentary mistake, although she couldn't help but wish the mistake would be permanent. Then she could call him Gabriel—but only because there were no *w*'s in Gabriel, of course.

"Brian, bring me the green bottle from the cupboard in the washroom." While Brian ran to fulfill his commission, he gave her his diagnosis. "Your ankle isn't broken, but I expect it's sprained, and that can be almost as bad. I'm going to put some liniment on it, then wrap it." He got up, took off his hat and his white canvas duster, tossed them on another chair, then crossed the room and began rummaging in the bag of rags hanging by the back door. Finding what looked like an old pillowcase, he began tearing it into strips. "You'll need to take off your stocking," he said, without turning around.

Of course you have to take off your stocking, ninny, Karin scolded herself as she reached under her dress to pull off her elastic garter and quickly roll her cotton stocking down and off. Ordinarily this whole situation would really be most improper. A woman could wear her décolletage cut down virtually to her navel, but allowing a man so much as a glimpse of her ankle was absolutely scandalous. Brian returned with a bottle of Good Samaritan Liniment, and she took a fresh grip on the chair as Gabriel squatted down again, picked up her bare foot and balanced it on his thigh—his very warm, very solid thigh.

He began to apply the liniment, and Karin felt a sudden suffusion of heat that made her wish she'd taken off her sweater along with her stocking. She wanted to blame the liniment, but the feeling originated nowhere near her ankle. He had shifted position slightly, causing the hard muscle in his thigh to bulge, and her foot—entirely without her permission—began rubbing.... She put a stop to it immediately, but her equally delinquent imagination was already speculating on what it might feel like without cloth between her bare foot and his thigh...whether it would be smooth, like warm satin, or hairy and tickly.... While she was dealing with that shocking misbehavior, her eyes took advantage, straying from one bulge up to— Squeezing her eyes shut, Karin gritted her teeth. Enough! He was behaving very matter-of-factly, his hands brisk and impersonal, behaving like a mature adult, which they both supposedly were.

Oh, Lord, he was going to melt. Which made sense, Gabe thought sardonically; melting came after stewing and boiling. He'd touched a hell of a lot more than a woman's ankle in the past and never felt like a piece of ice on a tin roof in the middle of July. At high noon. Her ankle was trim and graceful, making it too easy to guess what the rest of her leg would be like. And her skin... If her ankle felt this smooth and silky, how would her cheek feel, her shoulder, her— He tried to rub away the thought with another glob of liniment, and her foot flexed. Her foot was narrow and pretty, her toes were dainty, and if she stretched them just a few inches higher...

"That lim'nent stinks."

Brian wondered at the grateful looks his sister earned from both adults for her impolite remark.

"Yes, it certainly does," Karin said fervently.

"Really bad," Gabe agreed heartily.

As further proof of the incomprehensibility of grown-ups, Sarge earned even more grateful looks just for walking in the kitchen door.

"Sarge!" Gabe leaped up. "Just the man I—*we* need!" Grabbing the rag strips, he shoved them at the startled man. "Sarge is an expert at bandaging," he explained, not quite looking at Karin as he snatched up his coat and hat.

"What about Karin's hands?" Brian asked.

Freezing at the door, Gabe turned back to the woman in the chair. "What's the matter with your hands?"

After a short hesitation, she pulled them out from under her skirt and held them up, and Gabe snarled under his breath. Her lovely, white, soft hands were a mass of red scratches and bloody punctures.

"That nasty Attila did it after she made Karin trip and fall," Mary informed him.

At his furious look, Karin assured him hastily, "They won't keep me from fulfilling my housekeeping duties."

Far from seeming reassured, he looked even more furious, and she clearly heard the filthy word he muttered this time. The slamming of the kitchen door echoed it.

Half an hour later, her bandaged ankle and foot propped on a chair, her hands no longer stinging from a liberal dose of carbolic, and the children and Sarge off somewhere outside, Karin was alone with her sewing machine. Without warning, the door opened, and a freshly plucked chicken carcass landed in the dry sink a second later.

"We're having chicken for supper."

"All right." Karin eyed the big dark man warily, but only the usual frown was on his face now. A few red feathers clinging to the cuff of his pants provided "supper's" former identity. She couldn't say she was sorry.

Instead of leaving her to cook the chicken, as she expected, he hung his hat and duster by the door, filled a pot with water, plunked in the chicken and asked what else he should add. Bemused, Karin watched him bustle around the kitchen as he followed her directions—and he didn't look ridiculous doing it. When the lid was on the pot and the stove restoked with coal, he surprised her again by pulling out a chair and sitting down across the table from her.

"There was a letter for you when I picked up the mail."

"Thank you. It was thoughtful of you to ask if there was anything for me," she said, trying to keep the surprise out of her voice. He must have asked, because the postmaster didn't know where she was staying. He became engrossed in a sheaf of papers, so she opened the letter. It was from her mother and full, as always, of family news. Both Ria and Kathyl, her two younger sisters, were pregnant again, and she smiled to herself, ignoring a jealous pang that she refused to dignify with acknowledgment.

"Mary and Brian's adoption papers came."

Karin's head snapped up. It had only been two weeks since he sent for the papers; she had never thought a reply would come so fast. "When were they signed?"

"The day after Hiram and Marit died."

She stared at him unhappily. It was a fact of life that the children would have far more adoption value if they came with a substantial "dowry." "I guess there's nothing to do now but contact the foundling home and see what they want done."

"I already did." One long forefinger tapped several yellow telegraph forms. "They want the children sent back as soon as possible. They'll wire the fares."

"Oh, no!" Karin couldn't help her soft cry. Of course, now that he didn't have to buy the ranch from the children, there was no reason for him to keep them. And no reason for him to keep her. Hot, bitter tears burned the back of her throat. What a fool she'd been not to remember that she and the children had only a temporary relationship. She'd even blithely told Brian and Mary that Santa Claus would find them here, never considering that *they* might not be here. Her unthinking stupidity was going to bring them yet another awful disappointment. "V—" She tried again. "When is the next stage to Lamy, so they can catch a train east?"

He shrugged carelessly. "I have no idea. I wired the home back that it wasn't convenient to send them now, and that the weather was too uncertain, anyway. It will have to wait until after the first of the year. I also suggested the possibility of finding them a home here."

Now she was totally confused. If anything was inconvenient, she would have thought having the children stay was. And the weather was fine; it had been fine and looked to stay that way through next week, at least. And that last comment was the biggest puzzler. He'd said it as if it were a casual afterthought, yet the look on his face had been anything but casual. "What did they say to that?"

"What could they say? Yes." He grinned suddenly, and her brain stopped dead. It was, she realized when it started up again, the first time she'd ever seen him grin. The effect was—the word was ridiculous, but it was the only one she could think of—lethal. Sobering, he added, "They are amenable to an adoption here, but they're adamant that Mary and Brian stay together, and that any prospective parents meet their requirements."

"That's only reasonable," she said slowly, as an impossible idea began to form. "It would be criminal to separate them."

"Yes, it would," he said with peculiar intensity as he got up from the table and left the room.

Soon she heard him moving around in his room and turned back to her sewing. But after a few stitches she stopped again, her eyes drawn to the papers he'd left on the table. With a half-guilty ear toward the noises still coming from his bedroom, she grabbed the papers and began to read rapidly.

Gabe looked down into the open trunk. It was all he'd managed to rescue before his house went up in flames, and he still didn't know why, of all the things he might have saved, it had been this old trunk. All it had in it was junk, worthless stuff he'd thought was precious when he was a boy. His mother had packed it after he left for the War, and his sister had insisted he take it when he came west. The trunk was still useful, so he'd thrown it on the wagon, intending to dump the contents, but he'd never gotten around to it. He began to poke through the top layer. Maybe some of it might have some use after all, for Brian and Mary. His hand paused on an unfamiliar small velvet box stuffed in a back corner. Frowning, he opened it and felt the shock of a long-forgotten memory. It was a ring, his French great-grandmother's. Of rose gold, it was a circle of hearts, and she'd worn it as a wedding ring. Shaking his head, he closed the box and absently put it in his vest pocket. Whatever had possessed his mother to stick that in?

Karin glanced up from her sewing as he came back into the kitchen with a small trunk. Intrigued, she watched him set it down beside her and flip up the lid.

"Since you seem to have taken up schoolmarming along with housekeeping, you might find something useful in here."

The trunk was full of children's books, some obviously well loved, and tucked against a side were what looked like a couple of slates. Reaching in, she lifted out an old Blue-backed Speller. The name inside was inscribed in a child's hand that had shown signs even then of the boldness and strength of the man to come. She looked up. "You don't mind?"

His mouth quirked fractionally. "I figure it's the only way I'll get my tally slate back."

"You're probably right," she said gravely, then gave him a dazzling smile. "Thank you."

With a grunt, he shrugged into his duster, then reached for his hat. At the door, he paused to look back at her. "Stay off that foot."

# Chapter Six

A single woman with small children was not a "viable economic unit." Mr. Kaune's pomposity still rankled as Karin crossed the polished oak floor of the Roswell Territorial Bank. She was not the usual single woman, she had pointed out; she had an established career and a tidy sum in the bank—*his* bank. He'd hemmed and hawed, but she was walking out with the letter she needed, testifying to her fiscal soundness and responsibility and the probable success of a dressmaking establishment in Roswell—virtually guaranteed, since hers would be the only one.

Mr. Kaune's letter would go along with the postmaster's, which certified her moral character and fitness. She trusted that even in New York they knew that post offices served as a small town's gossip clearinghouse, so postmasters knew everything about everyone. A letter from a churchman would have been nice, but Roswell was served only by a circuit preacher who visited every third week, and she'd never met him.

She'd spent the past three days—and nights—endlessly turning over the idea of adopting Mary and Brian herself. The unexpected opportunity to come into town this morning had seemed like a sign from Providence, and she'd run to put on her best dress and hat and the pearl brooch her grandmother had left her. She'd been planning for the day when she would retire from the road and open a dress shop in one of the growing towns she traveled through, and although this was a little sooner than she had planned, she would succeed. She would never be rich in dollars, but she would be far richer than she ever could have imagined in other, more important, ways. She had lived with loneliness for so long that she'd no longer noticed it, but Mary and Brian had made her aware of it again, then made her see the possibility of combating it with love and the sharing of her life and herself. And if the love and sharing did not include all the possibilities, and there would still be one loneliness left ... Well—she laughed a little wistfully to herself—that was the advantage of coming from a long line of cold, dour people: You knew not to expect complete happiness.

She'd read the adoption agreement signed by the Ozbuns' proxies and seen nothing that would preclude her from adopting the children in their stead. She would support Brian and Mary until they were eighteen; she would see to their education, make them her legal heirs and faithfully report on their progress every six months. The only possible "preclusion" was her matrimonial state, but, she hoped, the board would overlook that to avoid the trouble and expense of transporting the children back to New York, then out again on another orphan train, because there was nothing she could do about that. A mental image suddenly presented itself as a solution to her single status—an utterly absurd, impossible and unwanted solution, she told herself roundly as she reached for the handle of the ornate frosted-glass door.

The knob turned in her hand at the same time that she saw a dark shape through the frosted glass, and she stepped back quickly to get out of the way of the incoming customer. The door opened, and the dark shape resolved itself into the living, breathing version of the image she'd just banished.

"I didn't know you were coming into town."

If they'd practiced it, they couldn't have performed the duet more perfectly, Karin decided as they both said the same thing at the same time. Gabriel took her arm to lead her away from the door, then dropped it immediately. It was amazing how quickly heat could travel through leather gloves, waterproof cloth, and wool.

"Sarge mentioned he was coming into town after you left, so Brian and Mary and I came along to get some groceries and visit the bank," she volunteered brightly, hoping to forestall any questions, such as why she wanted to visit the bank, or where Mary and Brian were, and also hoping that he wouldn't notice her edging toward the door.

"I had to visit the bank, too." He lifted his hat to her politely. "Well, I'll see you at supper."

Back outside, Karin reflected that he hadn't said anything about coming to town at breakfast, and that he'd been as eager to get away from her as she had from him.

"How would you two like to go on a picnic?"

"What's a picnic?"

Looking at Brian, Karin felt the small ache that came whenever he or Mary revealed ignorance of something most children took for granted. She supposed she was spoiling them, what with a trip to town yesterday and a picnic today, but they needed a little spoiling. "Well, you make a lunch—" she swung the basket in her hand "—and eat it outside." The children looked around the windy, mostly dirt yard, then back to her, with clear doubt. "It'll be fun," she promised, and started toward the line of trees along the river.

The river fell over a short waterfall into a wide, shallow pothole that eventually narrowed to a river again. Ruddy salt cedars grew along the banks, and on the opposite side a great blue heron ignored them as it speared its lunch from the silvery clouds of minnows drifting over the river bottom. They paused so that she could be suitably impressed by Brian's and Mary's stone-skipping ability. Mr. Gabe had taught them, they said. They showed off for him, too, she knew, reviewing the day's lessons from his old schoolbooks each evening, and he listened, seemingly with complete attention, then praised them for their efforts. Both children soaked up praise and attention like drought-thirsty flowers. When she had ventured a comment on how kind it was of him, she'd gotten his trademark frown.

He'd told the children that they would be staying a while longer, and they'd accepted it without question. She knew it might be crueler to let them stay, rather than send them back immediately, because the longer they stayed, the harder it would be for them to go. Gabriel knew it, too, from the bleak expression she sometimes caught in his eyes when he watched them, but she couldn't believe that care and attention and security—however brief—would really harm them.

The river turned right, but they kept going straight, up a gradual rise that turned into a broad mesa dotted with several sinkholes. Marit had shown her the spot one day when they were working out the kinks of three days of nonstop quilting. Most of the sinkholes held water, mirroring the clear sky like beautiful blue jewels, but the last one was dry, forming a little dell with a smooth, grassy bottom just perfect for a picnic. The children scrambled down, while Karin followed more slowly, mindful of her ankle, although it hadn't even twinged all day, thanks to the liniment—or the method of its application, a small, teasing voice added. She gave the voice the disdain it deserved.

The high red sandstone walls cut off the chilly wind, making the floor of the dell warm enough that they were able to take off their sweaters and coats and soak up the sun while they ate Attila sandwiches and drank the lemonade that she had made as a special treat. Glancing at Mary, Karin fought the urge to smile that she'd been fighting every time she looked at the little girl for the past two days. Gabriel had given the old set of lead soldiers at the bottom of the trunk to Brian before he realized there was nothing for Mary. Mary had solved the problem herself when she saw the coonskin cap. Holding the moth-eaten relic as if it were a solid gold crown, she listened as the former owner explained seriously how he had made it himself, while Karin tried desperately not to laugh. Brian had tried to trade her out of it, but Mary recognized a true treasure when she saw it, and wore the cap proudly, even to bed. There was no harm in it; the smell, after almost thirty years, was gone . . . mostly.

Mary looked back at her wistfully. "I wish Mr. Gabe was here."

"So do I." Karin heard the same wistfulness in her own voice.

They were finishing the last of the lemonade when Brian pointed to a spot just above the floor of the dell. "What's that shiny stuff, Karin?"

Karin looked over at what appeared to be dozens of smashed bottles reflecting the sun. "I'm not sure." She smiled at him. "Let's go see."

Instead of broken glass, they found what Karin guessed was some sort of mineral deposit. In some places the mineral had leached out of the red soil to form a saltlike crust; in others it had formed paper-thin, transparent layers, like isinglass, that shone brightly in the sun.

"Look, Karin, angel wings!" Discovering that the layers could be separated, Mary held up two large pieces that did indeed look like wings.

"And here are icicles!" Brian shouted, holding up several long crystals he'd dug out of the red dirt. "We could hang them on the Christmas tree."

"And use the wings for the angel on the top!" Mary added excitedly.

Poverty sharpened imagination, Karin thought. Their mention of a Christmas tree didn't catch her unawares, the way Santa Claus had, because she'd known the question of a tree would come up eventually; children who knew about Santa knew about Christmas trees, although she doubted their parents had ever been able to afford one. Having detected no softening in Gabriel's attitude toward Christmas, she was honestly glad that the tallest things for miles around were windmills and the poplars ranchers planted for windbreaks, because that effectively settled the question of a Christmas tree. The only evergreens were scrubby junipers no taller than Mary. "I'm afraid there aren't any trees around here that would make a good Christmas tree."

The children nodded sadly; then Brian's face suddenly brightened. "We could have a yucca."

With an effort, Karin kept a straight face, although she had to admire the boy's ingenuity. The yuccas were a good foot or two taller than the junipers, and they were green— the tops, anyway.

"We can't be bringin' a yucca into the house," Mary pointed out practically.

Brian's gloom lasted only a few seconds. "No, but we could decorate the one near the springhouse."

Mary thought that over, evidently decided it was acceptable and added her hopeful look to her brother's.

"If Mr. Gabe says it's all right," Karin said firmly. She would not go behind his back; it was a bad example for the children, and it wasn't fair to him to trap him into something he didn't approve of, whether she agreed or not.

Deciding to take the chance that he would say yes— probably because they couldn't imagine he would say no, Karin thought wryly—they began gathering "icicles" industriously. Karin took advantage of a rare opportunity to just sit. Leaning back against the sandstone wall, she closed her eyes, enjoying the sun and the peacefulness.

She realized she must have dozed off when something touched her shoulder. She opened her eyes to see Brian standing in front of her.

"Mr. Gabe's been calling you, Karin."

As she got to her feet, she heard Mary yell back to him. Shading her eyes, she saw him appear on the rim above them; then he started down at a near-run, a shower of dirt and small stones preceding him. She barely had time to worry what was wrong when he leaped the last few feet to the bottom, grabbed her and crushed her to him.

She'd only just begun to notice the heat radiating from him, the scent of cold wind and soap, the hard beating of his heart against her, the solid strength of his body and the fact that hers was trying to worm closer rather than away, when he jerked her back out of his arms, his hands clamped tight on hers. "Don't you ever go off like that again, Karin!" He gave her a hard shake. "You scared the—the sand out of me! I didn't know if Apaches had gotten you, or what!"

Dazed, Karin stared up at him, fascinated by the way his whiskey-colored eyes had turned to molten copper. "There haven't been any Apaches around here for years."

"Well, they could come back any minute!" He shook her again, then released her so abruptly that she almost collapsed.

Running up, Mary and Brian greeted him as if they hadn't noticed anything out of the ordinary.

"I'm sorry," Karin said, steadier on her feet but still trying to find her mental balance. "I would have left a note, but I wasn't expecting you or Sarge back so soon."

He took a deep breath, as if trying to control his jagged breathing. Hers was none too even, either, she noticed.

"I've got to ride over to Fort Stanton to…take care of some business. I'll be gone at least a week."

Sarge had told her that Swathwick beef fed the soldiers at several army forts, as well as the miners at Prescott and Jerome. "I hope everything goes well." The chill, lonely wind seemed suddenly to have found its way into the dell.

He said goodbye to the children, then looked back to her. "I'd prefer it if you stayed close to the house while I'm gone."

"We will," Karin said quietly.

They followed him out of the dell minutes later. On horseback, he was already halfway back to the house.

"Mr. Gabe was worried about you, Karin," Mary said.

"He was worried about all of us," Karin pointed out gently.

Mary nodded. "But you most."

Karin looked at her curiously. "Why do you think so?"

Brian gave her a patient look. "Because he was calling you over and over, and us just once."

Sarge leaned against the side of a stall. "When did you decide to go to Fort Stanton?"

"About fifteen minutes ago," Gabe muttered, tightening the knot tying down his saddlebags. "I need to check on the beef contracts."

"You said you'd worked them out when you were over there last month. Why do you need to go back?"

Gabe swore under his breath; Sarge could have the persistence of a horsefly. "Because I do." Picking up his rifle, he shoved it into the saddle scabbard. "By the way, Sergeant, I don't need you to shill for me." He had overheard Sarge regaling Karin with tales that made him into the hero of some dime novel.

Sarge hid a grin as his suspicions about the real reason for the sudden trip to Fort Stanton were confirmed. "Somebody has to, since you're doing such a damn poor job of it yourself."

Gabe swung up into the saddle, then leaned down until he was nose-to-nose with the older man. "Did it ever occur to you that maybe I'm not interested?"

The other man's loud laughter chased him as he rode out of the yard.

# Chapter Seven

She was going to be lucky if she didn't set her hair on fire, Karin thought as the juniper crown of candles slipped. Gingerly, she pushed it down tighter, smoothed down Marit's Saint Lucia robe, then picked up the tray again and began climbing the steps to the loft. Midway up, she began singing, wishing all the while that she had never told Mary and Brian about Saint Lucia Day, because she was far too old to be making such a fool of herself. Early on the morning of December 13, the eldest daughter, wearing a white robe and evergreen wreath with seven lit candles, and singing the Saint Lucia song, served each member of the family coffee and *lussekake* in bed. It was the official start of the Christmas season, which didn't end until a month later, Saint Knut's Day, when the candles on the Christmas tree were lit for the last time before the tree was placed outside with a sheaf of grain or "bread" cookies for the birds.

The children had immediately begun campaigning to celebrate Saint Lucia Day, but she had held out until Sarge got into the act. He was going to have to do without Christmas this year, he'd said mournfully, what with Hilda away and all, and at his age, who knew but what this might be his last one? His performance had been so good that Karin felt like applauding. She wouldn't have given in, of course, if Gabriel had been home, and she was still a little uncertain of his reaction when he found out, but she didn't think he would mind, as long as he didn't have to participate.

She entered the children's little room first. Brian and Mary were sitting up in their beds, their faces solemn, their eyes wide with wonder in the candlelight, and abruptly she didn't feel so silly.

He was back, and after only four days and a cold all-night ride, Gabe thought dryly. Letting his weary horse come to a stop, he studied the moonlit house. It was funny; he'd lived in his old house for over five years and in this one for only a few weeks, yet he had the odd sense that he was coming home after years of aimless roving. He nudged the buckskin toward the barn, frowning at the light in the kitchen. Was one of the children sick?

What looked like a flaming torch suddenly appeared in a side window, disappeared, reappeared in the small window at the top of the stairs, then turned toward the children's room. Jerking his rifle out of the scabbard, he jumped off his horse, then ran toward the house. On the porch, he paused to slip off his boots so that the jingle of his spurs wouldn't betray him, reflecting that there was a good chance he was about to make an ass of himself. Well, it wouldn't be the first time that week, Gabe thought sourly as he turned the knob of the front door. The door was unbolted, as always, and swung open with a squeak. Taking a deep breath, he dashed through the door, rolled across the floor and came up in a crouch beside the foot of the stairs. Cautiously, rifle at the ready, he looked up.

And saw Sarge's grinning face. Leaping to his feet, he was opening his mouth when Sarge put his finger to his lips, glanced over his shoulder, then motioned to him frantically.

"Just what the *hell* is going on?" Gabe demanded in a furious whisper when he reached the top of the stairs.

Sarge gave him a hard shove toward his room. "Quiet down!" he growled. "You're gonna ruin it."

Karin gave Mary and Brian each a sweet saffron bun and a cup of coffee—well diluted with warm milk—and the traditional kiss on the cheek. Returning their delighted smiles, she picked up both the tray and the song again, and started for Sarge's room.

The words clogged in her throat when she saw who else was in the room. He was supposed to be miles away, not plunked on the end of Sarge's bed, *grinning* at her. Inanely she remembered how much shorter Marit had been than she was. The fact that he was getting a really good look at her ankles this time was the least of her problems, Karin groaned silently. Then the expression on his face fully registered. A grin was the last thing she would have predicted. And it took a definitely wicked turn as he motioned for her to continue. Deciding that she'd already lost whatever dignity she might have had, Karin resumed singing and approached the bed.

Sarge smiled broadly as he accepted his coffee and *lussekake* and the kiss she gave him without thinking. Then she turned to the man at the foot of the bed. Soberly he accepted the bun and coffee she had intended for herself, the wickedness now confined to his eyes, which she took great care not to meet. Congratulating herself on her composure, she began to turn away.

"Where's my kiss?"

The soft whisper froze her in place as her eyes jerked to his before she could stop them.

With her big blue eyes, virginal white dress and gorgeous, sun-stepped hair floating free—finally—around her face and shoulders, she looked about sixteen. She wasn't the most beautiful woman he'd ever seen—though at the moment he couldn't remember who was—but she was the most insidiously appealing, even if he did get the sand-burr edge of her tongue more often than not. Which, Gabe admitted, was usually his own fault. He had survived Yankee cannons, Indian raids, rustlers, drought, fire and a range war, but he wasn't sure he was going to survive Karin Eklund. And, what was worse, he wasn't sure he cared.

A clear challenge shone through the deviltry in his eyes. Ever since she was a little girl, Karin had worked diligently to correct her faults, but there was one that, try as she might, she had never conquered: She couldn't resist a dare. Holding his gaze, she leaned forward with slow deliberation. Her lips were a breath away from his cheek when his head turned, and it was his mouth, not his cheek, that her mouth met.

The candles had finally set her hair on fire, Karin decided, unconcerned, as heat flushed through her. It didn't seem possible that a mouth that could frown so well could be so soft and gentle and welcoming. The kiss deepened and, with an unconscious murmur, she went willingly.

The small, inarticulate sound woke Gabe up to the fact that the woman he was kissing—and who was kissing him back—had a head full of candles in danger of falling in his lap, and that Sarge was enjoying the show, and that if he didn't stop within the next second or two, he wouldn't care about either one. He pulled back slowly, and she stared at him, her eyes wide and stark. Then she stood up abruptly, holding the empty tray to her chest as if it were a shield, and backed toward the door.

"Breakfast will be at the usual time." Starting down the stairs, Karin congratulated herself on regaining the ability to speak so soon—and at a normal pitch, too—and on successfully hiding the dreadful discovery she'd just made.

Giving Sarge a bland look, Gabe raised his cup of coffee in a hand that the other man wouldn't notice was shaking unless he looked closely. He was certain now; he didn't care if he survived Karin Eklund.

Yesterday's discovery wasn't really so dreadful. Karin laughed wryly to herself as she shaped another rope of dough into a figure-eight *kringla,* then slid the filled cookie sheet into the oven. What had happened was inevitable for any spinster worth her salt who was living in the house of an eligible, handsome, intelligent and kind—whether he admitted to it or not—man. Shaking down the clinkers, she added more coal to the stove. Naturally she had fallen in love with him, helplessly, hopelessly and irreversibly... and he would never guess, which was as it should be. But she wouldn't, Karin decided ruefully, as she began another sheet of cookies, take any more dares; reckless she might be, but not suicidal.

She was just transferring the cookies to a cooling rack when the man himself came through the back door. With the new bunkhouse, barn and corrals finished, he and his men had been back and forth all day, moving stock. She had given Mary and Brian permission to watch, as long as they promised to stay out of the way.

"I understand Santa Claus is coming."

There was nothing in his expression to tell her how he felt about that. "I'm planning that he will," she said neutrally, automatically squaring her shoulders. She had been wrong not to tell him sooner, but if he said no, he was going to have a fight on his hands.

"If you need money for presents, let me know."

The spatula clattered onto the table. "Th-thank you. I have what I need to make their presents but... thank you."

Nodding, Gabe reached across the table and snitched several of the cooling cookies. Her hair in a sensible bun, her hands sensibly folded at her waist, sensible green dress buttoned up to her neck, she had the sensible air of a no-

nonsense woman. After spending most of the night in most definitely nonsensible dreams, he resented it like hell, he thought wryly. Turning one of the eights into a zero, he chewed slowly. "Mmm...Good."

"Thank you." She sounded like a parrot, and not a particularly bright one at that, Karin thought dryly. A grin seemed to be lurking in his eyes as he pocketed the rest of the cookies and turned toward the door.

He paused with his hand on the knob, as if he'd suddenly remembered something. "My old striped shirt wasn't with the rest of my clean clothes yesterday. Mrs. Baca didn't mention what she did with it, did she?"

Karin kept her eyes from straying toward the blue-and-white ticking folded beside her sewing machine. "It came to pieces after it was washed." With a little help.

He grimaced ruefully. "I was afraid of that." As the door shut, Karin sat down hard in the nearest chair.

He really shouldn't be eating cookies, Gabe thought absently; he'd already let his belt out one notch, and was working on another. He nudged the buckskin into a canter to catch up with the last of the stock being moved to the new corrals. He had overheard Mary and Brian discussing Santa Claus's impending visit. Brian hoped Santa would bring him a penny and an orange, saying it as if they were a chest of gold and wondrous feast, and a large lump had suddenly stuck in his throat. A *penny,* for God's sake. And an orange.

He'd been easing away when Mary's comment stopped him. It was too bad, she'd said, that "Mr. Gabe" didn't like Christmas. It was probably like Karin said, Brian had answered; he hadn't celebrated Christmas when he was little. That was why it was best not to bother him about it. Swift anger had risen, both at her wrong assumption and for involving the children in something she thought he wouldn't like, but his anger had faded just as quickly. She had been going to tell him about her Christmas plans for Brian and Mary, he was sure, and he could understand how she might think he didn't like Christmas, remembering an exchange between him and young Billy Burcar that she had caught the tail end of.

Billy had sidled up to him, wanting to know if "Miss Karin" was going to the big Christmas dance in Roswell. And, remembering some sly looks directed her way, Gabe had known Billy wasn't asking just for himself. He'd given Billy an answer that he hoped had ended everyone's hopes about holding "Miss Karin" in their randy arms under the guise of dancing. She'd heard it and drawn her own conclusions, but he wasn't as heartless as she thought, and it hurt oddly that she did. The truth was that Christmas celebrations weren't anything he'd had time or money for, not when it had taken every second and every cent just to survive the first few years. Later, when he did have the time and the money, he'd gotten out of the habit, he guessed. After years of living hard, he'd changed, and maybe not for the better.

He knew the danger in making a change now, in celebrating Christmas—she would be part of it. It wouldn't ever be like that again, and the memory would haunt him.

Karin stuck her hand in the oven and mentally started counting. At twenty, her hand was starting to scorch and she pulled it out, satisfied that the oven was the right temperature. Quickly, she slid in the loaves of *julekage*, calculating the baking time. The beans cooking on the back of the stove—which she kept reassuring Brian and Mary were *not* chili—would be done the same time as the bread, so a 1-2-3-4 cake and one other could be baking while they ate supper. The cakes and they should finish up at about the same time, so she could make up a batch of *kringla* and finish off with one more pan of crackers, if there was enough baker's ammonia and oil of lemon left. While the crackers were baking, she would set the sponge for another three loaves of *julekage* and put dried apples and plums to soak for the pies she had to make tomorrow. Then she could go to bed, providing it wasn't breakfast-time, she thought, aiming an exasperated breath upward to blow a wisp of hair out of her eyes.

"Himself," as Mary and Brian would say, had casually announced this morning that they would be going to the Christmas dance in town. This morning! And the dance was the day after tomorrow! And Christmas was only two days after that! Men! They thought all you had to do was put on your clothes and go, which showed how much *they* knew. The dance would be just like the church suppers back in Minnesota; the food would be put out on the tables, and then the contest would begin, with the women subtly judging each other's contributions. Well, it was not going to be *her* who won the pitying looks of the other women!

She could have gotten an earlier start if he didn't insist on dragging her over to see the progress on his new house every day. In addition to being the housekeeper, she was now a "consulting architect." Before he'd broken ground, he'd asked her for suggestions, and before she realized it, she was describing the house she daydreamed about when she had too much time on her hands, one with a bay window in the kitchen, a large keeping room with built-in bookcases, instead of a small, relatively useless parlor, airy windows, a big back porch.... As the house took shape, it seemed he was incorporating every one of her suggestions, which was flattering—and also gave her a desolate feeling, because she couldn't help wondering if someday he would bring another woman to live there, in "her" house.

"Karin, will we have a spelling bee tonight?"

She looked across the table to Mary, sitting beside her brother, both of them shelling walnuts. Today's lessons had been reading recipes and measuring flour and sugar as she had pressed them into service as assistant bakers. Marit had dried wild grapes and gathered wild walnuts, and all afternoon the children had seeded and shelled without complaint. "Of course we'll have a spelling bee." Reaching across the table, she tugged on the raccoon tail dangling over the little girl's right ear. "And I suppose you think you and Mr. Gabe will win again, don't you?" she said with mock ferocity.

"Yes!" Mary crowed. "Like last night."

Her brother gave her a superior look. "Karin and I have won more."

One time more, Karin added silently, not that I'm keeping score. Spelling bees had become part of Mary and Brian's lesson reviews for Gabriel. To even up the odds for Mary, who had no chance of beating her brother on her own, she and Gabe had teamed up with the children. The bees were supposed to be for the children, but they had somehow degenerated into cutthroat competitions between the adults. She'd laughed evilly to herself the first time, thinking he would present no challenge for the winner of the Anoka County spelling championship three years running, but her smugness had died a quick death. Now she was having to resort to searching her books for obscure, difficult words that he couldn't possibly spell—but usually did. Her conscience was clear, though, because she was certain he was doing the same. She would never admit it, but she looked forward to their nightly contests even more than Mary did.

Well, the score was tied now. Dumping a cooled cake out of its pan, Karin stole a taste of the lemon glaze she'd poured over it after Mary had punched in holes with a knitting needle. What idiot had decided *escutcheon* should have a *t* in it? Hands on her hips, Karin surveyed the results of the day's baking frenzy, spread over the table. Secretly, she had enjoyed it, but maybe Sarge was right. It did look like she had enough food to feed a platoon. Gathering up pans and baking sheets, she began stacking them in the sink.

Gabe paused in the doorway. He knew she hadn't heard him come in; he should announce himself, and he would . . . in a minute. Her hair was coming down; as soon as she realized he was here, she would put it back up. She wrapped a loaf of bread in wax paper, her movements neat and graceful. Her hands had healed up fine, the faint red marks already fading. She wrapped another loaf; it was for the dance in Roswell, he knew. It had taken him a while to make up his mind about that dance, and when he had, then, of course, there had been a new worry: what he was going to do about all the men who would try to cut in. Well, they would just have to find their own woman, he decided suddenly, shrugging out of his sheepskin coat. Karin was his. The decision didn't startle him even half as much as it should have.

"Do you think you have enough food?"

Karin laughed sheepishly. "Just barely." Her hands lifted automatically to tuck in loose pins and tighten her bun. His eyes followed the movement, and she wondered at his slight smile. She'd realized he had come in when she heard him take off his coat, yet she had the sense that he'd been standing there for a while first. "Did you finish up in the barn?" Lately, after Mary and Brian went to bed, he'd taken to going out to the barn on some unexplained business.

"Pretty much." The past few weeks had been the happiest of his life, despite the struggle to keep his hands to himself. But the struggle was taking its toll, especially since he'd kissed her. He wasn't sleeping much, couldn't think straight half the time, couldn't get rid of the itch in his blood. Something had to give. He hung up his coat and moved to the other end of the table, picking up one of the teardrop-shaped cookies left over from supper. "What did you call these?"

"Cat's tongue cookies." Watching him from under her lashes, she wrapped another loaf as he lolled seductively against the table. Then he took a step to stand seductively beside her. You're hopeless, Karin told herself as she started stacking crackers in a tin, studiously avoiding the view.

"Mmm... What kind of cake is this?"

She had to look, to make sure he wasn't eating something for the dance. He was picking up crumbs with his...

"Kiss me," she said quickly.

One corner of his mouth turned up in an odd smile. "All right," he said softly, taking a step toward her.

She backed up hastily. "No! The cake, I meant... The name—"

His mouth was gentle and sweet...so sweet, seducing her into the kiss, capturing her mouth without a struggle. His tongue demanded that hers surrender, and she ransomed it back with tiny kisses. One hand glided up her spine and opened across her shoulders to lift her effortlessly to his questing mouth. Sliding her arms around his neck, she pressed closer, her body suddenly hungry for something only his could provide. Dimly she felt her hair loosening, falling free, and her hands borrowed the idea, delving into the rough silk strands at the nape of his neck, luxuriating in the feel of them between her fingers, against her palms, as her body luxuriated in the feel of his.

At the feel of her cool hands burning around his neck, Gabe's conscience finally got a word in edgewise. What was he doing? She was a woman alone, living in his house and under his protection. With a murmur, she deepened the kiss, and, consigning his conscience to hell, he started to take the kiss even deeper. Then, with a silent curse, he pulled back. His conscience, damn it, was right. Her eyes opened slowly, the lids heavy and sleepy-looking, giving her the look of a woman who had just been well bedded, testing even his conscience this time. Her hands fell away as she stared up at him, her eyes widening with shock. Her lips parted, and the tip of her tongue darted out, as if to moisten them so that she could speak, throwing kerosene on the fire he was trying to tamp down in his belly.

He grinned down at her. "What's the matter, Miss Eklund?" he whispered, amazed that his voice worked. "Cat got your tongue?"

Her eyes widened farther as shock began to turn to outrage. Dropping a quick kiss on the tip of her nose, he released her, then left her standing in the middle of the kitchen, while he still could.

"Lubricious."

It was the third word she'd said to him all day. Her mouth was still prissed up, which confirmed what he suspected was the meaning of the word he was supposed to spell. So she thought he was lecherous. He spelled it, saw her barest nod of confirmation, and gave her a word.

"Unrepentant."

Unrepentant, was he? Well, she'd— Abruptly, Karin could keep up the charade of outrage no longer. He had done nothing last night that called for repentance. She was the one who should repent, both for her lack of control and for then blaming him for it. She spelled the word, then gave him hers.

"Embarrassed."

Her quiet admission surprised him, but it shouldn't have; she was honest to a fault. Her outrage had been a cover for the embarrassment she felt for what she probably thought was wanton behavior. He smiled at her downcast head, spelled her word and said his, softly.

"Ensorcelled."

Karin raised her head slowly. He'd been *enchanted?* She saw his smile, and quickly lowered her head again before he saw hers. No man had ever thought she was the stuff of enchantment before.

Clapping her hands suddenly, she stood up. "This spelling bee is a draw," she declared.

Brian looked at her, puzzled. "What's a draw?"

"It means Mr. Gabe and I have run out of words for tonight, and it's time for bed," she told him with a smile.

"Who won?" Mary asked as they left the kitchen.

"We all did," Karin said.

Gabe stared after her. A draw meant two contestants were so evenly matched that there was virtually no difference between them. The slow grin that came made him glad Sarge was out in the barn. He was certain she had just told him that she'd been enchanted, too.

## Chapter Eight

On the day of the dance, the wind came up at dawn. The cloud bank on the western horizon advanced rapidly, rolling over the low hills and burying them in thick gray wool. The closer the clouds came, the weaker the wind blew, until it died entirely around noon. At about the same time, the watery sun vanished under the heavy blanket of clouds; it was the last they would see of it that day, Karin knew.

The snowflakes came singly at first, then faster and faster, thickening into a solid white curtain that blocked the view beyond the last corral, then the barn, then the end of the front porch. They fell silently, muffling all sound, as well— a still white storm that had buried the ground six inches deep by midafternoon.

Karin discovered that a house got smaller in direct proportion to the length of time two active children were cooped up in it. She was seriously considering proposing a screaming contest so that she could participate when Gabriel brought something into the house that settled everyone down, astounded her and coincidentally revealed that he hadn't been working on his house the day before.

"Ooooh, a real Christmas tree..." Mary breathed, her eyes as big as saucers.

"Where'd you get it?" Brian asked, dancing around him as he carried the beautiful blue spruce into the parlor.

"At one of the dry-goods stores in town." He glanced at her as he anchored the tree in the bucket of damp earth Sarge had carried in behind him. "A freighter hauled some in from up around Lincoln. I couldn't get any ornaments," he warned. "Just some candles."

"We can come up with some ornaments," Karin said solemnly.

"Can we light the candles?"

Smiling, Karin ruffled Mary's hair. "No, we can't. You're really supposed to decorate the tree on Christmas Eve. We have to leave something for tomorrow night."

Sarge came to stand beside Brian, Mary and Karin. "Sure looks pretty, don't it, Gabe?"

"Yes, it does."

He stood a little apart from them, looking at the tree. Reaching out, Mary took his hand and pulled him closer. "Doesn't the angel look beautiful, Mr. Gabe?"

He smiled down at the little girl. "Yes, it looks beautiful, Mary."

The angel was made of silver paper, with the crystal "wings" Mary had found, and Gabriel had lifted her up to place it on top of the tree. Karin had expected him to leave after setting up the tree, but he hadn't. Sarge had popped popcorn, and Gabriel had helped string it. He had hung the crystal icicles on the high branches, along with the bows she had made out of red calico from her carpetbag. He had even taken part in the candy pull and all its attendant silliness after supper. And he'd seemed to enjoy it.

Gabe gazed at the tree. He had never realized that he needed the trappings of tradition, of holidays, one of the things that turned a house into a home.

Brian pulled on Karin's hand. "Do you think the candy is ready to eat?"

She smiled at him. "I don't know. Let's go see."

The children raced out of the parlor, with Sarge and his sweet tooth close behind. Gabe put out his hand to stop her when she started to follow.

"Are you sorry you missed the dance?"

Just a touch and she was ready to melt, Karin thought on a silent, despairing laugh. "Not really." How could she be, when the only reason she'd wanted to go was to be with him? "I went to the one in Tres Ritos last year. The general store had five-gallon pails of candy, and the bachelors had picked out the little hearts with the romantic sayings on them to give to their favorite women."

"Did you get any?"

"A few," she admitted with a laugh, and he scowled as she stared dreamily at the tree. "There was a big Christmas tree, and people put presents on it for friends and sweethearts—magazine subscriptions, little boxes of candy, books. I got a box of stationery from the family I was staying with." Her gaze shifting to him, she confided with another laugh, "So I wouldn't feel left out, I think. The oldest daughter got a diamond ring from an anonymous admirer. She still isn't married, so I guess either he never found the courage to reveal his identity or she said no."

"Karin!" A plaintive voice called from the kitchen.

Watching her leave, Gabe fingered the small velvet box in his vest pocket with a wry smile. He could sympathize with the anonymous admirer.

Karin shrieked in mock outrage as small hands tried to stuff snow down her neck. Abandoning the snowman she was finishing, she reached behind her and grabbed the culprit, then held down a giggling, squirming Brian while she tried to wash his face with snow. Without warning, a very big, very wet snowball smacked her backside, and she straightened up with another shriek—of real outrage, this time—whirling around to find the perpetrator.

Gabe ducked back inside the barn. Waiting a couple of minutes, he composed his face into an innocent expression and strolled back out. A bigger, wetter snowball crashed into his chest. By the time he wiped the splattered snow out of his eyes, the thrower was nowhere to be seen. He scanned the snow until he found what he was looking for, then, grinning, began following the tracks.

A huge hay mound sat in the middle of the original corral. As the horses had eaten into it, they had created a shallow cave, and Karin slipped into it, still giggling.

A foot of snow had fallen overnight, but a warm wind had already blown the clouds away, and the sun was shining brightly, so naturally Mary and Brian had wanted to go outside and play. Secretly, she had, too, which was amazing considering she had spent most of her life despising snow. Marit's galoshes, with socks stuffed in the toes, had fit Brian, and Hiram's—without socks, unfortunately—had fit her. Sarge had wrapped strips from an old oilskin around Mary's feet and calves, which hadn't pleased her until he mentioned that they looked like the leggings Indians wore. Then Mary had run around war-whooping until she was hoarse, proving that Indians, as well as Santa Claus, must have been a topic of conversation at the foundling home. Thoughts of the letter she was waiting for intruded, but she pushed them firmly aside. It wouldn't come before the first of the year, and thinking about it would only raise her hopes more.

She gave a startled yelp when Gabriel suddenly materialized in front of her. Grinning, he held up his gloved hands to show her that he was unarmed, then crowded into the little shelter beside her.

Putting his hands in his pockets, Gabe looked out over a cold, snow-filled yard, while smelling summer sun and honeysuckle. What had put such a worried look on her face? Though as soon as she saw him—and realized she wasn't going to get a faceful of snow—she'd given him a big smile. She'd looked the way she had when she was showing Mary and Brian how to make a snowman, happy as the two children she was playing with. The ache to hold on to that precious moment had been so fierce it took his breath away. "Does this remind you of winter in Minnesota?"

"This is a fine spring day in Minnesota," she laughed dryly, then touched his arm and pointed. "Look," she whispered.

Sarge was heading for the house, unaware that he was being stalked. Suddenly a snowball sent his old bowler sailing, while another caught him squarely between the shoulder blades. With a roar, he turned and took off in hot pursuit of the throwers, Mary and Brian shrieking in delighted fright as they ran for the barn.

Eyes sparkling, cheeks rosy with the cold, wisps of gold escaping from under her scarf, Karin laughed up at him. He stared down at her, and her laughter died abruptly, a look of longing replacing it and annihilating all his fine resolve. "Aw, hell," he muttered, and reached for her.

There was nothing sweet or gentle in this kiss; it was hot and hard and rough. His arms vised around her, and despite all their clothes, she felt fused to him. He was holding her body and heart captive, and the only ransom was total, unconditional surrender. She was lost either way, had lost days ago. His head lifted, breaking the kiss, and without thought her arms twisted around his neck, her hands knocking off his hat to tangle in his hair and drag his mouth back. Vaguely, she was aware of his hand moving between them, ripping open his coat, then hers; then she was vividly aware of that hand sliding up and closing over her breast. She froze at the unfamiliar intimacy; then his hand spread, rubbing slowly, and, with a small moan, she melted.

At first Gabe ignored the small, hard square object digging under his ribs, but finally he remembered what it was and, more importantly, what it contained. The moment couldn't be much better. Pulling back, he looked down at her. Her eyes were still closed, her lips moist and rosy from his kiss, her breath trembling over them. A hot wash of desire purled through him, and he had to take a breath before he could trust his voice. "Karin, I—"

"Major! Major!"

Gabe swore viciously under his breath. If Billy Burcar lived to be twenty, it wouldn't be his fault. His hands slipped to her arms as her eyes opened, soft and hazed with desire, and he swore again. He would have ignored the damn kid, but he'd spotted them and was heading this way. His hands tightened involuntarily for a moment; then he released her. "Stay *right* here. Don't move."

Karin sagged weakly back against the hay. She couldn't have disobeyed his order if she'd wanted to. Vaguely she wondered what he had been going to say when Billy had called him.

Jamming on his hat, Gabe stomped across the yard.

Billy had apparently ridden into town and couldn't wait to share his news. "The dance got canceled 'cause of the storm, but they're talking about havin' it on Valentine's Day. I picked up the mail while I was in town, too, and a couple of telegrams." Impatiently Gabe held out his hand. "One was for Miss Karin." Billy tried to see past him. "Is she...uh...busy?"

"Yes." Gabe gave him a hard look, and Billy finally took the hint, handing over the envelope and shambling off.

From a distance, Karin watched Gabriel tear open a yellow envelope. She was grateful to Billy, although there had been a few moments before she regained her senses when she would cheerfully have wrung his neck, she remembered wryly, then sobered. Each time she fell deeper and deeper;

there couldn't be another time, she thought starkly. She couldn't take the chance of revealing her feelings and humiliating herself.

Gabriel wadded up whatever had been in the yellow envelope and jammed it in his coat pocket, then started toward her.

"This came for you."

"Thank you," Karin murmured, taking the yellow telegraph envelope, an envelope that looked identical to the one he'd just opened. Although both his face and his voice were expressionless, she sensed that he was furious about something. Saying nothing further, he left, and Karin tore open the envelope and scanned the brief message.

Refolding the yellow sheet carefully, she slid it back into the envelope and put it in her pocket. She wasn't furious, Karin noted absently; she was numb. Her character references were excellent and her financial resources adequate, but only married couples were suitable as adoptive parents. Suddenly, she realized her absentminded conclusion. No— it was crazy, but...? Yes, Gabe's telegram had said the same.

She wasn't really surprised that he had tried to adopt the children, too. The day she had met him in the bank, she'd had the crazy suspicion that he was there for the same reason. Apparently it wasn't so crazy after all. The only crazy thing, Karin decided sadly, was that both of them wanted Mary and Brian and could give them a good home, but neither of them was "suitable."

Determinedly, she dashed away the tears. It was Christmas Eve. Nothing was going to spoil tonight or tomorrow for Brian and Mary, not even the news that they were once again about to be orphaned.

As she had hoped, Gabe said nothing to them, although she suspected he had said something to Sarge, judging by the older man's uncharacteristic heartiness. She had worried that Brian and Mary would sense Gabe's temper, but he had managed to put aside his black mood. It was good that her own numbness held, she thought, because she wasn't nearly as good a dissembler.

Her numb composure slipped several times during Christmas Eve supper. The evening began with the traditional dipping to commemorate a long-ago famine in Sweden, when there had been only black bread and thin broth to eat on Christmas Eve. Karin would have skipped it, but she had already told Mary and Brian the story, and they were expecting it. Everyone dipped a slice of dark rye *vort* bread in broth and ate it to ensure good luck in the coming year. Mary and Brian ate theirs in happy ignorance; knowing what was to come in the New Year, Karin could hardly choke hers down. She didn't dare look to see how Gabriel and Sarge were managing.

Next came the *smörgåsbord,* followed by the traditional dessert of sweet rice porridge she'd made that morning. As she bit down and felt the crunch, she was glad she had forgotten to tell Mary and Brian another tradition; only she would be aware of the cruel irony. An almond was always cooked in the porridge; if an unmarried person got it, he or she would be the next to be married.

The blessed numbness suffered no more slips. In an attempt to celebrate an "American" Christmas, rather than a solely Swedish one, she had asked Mary and Brian what special things they had done for Christmas in Ireland. There hadn't been much, as she'd suspected, but they remembered lighting a large candle in the front window on Christmas Eve to welcome the Holy Family. It was supposed to be lit by the youngest child and snuffed out by someone named Mary. Carefully Mary lit the candle in the parlor window; then Gabe lit the candles on the tree. As the senior man, Sarge was given the honor of reading the Christmas story from her Bible; then Brian placed the baby in the nativity scene she and the children had made out of walnuts, wooden sewing-thread spools and quilt batting. Afterward they drank cocoa and ate Christmas cookies, and soon it was time for the children to hang up their stockings and try to go to sleep so that Santa could come.

She was just ready to turn out the lamp in the kitchen and go to bed herself when Gabe came in.

"I imagine your telegram said the same thing mine did." She nodded. "Yes."

"Well, I have a way to solve our mutual problem." Again he cursed Billy Burcar. This had seemed so much easier this afternoon. "We work well together, have common goals, both want Mary and Brian. I've been reasonably successful, and I'm financially secure. You are an exceptional housekeeper and would make an equally good mother, I'm sure. I think we should marry."

If it sounded more like a business proposition than a marriage proposal, that was because it was, Karin told herself as she fought a sudden, irrational urge to laugh. Maybe the almond had some magical power after all. Just as suddenly, she changed from laughter to tears. It was an awful temptation—a home of her own with a husband and children, a future she didn't have to spend alone...all the things she had secretly wanted, never admitting it, even to herself. There was only one thing lacking. The children would love her and she them, but there would be no loving husband. He did have feelings for her—only physical feelings, but from her customers, she knew many marriages started with no more than that. They also had respect and cooperation between them. Mary and Brian should grow up with parents who loved each other, but many children's natural parents didn't love each other, and they grew up fine. They both cared for the children and wanted them; many natural children didn't have that. He was offering her almost everything she'd ever wanted. Wouldn't "almost" be enough?

"It would certainly solve the problem, and you've made a ... generous offer. Unfortunately, I can't accept it."

She had said she would marry only for love. "I understand," Gabe said tonelessly. The words were there, the words he'd been about to tell her when that blasted Billy had interrupted, but they were stuck in his throat. Because he was sure he wouldn't hear the same words from her.

*No, you don't understand!* she wanted to scream at him. Instead, she willed her suddenly aching body to move. "Good night," she said quietly. "I'll see you in the morning."

Brian and Mary were up with the sun. As they gathered in the parlor, she noticed that there were considerably more gifts under the tree and more bulges in Mary and Brian's stockings than the night before, when she had set out her gifts. She glanced curiously at Gabe, but he didn't seem to see her look. After an obligatory nod of acknowledgment when he entered the room, he hadn't seemed to see her at all. But then, how could there be anything but acute awkwardness between them now? Karin thought bleakly. All she prayed was that Brian and Mary wouldn't notice anything that would spoil their day.

She didn't look as if she'd slept, either, Gabe decided. What that might mean, he didn't have time to ponder before Brian removed his stocking from the mantel.

"A penny! And an orange!" His eyes wide with wonder, Brian held up his bounty for everyone to see. His eyes got wider, if possible, when he dug deeper into the stocking and found a small pocketknife, a new pair of green mittens and an assortment of hard candy.

Mary had red mittens, along with an orange, a penny and a ball. She and her brother began discussing how they might spend their fortunes, and the adults realized they didn't understand the significance of the presents under the tree.

Sarge cleared his throat gruffly. "Mary, Brian, I think some of those packages under the tree have your names on them."

Karin watched Mary unwrap the new wardrobe for Bridget and the dress she had made, a silver ring set with turquoise from Sarge, and a lovely wooden cradle just Bridget's size. She glanced at the man sitting a few feet—and miles—away. Now she knew what he'd been doing in the barn every night.

Brian unwrapped three pairs of duckins—the long pants he'd coveted in place of the short pants and stockings small boys traditionally wore—from her, a pair of braces to help hold them up from Sarge, a worsted vest—which he had also coveted—from Gabe, and another item that had her giving him a disbelieving look before she could stop herself.

"A *drum?*"

"I always wanted one when I was a boy," he replied in the same undertone, "but I never got one."

"And you'll soon know why!"

He grinned, and she smiled back automatically, and the hideous awkwardness between them suddenly eased. Not entirely, Karin knew, but enough that she no longer worried about the children noticing anything.

Believing they needed to learn that it was important to give, as well as receive, Karin had helped Brian and Mary make gifts. The two men and Brian exclaimed nicely over the handkerchiefs Mary had embroidered with their first initial, and his sister and the men complimented Brian on his penmanship—of which he was inordinately proud—on the coupons they received, good for one shoe or boot polishing, promising to redeem them soon. They would have to, because... Karin did not allow herself to complete the thought.

In addition to a handkerchief and free boot polishing, Sarge had a new hat from Gabe, which was exactly like his old bowler—but respectable—and a winter shirt with a flannel-lined bib from her. Karin held her breath as he held it up. She wasn't sure he would appreciate the innovation she had made.

"Now, I don't know why me or Hilda didn't think of this." He examined the shortened sleeve with the lightly padded inset at the bottom. "It saves material; I don't have to mess with those consarned safety pins, and it'll be more comfortable." He beamed at her. "Thanks, Karin!"

She grinned back. "You're very welcome, Sarge." Her grin faded as she waited for Gabriel to open the last package in front of him. He had opened the children's gifts, and Sarge's pocket watch—to replace the one he had lost fighting the fire—and now he was ripping the silver paper off her present.

"Oh...Karin," he said softly as he held up the first shirt. It was a four-button pullover of blue and white ticking; the second was double-breasted, in blue flannel, and the third was another pullover of muslin, with a linen bosom and neck and wrist bands. "You must have worked until midnight every night to make these," he said quietly.

"I sew fast," she said lightly. "I used your old striped shirt for the pattern."

He frowned at her. "The one you said went to pieces in the wash?"

"It died for a good cause," she said gravely.

He laughed as he held up the ticking shirt again. "Yeah, I'd say it did." Lowering the shirt, he smiled at her. "Thank you, Karin."

"You're welcome, Gabriel." The use of her first name was more than thanks enough.

"Now open yours," he ordered softly. Hearing her finally say "Gabriel" was a present, too.

She had been enjoying watching everyone else open their presents so much that she had ignored hers. There were a startling number. She feigned surprise at Mary's handkerchief and Brian's polishing coupon, but her surprise was real when she saw the silver-and-turquoise bracelet from Sarge, and surprise became astonishment when she opened the next package and found a pair of fur-lined kid gloves. She looked at the man who had given them to her. "Thank you."

"Try them on to make sure they fit." She did, holding up her hands to show him that they fit perfectly. "Now open the last one."

Karin tore off the red paper and was past astonishment. "Gabe...it's beautiful," she said softly. He hadn't just been working on Mary's cradle those nights in the barn, she realized as she stared at the wooden box in her hands. The box was exquisitely carved, and polished to a finish as smooth as the finest satin. He hadn't tried to force the wood into a square shape, but had followed the natural lines of the tree, making no attempt to hide imperfections, instead somehow enhancing them, so that they became jewels set in a gold crown. In his hands, what might have been merely a pretty trinket became a minor work of art.

"It's mesquite."

She nodded, unwilling to trust her voice. Grasping a tiny knob, she pulled open a small drawer.

"There's a hidden compartment. Can you find it?"

Karin looked all around inside the opening, then shook her head. "I can't see it." With her finger, she felt for a crack, a button, something. Her nail caught under a small knot that had looked flush with the surface, and she lifted up. Another drawer, felt-lined, slid out of the box, and she laughed delightedly.

"Your pearl pin will fit in there, and—" he glanced at her wrist "—your bracelet should, too."

She slanted him a wondering look. He had seen her pin once, for maybe all of thirty seconds, and he'd remembered it? Sliding the drawer back in place, she tried to see it now that she knew it was there. She still couldn't, because he had carved it out so perfectly along the grain lines. Hugging the box to her, she gave him a dazzling smile. "It's absolutely marvelous, Gabe. Thank you."

"You're welcome, Karin," he murmured, feeling his heart break a little more. Why couldn't she have said yes?

Karin folded the dishrag and draped it over the side of the sink. Christmas dinner had been a success. Keeping with her plan to incorporate different traditions into an "American" Christmas, she had included one of each person's favorite foods in the Christmas dinner: soda scones for Mary and Brian, succotash for Gabe, fried apples 'n' onions for Sarge, *lutefisk* for herself. Afterward Sarge and the children had helped her wash up, while Gabe had taken the food she had made for the dance over to his men. When she had peeked into the parlor a minute ago, Sarge had been napping in the overstuffed chair, while Mary and Brian had each staked out a corner of the sofa and were sound asleep.

She looked over the neat kitchen. Women's work was undeniably hard—some of it was out-and-out drudgery—but it wasn't without its compensations and joys, she'd discovered. Like the smell of bread baking—it wasn't just the wonderful smell of the bread, but the smell of satisfaction for surviving and succeeding, especially here on the frontier. And the smell and the compensations and joys were even sweeter when the work was done out of love.... The ache in her chest, which she'd tried to ignore all day, abruptly became so acute that she almost cried out. How could she leave him? Leave Brian and Mary? Suddenly the question she'd been turning over and over since last night had an answer, and, hearing a rider outside, she grabbed her sweater off the hook and opened the back door.

\* \* \*

He knew who had come into the barn even before he could see who it was. Stepping out of a stall, Gabe walked to meet her.

Karin took a deep breath of air thick with the smell of animals, dust and manure. This was not where she would have chosen to do this, she thought wildly, but at least the only witness was a cow. "I've been reconsidering your offer, and, upon reflection, I've changed my mind. We each have skills that complement the other's, and we both want what is best for Brian and Mary. I think it would be a successful partnership."

Was that how his proposal had sounded, like they were discussing a pair of mules they were thinking of hitching to the same plow? So practical, so... cold? Until the children and then Karin had come, he had never realized he was lonely; so was she, he'd sensed. He'd thought if they joined together—"hitched up," he thought with a silent, humorless laugh—they could ease that loneliness, perhaps banish it entirely. If he said no, she would leave. So, too, would Mary and Brian, and he could bear to think of their leaving little more than he could hers. But were loneliness and Mary and Brian reasons enough to marry, when there was no promise that there might ever be more? He suspected a cold, practical marriage could be lonelier than being the last man on earth. Yet next year, and the year after that, on into the gray future, he saw himself still alone... and Karin, still alone... the loneliness aching and heart-deep. Getting married *had* been his idea first, and he *loved* her, damn it! The words still stuck, though, like a piece of cactus in his throat.

Karin felt like a clock with someone winding the key too tight. He was taking his time thinking it over. Maybe he'd been doing some reconsidering, too.

Finally he nodded, and she held her breath, not letting herself hope. "I think you were right yesterday in refusing my offer. A marriage between us would be a mistake."

"Of course," Karin said stiffly, and turned away.

She would have no talent for poker, Gabe thought absently as he watched her walk away; despite her cool answer, everything she felt was on her face—desolation, humiliation, anger. Extending his hand toward her, he was opening his mouth to call her back when she stopped.

"I'm scheduled to go on to the Paffetts up by Dunlap next," she said without turning around, her voice flat and rigidly controlled. "They always need more time than I can give them. Since the children will be leaving imminently, it won't matter if I leave early. If I catch tomorrow's stage, I won't have to wait a week for another one."

His hand fell back to his side. "As you wish, Miss Eklund."

# Chapter Nine

If there was a hell, it would consist of eternally reliving the past twenty hours, Karin thought. She gazed at the town buildings, seeing Mary's and Brian's faces, devastated, and Sarge's, suddenly old. Unable to help herself, she glanced at the face of the man standing beside her, scrupulously outside touching distance. His face was set in stone, even the frown absent. Since walking out of the barn, they had been like two exquisitely polite strangers, all rapport between them destroyed.

The stage pulled to a stop, and the agent stepped forward to accept the mailbag the guard handed down, then opened the door and let down the steps. Gabe watched the woman beside him indicate what was to go in the boot. Panic gripped him as his eyes started to burn and his throat swelled shut. She was leaving! He caught himself rubbing at the awful ache in his chest, bringing no relief.

Karin picked up her satchel. At the stage steps, she turned, her eyes carefully focused past his right shoulder. "Goodbye, Mr. Svathvick." It was going to take everything she had to get through the next seconds without humiliating herself further; accurate pronunciation was beyond her.

"If—" Gabe had to clear his throat, "—if the foundling home tells me their final placement, I'll let you know."

Swallowing a sob, Karin nodded. "You can send the letter to Mesilla, general delivery." She would never return to Roswell. Even the remote risk of seeing him was too great; she didn't think a heart could survive repeated breakings. "I hope they are adopted by people who are of love capable." Her eyes shifted to his face for one final look that would have to last her the rest of her life. After a moment, she turned away and, accepting the helping hand of the depot manager, blindly climbed the steps.

The manager flipped the steps back up; the driver released the brake and the stage lurched away. Gabe stood on the boardwalk, staring after it in helpless disbelief long after the dust had disappeared. She was . . . gone.

In vague surprise, Gabe glanced up to see a familiar house. Pulling up, he stared at the snowmen melted down to white stumps, and his mouth suddenly hardened. If the Children's Aid Society wanted Mary and Brian back, they were going to have to take them at gunpoint, and they'd better come with plenty of ammunition. He wasn't going to lose them, too. He would have at least that much love in his life.

Still staring at the remnants of the snow figures, he felt his mouth gradually soften into a faint smile. She'd looked like one of them herself, covered in snow, laughing and giggling, her hair coming down, her cheeks pink, her face shining with pure, simple joy. The memory of her face as she'd looked up at him when they were standing by the haystack came unbidden, then Christmas morning as she'd thanked him for the little box . . . her poker-talentless face that couldn't hide what she was thinking or feeling . . . Just as her English slipped when she was feeling something strongly, like this morning, with his name, and when she'd gotten the word order confused. . . "Of love capable," she'd said. . . . Love . . . *love.*

With an explosive curse, Gabe leaped off the wagon and ran for the barn. It had been staring him in the face—literally. She loved him! A blind man would have seen it—or at least heard it. But, since he hadn't, why the hell hadn't she told him? The answer came with the question. She was just following his lead, unwilling to take the risk of being laughed at or—worse—pitied.

He was tightening the cinch on his saddle when Sarge walked in. "I'll be back in a few hours," he said shortly.

Folding his arms across his chest, the older man adopted a belligerent stance. "Alone?"

Gabe swung up into the saddle. "No." He hoped.

Grinning, Sarge dropped his arms and stepped back. "I wondered if you were going to stay stupid all your life."

Giving him a wry look, Gabe swung his horse around. "Only the first thirty-seven years." Digging in his heels, he urged the buckskin forward.

"I'll take the kids over to my place for a few days," Sarge called after him.

It was fortunate that she had the stagecoach to herself, Karin thought absently. If she'd had to share it with the likes of Gerald Butterbaugh, she would have been forced to stuff his sample case down his throat by now. The first two hours had passed in numb misery, the last in a far more painful misery, as the numbness wore off.

He had been right to refuse her—a marriage with love only on one side would never work—but it didn't ease her heart's agony, the killing sense of loss. She sighed wearily. She wouldn't be surprised if he kept Mary and Brian after all. A man who had dealt with rustlers and Apaches wouldn't find an orphanage two thousand miles away much of a challenge. Brian and Mary would have him, and he would have them. And she would have nobody.

Suddenly there was a gunshot, but she couldn't rouse much curiosity, even when there were several more and the stage began to slow. She laughed blackly. A robbery—she'd never had that particular pleasure before; how fitting that it should be today. The stage rocked to a stop, and, hearing a single horse galloping up from behind, she glanced toward the window. The isinglass curtain had been down when she got in, and she hadn't seen any reason to raise it. A large shape appeared; then the door jerked open.

"Gabriel!"

He greeted her calmly. "Karin."

She stared at him. "What are you doing here?"

Instead of answering, he leaned from his saddle and reached inside the coach to pull out her satchel, slipping the handle over his saddle horn.

"Gabe? What are you—"

One long gloved finger sealed the rest of the words behind her lips. He reached into the coach again and, sliding his arms around her, lifted her out. With a gasp, Karin grabbed at him, her hands closing on his shoulders as he set her sideways in front of him on his horse.

His mouth crooked as she looked up at him warily. "We've tried this twice, Karin. Think we can get it right this time?" He saw the wild leap of hope in her eyes, then the struggle to keep it down. "I am 'of love capable.' I love you, Karin, and I can't bear to think of my life without you. Will you marry me?"

She regarded him soberly. "Are you sure you aren't asking just so you can adopt Mary and Brian?"

"Hell, woman! I just said—" He softened his tone and expression. "It's not to adopt Mary and Brian, Karin. After all, they'll be grown and gone someday, and I'll still have a wife." A corner of his mouth turned up. "I wouldn't choose one I didn't want to live with for fifty years."

Her mouth pursed as she considered him. "Fifty years may be a little ambitious, don't you think? After all, you are almost forty."

He threw back his head and laughed as he crushed her to him. "It'll seem like a hundred and fifty, with that sassy mouth of yours." Sobering, he held her away to meet her eyes. "Marry me, Karin, for me. Marry me and love me." The words caught as his throat constricted, and came out as a rasp. "And let me love you."

Suddenly unaccountably shy, Karin felt her cheeks flush as she ducked her head. "Yes," she said softly.

"What?" An implacable finger tipped up her chin. "I didn't hear you, and—" he glanced toward the guard and driver, who were avidly eavesdropping "—neither did the witnesses."

Karin looked directly into his eyes. "Yes," she said distinctly.

Anything else she might have said was lost in his kiss. After a minute or two the bored buckskin shook its head and started walking home.

"Hey!" The guard yelled after them. "What about her bags?" His conscientiousness earned him a hard elbow.

Rubbing his ribs, he gave the man beside him an aggrieved look. "Dang it, Bert, why'd you do that?"

"We'll put her things on the next stage back," Bert said equably. "They'll remember them in a week or two."

Karin studied the ring of hearts on her finger.

"We'll have a real wedding when the circuit preacher comes around again, but I didn't want to wait." He held out his arms, and she slid off the back of his horse into them.

She laughed up at him. "We'll have to. After having to cancel the Christmas dance, nobody would forgive us if we cheated them out of a party." They had stopped in Ely on the way back, where the saloon keeper–justice of the peace had married them, then treated them to huge steak dinners in honor of performing his first marriage ceremony. Finally realizing they were starving because they hadn't eaten all day, they had taken the time to accept his hospitality. She smiled inwardly. Some might consider their haste quite unseemly. The smile faded at the desire in his eyes. "I didn't want to wait, either," she said softly.

She truly didn't, but this was one time, Karin decided ruefully as he carried her inside, where having the knowledge but not the experience was a real disadvantage. She was expecting something extraordinary, something thrilling and something more than a little frightening.

Gradually, under his patient, tender tutelage, embarrassment became fascination, passivity participation, and hesitation eagerness. Delicious anticipation began to course through her as his mouth moved slowly downward. His hands cupping her breasts gently, his lips closed over a nipple, and her blood turned sluggish and hot. His wet, rough tongue curled around the hard nub as her hands made an intuitive leap.

He shuddered; then his hands moved lower and without warning her body was saturated with heat and helpless pleasure. He shifted, and a long, smooth glide began that ended in a glorious headlong rush of ecstasy.

Gabe watched the lowering sun shining through the window gild the hair sifting through his hand. "Promise me you'll stop scraping your hair back into that god-awful bun."

Her soft laughter was a warm gust across his bare chest. "I promise."

He tightened his arms around her sweet, boneless body as his heart expanded until it seemed to fill his chest. Suddenly he understood the significance of the secret compartment he had carved into the box he had made for her. It was the secret compartment inside him, where he hid away love, tenderness, all the gentle emotions he had denied for so long. Only she knew where it was, knew how to open it. In accepting his gift, she had given him back one far, far richer that he would cherish the rest of his life.

"How long will Brian and Mary be with Sarge?" she murmured.

"He said he'd bring them back in a couple of days." Privately he hoped it was more rather than fewer. He wanted the children back, but he wanted a few days alone with his wife first. He felt her push against his chest and, reluctantly, he loosened his arms.

She rose up on one elbow. How easily she had lost her modesty, Karin thought in amused amazement. She gave him an annoyed look, as annoyed as it could be when she was lying naked, her body still humming with fulfillment, in his arms. "You were that certain I would come back with you?"

Shaking his head, he brushed her hair back gently. "Taking the children was Sarge's idea. I wasn't certain of anything, but—" he grinned crookedly "—if two hours of solid praying had any effect, you had to."

Sliding her arms around his neck, she grinned back. Her face gradually sobered as she looked down on the face of the man she loved, remembering that day long ago when she'd stood at the rail of a ship, awaiting her first glimpse of the new country that held the promise of a new life and untold wonders. The promise had more than been fulfilled.

His expression changed, too, turning oddly whimsical. "I just remembered. I never wished you Merry Christmas yesterday. Merry Christmas, Karin."

Smiling softly, she lowered her mouth to his. "Merry Christmas, Gabriel."

\* \* \* \* \*

## A Note from Patricia Gardner Evans

*Dear Reader,*

As befits a nation of immigrants, Christmas in the U.S. is a rich stew, with each family personalizing the recipe by adding the unique flavoring of its own traditions. Those traditions may be ethnic, religious or just "family," but most of them immigrated to the United States, as well. One of the traditions in my family is raisin bread. The recipe came over from England with one of my multi-great-grandmothers, Sarah Hall.

My grandmother made the raisin bread every Christmas for as long as I can remember. After she no longer did, I made it some years and my mother others until I became the official Christmas raisin bread baker when my crafty mother decreed that I was heir to the collection of odd-size bread pans my grandmother always used. I've added a few odd sizes of my own and adapted the recipe to microwave and Cuisinart—the appliances may change, but women's work doesn't really, does it?

When I got out the recipe this year, I realized that the diverse ingredients that combine to make raisin bread come from all over the world—just like the diverse nationalities that have "combined" to make the United States. The older I get, the more I appreciate what a wonderful and unique "recipe" the U.S. is, and how fortunate I am to live here, free to celebrate whatever holiday in this season of holidays I choose.

I wish you the universal hopes that are part of all the holidays that will be celebrated this season—
Peace and Joy,

*Patricia Gardner Evans*

# VOWS
## Margaret Moore

Legend has it that couples who marry in the
Eternity chapel are destined for happiness.
Yet the couple who started it all almost never
made it to the altar!

*It all began in Eternity, Massachusetts, 1855....*
Bronwyn Davies started life afresh in America
and found refuge with William Powell. But
beneath William's respectability was a secret
that, once uncovered, could keep Bronwyn
bound to him forever.

Don't miss **VOWS,** the exciting prequel to
Harlequin's cross-line series, **WEDDINGS, INC.,**
available in December from Harlequin Historicals.
And look for the next **WEDDINGS, INC.**
book, *Bronwyn's Story,* by Marisa Carroll
(Harlequin Superromance #635), coming in
March 1995.

# LOOK TO THE PAST FOR
# FUTURE FUN AND EXCITEMENT!

The past the Harlequin Historical way, that is. 1994 is going to be a banner year for us, so here's a preview of what to expect:

* The continuation of our bigger book program, with titles such as *Across Time* by Nina Beaumont, *Defy the Eagle* by Lynn Bartlett and *Unicorn Bride* by Claire Delacroix.

* A 1994 March Madness promotion featuring four titles by promising new authors Gayle Wilson, Cheryl St. John, Madris Dupree and Emily French.

* Brand-new in-line series: DESTINY'S WOMEN by Merline Lovelace and HIGHLANDER by Ruth Langan; and new chapters in old favorites, such as the SPARHAWK saga by Miranda Jarrett and the WARRIOR series by Margaret Moore.

* *Promised Brides,* an exciting brand-new anthology with stories by Mary Jo Putney, Kristin James and Julie Tetel.

* Our perennial favorite, the Christmas anthology, this year featuring Patricia Gardner Evans, Kathleen Eagle, Elaine Barbieri and Margaret Moore.

Watch for these programs and titles wherever Harlequin Historicals are sold.

### HARLEQUIN HISTORICALS...
### A TOUCH OF MAGIC!

## CHRISTMAS STALKINGS

All wrapped up in spine-tingling packages, here are three books guaranteed to chill your spine...and warm your hearts this holiday season!

**#302 THE KID WHO STOLE CHRISTMAS**
Linda Stevens

**#303 I'LL BE HOME FOR CHRISTMAS**
Dawn Stewardson

**#304 BEARING GIFTS**
Aimée Thurlo

This December, fill your stockings with the "Christmas Stalkings"—for the best in romantic suspense. Only from

HARLEQUIN®

**I N T R I G U E®**

**Where do you find hot Texas nights, smooth Texas charm and dangerously sexy cowboys?**

Crystal Creek reverberates with the exciting rhythm of Texas. Each story features the rugged individuals who live and love in the Lone Star state.

"...Crystal Creek wonderfully evokes the hot days and steamy nights of a small Texas community...impossible to put down until the last page is turned."
—*Romantic Times*

"...a series that should hook any romance reader. Outstanding."
—*Rendezvous*

"Altogether, it couldn't be better." —*Rendezvous*

Don't miss the next book in this exciting series. Look for
**SOMEWHERE OTHER THAN THE NIGHT** by SANDY STEEN

Available in December wherever Harlequin books are sold.

# Maura Seger's
# BELLE HAVEN

Four books. Four generations. Four indomitable females.

You met the Belle Haven women who started it all in Harlequin Historicals.
Now meet descendant Nora Delaney in the emotional contemporary conclusion to the Belle Haven saga:

## THE SURRENDER OF NORA

When Nora's inheritance brings her home to Belle Haven, she finds more
than she bargained for. Deadly accidents prove someone wants her out of
town—fast. But the real problem is the prime suspect—handsome
Hamilton Fletcher. His quiet smile awakens the passion all Belle Haven
women are famous for. But does he want her heart...or her life?

Don't miss THE SURRENDER OF NORA
Silhouette Intimate Moments #617
Available in January!

---

HARLEQUIN®

*Temptation*®

THE HART GIRLS

Bestselling Temptation author Elise Title is back
with a funny, sexy trilogy—THE HART GIRLS—
written in the vein of her popular miniseries
THE FORTUNE BOYS!

In December 1994 tune in to
#517 HEART TO HEART....

Kate Hart *desperately* needs a new program director to
save her ailing TV station. But she feels like she's
made a deal with the devil when she hires "bad boy"
Brody Baker! Stay tuned for the juicy details....

**Available wherever Harlequin books are sold.**